FRACTURED

FRACTURED

ELLE CHARLES

FRACTURED

Cover design by Rachelle Gould-Harris of Designs by Rachelle

www.designsbyrachelle.com

For all enquiries, please email: elle@ellecharles.com

www.ellecharles.com

ISBN: 978-1-69-313520-0

First publication: 7 May 2014

First Edition
Version 1.5
November 2019

Contents

Prologue

6th MARCH.

7.15am.

Today is the second most anticipated day I have been counting down to for as long as I can remember. It's a day that should bring me great happiness. A day I should be rejoicing in. The start of a new year to define me, another year to bring me that little bit closer to becoming an adult.

The passing of today means I'm only another three hundred and sixty-five days away from my goal.

The ultimate prize.

My freedom.

I should be elated that the foreseeable end is finally within reach. But I'm not. And unknown to me, in my young naivety, this is the day that my real nightmare will begin, with no foreseeable end in sight.

10.45pm.

Today should have been the penultimate birthday of my being able to escape.

Today, I should have been out celebrating with friends I don't actually have.

Instead, I am in my room, curled up in a ball, trying hard not to make a sound as the music flows through the house from downstairs, leaking out loud, and bleeding into my tender eardrums.

This is a party, but it's not for me.

Clutching my chest, I rush to the door and prop my chair underneath the handle. I bite my lip and stare, wondering if it will be enough this time. Past experience mocks me because it's another useless act, but I conciliate myself, believing it will save me. Truthfully, I know the only thing that will be my saving grace is death. I embraced that fact a long time ago. One day the Reaper will come calling, and when he does, I will hold my arms out to him, because in death, I will finally find the peace I long for in life. Turning around, I curl back up on my bed and continue to stare straight ahead.

As I tap my foot nervously to the beat, my heart hammers out of control, and my lungs work hard to catch up. My hands bunch tight into the duvet as I continue to stare blankly at my bedroom door. Watching. *Waiting*. I know that by the end of tonight, someone will open it, and when that moment transpires, a small part of my soul will be destroyed. Come morning; I will have lost yet another part of myself that makes me whole. A part of myself that was once clean.

Innocent.

Tears leak from my eyes as I think back to the last party they held.

Two nights ago, I was left devoid of all emotion in the harsh light of day. My mind is strangely blank, but I understand the level of unknown depravity because my body is still sore, and in the long, painful process of recovery. Not that my broken, malnourished, skinny self was ever whole or unblemished to begin with.

The smell of stale tobacco and alcohol permeates through the air, and I retch, consuming the foul stench hitting the back of my throat. The sound of heavy footsteps plays on the stairs repeatedly, as my parents' *friends* come up and down from using the rooms beside mine. I shiver in fear, as the various noises sound out loud and unashamed. Random moans, screams of more, verbal vulgarity, water flushing and running taps in the bathroom. The noises are as often as the pounding on the stairs is.

Picking myself up, I shuffle uncomfortably into my tiny cubbyhole. Curling myself into a ball, I pull my knees tight into my chest in a bid to protect myself.

Except, I know it's no use. It doesn't matter where I hide because he finds me.

He always finds me.

Sitting in my usual spot, I throw down my old cushion to provide some extra comfort to my lower body, which still feels fragile from whatever abuse I don't have a recollection of, even though it was only two days ago. I am still undecided as to whether or not that's a good thing. The intermittent, subdued pain is yet another stark reminder of the latest *incident* in a long line of failures at the hands of my parents.

Feeling around the immediate space, the book I was reading the last time I was reduced to hiding in here is thrown haphazardly to the other side of the tiny box. Two nights ago, I had long since abandoned it and the torch I was using to illuminate the darkness surrounding me. It was just another indicator of where I was hiding.

But it didn't matter, because he found me, the same way he always does. The nameless, faceless man of my nightmares. The silhouette of doom, the harbinger of death. The man who haunts my dreams and pulls me into a bottomless pit of despair.

He found me.

Loud, heavy footsteps stop abruptly outside my bedroom door. The voices are hushed, and I hear the tell-tale squeak of the knob turning slowly. The sound of the lock twisting is my impending doom. It is the noise that keeps me awake at night, and the noise I fear more than anything else in the world.

"She's locked the fucking door! Get it open!" The sound of brute force being levied on my door from the outside is deafening. My hands clench tight over my ears as each body blow hits it. Eventually - predictably - the structure weakens, and the sound of splintering wood and twisting metal resounds loudly, echoing my fate.

My breath quickens as the sound of feet enter the room, drowning out everything else happening around me. I tense up and force myself to remain quiet, as the door creaks open and the owner of the voice, one that should be protecting me, calls me out with fake compassion.

"Sweets?"

I don't answer, and I don't dare move. This has been my life for years, and I am counting down the remaining days until I can either finally run free or rest easy for eternity. Until I can sleep at night and not dream of nightmares that psychologically slay me each time I close my eyes.

"She's not fucking here! You promised me, and you know I always collect. You find her or suffer the fucking consequences!"

The door slams shut, and I let out the breath that I'm holding so ardently, so fearfully. My lungs constrict and release. Reaching my hand out to the cubbyhole door, I rattle the handle. *Thank God I remembered to lock it this time.*

The footsteps retreat from outside my bedroom, and are drowned out effortlessly by the volume of the music drifting up from downstairs, and a couple moaning relentlessly in the room next door.

I slap my hand on the floor, feeling for the torch and switch it on to see what time it is. Brilliant, I sigh at my watch. I have been hiding up here for hours. I flick the switch off again and rest my head back, counting the invisible sheep under a shroud of darkness in the tiny space.

My eyes feel heavy, and I make myself as comfortable as possible for the long night ahead. The party doesn't sound like it is dying down anytime soon, as a matter of fact, it sounds like it's getting louder. Surely it can't be going on for much longer? My only consolation is that my father will most likely be stinking drunk, or high, or both, by the time he is ordered to find me again.

I can only hope.

Holding myself tight in the darkness, my mind wanders through all the things I should be doing right now. How I wish I'd had a normal life and not the one given to me. How I wish I had parents who actually cared.

Regardless of what occurs inside this house of horrors, my main priority is school and homework - which I stupidly left downstairs. If I'd have known I was going to be in this godforsaken room for hours, I would have brought it up with me, rather than wasting precious time. The only way I am escaping this shithole of an existence is with good marks. My life might not be my own inside these four walls, but I don't let what happens in this house dictate how well I perform in school. Naturally, it dictates my ability to make friends and to interact. I have been hauled into the head teacher's office on more than one occasion for fighting and back chatting, but attitude is the only way I can protect myself. I know the other girls at school look at me like I'm shit they walked in, while the boys speak loud and clear that they think I'm some cheap slut. Judging by the way my body survives broken and bruised on a daily basis, they are probably right. I am a self-inflicted loner with only one friend to my name, but that's how I prefer it. The less anyone knows about me, the safer I am.

A tired sigh escapes my throat, and my eyes are unquestionably heavy. Groaning, I realise that if I make it through tonight - undiscovered *and* unscathed - I am going to look exhausted tomorrow. Some of my teachers have already started to ask questions, tentatively testing the proverbial waters as such. It would just be the icing on the cake for them if I arrived tomorrow looking half-dead. It would prove their suspicions are not just unfounded fantasies.

My eyelids begin to droop as sleep beckons me, but I can't let it tempt me. I have to stay awake. I have to fight. And I do. I fight so hard not to let it take me away with it, but I lose the battle when an almighty yawn ripples from deep inside, and stupidly, I allow it to.

The cubbyhole door flies open at speed. The sound of wood and metal cracking snap me out of subconsciousness. Rubbing my eyes as I come to, the frame of a large man fills the doorway. The light of the room floods in behind him. Ironically, I might have mistaken him for an angel, if I couldn't already see he has the face of the devil. His mouth contorts into a wry grin, and his arm reaches inside towards me. I push myself back against the wall, but there is nowhere left to hide in this six by three space. His hand grabs me, and I fight with all I've got for him not to touch me. Unforgiving fingers tighten around my wrists, and with one swift pull, I'm up on my feet, and he drags me to him. I tilt my head to the side, as far back as I can manage, while he sneers at me and licks his lips.

"We're gonna have some fun, sweets!" He hauls me out of the cubbyhole and throws me on the bed. I turn just in time to see a familiar figure closing the door behind him, leaving me to my fate. I scream at the top of my lungs, praying he will come back.

But he won't.

He never does.

Tears form in my eyes, realising my safe haven is no longer safe, and I have just been sold to repay his debt.

I crawl back into the bed until my spine hits the wall, and the pain reverberates up and down each vertebrate.

There is nowhere for me to run.

The man standing in front of me, still with a grin on his face, shrugs off his jacket and begins unfastening his belt. A strange sense of déjà-vu overcomes me, and I know, somewhere deep inside, this is not the first time I have met him.

"Please, don't!" I cry at him. "Please, I'm begging you!" I scream out as my tears fall like a river, burning everything in their path. I reach my hands up to try and push him away, but it's pointless. I already know what the outcome will be tonight.

I silently pray not to see daybreak.

The man reaches over and yanks the back of my neck, and my body turns limp. He's holding me prone by my ponytail, as he looks me up and down. The burn developing at the back of my head, from my hair stretching at their follicles, is agonising.

"Don't struggle you little bitch; you'll only make it worse. Or maybe you fucking like it rough?" he says, a little too satisfied.

An eternity seems to pass by, but finally, my instincts kick in like a wrecking ball, and I slap him hard across the face. My hand burns in the aftershock of the action. My arms flail out, and I scratch him repeatedly, clawing like a dog, trying to escape him. Beyond angry, he tosses me back down like a rag doll. Bringing his hand to his mouth to inspect the damage, he spits the watery blood onto the carpet and turns back to me enraged.

"You little fucking bitch! What did I tell you?" he screams at me.

I scramble off the bed, not knowing where to turn. I spy the open window, knowing it's my only escape. But before I can put my plan into action, a large, unforgiving hand restrains my ankle and jerks me back. Flipping me over, I am now underneath him. *Trapped*.

He smashes his fist over my face, and I feel my jaw dislodge. Screaming out in agony, he leans over and drags my arms over my head, securing them in one hand. I kick my legs out, and he shakes his head as a sudden, white-hot searing pain engulfs the top of my thigh. Looking down the length of my body, my eyes widen when I see the knife, its tip coated with my blood. He brings it up to my face and then presses it into my neck until I can feel the sharp edge begging to penetrate the surface of my skin. I quiet down instantly, sobbing at the inevitable that will come to pass before tonight is through.

Defeated, I close my eyes, struggling in vain to try and shut him out. His hands rub over my middle and bile seeps into my throat. The acid burns and vomit enters my mouth. I swallow it back down, blocking out the putrid taste of my own stomach. If only I could block out the feeling of him touching me, violating me.

I whimper, as he starts to drag my jeans down my legs and rips the t-shirt from my torso. The ringing in my ears is loud, but all I can hear is the flimsy, cheap fabric being shredded under his hands. They then roam over my body again. I feel sick - not that it went away in the first place - and I dry heave, as his hands touch me in places they shouldn't. I want nothing more than to die this instant.

My breaths come out in long, fear-infused pants, while my heart beats out of control, thundering hard and painful against my chest. I fear I'm going to have a heart attack, and I pray that if I do, it takes me quickly.

My eyes are still closed in the final minutes before the last remaining items of my clothes are forcibly removed, and another set of footsteps enter the room. And somewhere between the second heavy punch to my face - which annihilates my sight completely - and his hand getting higher and higher on my thigh, my ankles and wrists are being restrained by another set of hands that I cannot see.

Something then pricks sharply at my neck, and I pass out.

"You son of a bitch!"

"Say what you want, pussy! I'm fucking done here!"

My body feels broken and ravaged. This pain is far worse than anything else I have ever felt before. It seeps through my limbs at an excruciating rate, and I scream out in agony, trying in vain to position my arm underneath myself to lift up. The weight is too much to bear, and I drop back down with a soft thud. My body feels incapacitated and unresponsive.

Two nights ago was tame in comparison to this.

This feels like torture.

The sound of sobbing and whimpering in the room sobers me instantly. It's too easy to identify the pitiful, mournful sounds of my own broken voice, laced with the tears of a freshly fractured and abused girl. I want to speak and beg him not to hurt me again, but I'm unable to make a sound. My mouth refuses to open; my jaw is heavy and sore.

I wince under the soft, caring touch of a stranger I can barely see. My eyes are partially closed - and it's not because I am squeezing them shut. The pain coming from every nerve ending and muscle tells me I have not only been raped, but beaten beyond comprehension.

"Easy, don't move. I've got you. I've got you." The stranger's arms hold me gently, but firmly, as he lifts me up. My body stings with every step he takes. Even the smallest jolt is a complete shock to my system. I'm trapped in a dark place of never-ending pain.

The cold air of early spring whips around my body, chilling me to the bone. The indicative signs of my skin breaking out in goosebumps implies that I am completely naked now. The scattered memories of what the man did start to break out clearly inside my head. I replay them over and over in order to block them aside. It's the first step in my mission not to remember.

"Hey, man, get the door! Get those blankets and layer them over the back." I cry harder at his words and turn my head slowly towards the sound of his voice. His familiar dark hair causes me to panic. I know it isn't over; he is giving me a cruel reprieve before he starts all over again.

Please, God, no, not again. Not again.

"No, baby, we're not going to hurt you," he speaks again, as I feel something being wrapped around my abused body. "We're going to get you to a doctor. Just sleep, okay?" He places me down, and the hard surface beneath my back is too painful. I feel a big hand stroke over my cheek, and it is the most tender anyone has ever been with me, from what I can remember of the montage of childhood memories currently flooding my brain.

The car roars to life and moves off. Each jolt or brake feels like I am going to shatter, and the blankets do little to protect my broken body. It is too reminiscent of being punched and repeatedly kicked, as the vehicle lurches forward, faster and faster. I have no idea what time it is, nor where I am. I hear nothing except the sound of an engine rumbling, hushed voices of various different men, and the tears of my own heartbreak.

As someone begins to touch my limbs, my eyes close under the swelling. I grow numb and block out the way he touches me. I can't fight him off a second time; I couldn't even do it the first. Only this time I pray that I will never have to wake again.

Shifting under the hands of an unknown man, I finally concede that I can never trust anyone from this day forward. Making a promise to myself, I vow to never weaken my resolve again, or to rely on anyone to get me through life. Provided I survive this torture, I know I can never learn to love again because my heart is now dead. It died the moment my father closed the door and left me with a monster.

A truth I have known for so long, but never dared to fully acknowledge, seeps to the surface of my damaged and permanently scarred soul - my own parents have failed me. They have failed to keep me safe in every way a parent should. They have failed more times than I can even begin to count. It is their mistakes that have led me to this place of unimaginable pain and suffering.

With a slow, heavy beating heart, the first brick of an invisible wall drops into place. Each one thereafter falls in line, forming an impenetrable structure around me. Standing on the edge of no return, the darkness in my mind is heavenly. With open arms, I finally give myself over to it, and it takes me under.

Happy fifteenth birthday.

Chapter 1

"YOU'VE GOT A foul fucking mouth, Petersen!"

"Screw you, arsehole!"

"You better have it by the end of the week, or I'll get it my own way!" Danny says suggestively, leaning his full weight on either side of the architrave.

"Fuck you!" I throw back, watching him finally retreat from my front door. I have listened to him bitch about late rent payments all week, and I've had enough. Slamming the door shut behind my irate landlord, the wood creaks ominously under the unnecessary force imposed upon it.

Marching down the small hallway with determination, I stand in the doorway of the living room with my hands on my hips. My foot taps wildly, vexed and out of control. Sam moves slowly, bringing her forearm over her face and rubbing the sleep from her eyes. Picking up the cushion from the chair beside me, I throw it at her with as much force as I can muster. She shoots up the instant it bounces off her stomach and gives me a look of pure annoyance. My hands ball into tight fists. She's so goddamn lucky it isn't something harder!

"What?" she asks, bleary-eyed, and as innocently as she can in her current condition. She's pushing her luck. And, by acting like she doesn't know what I am so angry about, she's insulting my intelligence as well as her own.

"Where the fuck is the rent money, Samantha!?" I glower at my roommate. She lifts up and stares at me, glassy-eyed and vacant. She has undoubtedly been high all night - *on our rent money.*

"For God sake, Kara, I will get the fucking money. Stop complaining," she grumbles into the pillow, repositioning herself for the impending sleep that her body is most likely screaming for.

I have lived with Samantha Jones for over three years. We first met in nursery nearly twenty years ago. She was the little girl who lit up the room, all long blonde hair, and sparkling, blue eyes. But all that changed as we grew. Over the last few years, I have witnessed her slow decline into oblivion. I've known for a while that she has been using more regularly, but I choose to turn a blind eye for far too long.

Now, it was paying me back tenfold.

After not seeing her for days on end, she finally resurfaced and came home around three this morning. I didn't need to see her to know she was coming down from being high all weekend. I heard it loud and clear when she fell into every piece of second-hand furniture we owned, before finally passing out on the sofa.

"You said that five days ago! You know, this may come as a surprise to you, but if we don't pay the rent, we get evicted! Remember it was your idea to move into this privately let shithole together, so I suggest you get whatever is going on sorted because I'm tired of financially bailing you out, Sam. It's not fair!"

"So, what the hell are you going to do? Walk out and not come back? It may come as a surprise to *you* that *we* are jointly and severally liable!" she spouts out the tenancy wording sarcastically, raising her head up to look me in the eye.

"Well, *we* are going to have some serious issues, if *you* don't get off your arse and sort out the shit you have put us smack bang in the middle of!"

Unable to control my frustration any longer, I throw my hands in the air. I am thoroughly pissed off, not just with the money situation - which seems to be escalating deeper with each passing month - but the fact that she has a reckless, devil-may-care attitude regarding it.

Leaving her where she lies, I stride into my bedroom, drag my coat and bag off the bed and storm back into the living room. Passing her by, I grip the handles of my bag tightly, because the urge to wrap them around her throat is too strong to ignore.

"I'm going to work. I suggest you use the time to figure out how to pay our rent arrears. And you better be sober by the time I come home, or I swear I will do fucking time for you, Samantha Jones!" I scream back at her while stomping down the hallway and out of the flat.

Taking the stairs two at a time, my blood is hovering at boiling point. I'm so fucking fed up of her lies. *Two weeks*. Two weeks of listening to her lie about the whereabouts of our missing rent money. Except, we both know it isn't missing - it has long been snorted up her nose.

Gone forever.

Her penchant for the old blow was more than a weekend jolly folly these days. She was dependent. When faced with the truth that I choose to ignore, it is crystal clear she has been addicted for far longer than even she realises. It is also an addiction that I'm not sure I can live through with her. Drugs had inadvertently destroyed me, and it's a path I fear to tread again. Yet I have no one to blame for this but myself. I had trusted her to hand over the payments on time, even when I knew she was a certified addict. I knew the signs; I had seen them growing up.

And I had paid for them growing up, too.

The morning chill of the mid-March air feels good against my overheated skin as I try to calm down. I lean against the outside door and let out a resigned huff. Unlocking my piece of shit car, I plop myself into the driver's seat and smash my hand against the steering wheel in frustration. I press my back into the seat and look up, needing to find a way out of this mess with her.

All our money was currently being spent on keeping her lows high, and now I'm running out of options. I earn a decent living for myself, and have worked hard to get where I am. If it wasn't for my wayward friend and the constant need to bail her out financially, I would have more saved. But sadly, I didn't, and what little I did have was diminishing alarmingly.

Turning the ignition, the car refuses to start. "Oh, come on! Don't fucking do this, you bitch!" I curse at her. After threatening her with the scrap yard, she finally garners some life after three attempts. I pull out of the car park and join the rush hour traffic.

The drive into the city is a nightmare, not that it's different from any other day, but Monday's always seem to be the worst. Why there is consistently more traffic on the roads on one particular day of the week and not on the others, is anyone's guess. I watch the scenery change from the partially rundown area of East London that Sam and I live in, to the built-up, sophisticated, metropolitan towers of the city.

It takes me ten, profanity-laced minutes to find a free space - one which I've had to pay for - since someone has so kindly parked in my reserved bay. Thank you very much.

Flashing my security card at the automatic door lock, I make my way up the stairs. Unlocking the door that is home to Dawson's Catering, I hang my coat on the rack and make my way into the tiny box kitchen. Filling the kettle to boil, I walk back out, switch on the two computers and wait for them to boot up. I fish out my mobile to let Marie know that I'm in and to call me back.

Marie Dawson is the owner, my boss, and my *aunt*, for all intent and purposes. She was the first person who had taken a chance on me eight years ago when I had turned my back on my old life at the tender age of fifteen.

Waiting for the computers to load up, my mind drifts back to those dark, lonely days.

I had been offered a ride from Manchester to London. I arrived with nothing, except the clothes on my back, and what I had managed to salvage in those last desperate minutes, after running away from the hospital, the Social Services, and the Manchester Metropolitan Police. I had no idea what I was going to do. My first plan of action was to find a women's shelter and take it from there. I knew they would call the authorities once they discovered I was underage, but at least I would have a warm, *safe*, bed for the night.

Needless to say, that didn't quite work out as well as I had originally planned.

After roaming around the city for long, lonely hours, I had run into some other teenagers who were squatting together in an old, derelict house, which was definitely not fit for human habitation. As in any normal situation, I had been wary at first and tried running from them. One of the girls, Sarah, took me under her wing, and she became my friend. The others warmed to me slowly. I was grateful when they shared their food and gave me a place to sleep. Even though I was off the streets, it wasn't safe. I saw things that were no different from the council estate I had grown up on. Most nights, I slept fully clothed with a knife clutched to my chest in fear that I might be raped.

Again.

Every day was a struggle, a battle to stay safe and whole, and to ensure there was enough to eat. The other teens I lived with managed to steal enough food on a daily basis, and somehow, kept the water at the house flowing - albeit it was cold. They had also hacked into the electricity supply from the street level, I don't know how, but we never went overboard with it. A surge in electricity at a condemned house would've had the authorities crawling all over us, and we all knew what that would result in. Regardless, it still couldn't compare to a proper hot meal and constant warmth.

Then one night, my life changed completely. I met Marie.

I was waiting with intent in an alleyway at the back of a plush hotel. There was some function going on that night. According to the sign on the placard outside the main entrance, it was a gala for the rich and famous to get wasted while emptying their pockets of any excess change. I waited for ages in the cold night, watching the kitchen staff regularly come and go for a quick fag or a drink. The grand plan of execution was to sneak in and sneak out with my pockets full of food, preferably without them noticing. It didn't quite play out that way, and fortunately for me - or unfortunately, depending on your point of view - Marie caught me in the act before the hotel manager did. Although I didn't come across as it, I was terrified. She was observant enough to notice that I was homeless, cold and starving. After ordering me to stay put, she kindly gave me my first proper meal in months, followed by a stiff talking to. She made it clear she would call the police unless I gave her a good reason not to. My reason was damn good. Softening towards a teenage girl with a painful past and little to no future, she gave me a place to stay. She made me go back to school to get my GCSE's and then to college.

She gave me a chance to live, and I will always be grateful and indebted to her for it.

Now, eight years later, I'm her assistant, except she always introduces me as her office manager, which is actually a more accurate description, considering these four walls are pretty much my domain.

Reaching my small, but perfectly coordinated desk with a fresh coffee in hand, I glance at my effects. My flat might be messy at times, with various levels of clean and dirty, but my desk is immaculate.

Opening my calendar, I trawl through my diary to see what is scheduled for today. There is a meeting at eleven at the Emerson Hotel for a function being held there in a few months' time. Digging into the filing cabinet, I shake my head when I see she has forgotten to take the bloody file with her. This is so typical of Marie – always disorganised.

I remember the day I first walked into the office. It was the day after I left college, and the sheer dread that I was faced with was insurmountable. Initially, I was pleased when she told me she had a nice job for me over the summer since I was still undecided whether or not I was going to university. I thought I would just be sitting around, answering the phone, ordering sandwiches and reading magazines. My heart sank when she dropped a two-foot stack of paperwork at my feet and told me to organise it. I thought I was doing very well by day four, seeing as I had miraculously managed to clear it all and categorise it correctly. You can imagine my horror when she pointed into another room, and I saw more of where it came from.

It still makes me smile to this day.

Quickly scanning through the Emerson file, I let out a frustrated breath. She always manages to mix up my bloody files. I have a system in place, it's not hard, but it's one she still fails to abide by. She forgets it's me who has to book and pay for all the stuff that gets ordered. Reorganising the folder to my liking, complete with my colour coordinated wallets, I elastic band it and put it back in the filing cabinet.

I quickly type up a text to let her know I still have the working file here, and, in bold, shouting capitals, I admonish her for the state of it, and also for thinking she could sway my resolve in such a deceitful way. The truth is, she was actually hoping I would go with her. By leaving the file behind, she probably expected I would hot-foot it over to the hotel, but we both knew that wouldn't happen, considering my preference of existing under a cloak of invisibility.

As far as I was concerned, I answered the phones, dealt with any queries, and God forbid, any complaints. I booked the five-course dinners, and made sure the free champagne was delectable and supplied on tap - she did all the leg work!

Opening the monthly accounts spreadsheet, I quickly start to input the figures from the last two functions. My fingers glide over the keys furiously, and I bite the inside of my cheek, praying to all that is holy the numbers add up. If they don't, I will be paying a grovelling trip downstairs to our friendly accountant, who seems to avoid everyone in the small building at all costs.

"That's not right!" I mutter to myself, dropping my head in my hands. I swear if she messes up the formulas on my spreadsheets again, there will be some matricide being committed in this office.

Glancing at the clock, it has gone ten, and the numbers are still not adding up. Frustrated, I throw my pen on the desk and pick up my mobile. I ponder to myself if it is too late in the morning to be arranging lunch in a few hours' time?

What the hell, it can't hurt to ask.

I send a text to Sophie to see if she wants to meet. Her response is almost immediate:

Yes! Ned 2 tel u sumting. 12 x

Re-reading the message again, I consider myself lucky that I can actually decrypt and understand it. I flaming hate text talk and she is the worst offender for it! She knows how much I despise it, and thus, she makes it all the more cryptic at times. But I do love her, so I allow her the indiscretion of forgetting every now and again.

Sophie Morgan was the first girl I met when Marie made me go back to school to finish my final year. She had taken me under her wing, much the same way Sarah once had, and we became inseparable. I'm glad that we have remained close friends ever since and not drifted apart. She now works for a large firm of solicitors in the city. She is the personal assistant to, in her words, the biggest arsehole walking, but she tolerates it because there is nothing else out there at the moment. Far too many in her sector are unemployed, and as much as she dreads going to work each morning, she also has to keep a roof over her head. Many nights have been spent debating the pros and cons of being unemployed over a bottle of wine or two.

Putting the phone back down, I slouch in my seat, thinking about what she is so desperate to tell me. I'm more than aware of the rumours circulating lately, and they all come back to the same person: Samantha. Shaking the thoughts of her from my head, I bury myself in work.

Time flies by, and the next time I glance at the clock, it's nearly midday. I can feel a tension headache starting to build due to staring at the screen for long periods, and my coffee has long since turned cold and stale. This morning has actually been quite productive after I finally managed to balance the books and reinstate my well-formatted spreadsheets to being golden again.

Stretching in my chair, I feel the pressure building uncomfortably in my lower body. I pad down to the shared ladies' toilets and lock the door behind me. After doing what I need to, I stare at my reflection in the mirror while washing my hands, noting that my appearance is very lacklustre as of late. Not that it has ever sparkled in the past.

My long, medium brown hair is in need of a trim and maybe even some colour. My skin is still dry looking and chapped, from the long winter that has finally come to an end. And my green eyes look dull, even under the harsh fluorescent lights. I remember back to the time they used to glow, and were more emerald than the drab moss shade staring back at me.

I smile at my pathetic reflection and feel satisfied. My aim to achieve invisibility in life has succeeded.

This is exactly as it should be, and exactly as I want it to be. I'm nothing special. I don't stand out in a crowd. I rarely attract anyone, and in equal measure, I've never really been attracted to anyone. Not to mention, the fact that I avoid physical contact like the plague. These are also the reasons why I have rarely dated, and the few times I have, well, they proved to be disasters of epic proportions. I guess it doesn't help my cause that I can't stand to have anyone within a few feet of me, or to some I come across as asexual, and not worth the time or effort. The only thing the past, mentally demeaning, disastrous dates had afforded me was the ability to still feel something, even if it did hurt to let someone try and touch me. I roll my eyes, thinking back to the many times I've been called a tease or a slut. The few times arseholes thought *no* really meant *yes* when I was unable to give them more than I physically or emotionally could.

I'm consciously aware this isn't the best way to exist, but it is another layer of the wall that blocks out everything and everyone. I've been told on more than one occasion I have underlying issues. Each time I would wave it off because I knew exactly what those issues were. I live with them every second of every single day. They defined me, they shaped me, and they have made me what I am. I didn't need some overworked, underpaid NHS funded shrink to spell it out to me. I've frequented more one-on-one therapy sessions than I care to admit to. Some might think I need sectioning, and God knows there have times when I've felt the need to sign myself over, but truthfully, I just want to be left alone.

Permanently.

I stare down at my wrist, and the light catches my scar.

It hasn't been easy.

Life, that is.

Everyone thinks I've finally achieved peace, and therein found my place in the world. But it's all lies. No one knows; not Marie, not Sophie, and definitely not Sam. They don't realise that the darkness of my life is still so deeply ingrained in me, that some days I fear I won't make it through if I allow the truth to consume me. They don't know the truth. They don't know what I lived through, and the worst part of it all, I don't either.

I made sure I would never remember.

Over the last eight years, I have carefully constructed invisible walls to keep myself safe inside, and to keep everyone else out. I can still remember it like it was yesterday when the first brick fell into place - the second the foundation became set in stone. There is no going back now – I couldn't even if I wanted to. It's beyond the ridiculous and extreme, and I'm well aware that I'm setting myself up for a fall later in life, but I can't go back there again. I can't.

I won't be that girl I desperately want to forget.

The one crying in pain in the darkness.

The one begging for God to take her because surely death has to be better than living.

Quickly and harshly, I brush away the stray tear and the memory that accompanies it. I hate myself for having such a moment of weakness. Weakness equals pain in my book. My father's weakness brought about my pain.

Straightening up and taking a few deep breaths, I collect my things from the office and pull my coat on. I swing my bag over my shoulder and grab my umbrella - since the heavens have opened heavily outside - and make my way downstairs for a social lunch.

The five minute walk to meet Sophie is an effort in itself. The rain is unforgiving against my face, and I can already feel the burn of the cold against my cheeks. My hair is now more than a little damp, due to the long queue at the cash machine, and the fact that my brolly wouldn't stop blowing inside out. Needless to say, it now resides in a bin since it was about as useful as a chocolate fireguard. Then again, you do get what you pay for, and a one-pound umbrella was never going to stand the test of time against the English wind and rain.

I finally hustle into the café, looking like a drowned rat, with my hair now soaked and plastered to my face. Sophie is already sat down, twirling her highlighted, light brown locks in her fingers and flicking through a magazine, wearing a bored expression.

"Hey chick!" she calls me over, pointing down at the table where lunch is sat ready and waiting. My stomach growls when my eyes register the food. Stripping out of my wet coat, she smiles brightly and hands me a few napkins. Patting my face dry, I grab the mug and take a sip, relishing the heat the drink is providing.

"So, how was your weekend?" She's all light and optimism. *Always*. Unlike me, her glass is always half full.

"Interesting," I answer nonchalantly. She spies me curiously, and I know she is dying to talk about whatever she was so desperate to convey this morning.

Taking a bite of my ham and cheese, I really don't want to talk in any great detail about the tragedy currently comatose on my sofa. I'm positive by the time I get home this evening, rigor mortis might have even set in. I avert my eyes, knowing full well Sophie can read me like a book - everyone who knows me can. I'm aware that I am facially expressive, but I didn't think I was that clear-cut.

Sophie's eyes sadden a little at me. "That's what I wanted to talk about. Some of the girls had seen her out with a few scary-looking guys the other night, and they said she looked high. Is she still using?" she asks in a hushed tone, glancing around to make sure we're not overheard. I nod, swallowing hard.

There's no point in speaking of it, trying to find a way to evaluate and justify it, the truth hurts too much. I have spent my entire adult life trying to escape the pitfalls of addiction and pain. Just when I thought I was finally arriving at a good place in life, another obstacle would be thrown my way. Looking around the café, the few people who were in here have now gone, and only a few customers are waiting to be served.

"I hadn't seen her since the last time we spoke. She finally resurfaced around three this morning. She looks awful, but I don't know what to do anymore. I can't turn my back on her, but at the same time, I don't want to help her. I know that sounds really cruel, and I'm not being a bitch, but I just can't do it any longer," I say, my hand shaking softly on the tabletop. Sophie's fingers come over mine, and my breath catches in my throat, as the slow burn starts to envelop my hand.

"It's not cruel, Kara. I would feel the same. I know you want to help her, but if she doesn't want it, you can't force it. Look, if you need somewhere to stay, give us a ring."

"Thanks, but I don't want to put you out."

"Don't be stupid. It'd be nice to have some company, instead of going home to an empty house and a cat that uses me for food." I chuckle. Like I said, always on the bright side.

Sophie doesn't push any further after imparting her views, and I sit and stare out of the window. The sky has darkened considerably, and I'm mesmerised by the way the rain pelts against the glass. Glancing back at her, seeing her lips move, my own thoughts run rampant through my brain like wild horses. And for the second time today, my mind drifts back to the terrified girl that used to hide in her cubbyhole. The one who used to lock her bedroom door in fear every night.

I drain the contents of my mug, ask Sophie if she wants another - she doesn't - and move to the counter for a second coffee. My mind is still awash with emotions, as I attempt to dam the torrent of unwelcome memories and horrors I can recall a little clearer because I have finally let a handful resurface.

Fresh coffee in hand, I head back to the table and sit. I give Sophie a weak smile. "How much do I owe you?" I ask, needing something other than the train wreck at home to speak about.

She waves her hand very blasé. "You can pay next time. Or maybe we'll call it your birthday lunch since you skipped out on drinks last week," she says, clucking her tongue at me.

"Soph, in the years you have known me, how many times have I skipped out on drinks with you? Hmm?"

"Last week!" She smiles broadly. I groan when I realise what she's doing.

"No!"

"Yes!"

"No. N. O. No!"

"Fine, I'll just drag you out!" I roll my eyes at her; we both know she wouldn't dream of it. She sits opposite, giving me a pouty, innocent look, knowing full well I will eventually break under the guilt trip.

"Fine! Birthday drinks it is, then! I'm guessing the usual suspects will be making an appearance?"

"Of course! Don't worry, I'll make sure they don't hire you a stripper or anything!"

My mouth falls open in shock. "*Sophie,*" I say in warning.

"Seriously, just a few quiet drinks with friends, belated birthday girl!" she says, clapping her hands together.

We eventually finish lunch and start to go our separate ways. Sophie makes me promise to call her if anything happens when I get home, and also not to cry off on my birthday drinks. After yielding that I will, and also that I won't, she lets me go. I walk steadily back to the office in the rain, my mind a blur with an abundance of emotions and feelings consuming it.

It is far too easy to become lost in life.

The only trouble is, I have never been found.

A little after two, my phone starts vibrating across the desk. I eye it suspiciously. The only people who know my number are my parents, Sophie, Marie, and Sam.

I have no internet accounts and only my work email address. I'm also not registered with any social media network sites. The fewer people know about me, the better. It's my safeguard, the way I keep people out and myself safe inside. My only real friends are Sam - if I can still call her that at the moment - Sophie, and a few girls that we both went to college with.

Picking up my mobile, I groan when I see the name on the screen. "Yes?" I snap out, tapping my finger, waiting for the latest round of lies to leave his lips.

Pleasantries are not something that will ever pass between us, no matter how hard he tries to come across as caring. Even as a child, his presence stirred something inside me that I could never explain. Now I know better. Yet I just don't seem to know when to sever all ties completely.

"Kara, don't be like that. I just want to talk," his voice slurs on the other end of the phone. "I thought that maybe you could come up and see us, your mum has been asking about you for days."

My mum! *How dare he use her as an excuse!* I scoff at his audacity, and his obvious, but failed attempt at hiding behind the true nature of his call.

"*Really*? The only time you want to see me is when *you* need something. So how much is it this time, Ian?" I'm beyond irritated, and I half-listen while he rattles on about getting a new job, saying he will pay me back. He's been paying me back for years. As much as I despise him, and what he allowed to be done to me all those years ago, I still love my mother. How could I not, knowing her life isn't much better than mine had been back then?

"I don't need much, just a few hundred quid will do," he says, a little more perceptive this time.

"*A few hundred quid?* Where do you think I'm getting that kind of money? Look, whatever mess you're in, you better find your own way out. I'm done with you. If Mum needs anything, tell her to call me herself." I wait for him to hang up.

He doesn't.

"Come on, Kara, I'm in trouble up here. I owe some money to Franklin, and he's coming to collect. *Soon*."

I sigh.

Rigidly, I stand, and walk away from my desk and into the kitchen, with the phone still nestled against my ear. Even as an adult, the mere mention of *that* man still makes my skin crawl. I lean against the worktop, listening to the silence thicken between us. Hundreds of miles might separate us now, but it doesn't make me feel any more relaxed.

"No, I can't help you, Ian," I say with conviction, my resolve final.

"They're gonna kill me, sweets."

I say nothing.

"Please, I'm begging you!"

He's begging the wrong person.

The silence is deafening as he waits for me to cave. He'll be waiting for a very long time. Realising I am not wavering, he starts swearing at me and calling me by *that* name. I despise it more than anything else in my life.

Sweets!

"Don't call me that!" I hiss.

"You just fucking killed me! You've fucking killed me, Kara." The line goes dead.

I brace my hands on the sink, fearing my legs might give out from under me. I gulp in a few deep cleansing breaths; only nothing will ever be able to clean out the shit from my past. I lean forward and splash some cold water on my face, then pat it dry with some paper towels.

A rustling in the entranceway tells me Marie is back. I straighten and leave the kitchen, just in time to see her bluster in. She looks fantastic in her black tailored skirt suit, with her short blonde, bobbed hair perfectly in place. I know I look a complete mess in comparison. One simple, fleeting glance my way will easily tell her of my newly formed distress.

"I have to tell you all about the man I met today at the Emerson. He was so bloody rude! An arrogant little bastard! Didn't seem bothered in the slightest at what I was offering! Just wait until I tell-" She quietens immediately when she notices me lingering in the doorway. A frown of concern replaces her welcoming smile. "Oh, no, what has she done now?"

I don't even bother trying to hide the anguish I know is written all over my face, clear for her to see. Disappointment slices through my insides. It has taken me years to try and perfect the false façade that screams I don't give a damn, but lately, that guise is disintegrating fast.

"No, it's not her. My dad just called," I say quietly, allowing my hatred for the man to devour me. I bring my hand to my eyes, trying to hide the despair I am currently feeling for myself, and the life I have been bestowed with. The sham of an existence I have to live with.

"Want to talk about it?" she asks sympathetically.

"No." What's the point? It wouldn't change anything. It wouldn't remove the bad elements. Talking just makes it more destructive.

Putting one hand on her hip, she starts to shake her head. "Look, go home. You've done more than enough this morning," she says warmly, putting her bag on the desk. "I suggest you have a chat with Sam, too. I've heard some stuff lately, but I'm not quite sure how true it is." She gives me the same sad eyes that Sophie had only a few hours ago.

I nod knowingly. I'd also heard the rumours swirling around regarding Sam's current lifestyle, and it wasn't just the mention of over-consumption of illegal drugs that were being tossed out there. The small group of friends I occasionally went out with had mentioned her in passing a few weeks back, and as usual, I brushed them off. At the time, I prayed it wasn't true, but judging by the way she was this morning, and the fact she had disappeared for the whole weekend, I can't deny it anymore.

"I know; I've heard the same. I spoke to Sophie at lunch, and I... I don't know what to do anymore," I whisper. Watching as she rounds the desk, her arm stretched out to me. I quickly get up and make my way to the door, and she sighs in defeat.

Touching makes me uncomfortable. Seriously, physical touch feels like I'm being slowly eviscerated. For me, it's parallel to a small burning sensation that starts on the surface and burrows itself deep into my soul. It doesn't matter who it is; it always drags me back to a place that I never want to go back to again. Normally, Marie is the only one I can tolerate touching me, but lately, my condition was becoming worse.

"Promise me you'll call if you need anything, honey."

"I will, thanks," I murmur softly, grabbing my bag and coat as I head out of the door.

Chapter 2

IT'S STILL EARLY afternoon, and the rain has finally eased off. Luckily, traffic is relatively light, apart from the bus drivers who honestly thought they owned the roads, and the irate Hackney cabbies, who fisted their horns at whatever annoyance irked them - usually the bus drivers.

As I sit in traffic, contemplating, riding the biting point, I wonder if it would be advantageous to get the Tube or the bus home. If I did, at least I wouldn't be sat burning money on petrol and moving at a snail's pace for miles. The bus in front of me pulls up to its stop, and I wait further back, seeing the mass exodus of bodies alighting and boarding. My skin feels itchy just watching them.

No, I definitely wouldn't do well with public transport.

My *condition* isn't just becoming worse; it has already exceeded that stage. It is now bordering on the line of clinical expertise. I'm not ignorant to it, but it will be a cold day in hell when I openly offer to find help. The only reason I have a long list of numbers pertaining to London shrinks, albeit the NHS ones, was because Marie would put me in the car and spring it on me as late as she could, namely when we were already in the building, and I was speculating. It would take something, or someone, amazing and exceptional, to get me to seek help of my own free will in an attempt to finally cure myself of this self-loathing.

I make it home ten minutes earlier than I usual. Slowly pulling into my parking space, I notice a very expensive black Mercedes in the space next to mine. I can't ever recall seeing it before, and naturally, I'm curious. This isn't the kind of area you leave a beautiful machine like that. I carefully open my door, ensuring I don't scrape the side of it. I stare at it for a few more moments, knowing I will probably never own anything as stunning in my pathetic life.

Pushing open the main door to the dilapidated building, I boycott the lift and start to take the stairs up to the flat. A few months back, the owner - Danny's father - decided the staircases needed to be freshened up in order to procure himself some new tenants. Under duress, I was resigned to get in the bastard thing. As my luck would have it, my reasons for avoiding them were strengthened when it suddenly stopped. Given my fear of confined spaces anyway, it's not an experience I want to relive anytime soon, if ever again.

Approaching my flat, I hear voices coming from the other side of the door. I turn the handle, and it opens in my palm. *She didn't even lock the fucking door!* My patience for her is wearing thin as the day goes on.

Marching into the living room with purpose, I'm stopped short by its occupants. My eyes expand in shock at what she has done.

She has broken rule number one: no men in our home. *Ever*.

I look over the two men sat on our sofa and tilt my head up in acknowledgement to them. These could easily be the two scary guys Sophie had spoken of at lunch. Both large in stature, they are dressed head to toe in black. They each have dark hair and dark eyes, and I have to admit, they are very easy on the eye. The bigger one is grinning at me, and fear starts to course through my body under his relatively attractive, but watchful glare. His companion's eyes are trained on the floor, never abandoning the spot they are fixated on.

A strong feeling cuts through me, and a bizarre sense of familiarity is too intense to brush aside. Except, I am absolutely positive I've never laid eyes on these two prior to today.

"Hey! My friends came by. Hope you don't mind," Sam says cheerily, literally bouncing into the room, obviously forgetting our unfinished argument from this morning. It's more than likely she probably doesn't even remember.

Drugs will do that to you.

She's all big smiles and optimism now, whereas I'm as angry as hell, balancing precariously on the edge of sanity and reason. She knows she isn't allowed to bring anyone back here, and I sure as hell don't want these *friends* thinking we have an open-door policy and dropping by whenever they see fit.

"Sam, can I talk to you for a minute?" I calmly walk down the hallway and into the bathroom, with her following a few steps behind. She closes the door, and I quickly spin on my heels.

"What the fuck?!"

"I'm sorry, they just came by," she says, her pleading tone laced with guilt, which is corroborated when her eyes widen, and she starts to wring her hands together.

"Sam, nobody *just comes by*! Nobody knows where we live, not even my parents! You gave them our address, didn't you?" I ask, feeling the pressure of the day finally spilling over the surface. Her head drops down in confirmation that she most certainly did. I bring my hand to my forehead and rub it firmly.

"Get them out now! I can't take any more of your shit today!" She reaches out to me, but I flinch at her action and quickly move away. "Don't."

"What's happened now?" she asks, apparently forgetting *she* is what happened this morning. She crosses her arms over her chest, clearly pissed off.

Well, that makes two of us, because I feel ready to commit murder!

"The bastard called. He owes money to Franklin. *Again*!" I answer, turning to the sink to stare at my pathetic reflection in the mirror above it.

"Oh, shit! What does he want now? You to bail him out? Fuck him, you've been doing it for years. He needs to learn to deal with his shit himself. He's not down here, is he?" It's times like these I could almost forget the rumours I've heard about Sam. The same way I could almost forget that my father isn't the only person in my life who is a financial drain on my resources.

Almost.

"No, he's still in Manchester. Well, at least I think he is." I turn to look at her, hesitant to ask my next question, but the time for ignorance has been and gone given the men currently sitting in our living room. "Sam, I've heard some stuff recently, and I want you to tell me the truth-"

"Leave it, Kara!" she says defiantly, twisting her head towards the living room. "Look, I'm going out. I'll see you when I get back."

"And will that be tonight, next week, or next month? I don't know, next year, maybe, if I'm lucky?" I mutter sarcastically. She doesn't respond. Instead, she just glares at me and shakes her head. She walks out of the bathroom, and I follow.

I hang back in the living room doorway, watching as she collects her things. I cross my arms over my chest and look at the men on the sofa again, their eyes trail me from head to toe while I wait impatiently for them to get out. Their perusal makes me shiver. Something just doesn't feel right.

"Hey, I'm Deacon," the larger of the two says. He stands and moves a little closer, and his body casts a shadow from the sunlight penetrating the room. I inch back discreetly under his evident curiosity. His eyes are judging me closely. He licks his lips, and his pupils dilate, pinning my body with invisible barbs. I feel nauseous. The look is all-knowing and all-seeing.

"And this is Jeremy." He jerks his hand towards his companion, who is a little smaller, but no less intimidating. He merely looks into my eyes once, then drops them back down. *Very strange.*

I tilt my head a little but don't say a word; they don't deserve anything from me. I look at Sam, her eyes appear weary, old before their time. She walks over to me, and I stiffen when she grabs me and kisses my cheek hesitantly.

"Don't wait up."

A few moments later, the door closes behind them, and I put my ear to it, listening to their collective footsteps retreating further down the hallway until the lift pings faintly. I quickly lock the door and rest my head against it. At last, I'm finally left alone, with nothing but the hum of the refrigerator, and the burning sensation slowly dissipating on my skin.

I kick the wood in frustration.

This is bad.

This is very, very bad.

A buzzing resounds in my head, and I shift in bed. Slowly registering the noise, my eyes feel heavy, and my mouth is dry as I fumble for my vibrating phone. Disorientated and tired, I look at the screen wearily.

"Sam?" Still half asleep, I roll over to see it is two o'clock in the damn morning.

"Kara, please come and get me, I'm scared! Please come!" Oh shit, she doesn't sound good. Her voice is shaky, interspersed with tears.

I am instantly on high alert, wondering what the hell she has been doing for the last ten hours or so. I hate to say I told you so, but I knew it would end badly.

"Sam, where are you?"

Cradling the phone between my head and shoulder, I dash across my small room, throwing on my battered, old jeans and a t-shirt, listening to her mumble incoherently the name of the hotel. I grab my keys and wallet, lock the door behind me and bolt down the stairs.

I turn the key in the ignition and will my Fiesta not to be a bitch, and thankfully, she cooperates. I reverse out of the space at speed, quickly checking my blind spots and mirrors to make sure no police are about, then plough out of the car park faster than I usually do.

Turning onto the main road, I run red lights where I can, well aware I'm breaking a dozen traffic laws and at risk of getting caught by the cameras, but all I can think about is Sam. As much as she made me want to do time for her earlier today - *yesterday* - I couldn't care less, because right now, she's all that matters. She's in trouble, and I know I should turn and walk the other way, but something inside won't let me.

I won't let her down the way that others have done to me. It just isn't an option.

Driving into the city, I ease down on the accelerator slightly and maintain a speed just above the limit. My hand grips the steering wheel tightly, as I wonder what situation might face me when I eventually find her. I want to scream out in frustration that she keeps getting herself into these shit predicaments. That, no sooner does she have a good thing going on, she screws it up disastrously. Nearly three years of living together have taken their toll on me. I have witnessed her drift through life without a care in the world, going from job to job, and man to man, while I was left running behind her, picking up the pieces each time the shit hit the fan and blew up in her face.

My head is on the verge of exploding with thoughts of what state she might be in as I get closer and closer to the hotel. And more importantly, what she has got herself involved in this time.

Except, in my heart of hearts, I already know.

Chapter 3

I PULL UP outside the Emerson Hotel and run inside, leaving the car engine running and effectively blocking the entrance. I wouldn't do it under any other circumstance, but it is very early morning, and no one would want to steal my piece of shit anyway. Or at least I hope not.

Sprinting through the lobby, there are only a couple of people milling around and a few night staff working. I halt abruptly at the grand reception desk and wait for the smart, suited man behind it to slowly make his way over to me.

"Hi, I'm looking for my friend. She said she was here."

"Name?" he asks rudely, while he eyes me with undisguised revulsion.

"Kara Petersen."

"Your friend's name!" he counters sharply.

"S-Samantha J-Jones," I say, suddenly developing a stutter that I've never had before.

The man looks me up and down questionably, taking in my dishevelled appearance and cheap clothes before he picks up the phone. He turns his back to me, and I hear him whispering something to whoever is on the other end. After a few moments, he hangs up and turns to face me, assessing me from head to toe yet again from behind the safety of the marble reception desk. My skin prickles under his unnerving, critical scrutiny, but my shame, in this grand and opulent setting, is battened down in light of why I am here.

"Take the lift to the tenth floor, Miss." Taken aback by his rude and judgemental attitude, I nod and turn to where he is pointing.

I jog quickly to the lifts, prodding the up buttons until one arrives. My fear of confined spaces has taken a back seat as my thoughts fix purely on finding Samantha, and getting the hell away from these snotty, ungrateful people. Pressing the button to the tenth floor, my stomach lurches as the box moves, and I brace my hands on the highly polished brass railing running around the perimeter.

This is one of the three things I hate most in life: the word *sweets,* touching and confined spaces. In that order.

"One, *breathe,* two, *breathe,*" I say to my reflection in the mirror encasing all four sides. I grip the bar tighter, while my stomach does somersaults and threatens to empty itself all over the pristine, black granite floor.

The doors open and I find myself in a private foyer. It is beautifully presented in warm shades of cream, with red accents. I look around in admiration at the grandeur, wondering what on earth the stupid cow has gotten mixed up in this time. And more worryingly, what might meet me on the other side. Even I know this isn't the kind of place you tout for personal services and peddle drugs in.

My stomach recoils noticing the floor holds two suites. My eyes shift between the two doors in front of me, and I press the first doorbell with determination. Straightening my shoulders, I aim to appear confident, yet I feel anything but. There is only one thing filling my head right now: please don't let that sneering, dirty bastard from earlier today be inside this suite. *Please…*

I'm in luck when the door opens, and I just walk straight on in. I don't even stop to see who has opened it, or if I am even in the right room. The first thing I see is Sam, curled up in a ball on an expensive-looking leather sofa. She appears to be sleeping, and I breathe out a sigh of relief until I notice my surroundings.

I slowly take in the room; clean lines of glass and dark wood, expensive fabrics and leather. Opulence seems to be a running theme here from what I can see. Rich shades of cream and brown finish the room beautifully. The whole place screams money and success, and it's absolutely stunning. Suddenly, I realise why the man downstairs eyed me like shit; I don't belong here, and neither does Sam. I bite down on my lip to suppress the panic rising up from the confines of my stomach.

Then the door clicks shut behind me.

I spin around, and my mouth dries out almost instantly, as I prepare myself to come face to face with the sneering, dirty bastard again.

Oh. Holy. Fuck!

It's not the sneering, dirty bastard.

I wilt where I stand. My lungs actually stop operating momentarily, and my heart shudders like it has been finally shocked from a long, deep slumber. My whole body currently feels on fire for some unknown, inexplicable reason.

"I have already had my doctor take a look at her. She seems to be fine, just, well...she's high."

He folds his impressive, muscular arms over his equally impressive, muscular chest, and he leans back against the closed door. My eyes drop to his feet, and ever so slowly, work their way up his body. Tanned bare feet, long muscular legs and thick thighs, wrapped up in worn, faded blue jeans. The fitted white t-shirt encasing his torso does nothing to hide the perfectly defined ridges of his stomach, chest and shoulders. The outlines are more than visible underneath the stretched fabric. I gulp excessively, open-mouthed and speechless, at the faultless specimen of male perfection towering over me.

I stare up at him, my lips part and my eyes widen. His face is heavenly; beautiful, naturally bronzed skin, a strong, chiselled jaw, set under perfect cheekbones. His nose is straight and flawlessly proportioned. He has the darkest, yet clearest midnight blue eyes I have ever seen. In fact, I'm positive I have never seen such a colour before. He seems piqued by my stare, and there is nothing I can do to stop it.

My hands clench at my sides in desperation, and my tongue slides over my bottom lip. All I can think about is running my hands over his sexy, slightly too long dark locks, while his tongue…

Oh my God! What the hell?

A nervous feeling wells up in my stomach, twisting into knots deep in my gut. I place a hand over my belly, but the feeling shifts south and suddenly, I can feel heat pooling in my core profusely. His eyes remain locked on mine, and I'm dying to rub my thighs together to alleviate the tension that is building immensely.

I chew my lip timidly. Is he aware of what I am doing and that he's instigating it? He smirks a little. Of course, he's aware! Look at him! Any woman would be brain dead not to want him. Even my asexual self is not immune, judging by the way my body is reacting to him.

He arches up an eyebrow over his stunning dark blue, now virtually black eyes. He is fully aware that I am shamelessly checking him out, amongst other things, while my poor friend is lying in pain only a few feet away. I mentally scold myself for such uncharacteristic behaviour. Yet I can't help it, this man has ignited something in me. I can't even begin to fathom where it is coming from.

I need to get out of here.

I need to get away from *him*.

Feeling painfully aware, I wrap my arms around my middle and shift from one foot to the other, desperate to eradicate these alien sensations bubbling copiously inside my body. He remains motionless watching me, leaving me feeling exposed and vulnerable under his roving eye. The way he's studying me makes me want to run for cover. I don't know what it is, but there is a familiarity in his eyes that is unmistakable. I also don't misinterpret the ghost of a smile forming on his lips.

Somewhere, I think I have seen him before.

"Thank you," I whisper, averting my eyes, desperately trying to control the heat my body is emanating. I don't know what else to say. All words have left me, and for the first time in my life, I actually feel something I can definitely say I've not experienced previously.

Sexual attraction.

It's something that no man has ever elicited in me, not even come close to.

Well, maybe once, many years ago.

He moves towards Sam, bends down and puts his hand on her forehead. "She just needs to sleep. I found her wandering around on the floor below..."

I listen to his voice rumble from his chest. It's like velvet and chocolate mixed together. Baritone, smooth and hypnotic. I am having a hard time placing what part of the country he is actually from. He doesn't sound particularly southern or cockney. He's definitely not northern, I should know. There is a lilt of an accent there, possibly American or Canadian. Might even be Australian. But what do I know, I've never set foot outside of England.

He stands suddenly, and marches into the open plan kitchen which adjoins the living room. I blatantly stare at the muscles in his back, which flex deliciously with each movement under his t-shirt. His denim-covered arse is tight and mesmerising. I avert my eyes away for a second time, fearing he will see me again, and the way my body is fighting a battle not to wrap itself around him. He pulls out two mugs and puts on some coffee.

"I think she should stay here, she's not in a fit state to be moved." His tone is firm and commanding. He turns to me with a cautious, yet confident stare. It penetrates deep inside me and awakens the dormant, feminine parts of myself I was sure had died long ago.

God help me he really is beautiful. But why is this happening to me? Why now? I mentally whine.

The ache deepening in my body adds further justification to the affect he is genuinely having on me. My thighs clench tight, while my hormone levels begin to rocket off the scale. I have no idea what is going on underneath my skin, but I do know I need to leave, so I use the only defence mechanism I possess - anger.

"Sorry, but who the hell are you?" I ask, hot and flustered.

"Sloan Foster," he replies, a little too confident, holding out one of the full mugs. I shake my head, refusing his offering. He stares at me with intent, and I wring my hands together apprehensively.

"Right, Mr Foster. Tell me, is it common practice for you to invite drugged up, half-naked women into your hotel room and beat them?" He looks shocked at my outburst. And so am I.

Oh shit, did that really just come out? I could slap myself for it, but in my shame, I don't stand around to await his response.

Walking over to Sam with determination, I delicately place my hand on her forehead, satisfied she is still breathing and sleeping peacefully. Her make-up is smudged, and the purple bruises forming rapidly are evident under her heavily applied, and now ruined, face. Her clothes are bloodied and torn, and she has bandages around her knees and hands.

"No, it isn't, Miss?" his voice speaks up hoarsely from behind me.

"Petersen. Kara Petersen," I answer, standing to face him. He is now only a few inches away from me. I feel lightheaded and uncomfortable being this close to him, being able to identify his unique scent so easily. His brow furrows slightly, then he gives out a small sigh. I have no idea what is going through his head, but all I want is to get the hell away from this hotel room. *Now.*

"Miss Petersen, I will have my driver take you and your friend home."

Amazed at his nerve, I'm unable to conceal my abhorrence for what he has done and the nonchalant demeanour in which he can dismiss her so easily, without taking any responsibility for his actions.

"What, so you just fuck and beat defenceless women and send them on their way. Use her and then discard her?!" My eyes burn holes into him, and it's not because of what he has done to Sam, it's because I can't control the heat flaring inside me for a man who equals my father. It's masochistic to want a man who has done such a degrading thing to my friend, *my sister*. Usually, it would make me recoil and lash out.

I start to move away from him, but his fingers cut into my wrist, halting my escape. A shock of something sends a powerful surge down my arm and deep into my body. Not possessing the wisdom to understand what I am feeling, I look up at him, mouth open and eyes wide. Captured in his gaze and hold, I wait impatiently for the prickly burn to come, but it doesn't materialise. Whenever anyone touches me, I feel it. Yet with him - setting aside the static shock from my cheap top - it feels natural to have his hand on me. It feels like it belongs there. It's a calm feeling I have only felt once before.

"Now, let's get one thing clear in your head, Miss Petersen," he says, his tone dripping with anger. "I did *not* fuck her, and I did *not* beat her," he responds, levying his resentment on me. "I was told there was a woman pounding on the doors of the guests. This is not the kind of place that has an hourly charge, regardless of what ridiculous and twisted ideas you may have filling your head right now." His eyes flick to Sam, then back to me. They soften slightly, and I now feel something else that has also been alien to me for many years.

Guilt.

I haven't experienced that particular emotion in a long time, but damn, do I feel it now. I'm so confused at his ability to make me feel. I hate these emotions that are welling up inside, and he is the bloody cause of them.

I look down at my friend and then back to him. Shame washes over me in abundance. "Sorry," I apologise a little too quietly, trying to avoid his gaze.

He doesn't say anything further, and I don't expect him to. He merely nods and hands the coffee back to me. Feeling self-conscious, I accept it while he continues to watch me closely, seemingly satisfied with himself. The tension in the room is thick, and I shift nervously under his penetrating stare. Sam murmurs in her drug-induced state, and I love her for the brief reprieve she has just afforded me. Holding his hand out to take the mug from me, his finger brushes against mine softly. The electricity piques and surges once again. The pleasurable heat flaring from such an innocent touch feels like I am being burnt alive from the outside. The intensity of it is indescribable, and I have to hold in the gasp that I am dying to let out.

"I'll call my driver and have him take you both home." His eyes linger on mine for far too long until I break the connection. Maybe I'm imagining it, but I could have sworn I heard a disappointing huff coming from his direction.

"You don't have to do that. My car is outside. We'll be fine," I reply, training my eyes on the floor - anywhere - to avoid his piercing and smouldering gaze, which is figuratively burning me alive, and causing all kinds of things to awaken inside my dormant body.

"Please, don't fight me on this. I will have your car put into the secure car park, and you can pick it up later." He is firm and commanding again. His eyes continue to search my face, and I wonder what it is he is actually searching for. He seems to want to say something, but the words don't come out, and I don't dare press him for more.

He leaves the room, presumably to call his driver, while I pace the living room, my attention divided between my friend and him disappearing upstairs. *Do hotel suites have an upstairs? Apparently so.* I mentally muse to myself while I look around his lavish suite until he appears in front of me again and he hands me a card.

His business card.

"What's this for?" I ask suspiciously, but not completely unaware. My eyes flick towards the door, praying that his driver arrives soon and stops whatever madness is about to materialise.

"I feel awful that this has happened here. I would really like to make it up to you. Dinner…maybe?" I let out a nervous laugh, and he steps back slightly, frowning.

Is he serious? He can't be serious!

"You're joking, right? My friend is lying there broken, in your hotel room no less, and you want a *date*?" I shake my head for emphasis, but I know I am in trouble.

I knew it the first moment my eyes met his, and the moment he touched me. The moment I felt an attraction that I have never felt before. I had made it my life's mission not to depend on anyone but myself. I had become disjointed from reality and felt safe in my absolution. I know if I agree to this, my walls will be penetrated, and there will be no coming back from it.

"Sorry, no. I just want to get my friend home safe." I hand his card back to him, praying he will take it without issue.

He looks at me like I have just spoken a foreign language. Something tells me that this man is not used to being told no. I take another glance around the room and realise the world's successful and wealthy are most likely never refused anything they want or desire.

Well, tough shit!

The doorbell pierces through the tension hanging thickly between us. The door opens, and we are still standing in a face-off, staring at each other, neither of us wanting to back down. His driver; tall, stocky built and appearing to be in his fifties, walks over to the sofa and gently picks Sam up. Sloan gives him a look, and he leaves the room, carrying her without so much as a second glance my way.

"Please keep my card." His eyes are full of determination, and the sharp, chiselled lines of his face are taut.

He isn't asking me; he's telling me.

I shake my head again because his intentions are clear, and I want no part of whatever he is promising. What I wanted, wouldn't be what he wanted, and I could never lower myself to be a rich man's plaything. My dignity might have been stripped from me forever, but I'll be damned if I allow someone to take my pride.

"Why are you doing this? Why do you even care?"

Without answering, he ushers me towards the door. Placing his hand on the small of my back, the heat spreads through me again like liquid fire, eviscerating everything in its tracks. His brow raises, and he eyes me up and down, deep in thought, before picking a jacket off the rack, then following me out too close for comfort.

We approach the lift, and my blood runs cold, as though a bucket of water has just been thrown over me. A cold sweat overcomes me as we stand in silence waiting for it to arrive. The bell dings and the doors open, relief and sheer dread fill me simultaneously. As uncomfortable as lifts make me, it's nowhere near as uncomfortable as being in his haughty sight. Still, I'm safe in the knowledge that within minutes, I will never have to lay eyes on him again.

The doors open and I enter cautiously. I practically jump for joy when he appears to remain outside the box. The doors then start to close, and with a sigh, he shakes his head. Reaching his arm out to stop the doors, he steps in, filling the small space in front of me. I stare at his back, pretending not to be affected by this new turn of events. I only hope he doesn't notice my skin starting to perspire alarmingly.

"To answer your question, Miss Petersen, I care because I don't like to see women hurt." The words are blunt, honest and straightforward, but they cut right to the heart of my soul.

Old memories bounce to the surface, while we ride down all ten floors. I can't bring myself to look at him, and the feeling is mutual apparently since he is staring straight ahead. It's disturbing, even to myself, that I want him to catch my desirous gaze in the mirrors, but his eyes never deviate.

When the doors open at the lobby, he gently places his hand on the small of my back, and yet again, the powerful current runs through me as soon as his skin connects with mine. I want to run and hide, but he keeps his hand firmly in place, leaving me with nowhere to turn. A small shiver runs through my limbs, and I bite down on my lip. I can't let him see how much he affects me, so I endeavour to compose myself the best I can and hold my head high.

Proceeding through the lobby in silence, there are more people down here now. I glance over to the rude man on reception, noting the look of shock on his face when he sees Sloan's hand on my back.

Who the hell is this guy?

Chancing a peek at him, he exudes confidence like I have never seen before. His demeanour could even be classed as bordering on arrogance. I stare, captivated until his eyes lock with mine. I quickly turn, knowing I have been well and truly caught.

The front doors are opened for us, and the doorman tilts his head at Sloan in acknowledgement. The cold, icy night air assaults my senses, and I shiver as the wind chill picks up, and an unforgiving breeze wraps around my uncovered, naked arms. Sloan drops his head down to me with a knowing smirk. Clearly seeing my aversion to the cold, he removes his jacket and wraps it around me.

"Thanks," I say, holding it over my shoulders, acutely embarrassed that I am silly enough not to bring a coat and that he feels obliged to take care of me. I have no right to ask him to care, and I sure as hell don't want him to. I already made my thoughts on that subject known to him upstairs.

Walking towards Sloan's driver, I notice a porter getting into my car, which is still parked at the front entrance - with my keys still in the ignition. The porter then comes over, takes the car key off the ring and hands the rest back to Sloan. I watch the man walk back to my car as Sloan folds my flat keys into my palm, clamping his over mine for longer than necessary. Thanking him, I climb into the limo, and he bends down to eye level. His face is now softer looking, and he even appears to be smiling a little.

"Your car will be here for you when you come to collect it." He reaches out his hand and lightly brushes my cheek. A shiver ripples through me again, and I can no longer deny that I feel something. He closes his eyes slowly, appearing to absorb the moment, but when he opens them again, his expression is back to firm and stoic, and his jaw is tight. He closes the limo door, still looking past the darkened windows and straight into me.

The car pulls out onto the street, and I'm compelled to look back. I stare at him, in all his beautiful, masculine perfection, as he stands tall and proud outside the entrance, watching as we drift further away.

I let out a long overdue sigh and lean over to Sam, placing a soft kiss on her forehead. She fucks up - *a lot* - but I love her like a sister. She lets out a content sigh, and I stare into the privacy screen numbly. Pulling the jacket around my body, I sniff the exquisite fabric longingly. He does smell good, but this feels far from good.

I know from the horrors of my past the only person I can rely on in this world is myself, and this, whatever it might have been, would only lead to pain and destruction.

Or maybe it would have been something else entirely? Something amazing, something I deserve, perhaps?

What on earth am I thinking? I have nothing to compare anything to! But what I wouldn't give to feel his hands on me, just once more...

Or his lips on mine…

I slowly close my eyes and savour the image. My brain is bombarded with visions of Mr Foster, his beautiful blue eyes, and strong, muscular body. My imagination is now running away with me, as I think of all the things I really want to do to him. I don't even know where half of this is originating from, considering my self-imposed celibacy. All I know is that I shouldn't be having these kinds of thoughts, yet I'm unable to rein in the sensations that he has helped to restore life to inside me.

Leaning back into the supple leather seat, I put my hands in the pockets to warm them. My fingers connect with something stiff and square. I tentatively pull it out and realise he has discreetly given me back his business card. I chortle; the arrogant swine knew exactly what he was doing when he brought his jacket with him.

Years and years of building myself up, and hardening my emotions, have just wilted spectacularly in the space of less than an hour. All because a man, a beautiful, mercurial man, has just entered my stratosphere. I flip the small card through my fingers, tracing my thumb across the black embossed letters and numbers.

I can feel my world tilting into the unknown already.

I knew tonight was going to be bad.

I'm *definitely* in trouble.

Chapter 4

THE LAST THREE days have proved uneventful, and I've never been so thankful in my life. My world has reverted back to some degree of normality, and work is the only thing that is keeping me sane at the moment, in between worrying about Sam and thinking about *him*.

Him, who has, unfortunately, plagued my dreams, or possibly my nightmares, whichever way you want to look at it. He is all I have thought about since collecting Sam on Tuesday morning. Every time I close my eyes, he's there, staring at me with that slight smirk and those deep blue pools. There has also been more than one occasion when I have woken up in desperate need of...something!

Sitting at the old wooden table in my kitchen, I am lost in thought, fixated on last night's dream and his business card, when Sam walks in.

"Good morning, sunshine," she says with bright enthusiasm.

"Is it?" I reply with a little too much cynicism. She narrows her eyes at me in disbelief.

I acquiesce. "Sorry." A forced smile tugs at my lips.

Since Monday, I've seen more of her than I have in weeks, maybe even months. She hasn't been out transgressing, and curiously, she's even picked up a few more shifts at work. Just like me, she also works for Marie. Whereas I don't wait hand and foot on the rich and ungrateful anymore, Sam is quite happy to be one of Marie's girls on the ground.

"Isn't it the Emerson function tonight? Why are you up so early?"

"Yep, it is," she says cheerily, grabbing a bowl and a box of cereal from the cupboard. She sits opposite me, and her eyes instantly fix on *that* business card, which I've intentionally left on the middle of the table for the last three days.

She nudges her head in its direction. "Are you ever going to call him?" I shrug my shoulders. I know the answer should be no. I know that is the right decision. But why does it feel that maybe I am wrong? Everything has felt different since Tuesday morning.

I feel different.

"I think you should," she replies, in between mouthfuls of Cheerios. I roll my eyes.

Words have long since been abandoned on the subject of Sloan Foster. He is all she has talked about since finally regaining consciousness late Tuesday afternoon. After hearing his name mentioned for the thousandth time, I snapped. Needless to say, for the last twenty-four hours she has skirted around the subject, just barely, but she doesn't fail to get a dig in whenever she can.

"Don't roll your eyes at me! I know you, remember. You can't let every guy you meet go because you're frightened they will be like him. He's a bastard. You might think you left it all behind up north, but you haven't, because he's still there at the back of your mind, controlling everything and still poisoning your future."

God, how I wish she was wrong, but she never is. Truthfully, I would always be running from my father, and my other demons, while we still lived and breathed the same air. My thoughts take me back to the last conversation we'd had. I haven't heard from him since Monday afternoon, and although I couldn't give a shit about what mess he has landed himself in this time, it will be my mum that is on the receiving end of his hatred.

"So, anyway," I begin, blatantly changing the subject. "Why are you up so early?"

"Well, actually, I wanted to ask you about that." She smiles far too sweetly, and the girl I grew up with begins to shine through. I move my head slowly from side to side because as hard as she may try, she could never fool me before, and she still can't do it now.

"No, I'm not doing it for you!"

"Please, just tonight. I have something that I need to do. This gig tonight was so last minute; I don't even know why she accepted it on such short notice. Seriously, two days warning? I didn't want to refuse Marie, it's such a coup for her reputation."

"Where are you going tonight?" I don't even want to think about it, but I have to ask. The thought of picking her up beaten again is too much to comprehend. She obviously recognises the look of concern on my face.

"I have a date." She peers at me, her eyes huge and pleading.

She is also lying.

"A date? *You*?" She nods her head quickly.

We are both more than aware she's not telling the truth. She is just like me; keeps everyone at arm's length. But unlike me, she will play ball if they can give her something she needs. I huff. She must think I was born yesterday.

"Yep. One of the guys at work has been asking me out for some time, and I think, after what happened-"

"Stop, just stop! I'm not stupid, Sam. Look, just promise me you'll be safe, okay? That's all I ask."

"I will; I promise. But it's not what you think, though."

"Really? I don't want to know." She jumps up from the table, coming around to hug me and every muscle instantly tightens. "All right, you know how I feel about personal space and…hugging." She steps back, cooing how much she loves me and repositions herself in the seat opposite me again.

"So, the Emerson is pretty plush, isn't it?" she says, grinning knowingly. I shrug my shoulders. I don't want the conversation to go there again. Not now, not ever. The man was already making a nightly appearance in my subconsciousness. There is no way on this God's green earth I was going to call him, or at least that's what I told Sam, not that she took any notice, of course.

"I guess so," I mumble. Sam's spoon clatters against her bowl, and her mouth falls open.

"You guess so? I suppose you think the owner is *just* okay too, huh?" She folds her arms over her chest and raises an eyebrow.

"Well, it looked okay from what I saw at silly o'clock on Tuesday morning." I level a look at her, making her remember it was her fault I ended up there prematurely in the first place.

"Right. Well, the function there tonight is for abused women-" She stops instantly, no doubt realising that three days ago, she had become a new member of that particular club. Looking at me sadly, her face drops all emotion, clearly remembering I had been initiated many years ago.

While we both had shit parents and equally shit childhoods, she never suffered the way I did. It's a sad fact that her father battered her around a lot when he wanted a drink, but he never did what my dad did. Well, at least the little I can remember of what he did.

"Okay," I agree, knowing I can't get out of it. I get up from the table and head into the bathroom.

"I have a spare uniform in my wardrobe, or just wear a black skirt and white shirt if mine are too short!" she shouts after me.

I finish up in the bathroom, deciding since it is going to be a long night, I'll try to get a few hours' sleep. It has been a couple of years since I've worked for Marie Dawson in a non-clerical capacity, but I remember how exhausting covering these events truly was.

Sam is nowhere in the flat when I wake a few hours later. It is late afternoon and my phone chimes with a text from Marie telling me not to be late. I shake my head, that's rich coming from her. She hasn't managed to make it into the office on time a single day this week.

I pad into the bathroom to start the long prep to look relatively normal. Standing under the hot spray, I attempt to gather my thoughts. I wrap myself in a towel as I examine my reflection. I am about to willingly spend six hours plus at a function that will, without a doubt, take me back to my childhood. I might not be that child anymore, but my future will always be influenced by it. I let out a long, controlled breath, then pick up my foundation.

An hour or so later, I look presentable. The black, knee-length, pencil skirt I'm wearing hugs me in all the right places, while the plain white, fitted shirt fits like a glove. I slide my feet into my black four-inch heels and wince. I had forgotten how much they pinch my toes, and I still had a long night of being on my feet ahead of me. I style my unruly mass of hair into a bun, it's kind of messy, in a fairly professional way. Sort of. As per usual, I've kept my make-up natural and barely noticeable. Overall the look is presentable and utterly forgettable.

Walking back into the living room, I gather up my bag, black jacket and my old Converse trainers - I will definitely be needing them later tonight.

Crossing the distance to my car, I admire her fondly. She has never looked so good. In the forty-eight hours it had been at the hotel, it has been cleaned and valeted, both inside and out, and drives better than the first time I'd ever set foot inside it. And again, I feel guilty that Sloan felt the need to look after me. I also still had to thank him for it. I just didn't know if I could. He conjures up feelings in me that are borderline dangerous. I couldn't face going to collect it on Tuesday, and instead, ended up begging one of the admin staff who worked in one of the other serviced offices in the building into going for me. He drove a hard bargain, and even though he had bartered morning coffee and lunch every day for a week, it really was worth my sanity and solitude.

Sliding into the seat, the ignition turns on the first attempt – something it hasn't done in a long time. Cruising through the late afternoon traffic, I blast the radio on my way into the city. The traffic, thankfully, isn't too heavy, yet I'm still cut up by other overzealous drivers. Taking exactly the same roads I did three days ago, my stomach twitches with both anticipation and nerves.

Arriving at the hotel, I pull up into the public car park adjacent to it. I glance in awe at the chic, beautiful nineteen-twenties style exterior brickwork and ornate features, finally getting a chance to see them properly for the first time. My eyes catch the doorman, who happens to be the same one from the other night. I halt in sheer dread. I pray he doesn't remember me. With my head down, I quickly march around to the side towards the staff entrance, avoiding him completely. As I show my ID to security, I see the rude sod from reception, laughing with a couple of female staff down the corridor. I turn inconspicuously, hoping he doesn't recognise me. How would I ever explain it to Marie if he did?

With my mind conjuring up every worst-case scenario, the next thought pops into my head. *Oh, shit, what if he's here? No, he was a guest, it was the penthouse!* I try to convince myself. With any luck, he's checked out already and won't be here tonight – I'm sure of it.

Exhaling steadily, trying to dispel my vivid imagination, I smooth down my skirt and head inside. My paranoia is working overtime, as my thoughts continue to run amok. I'm too busy remembering the man who had provoked a torrent of emotions in me on the tenth floor only a few nights ago, when Marie comes into view.

"Well, look at you!" Marie sings the instant she lays eyes on me. "I couldn't believe it when Sam called to say you were covering for her." I turn slowly to give her the full show, with a genuine smile on my face.

"Good evening, Marie! I bet you didn't think you'd get me back into the penguin outfit anytime soon, did you?" I respond with a curtsy, standing as far away as I can, intentionally evading her impending touch. It has gradually gotten worse over the years, but it's never been as prominent as this. It is obvious she can identify it because when I lived with her, she was the only one I could stand being this close to me. Since I'd moved out, it was mutating to epic levels as the years passed by.

Ignoring my attempt to keep some distance, she puts her arm on mine, guiding us through the labyrinth of corridors and into the staff locker room. All the while I feel a dull prickle run down my spine.

"Right, you can put your things in here," she says, handing me a key. "Let's get started."

Chapter 5

STRIDING THROUGH THE kitchen, I pass the empty tray to the poor kid on dishwashing duty and give him a small smile. I swipe my arm across my brow and snag a bottle of water from the fridge. I swallow back half of it in one long gulp. Looking around the busy kitchen, the staff pay me no never mind. Two chefs approach, and I have to breathe in to allow them to pass. one of them winks at me, and I frown. I'm really not comfortable with being noticed, or openly admired, as a matter of fact. I give him a small, friendly nod in return and quickly exit the hot, busy kitchen.

Standing at the bar, sipping my bottle of water, I am under absolutely no illusions as to why I constantly refuse to assist Marie in manning these events anymore. I am so much more comfortable in the office ordering the hors-d'oeuvres than I am serving them. It had taken me all of five minutes, from the moment I walked through the French doors, to remember the real reason why I used to bite my tongue when Marie made me work my way through sixth form and college - my feet are on goddamn fire!

The guests started to arrive an hour or so ago, although the main event doesn't actually start for another forty-five minutes, I'm already a hot, sweaty mess. Escaping into the safety of the staff room, I ease my sore feet from the constricting heels, hissing as my toes finally feel temporary freedom. As I rub them soothingly, I see Marie standing at the door smiling.

"I'm sorry I haven't been in the office much this last week."

"That's okay. It's probably a good job since you keep screwing up my files and spreadsheets!" I smile at her. She laughs and inches closer until she is sitting next to me. She attempts to remove a tendril of hair away from my face that has bounced free, but I pull back fast.

"*Kara...* I wish you would assist more often. I remember the good times we used to have at these things." I raise my brow, wondering which events she was referring to because I can't remember any good times. I remember sweating like a pig at the butchers, and getting covered in crap, but never good times. She nudges my side playfully. "Sure, Sam's a laugh and all, but we both know that's a disaster waiting to happen." I roll my eyes. It was no longer waiting to happen, it already had, and I now had to deal with the fallout. I feared it would get a hell of a lot worse before it got any better. The brief respite of the last three days was just the calm before the storm.

"I know; I know. It's just hard for me, you understand?" I look into her stunning, icy blue eyes. She looks nowhere near her forty years. She has been like a mother to me since my own had let me walk out at fifteen without so much as a second glance. She has always treated me like I was her own. I love her more than I know how to express.

"I do understand, honey, and my door is always open to you. It's your home, too. Anytime you need anything, all you have to do is ask." I smile at her, and she gives me a look that speaks more than words ever could. She is offering me a way out of the current mess that Sam was dragging me into.

"I'm glad you agreed to do this tonight. Sam has been...different lately." She raises her eyebrows, waiting for me to divulge whatever she thinks I already know.

"She's involved in something, I'm not sure what exactly. When I got home on Monday, she had two men in the flat. Then later in the night, she called to say she was in trouble, and I had to come and get her. She was beaten and unconscious." I sigh. Marie drapes her arm around my shoulder, and I allow her to. As much as it disturbs me, I need something right now.

"Brings back memories," Marie states. It's not a question, it's a fact, and I squeeze my eyes tight against the tears that are forming.

Marie lets go and tugs my arm. "Come on. I gave you table one. They shouldn't give you any trouble, but if you need anything, you come and find me. Let's go, honey."

We walk back into the main reception room, which is now filled with double the number of bodies. My breath lapses, realising I might have problems keeping people away from my personal space tonight. There appear to be more attendees present this evening than at the events I have waited on in the past. I turn to Marie in question, but she just smiles, squeezes my arm, and goes back to instructing her other staff.

I stand back and admire the beauty of the ballroom. It is clothed from floor to ceiling in shimmering, pale cream and dark beige silks. The tables are beautifully presented with arrangements of pink roses and white lilies. The only thing missing is the real reason behind this event; the victims. I haven't seen one single piece of information or insignia surrounding the uncomfortable subject and, unlike past functions, there is no auction going on to raise money for the cause benefiting the event. I can't quite make my mind up if it's a good or a bad thing. There is nothing worse than having it swept under the carpet, or heaven forbid, shoved in your face.

The service is in full swing, and within an hour the guests are seated for dinner. All of London's successful and wealthy are out in force, with designer gowns and tuxes at every turn. I am standing at the bar, waiting for my drinks tray to be filled, when one of the other waitresses catches my attention.

"Oh, my goodness, look at her dress!" The girl squeals beside me in delight. I turn around to see what she is gawking at. If you've seen one dress, you've seen them all.

Sauntering through the entrance, is one of the most beautiful women I think I have ever seen. She is model tall; beautiful and slender. Her long, strawberry blonde hair hangs in immaculate curls down her back. The multitude of diamonds adorning her body reflect the light spectacularly. She is everything I wish I could be. I've never really cared for looks, but it's the way she carries herself; confident and vibrant. I turn back to the bar, and wish I could run far, far away and hide.

My tray is just about ready when the girl squeals again. At this rate, I am going to be deaf as well as exhausted by the end of the night. I turn around and pierce her with my most thoroughly pissed off glare.

"Oh, my God! Have you ever seen anyone so beautiful?!"

God, if I had to look at that woman once more, I was going to throw up. I continue to glare at squealing girl until she does the absolute unthinkable - she grabs my arm forcibly and spins me around. Furious, I shake out of her hold and narrow my eyes at her in disgust.

How dare she fucking touch me?

Beyond pissed, I follow her line of sight.

And, there, at the other end of the room, is Sloan Foster.

The whole beautiful, mesmerising, six-foot-plus, sexy package of him. His lean, tanned, muscular body is encased in what is probably the latest designer offering. His dark hair is styled half-heartedly and is still slightly long at the sides, skimming the collar of the crisp, white shirt, peeking through the form-fitting suit hugging his perfect, hard body. The same body that mine has been craving for the last few days.

Desire spikes every nerve ending inside me, firing them up and keeping them burning. I can feel myself starting to become damp in between my legs, and I rub them together inconspicuously, in a bid to calm the chain reaction his presence alone has initiated deep inside. Licking my lips, I close my eyes involuntarily, remembering the way electricity surged through me when he put his hand on me. I initially put it down to the cheap top I was wearing, but now I know better. My eyes start to feel heavy, and the sensation building inside my belly deepens dramatically.

Snapping my eyes open, I turn and grab a bottle of water from the bar and all but drain the contents; trying to cool myself from the inside out. I salivate copiously, but I still feel like I am swallowing sandpaper. I survey him attentively from the safety and anonymity of the bar, while he moves through the ballroom with complete confidence. He is stopped every few minutes by other guests wanting to talk to him. I watch a little too closely as he converses with each person and then moves on to the next vying for his undivided attention.

The girl next to me has long since left my side and is now serving drinks at her table, which is, unfortunately, next to the one I am allocated. Her head bobs around comically as she tries to serve and ogle Mr Perfect now taking his seat.

At my bloody table!

Oh, for fuck sake, this isn't happening! Only it is, and my lungs have stopped functioning, and my heart is failing to beat. And there's not a damn thing I can do about it.

Performing a quick recce of the room, Marie is standing in a corner, talking to one of the guests, no doubt touting for more business. Another member of staff walks by, and I quickly ask if he can deliver my drinks tray. He agrees with reluctance, and I thank him profusely, before briskly walking towards Marie.

"What's up, honey?" she asks concerned, once I'm within speaking distance.

"I can't serve at table one, Marie!" I blurt out breathlessly. The man she is conversing with shakes her hand and walks away smiling.

"Oh, I'm sorry."

"Never mind that. Has someone said something to you?" she asks annoyed. I shake my head and pull her back into the now empty corner, forgetting I'm the one that generally avoids all skin-on-skin contact. This unfortunate situation is taking precedence right now.

"No, no, no. Monday, when Sam was... Well, she was here, and he was here...and he gave me his number and…and..." I'm in deep shit and sinking fast!

Marie puts her hands on my shoulders ever so lightly to calm me down. I flinch, but catch my breath long enough to inform her of the entire tragic debacle in a more coherent fashion. Her mouth turns up into a sly smile before I have even finished imparting the whole sorry affair, and she shrugs.

She flipping shrugs!

"For as long as I have known you, no one has ever affected you this way. Well, only one person, if I remember rightly." She takes a look behind me, no doubt scanning the occupants of my table, to see who has got my knickers in a twist. She makes a surprised face and then turns back to me. Her returning look is coy and smug, and I know exactly what is coming.

"Call me a bitch, because I know you will, but no. Sorry, table one is yours."

There is no battle, and yet the war is already lost. Marie's word is always final, and I know better than to argue with her. I had never gotten my own way when I was a teenager living under her roof, and there is no way she would let me have that advantage now. Blowing out my breath, I turn in defeat and discreetly pat my skirt down, simultaneously wiping away the Sloan Foster induced sweat from my palms. I already knew she would refuse, but it was worth a try. The heat of her breath tickles my neck as she stands close behind me.

"Go on, say it!" The smile is evident in the tone of her voice.

"Bitch!" I respond playfully. Putting on my best game face, I walk away with my head held high, leaving her laughing behind me. I slowly approach table one, focusing on my breathing.

In and out. In and out. Deep and even.

"Excuse me, girl. Can I have a refill?" I scowl, as a woman's voice cuts through my technique. I turn sharply in the direction the sound originated from, the irritation coming off me in waves at being so rudely interrupted. A woman is holding out her glass to me expectantly. *Girl?* She looks younger than I do! Well, she would if she didn't have a face full of slap on.

And, unfortunately, she is also the woman who is the vision of perfection.

"*Please!*" I mutter quietly, clenching my jaw. Her face scrunches up, and I know she has heard me loud and clear. I might have a less than a desirable existence to these people, but it's evident that money definitely doesn't buy manners.

"I'm sorry?" she counters, in a tone that says she is not customarily pulled up on her social grace, or politeness, if at all.

"Yes, of course!" I reply over-enthusiastically, and give her a sickly-sweet smile.

Walking back to the bar to collect her drink, I'm half-inclined to get it laced with a triple vodka, just to knock her out for the rest of the night. I catch Marie staring at me from the other end of the bar, shaking her head to tell me no. It wouldn't be the first time I have done it. Many a forward, touchy-feely man has fallen foul of my secret vodka stunt in the past. I smile innocently at her and mouth the word *bitch*. She simply sticks her tongue out and laughs.

Straightening my shoulders, I hold my head high, slap a fake toothy grin on my face and glide through the bodies blocking my way. More than once I am touched, and it's a miracle I haven't gone arse over tit and spilt the bitch's drink down me already.

A faint glimmer of calm flows through me as I get closer and closer to the table, and I notice that Sloan has now taken his seat. Or maybe he has been there the whole time? I have absolutely no idea. Trying to breathe as normally as possible, I subtly peer at him through my lashes, wondering how long he has actually been sat down. I place the drink in front of the obnoxious cow, and see the way his eyes flit between me and where Marie is standing, appearing both amused and annoyed.

Oh, my God, I am so screwed! Not only does he recognise me, but he has most likely been sitting here the whole time.

I raise my head up to the table and ask if anyone would like any more drinks. They all shake their heads and look at me ludicrously. And that's when I notice the various different bottles, both open and sealed, covering the centre of the table. The bitch did it on purpose to prove I am below her in the class ranks! I narrow my eyes and see her glaring at me, searching my face for whatever keeps vapid, silver spoon women entertained daily.

I square my shoulders in annoyance. She smirks and places her hand on top of Sloan's, who is staring at me with such intensity, I fear I may burst into flames any minute while trying to work efficiently. Quickly shifting my eyes, which I'm sure will tell him what I am feeling, I look at her preposterously. She taps his hand with affection and gives me an unimpressed pout.

God, she can piss on him for all I care!

And that's the real problem, I do care. More than I am willing to admit, even to myself. But why do I care? I ask myself the question that has plagued me since he put me inside his car and closed the door.

As I walk away from the table, in the corner of my eye, I see Sloan snatch his hand out from under hers, and he whispers something in her ear. She looks crestfallen, but delicately picks up her champagne and drains the flute, trying to come across calm and unaffected by whatever pearls of wisdom he has spoken to her. Her eyes sadden, and for a moment, I can see through them in a way that I'm sure she doesn't even realise. I can see the pain in them.

I shake the sorrow from my head. I don't want to feel sorry for a woman who apparently thinks I am something she stepped in. I turn, and Sloan's eyes snare mine fiercely. A combined look of agitation and, dare I say, admiration, is definitely playing on his features. I hold his penetrating stare with confidence, as a multitude of sensations surge through me at the speed of light. My head feels fuzzy, my blood is tingling, and my skin is perspiring. My body heat is definitely rising a few notches a minute being this close to him. I don't even want to admit to, let alone attempt to pick apart, the awareness that is burgeoning between my thighs and pooling deep in my abdomen. I'm not brave enough to acknowledge it just yet.

I need a minute - a long one - and instead of running outside for some fresh air, I position myself on the outskirts of the large room and shuffle into a corner. Under the guise of composing myself and rejuvenating my appearance, I straighten my blouse and adjust my skirt hem. Glancing around the area, confident I am well concealed in the dim space, I subtly rub my legs together. I'm a little shocked, but not entirely unsurprised that *that* awareness has developed into more than a subtle tingle which has never made an appearance before. Well, not without my assistance anyway - and definitely not because of a man.

I lift my head up and blow a strand of hair from my face. Big mistake. Sloan is openly gazing at me with a look that could cause dry tinder to go up in smoke. Trust me, there is already enough electricity flowing through me at his close proximity, that I fear I may spontaneously combust with just a fleeting look from him. Gifting him a small smile, one that causes my cheeks to flush liberally, I move towards the bar. I can sense his eyes following me and miraculously, I manage to make it the last few feet without falling flat on my face. Feeling the embarrassment pulling to and fro in my body, I shrink back into the anonymity of the busy room, still trying to rid myself of my deepening sexual desires.

Approaching the bar, the bartender acknowledges my presence and passes me a bottle of water. I swallow a large mouthful and turn. Inadvertently, I pin my eyes on the one person in the room I desperately want to run away from, and then wish I hadn't.

Oh, how I really wish I hadn't!

A buxom blonde is leaning over the table, her large and rather exposed breasts are almost horizontal with his head. He might just be being courteous, but he seems utterly oblivious to the mammoth tits being virtually pressed into his face. He smiles at her warmly with an air of recognition. Slowly concealing myself behind a couple of men now taking up occupation at the bar, I can feel my soul sink. I mentally scream and tell myself I should turn and walk away, that I should forget all about him, but I can't. Something inside won't allow me to.

The woman pulls up a vacant chair at the table and starts to paw him. Her hands slide from his forearm, slowly creeping up and up until they linger on his shoulder. I can barely watch as she reaches his hair and tangles it gently between her fingers. Sloan, the gentleman he is, or at least it's the impression he gives, gently stops her perusal of him. Bringing her hand down to the table, he leans in close to her. Her face instantly lights up, then she frowns and stands, before tottering away on her ridiculously high heels – not that I've got much room to talk, considering the monstrosities housing my tender toes this evening.

Grabbing my tray, I realise I have been neglecting my patrons. Walking swiftly back to the table, I collect up the dirty glasses and empty bottles. My concentration is fixed on not accidentally throwing alcohol over anyone, but my mind is filled with the scene that has just played out before me. I jolt and gasp, ready to scream blue bloody murder when I feel a hand on my leg. Except, my gasp is generated from arousal and sensation, rather than one borne of the bone-chilling prickle that generally accompanies unwanted touch.

I tilt my head over my shoulder and look down to see Sloan's hand slide back onto the table. A sexy, naughty grin spreads over his face, and he brings his finger to his lips. I glare at him, but such an innocent touch, or maybe not so innocent, has just fuelled my already smouldering embers. His touch is something, which aside from our first meeting, I have only experienced in my dreams. I feel my face becoming flustered - I don't need a mirror to know that I am glowing bright red. Just looking at him, wearing his self-assured, satisfied grin, tells me he's achieved what he hoped to by touching me without my permission.

He wanted a reaction.

I gave him one.

He wants to see what I will do.

Well, *I* am not going to do anything, other than discourage him and walk away. My body, on the other hand, has plenty of other things to contend with. Namely, the sexual tension scorching every cell, and my other needy parts that want his hand back on me, reaching higher and higher.

Slowly shielding my face, I ignore him, and quickly pick up the tray and turn around. As I walk away, a redheaded woman approaches the table, and Sloan suddenly appears uncomfortable. He shuffles in his seat and gives her a pointed look. I watch from the comfort of the bar again, still rapt, by how his posture hardens inexplicably, as he stands and pulls her away. My eyes follow them until they stop at the edge of the room. The woman is unmistakably aggravated, throwing her hands in the air and gesturing wildly, as he stands there with his hands on his hips, motionless, not looking the slightest bit impressed.

Like a train wreck that you know is going to happen, compulsion forces me to watch the spectacle. Well, that and something else I'm too terrified to confess to. The woman leans into him, endeavouring to kiss him. My breath halts, curious to see how he will react, all the while I berate myself for thinking that he was ever interested in me.

He probably thinks I'm cheap like Sam. An easy shag - that's why he asked me out.

My foolish heart is propitiated moments later when he locks her wrists in his hands and pushes her back. The woman is clearly upset, but in a split second, she regains her composure and walks back to her table on the other side of the room.

Sloan runs his hand through his hair and turns back towards his table. I quickly shift position, so he won't catch me spying. When I look back, he is slumped in his seat, his eyes trained on the floral centrepiece, downing a shot of something dark.

Studying him carefully, I can see the vacant look in his eyes, one born of defeat and pain, and it makes me wonder what, or who, put it there in the first place. I snort to myself; a simpering idiot feeling sorry for someone like him, who, at any other time, would probably blatantly ignore me.

Sucking my bottom lip between my teeth, I see his nasty little companion gliding across the dance floor with a large, dark-haired man. She smiles and giggles, and I watch a little too intrigued that Sloan is allowing his date to dance with a man, who from my distance, is definitely level pegging with him in the good looks stakes.

As I take another glance in Sloan's direction, I screw up my face and laugh to myself, as yet another woman saunters over to him. Now, I understand. I understand very well. As if I ever thought I stood a chance with him. There are already numerous, walking, talking examples of the type of woman he desires in this ballroom. I'm only misleading myself if I honestly believed he would ever look at me as anything more than an easy one-night stand.

But if he offered, would I be able to refuse? And that was another unspoken truth that had been causing me internal stress for the last few days, too. It's also the real reason his business card was still sat on the centre of my kitchen table and not decomposing in some landfill.

But honestly, could I refuse him?

Evening blends into night effortlessly. The multitude of laughter and conversation flows freely between the patrons. I do a final check of my table - not an easy feat when you're trying to remain invisible. It has worked out well for me for the majority of my life, but tonight, I am failing miserably, under the intense scrutiny of a man who makes me want more than I ever imagined possible. And, not to mention his wayward hands, which have taken every available opportunity to touch me, whether it be while I clear away the empties, or simply walk by him.

Positive I'm not going to be missed for a while, I head over to Marie, who is observing the room with quiet confidence. She looks thoroughly impressed, and she should, considering she has managed to pull it all together in only two days. I just hope the bastard manager she was so angry about is grateful. Hopefully, his attitude will have improved before our next gig here in a few months.

"Hey, do you mind if I take five?" I ask.

"No, go ahead. Grab a drink on your way. Only a small one, though!" She holds up her finger and thumb to indicate just how small. I roll my eyes and smile lovingly at the woman who has shown me, on more than one occasion, that she loves me more than my own parents ever did.

Standing at the end of the bar, waiting for my *small* white wine spritzer to be poured, I turn around to take in the room and am captured by Sloan's penetrating, lust-filled stare. A smile tugs at his mouth when he sees I am ensnared. How can I not be? He has made it his mission this evening to ensure I will not forget he's there. Trust me, that isn't even a possibility! I definitely cannot forget someone who makes me feel the way he does.

Shifting my eyes over the table before I make my escape for ten, his rude date - *the bitch* - looks to be away with the liquor fairies, until it dawns on her that he isn't paying her any attention whatsoever. Her head turns, and she follows his line of sight. Her eyes narrow in anger the moment she recognises me. Holding my glass tight, I twirl around as quickly as I can and vacate the room.

Approaching the kitchen door that leads to the back alley of the building, I hear the murmur of voices carrying over the slight chill of the evening breeze. The scent of burning tobacco is rife, and I smell the cigarette smoke before I see it.

"Hi." The chef who smiled at me earlier is outside with one of the kitchen's dogsbodies. He turns, and his friend grins at me, before dying out his smoke and heading back inside. I'd like to say I miss the look of insinuation that passes between them, but I don't. Feeling somewhat uncomfortable, I stare down at the ground.

Peeking at him, his chef's cap has gone, and his dark, blonde hair is stuck up all over, looking a bit greasy and matted. Except, I'm not a complete bitch that I'd hold that against him. I wouldn't like to work long, arduous shifts in the equivalent of hell's kitchen. I guess he's not a bad looking guy, but there's no prospect of anything more than polite conversation when his touch makes me feel like spontaneously combusting. And not in a good way.

"Hi, again," I reply politely.

He holds his cigarette packet out to me, offering me one, but I shake my head shyly. He makes no attempt to even pretend he isn't looking at me in a capacity that is no more than brief acquaintances, and it's making me feel very anxious.

Moving to stand a few feet away from him, I slip off my killer heels and stand barefoot in the dirt, and God knows what else, while I slowly sip my wine. I think back to the time when Marie found me, virtually in this precise spot. Letting myself be taken back to the best of worst times, I sway to the soft music drifting from inside.

"I haven't seen you at these things before, are you new?" His eyes openly roam my body, and I mentally chide myself for not fetching my jacket. At least if I had, he wouldn't be staring at my breasts like a starving man. I seem to be good at setting myself up for unwanted attention lately.

"No, my aunt owns the catering company. I'm just filling in for the night," I say, looking down the alleyway, my mind caught up in visions of my fifteen-year-old self.

"Ah, family favour, something you can never refuse," he replies with a laugh.

"Something like that." I'm still staring past him, but again, I don't mistake his look of appreciation in my peripheral vision.

"I'm Carl, nice to meet you…?"

I turn in order to be hospitable. He holds out his hand, and dread washes over me as I stare at it.

I hesitate.

Touching Sloan wasn't so bad. Actually, touching him was really good. So good, in fact, I can't get the man out of my head - or my subconscious bed. Is it possible he has single handily managed to eradicate my aversion at long last? Is it too premature to believe I might finally be cured? Maybe it's time to test my theory.

Tentatively reaching out to Carl, I wait for tranquillity to replace the wretched feeling of anxiety. His fingers graze mine, and I hold my breath… Nope, the dull prickle is still alive and well, and I quickly snatch my hand back. He looks annoyed, but I can't do something I'm not comfortable with.

"Kara. Kara Dawson," I reply, reverting back to the name I had used for years whilst evading the police, the social services, and any other authority that could either cart me off to foster care or throw Marie's arse in prison.

"Ka-ra," he says, testing the sound of it, letting the two syllables roll off his tongue. He thinks he's flirting well; I think he has lost the plot. I couldn't even tolerate his hand on mine for a split second, heaven knows what on earth he is expecting from this.

"So, what do you normally do then, Ka-ra?" And there he goes again.

I want to tell him to fuck off, but since he is one of the hotel's chefs and I am the hired help for the evening, I best keep my big gob shut. The last thing I want is for Marie's name to be trawled through the mud because I can't keep myself in check. Carl is still watching me, and I quickly take another sip of my spritzer, turning away from his lusty, lecherous grin.

"Clerical." Short, one-word answers usually do the trick.

"What kind of clerical? Where do you work?"

Maybe not this time.

I am about to answer when, suddenly, I feel at ease for the first time since I stepped outside. I close my eyes in provocation, already aware of who is standing behind me. I rotate on the balls of my feet slowly; if I move any faster, the contents of my glass won't survive. The pleasurable sensation eases through me, but in a split second it's destroyed, when Carl turns suspiciously and moves closer. He puts his hand on me, and I tense as the atmosphere shifts around me - from desirous to desolate in less than ten seconds flat. I step away from Carl, and his expression turns from pleased to pissed off. He looks from me to the man behind me, and his face purses into a scowl. Electricity then ripples inside me, adding further fuel to the already smouldering fire, when the soft, yet firm caress of a hand at my waist, and warm breath on my neck, come into contact.

"Is the kitchen not busy tonight, Carl? Are there not a hundred or so guests waiting for their desserts, Carl?" Sloan's hard voice punctures the silence of the night, and his hand tightens its hold on me. His fingers cut into my flesh, and I'm on the verge of telling him to get off me, when I turn around to look at him, and he is seething, absolutely furious. Whether it is because of me, or Carl - or both of us - I'm not entirely sure.

"Erm, sorry, Mr Foster, just having a quick fag." He looks ashen like he is about to face the firing squad. Not bothering to die out the butt, he throws it into the darkened space in front of us and turns to leave.

"I'll see you later, Ka-ra." He smiles expectantly.

"No, you won't, Carl!" Sloan replies with venom. The door slams shut, and timidly, I stare at the burning ember on the gravel, unable to look at him any longer.

I stand, staring with an open mouth, shocked that he has just treated one of the kitchen staff with such disrespect, and equally pleased with the new revelation that only he can affect me in such a sexually charged way. He tips my chin up to shut my mouth. Bringing his hand from around my waist, he pulls me close. So close, in fact, I'm sure he is...*hard*. I squeak a little when I feel *that* on my stomach. His face looks stormy, and I mentally brace myself, ready to see him up close and personal for the first time since Tuesday morning.

"Was I disturbing something?" his deep, hard voice asks. I quickly shake my head, and he breathes out content. "Good, I'm pleased to hear that."

He studies me carefully with a slight smile on his face. His beautiful eyes are dark, full of mystery, while his fingers move, attempting to run up either side of my waist. Shaking my head a little, realising I am in trouble here, I step away from his rebellious hands, creating some much-needed space. He looks both dejected and pleased. *How very peculiar.*

Holding out his hand to me, he asks, "May I have this dance, Miss Petersen? Or do you prefer Miss Dawson?" My eyes narrow at his insinuation. Was he out here when I said that to Carl? If not, how would he know that?

He presses me closer to him, waiting for my answer. His smile and beautiful face do things to me no other man has previously. It's a look that makes me want, in a primal, basic instinct, kind of way. I quickly memorise him from head to toe and back up again. I shift a little further, because in this extraordinary, beautiful moment, I can't decide if I want to flee from him faster than an Olympic sprinter...or devour him on the spot. My blood flows quicker into every major organ, while my skin perspires under his scrutiny. Feeling the heat begin to flame higher in the hollow space between my legs, I want nothing more than to rub my thighs together again to assuage the growing throb.

"No, thank you," I decline, hoping to sound more controlled and blasé than I actually feel.

Coolly, I take a sip of wine, determined to lie convincingly and show him he doesn't affect me in the slightest. But in his presence, it's easier said than done. I tip my head back, allowing the cold liquid to run down my throat. It doesn't douse the fire that is mounting deep within; if anything, it only incites it to burn stronger.

He steps closer, and pushes back the errant strand of hair that has been doing its own thing all evening. The touch kindles something inside me, and I tremble, as his flesh comes into contact with mine again. My eyes close involuntarily, and pure desire pulsates through my body. Instinctively, I find myself leaning into him, absorbing his individual, intoxicating scent, committing it to memory; woody, masculine. *Sloan.*

All my senses are heightened in a way they have never been subjected to before. Usually, I wouldn't allow anyone this close to me - *ever* - but I can't stop it. I can't stop him. And truthfully, I don't want to. I hear his sharp intake of breath when he realises I'm not going to resist him.

I open my eyes and look straight at his beautiful face. It's only now I notice his eyes are virtually black. He lifts his palm up, then brushes my cheek with the back of his hand. My core undulates furtively from his touch. Shying away with embarrassment at my abnormal behaviour, he smirks in satisfaction. His eyes cast over me a little too carefully. Shifting back once again, I have never been good with being admired. For me, it is right up there with showing emotions - it makes me feel both uncomfortable and exposed.

"Don't ever be ashamed of how you feel." He grasps my chin, incapacitating me on the spot. "Have dinner with me." Again, it's not a question, and a part of me knows there's no use in fighting the unavoidable any longer. Deep down, I know this is going to happen, whether it is the right thing to do or not.

And he knows it too.

I sigh and wiggle out of his hold. I'm confused by both his unwelcome, yet wanted touch, and the fact I don't want him to stop whatever it is about him that makes me feel calm and tingly. Inside, I'm torn between doing what is right for me, and doing what my body desires. I raise my glass and drain the contents, then set it down on the step beside me.

"You don't hear the word *no* very often, do you, Mr Foster?" I probe rhetorically, already knowing the answer. My confidence is firing on all cylinders, fuelled namely by the little alcohol running through my system - which is emboldening me beyond belief - and the fact I'm acutely aware that I hold all the power right now.

His face pales, and he frowns, and I wonder if he's searching his memory for all the times he has been told it before. I'm slightly shocked when he opens his mouth.

"No, Miss Petersen. I don't," he replies honestly, pulling me back closer to him. He guides his thumbs across my cheeks and mumbles quietly to himself. My skin catches on fire under his touch, and my body betrays me by responding, as my core fills with liquid heat and dampens profoundly.

"Well, I've heard it my entire life, and I've said it more times than I can remember, Mr Foster." My mind carries me back to the multiple times I have said it – no – *begged it*. Why it chooses this moment to come flooding back in full force is unknown to me. The tears are already fully formed in my eyes and squeezing them together is futile. *Too late, I remember*. A lone tear flees and runs down my cheek. I open my eyes to see Sloan's features twist in anger, and his look of pure hatred makes me flinch.

"I'm sorry," I whisper, as he slowly drags his thumb up my cheek, ensnaring the wetness and wiping it away. I attempt to slap his hand away, but he is having none of it. I'm angry at him for weakening me in such a way after only meeting him once, but I'm even more pissed off with myself for showing him the easiest way to do it. I'm actually letting my walls down for him. *That*, I didn't realise until a moment ago.

Without warning, he wraps his arms around my waist. I gasp out loud when one hand splays wide over the middle of my back, and my front is pressed up against his, hard and tight. "I want to hold you Miss Petersen, please stop moving away from me." I stop, and he continues. "Kara, listen to me, I would never tell you no, and you would never have to beg me for anything," he says assertively, withdrawing a little to evaluate my expression. "Please, have dinner with me. I really would like to spend an evening getting to know you." The hand on my back eases its way up to my neck. He supports my head at my nape. I don't know what the hell is happening to me, but all I know is that I really do loath to be touched, especially like this, yet this feels so natural, I'm intoxicated by it. Somewhere inside, it feels right. *He* feels right.

"I'm sorry, but I need to get back," I tell him, struggling to get out of his grasp, but it's nearly impossible. He has me where I stand, and his satisfied grin confirms it.

"Please, say yes. You know, as well as I do, that this *is* going to happen," he tells me in an undeniable tone. His eyes burn into mine, the intention and meaning behind them is crystal clear. "You're going to be mine in every way imaginable, and there's not a thing you can do to stop it. You know it, and I know it. It's merely just a matter of time. Now, we can do this the easy way, to which you say yes, or we can do it the hard way, in which I will wear you down until you have no choice. Although I would rather you say yes to this willingly."

My unspeakable parts seize up in desire as I stare into his eyes; they mean every single word he has just said. If I say no, I know he *will* pursue me until I'm too tired and defeated to fight anymore. In truth, I don't want to say no, but if I say yes, I know he will break me more so than I already am.

His breath fans my heated face, and the way the strong flow washes over me, I feel his patience is wearing thin. His eyes smoulder with the same intensity that I'm currently experiencing coursing throughout my body with dominance. His soft, parted lips are mere inches from mine. So close, in fact, all it would take is a small flick of my tongue…

Except, regardless of how much his statement has turned me on, I am verging on the edge of anger at his blunt presumption. *The beautiful, arrogant bastard!*

He honestly did think I was exactly like Sam. That I would put out for in him every way possible, like the cheap whore she claims not to be.

But who am I trying to convince, him or me? Honestly, I gave up on myself days ago. And despite how much I want to scream in his face, I can't deny the feeling in my belly at hearing him say such innuendo-laced words to me. My body exudes liquid heat and screams at me to say yes. Telling me that it can just be one date…and sex.

Sex, that I've never actually *willingly* participated in before.

Predictably, there is the hidden, feminine side of myself that desperately wants to finally feel something tangible. Irrespective of the fact I have denied myself the ability to form a relationship over the years, deep inside, it is still something I will always want, and typically, that is proving to be the governing voice inside my head. But sensibly, the smart, logical side of myself, tells me he already has a girlfriend, who is sitting just two rooms away. Not to mention the abundance of women who have approached him tonight. I've seen first-hand he is not the type of man to settle with one person. I might be judging him unfairly, but I can only go on what I have seen so far.

"What about your girlfriend?" I blurt out, hoping he doesn't realise I am actually a tad bit jealous. His pupils dilate in surprise, recognition dawns on him, and his eyes fill with understanding.

"Are you jealous, Kara?"

"No!" I spit out too quickly. And, yes, of course I'm bloody jealous! He's insulting his own intelligence by even asking me that.

He grins at me in triumphant. "Kara, she's not my girlfriend, she's my sister." My mouth forms an O, and I shut it firmly. I can feel my cheeks tinge pink, and I feel utterly ridiculous. "So, now that we have cleared up that little misunderstanding - dinner with me." His command is firm.

"No." My reply is unconvincing.

"You have a short memory; I don't hear that word very often. I must admit I don't like it very much, either."

"I don't care, that's not my problem!" I wriggle out of his grip, bend a little to slide my feet into my heels, and head towards the door.

"Oh, but you do care! I know for a fact that you do, because I can see it, I can feel it. I can smell it, Kara. I can smell the way you react to me. The way your skin flushes and heats when I am close. The way your eyes light up. Now, stop being so frustrating and downright ridiculous, and have dinner with me. *Please*," he says, allowing the word to linger in the air.

And so the wearing down commences.

I spin back around to him. I know he won't let it go until I say yes, and the only card I have left to play is to let him have what he wants. Maybe then he will realise I'm not worthy of the chase, like the few that have tried before him. I've already mentally persuaded myself it will be just dinner, and possibly something else that scares the living shit out of me. Honestly, I knew this would happen when I found that damn card in my pocket. Exhaling deeply, I say something that is completely out of character.

"Fine! I will have dinner with you, and that's it!" He smiles like a Cheshire cat, and I am at risk of losing my sanity. "I need to tell you where I-"

"I already know." Of course, he knows where I live. How could I forget? A broad smile stretches across his face triumphantly again. I nod, and purse my lips together. I really didn't stand a chance fighting against him, but I know it's better this way, or at least I hope it is.

"Tomorrow night. Seven o'clock." He fills the space between us, takes my hand and brushes his lips over my knuckles. "What time do you finish tonight?" his voice is firmer now; controlled and powerful, causing all kinds of emotions to rush out from inside me.

I shrug my shoulders. I knew from past experience I would be finished whenever the last guests left, and we could clean away our equipment. "It depends; could be two hours, could be four," I tell him honestly.

"Did you drive here?"

"Yes. And thank you, my car drives better than it has in years." Watching his happiness gradually die, I know that was the wrong thing to say. He is visibly unimpressed with my gratitude. He presses his lips together and looks thoroughly pissed. He closes his eyes with a roll of his shoulders, but when he opens them again, the intensity has vanished, and he looks happy. He doesn't reply, just grunts something incoherently.

He is one strange man.

No more words are spoken as he walks me back towards the main room. Pausing at the grand French doors, he turns me to face him. "Tomorrow night." He bends down and swipes his lips over mine. His kiss is soft and light, but there is nothing innocent about it. I flush with headiness, secretly enjoying the throbbing in my core, as his tongue runs the seam of my mouth. Instinctively, I open to him without a second thought. His tongue swipes over mine - just once - then he cups my chin in both hands and reluctantly pulls out of the embrace. I mewl in protest, and drag my tongue over my bottom lip, savouring the last remnants of him.

I stare at him with new clarity. I'm a quivering, hot mess, realising I have just technically had my first real kiss. One that I didn't want to stop. He grins, rubs his thumb over my bottom lip, and confidently makes his way back inside to his table.

The dining room is a lot quieter now, and it's apparent many of the patrons have already departed for the evening. I watch Sloan take the woman's hand - his *sister's* hand - and he leads her from the room. He stops at the main doors and looks over his shoulder at me, leaving me with a smile that makes my insides turn to mush. Even from this distance, unforbidden promise sparkles inside his dark pools.

I lean against the door where he has left me, confused and frustrated, wondering if I really have just made the right choice. And whether or not I could really go through with what he would be expecting of me.

"So, what did Mr Beautiful want?" Marie asks knowingly. How long has she been standing there? I leave her question unanswered. "Hmm, hmm, thought so. When?"

"Tomorrow," I say quietly, never removing my eyes from his retreating form. Marie moves in front of me, and I glare at her for blocking my impeccable view.

"You do know this was his event tonight?"

I shake my head. Now I just feel as sick as a dog.

"The rumour mill says that his mother suffered from domestic abuse, so he devotes a lot of time to it, and some rather substantial donations, apparently. He also owns…no, never mind. Come on, let's start cleaning up."

Two hours later, with my feet filthy from being bare, I finally leave the empty ballroom. My head has been swimming in the aftermath of Sloan's kiss, and also from the revelation that the charity benefiting tonight's event was his - in respect of his mother, to be more precise.

I now realise when he made his comment the other night about caring, he meant it. True to his word, in my heart, I know he will never tell me no, and I know I will never have to beg him. More so, I believe him.

I also can't seem to shake the feeling that I've met him before. The way he touches me is pacifying and more than familiar. It induces a calm that has never really been mine. Dropping my head, I remember the first time I was touched by a man. I quickly push it aside, and go off in search of Marie.

After finally locating her to say my goodbyes, I collect my things from the staff room. Slipping my heels back on, my feet protest at the constriction. I seriously cannot wait to get back into my trainers.

Reaching my car, I kick off my shoes, and my feet rejoice when they slide comfortably into my battered old Converse. I sigh in happy relief, and toss my bag and jacket onto the passenger seat. Starting the engine, it doesn't turn over. I slam my hand over the steering wheel in frustration. Checking my mirrors, I see a black Mercedes parked a short distance away. I look at it ominously and instantly activate the locks. Now is not a good time to be broken down – I don't even have cover.

"Please!" I beg, turning the key again. "Don't be a bitch, *please*!" I will it. On the second attempt, the engine roars to life, and I have renewed faith. Driving out of the car park slowly, I recheck my mirrors and notice the Mercedes trailing a couple of cars behind me. My anxiety starts to get the better of me, and I press the accelerator harder, defying the speed limit, and endangering myself due to the fear of God the car behind is instilling deep in my already damaged mind.

Arriving home, I dart out of the car and fumble with the lock on the communal entrance. The sound of a car slowing down and finally stopping, sends me into a full-fledged panic. I refuse to look back; somethings really are better not knowing about. I finally get the door open and race up to my flat, taking the stairs two at a time. The lift would have been quicker, but it isn't safer - not in my opinion.

Safe inside, I race to the living room window that overlooks the street, and the car is still sat there idling. I grab my mobile, letting it turn over and over in my hand, wondering if I should call the police. But what on earth would I tell them? That I had come home from a high society dinner with London's most elite and wealthy, and there's an expensive Merc sat outside on the publicly adopted road? Or maybe I could say I'm worried they are trying to break in - best not to mention I'm on the fifth floor! I laugh out loud to myself, musing over what bullshit I could spout out if put to the test, when the mobile screen lights up and vibrates in my hand. Incoming text. I touch the screen to view it.

Tomorrow seven. I will pick you up since your driving skills leave a lot to be desired.

How the hell did he get my number?!

I look back out of the window at the black Mercedes and shake my head. He followed me home. It begins to move away, and the red taillights eventually disappear into the darkness. I stand and stare at the vehicle until it is gone.

Until *he* is gone.

Drawing the curtains, I toe off my trainers and strip out of my shirt. My hand drifts up to my neck, the memory of him plays havoc on my senses. My hand lowers to my chest and over my breasts, and I still my palm when I realise what I am doing. I'm pretending. I huff out, flustered and ashamed, and head into the bathroom.

Pushing my bedroom door open, I pat the towel over my damp face. Digging through my drawers, I pull out my pyjama shorts and vest, and change into them. Looking at my bed, I suspiciously glance towards Sam's room. Slowly walking down the hallway, I slide her door open. She is sound asleep. I tiptoe back to my room and curl up in bed. My mind is overwhelmed with emotions and feelings. They were all foreign to me once, not so much anymore. Dragging the duvet up to my neck, I try to block them out as much as possible, but it's impossible.

The only thing I can think about is Sloan Foster.

Sleep doesn't come easy, if at all.

Chapter 6

AFTER TOSSING AND turning all night, fearing that sleep would evade me, the sun shines through the thin curtains that cover my bedroom window. I blink a few times and rub my eyes. Sleepily moving my hand across the bedside table, it eventually locates the alarm clock. I groan loudly, seeing it is two-thirty in the afternoon. I throw the duvet off and drag my still exhausted body across the room. I open my door to find Sam simultaneously raising her knuckles, ready to knock. She looks excited, and I brace myself for whatever she is so deliriously happy about today.

I'm also surprised she was already asleep when I arrived home last night. I actually anticipated her being out. She may have told me she was done with how her life was heading down the toilet, but saying it and doing it, were never two things that went hand in hand with her.

"Oh, my God! You have to see what's just been delivered!" she exclaims.

The tinge occurs before she even seizes my hand and pulls me towards the living room. In the space of less than fifteen seconds, I have gone from still exhausted, to seriously annoyed and exhausted. She knows how I feel about personal space. Admittedly, she does her best to not touch me the majority of the time, and in turn, I do my best to ensure I stand well enough away. But this morning, she has forgotten that little snippet of information - a lot like everything else she has forgotten lately.

She stands in the living room doorway, waving her arm over at the sofa manically. I swear if I didn't know her any better, she's so excited, she might actually wet herself. I step towards the sofa to find the biggest arrangement of flowers I have ever seen. I can't even begin to tell you what most of them are. My eyes narrow suspiciously at the Armani dress bag and the Jimmy Choo shoe box. *Ah, shit, this isn't good.* I run my hand around the flowers, trying not to damage the tender petals, until I find the card and pluck it out.

Past, present and future.
Seven...
Sloan. X

"Past, present and future? Oh, how unoriginal is that! Not too smart for a classy, rich guy, is he?" Sam says from over my shoulder. I don't answer.

Unoriginal or not, the cryptic card sucks all the air right out of my lungs instantly. I stumble back, grabbing the sideboard for support. Curling my fingers under the edge of the wood to steady myself, the words are like a kick in the stomach. But there is nothing I can do regarding it because he doesn't know me. He doesn't know anything about the painful past I hide, the present that is non-existent, or the future that I know I will never have.

Casting my gaze towards Sam, she is now looking dreamily at the expensive gifts taking pride of place on our sofa. I'm not an idiot; I know these items cost more than what I make in months. Sam's face beams full of hope. *Hope*, that at least one of us will finally have a normal, healthy relationship. Shame, I already have a feeling this *relationship* is going to be anything but healthy. I recommence studying the words on the card as Sam peers over my shoulder once again.

"I can't believe he bought these for you! I so wish I hadn't passed out on his sofa on Monday night. Such a waste. These could have all been mine!"

My mouth falls open at the same time my eyes bug out of my head. Trust her to become the pillar of optimism when faced with obscene wealth. Not that I blame her, I'm feeling a little overawed by it myself. Or it could quite possibly be the after-effects of last night, and the fact that I shared my bed with an invisible man. *Again*. I swear, at this rate, I am going to be heading for the loony bin.

"How does he know your sizes?" she muses to herself.

I shrug my shoulders. "I have no idea," I say, surprised that she has pointed out the most irrelevant fact that I have failed to see.

"Sam, he probably only bought these so I don't embarrass him in whatever fancy place he intends to take me to. Seriously, I wouldn't read too much into it. It's not so farfetched that a guy will buy expensive dresses and shoes so that he has a reason to sleep with you. Think of them as a down payment." I drop the card and head into the kitchen. The kettle is almost boiled, and I reach for my mug and a tea bag.

"Not every guy just wants a quick shag, you know!" Sam states from behind me, making her presence known once more.

"Oh, yeah? Tell me one? One guy that you know who has bought you something and didn't expect sex? *One!*" I bait her. She stands there, a vacant expression spreading across her face. I know this look; it's the look of *I can't think of one now, but I can't let you know that.* I have her, and she knows it.

"What about that Timothy guy you had a date with a few months back? He didn't expect anything in return!"

I grimace at the memory of the last disaster. "Sam, he already told me if he paid for dinner, I was dessert! I went into it headfirst with my eyes wide open. No different than any other date I've had," I say with exasperation. She really can't see what is in front of her at all. Pouring the boiling water into my mug, I keep one eye on her. She wears the same look again as she rattles through her brain. She evidently comes up empty because she doesn't retort.

"Exactly," I say with confidence, raising the large mug of tea to my mouth. "Every guy wants something, but that's not bad because I want something, too. Tonight is going to be no different than any other night I've had for the last two years; dinner and home. In that order." I take a long swallow, hoping she believes me.

Even though Sam and I have lived together for a few years, due to the 'nobody invited back home' rule, she isn't aware of my inability to see a date out until the end of the evening, or my sexual deficiency, and I have no desire to divulge otherwise. Ignorance is sometimes bliss.

Sam glares at me. "Well, I just think that you need to start looking at this differently, that's all. He seems nice from what I've heard-" I gasp, but she doesn't shut up. "And maybe he really likes you. I bet you fifty quid he does!" she says proudly.

"Hey, if you've got fifty quid, you better hand it over for the rent before the ugly bastard comes knocking!" I say it playfully, but I'm completely serious. Sam looks down ashamed, and I know instantly that everything she has promised me for the last four days was fabricated to make the situation seem less bleak than it actually is. I sigh out loud and shake my head at her.

"Look, I've got to go," she says quickly and bolts to her room. I start to open my mouth to ask where, but think better of it. The less I know about her downward spiral, the better. The last thing I want is *those* men sat in my living room again.

"Hey, Sammy," I call, knocking on her door. She opens it and looks at me with regret. "If it doesn't work out, at least we can sell the dress and shoes to pay the rent arrears!" Sam cocks her head to the side and gives me a forced, half-smile. The door then closes hard in front of me.

I stand and stare at the wood that has just been slammed in my face. As a naturally pessimistic person, my suggestion seemed like one of my better ideas a moment ago. No point in owning something that costs more than my entire wardrobe, if I might not – no, will not - wear them again. I walk back into the living room, set down my tea and lift the suit bag. Unzipping it, I ease the dress out carefully.

Wow, it's breathtakingly beautiful.

It's amazing what a gorgeous, unpretentious black, strapless, knee-length dress can do to you once it's in your grasp. I sigh. It's divine. Simply stunning and I'm completely in love with it. It would be exactly what I would buy for myself if I had the money - and the ability - to shop in those kinds of places. I hold it up to myself and stare down the length of my body. As expected, I don't feel elated. I place it back in the bag and notice that the price tag has been ripped off.

Typical. Nothing like making a poor girl feel worse, is there?

I sit on the coffee table and reach for the shoe box. They are a simple looking pair of black heels. If you can call five-inch spike, peep-toe heels, simple, that is. I bite my lip nervously. The overall effect screams elegance and sophistication. It's such a shame that I am so far from it, it exists in another universe entirely. I begin to pack the shoes back into their box, when I touch upon another card languishing innocently at the bottom.

I pluck it out and twiddle it between my fingers. Am I brave enough to read it? It was hidden in the bottom for a reason – for my eyes only. I stare at the plain white back for long minutes, debating if I really want to see what he's written on the other side. Feeling both brave and terrified, I inhale deeply and flip it over.

I can't wait to hear you scream my name wearing only these.

X.

The presumptuous, arrogant, self-confident, beautiful bastard!

But I'm only fooling myself.

This is precisely the reason why I agreed to see him tonight. The words merely confirm what we both already knew the moment I walked out of his hotel suite almost a week ago. Fear suddenly comes back in full force, and I shiver. I know if I'm going to do this, I have to be physically, and mentally, prepared to have someone touch me *there* - anywhere, as a matter of fact. I have to be strong enough to endure his flesh on mine and not compare it to that of the past. It has been just over eight years since anyone has touched me intimately. Since a *man* has touched me that way.

Except, rape can never, *ever*, be classed as being touched intimately. Violated, attacked, abused, defiled, debased – all words that can, and do, describe such an act, but never intimate.

I put the card back in the box and carry them, and my new dress, back into my room. Sitting on the edge of the bed, I look over at them again. Never have two such innocuous items ever been so terrifying.

I'm showered and shaved, exfoliated and moisturised. I've blow-dried my hair and styled it up, not very dissimilar to the way I wore it last night, and again, my make-up is light. This is intentional, the guy has already seen me at my worse almost five nights ago. He obviously didn't mind my au naturel appearance then, so it's good enough for him now. I stare at my reflection, noting the time behind me; six-thirty.

Thirty minutes for it all to go terribly wrong.

I study myself for longer than I'm generally comfortable with. I have gone over and over in my head what I will say if the worst happens - that's if I lose my shit entirely, the moment his hand touches more than it has already. If I turn completely ballistic, I need a plausible reason to justify it. Having already rehearsed my potential lie to death, I blow out my breath and close the bathroom door behind me.

Laying my bag and jacket down, a heavy knock rattles the front door. I tentatively walk out into the hallway, cursing him for being early, while testing out the ludicrous high heels. *Well, maybe they're not as ludicrous as I first thought,* I think to myself. I'm too busy admiring the way my legs look in them, and distractedly, I open the door without checking the peephole first.

Catastrophic mistake.

The ugly bastard.

"Petersen, you promised me! Now, where the fuck is my money? Don't make me come in there and get it!" Shit, he's furious. More so than I can ever recall in the few years that Sam and I have lived here.

Putting my body weight between the frame and the door, Danny pushes it open with little to no effort. He quickly looks behind me, before his eyes fall upon my body. They travel from my feet to my neck, and stop for far too long at my chest. My skin crawls sickeningly under his salacious grin. He leers and licks his lips, crossing his thick, rounded arms atop his equally thick, rounded stomach. Danny is about five stone overweight, and he uses it to his advantage - especially when it is female.

"I told you; I'll get it!" I tell him firmly, unintentionally pushing my chest out. It's a brave reflex action, but right now, it's the wrong one.

He lifts his hand and traces a finger down the naked skin of my forearm, making every tiny hair stand to attention. "You know, there are other ways you can pay me. If you know what I mean." His eyes sparkle with apparent kinky perversion, and as tough as like to think I am sometimes, I freeze, and shut down completely. The last time someone touched me like this - against my will - I did what I had to do for survival. I didn't - or rather couldn't - fight back, and the outcome destroyed me. Here and now, I feel like it's that night all over again.

"I-I will g-get your money. *Please d-don't!*" I stutter, my mind bombarded with the few jumbled, distorted images I still remembered from that soul-destroying night eight years ago. I am on the verge of begging, and that is also something else I haven't done in the last eight years and swore I never would again.

Until now.

Danny's smile grows wider, and his eyes glaze over. I can see in his expression this is something that has been eating away inside his head for a long time. I've had over two years of him and his lecherous, snide comments. The way he would always find a way to brush up against me. The way he would instinctively lick his lips whenever he saw me. The fact he would use pathetic reasons to come up to the flat; issues with the gas supply, the neighbours have complained about the water pressure, so on and so forth. All pathetic excuses to worm his way in. Yes, he knew this day would one day arrive, maybe not in this context, but having me this way, I'm sure it isn't something that has just popped into his thick head in the last five minutes.

With glassy eyes and shortness of breath, he abruptly slams me back against the wall and kicks the door with his foot. It bangs shut hard, the sound echoes down the small hallway, and my facial muscles clench as the sound grates on me. "Now, let's see how many ways you can repay me, shall we?" He advances on me, and I shift sharply.

Running back into the living room, I snatch up the lamp from the sideboard, ripping the plug from the socket, and hold it out in front of myself like a weapon. "I swear to God if you come any closer… I mean it. Don't!" Clutching the lamp in self-defence, I hold my other palm up to him. The panic in my own voice terrifies me. The sound is something that I've not had to identify in so long, it hardly sounds like me. Ignoring my pleas, he continues to advance on me. "Don't, *please,*" I whimper pathetically. My breathing is coming out loud and pained. I pray for someone to hear me; for someone to magically come and save me. Sloan won't be here for another twenty minutes or so, and deep inside, I guess I knew, somehow, it would all turn terribly wrong tonight.

Danny grunts as he slowly stalks me, backing me into a tight spot. I'm ready to beg; I will get down on my hands and knees if that what it takes. There is no way in hell I'm going to let someone use me like a prostitute again. The memories of nearly a decade ago linger at the surface, and tears begin to form in my eyes; not enough to fall away, but enough to know I won't be able to hide the redness. In the watery haze distorting my sight, I see the bastard reach out to me, and then, in a split second, he's lurching back into the hallway.

Then I see *him.*

The sound of the air shifting is deafening. I drop the lamp and start to move away. Danny groans loudly, as the sound of flesh upon flesh rings in my ears. Sloan raises his fist repeatedly, raining blow after blow on his face. A crack resounds loudly, and Danny's hand shoots up to his nose.

"You son of a bitch. I'm gonna fucking have you for that!" he yells, scrambling off the floor and slowly edges towards the safety of the door.

Sloan glares at him; rage emanating from every angle. His entire body hardens with fury, his fists are still clenched, and his face is tight and unreadable. I continue to slink away slowly in the face of his anger because this is too much for me to handle. Danny starts walking backwards down the small hallway, and Sloan stalks after him. Standing at the door, he grips the wood in his hand until his fingers turn white under the pressure he is exerting.

"You dare come back here again, and even think about touching her, you'll be fucking dead! I doubt anyone will miss you, you filthy, rapist bastard!"

The door slams shut, and the sound of wood splintering echoes momentarily throughout the deathly silent flat. I stand in the living room doorway, staring at his back in shock, with my hand over my heart. He twists around, his features change from enraged to concerned, and he's on me in seconds. His hands cradle my head affectionately. He looks into my eyes, then up and down the length of my body, before finally coming back up to my face. I sigh out in relief at his presence.

Danny has just managed to fracture a small part of the invisible wall I have carefully, and painfully, constructed around myself for all these years. Eight years of fighting back memories are now pointless, as they saturate my muddy, nightmare riddled mind like it had all happened yesterday.

The tears fall from behind my lashes freely, and Sloan urges me closer. He circles his arms around me as I let go, and the warmth of his body feels too good against my frozen flesh. His hands upon my back strengthen my current sense of security. Tucking myself into him, I cling tightly, without a hint of shame at my conduct. He holds me for a long time, or at least it feels like it, until he eases his grip.

I gaze at him. Apart from our first meeting, not once in my twenty-three years have I really appreciated the male form in its full glory, until now. It's definitely the wrong moment to appreciate it, especially considering I nearly just became a victim for a second time, but he does things to me I can't comprehend. I shuffle out of his hold and stare down at his body. He is dressed in black jeans, a black jacket and a white shirt, unbuttoned at the neck. He is a sight to behold, and I'm already feeling the effects of his nearness deep inside my core.

"I guess dinner is ruined for tonight," he breathes out in annoyance.

Evaluating the full meaning behind his words, there is nothing I can say to counter because it's true. Dinner is the last thing I want tonight if I'm honest. But at the same time, the last place I want to be is here. Not to mention the unspoken fact that Danny - as my landlord - has a master key, and stupidly, I don't have any additional locks or security on the inside of my door. Wriggling out of his grasp completely, he looks down at me with apprehension, like *I* have just punched *him* in the face.

"I guess so," I reply. His eyes sadden somewhat, and he grips my hand tightly, before starting to let go. He touches his lips to my temple, the tender action soothes me, and then he slowly begins to turn. Pulling at his wrist, he looks shocked at my assertiveness.

"Please, I don't want to be here alone tonight," I confess, my voice undecidedly croaky.

He pauses and studies me, then looks around my meagre living room. It's a look of disapproval, and I shrink back into myself. I've never before in my life felt embarrassed about where I live, but having this immaculate, beautiful, and extremely wealthy man here, I feel humiliated. Humiliated and ashamed. His eyes flick back to mine; his look of understanding identifies my discomfort.

"Where's your flatmate tonight?" he asks softly. I lift my shoulders and shake my head. I honestly have no idea where she is. After our little spat this afternoon, she had gone to her room, and sometime while I was getting ready, she disappeared for the evening. I don't know when, or *if*, she will come back tonight. No note, no text. *Nothing.*

He glances around again, until his eyes settle on the flowers I have actually managed to arrange and have placed in the centre of the coffee table. I regard them sadly, then rotate on my heels back to him.

"Oh, thank you, they're beautiful. The dress and shoes, too," I say, casting my eyes down my body all the way to my feet.

His face slackens, and his lips start to turn up, slowly following my line of sight. "Good, I'm glad you like them. You look beautiful by the way, absolutely stunning. I knew you would." His fingers massage my jaw. It feels good. Really good, actually. I can already feel the stress exiting my body, even if the newest memory is not.

"Go and pack a few things, I'm not leaving you alone tonight." His tone tells me not to argue, but my nature is fight or flight. Unfortunately, men had bossed me around more times than I'd liked in my young life, and I wasn't about to let another one do it.

"What do you mean? Where am I going?" I query sharply. I imagined he would take me to dinner, and that would be the end of it. Over. I mean, come on, he can't possibly expect me to be able to do *anything* in light of current events.

"You're coming with me." Now it's more of a command. It's something I realise comes naturally to him – commanding, ordering.

I gasp out a laugh. Who the hell does he think he is? "No, I don't think so."

He tilts his head, his eyes narrow and then he grips my shoulders hard. "Do you really think I'm going to leave you here, *alone*, with the rapist bastard out there? Hmm?" My body shudders, and my muscles begin to tense up thinking about my little to no security. I'm sure my lamp wouldn't protect me completely should he decide to come back again. Sloan clearly notices the effect his words have on me because he relaxes his hold. His face, however, does not, and is now stoic and assessing.

"Don't take this the wrong way, but I don't even know you! You could be no better than he is!" I shout, throwing my hand towards the closed door.

Watching him absorb my insinuation, he stiffens and appears tortured. Slowly, he starts walking me backwards, until I'm up against the wall; chests pressed together, noses practically touching. His lips are fractions from mine as he vents his anger. "Do not ever, *ever*, compare me to him! I don't beat or rape women! Now, either you go and pack something for the morning, or I will do it for you. You've got five minutes!"

Holding my breath, I slide out from between him and the wall. I throw my hands in the air in amazement, let out a loud, disapproving huff, and then stalk into my bedroom. "Fuck you!" I spit out viciously, the same second I slam my door shut.

Seconds later, the door swings open and Sloan's large frame fills it completely. I gulp in a long breath as this mercurial, sexy, and extremely vexed man edges towards me. His dark, brooding features are stunning in this moment. My breathing fails me when his eyes darken to a deep, rich black, as they flash over my bed.

"You've got a naughty mouth, my love," he says softly. He doesn't come any closer, just stands and watches me with crossed arms.

I rifle through my wardrobe and pack some jeans, a t-shirt, and then begin rummaging through my underwear drawer. Hesitating under his watchful eye, I make sure to only pull out the best that I've got, which isn't a lot. A black lace thong lands on the floor in my haste. Horrified, I make an attempt to grab it, but I'm too late when he approaches quickly, and lifts it up on the tip of his finger. I roll my bottom lip into my mouth. His irises widen, and his chest expands. The desire radiates off of him in spades, and the air in the room is turning heavy and palpable. I wait in pained silence, watching him examine the harmless, inoffensive, scrap of cheap lace and synthetic silk. He tilts his head to the side, spears me with a look of longing, and then inhales.

"Make sure you bring this." He carefully places it back down on the duvet, and leaves the room just as quickly as he had entered it.

After packing only what I need, I grip the bag in my hand and close my bedroom door behind me.

Sloan is in the living room when I enter, holding up a picture of me when I was younger with my parents. It depicts a time before it all turned to shit. Dropping the bag with a thud, he spins around, and I snatch the picture from his hand and set it back down. His face contorts, and I know he has questions.

Well, he isn't going to get any answers!

He has no right to know anything about my past. Any progress he might have made with me in the last handful of days vanishes. Knowing my past will always dictate my future, my resolve snaps firmly back into place, and I decide tonight, regardless of what has come to pass thus far, will be no different than what I'd already anticipated it would be.

I stand in front of him, and he reaches out to me. He growls low and deep in his throat when I allow him to run his hand over my neck and up my cheek. I lean into his palm, recommitting to memory his scent and touch, as well as the peace and tranquillity that is newly synonymous with him. I don't know how I've become so strong in the last thirty minutes. Danny nearly switched something back on inside me, he almost made me regress, but Sloan manages to eradicate everything and bend me to his will.

My mind is in absolute disarray. Sensing my bewilderment, Sloan silently picks up my bag and tucks me into his side to leave. The lock of my flat door turning is final.

We are standing at the small lift, waiting for it to arrive. He tips his head down, and studies me for long, hard minutes as the old, dilapidated lift lets out a drone that's meant to be akin to a bell. I hold my breath; he's going to make me get in the damn thing! The urge to run back into my flat and lock the door is intense, but I bite it back because Mr Foster is unaware of my *problem*. I chance a quick look at him. Hell, he's noticed my discomfort. I roll my shoulders, preparing for the inevitable, but he surprises me completely when pulls back, grips my hand tight, and guides us out of the corridor and down the multitude of stairs.

The light bleeds into the night as Sloan throws open the fire exit door. The cold chill of the evening wraps itself around me, the same moment his arm comes across my shoulder and pulls me close again. He leads us towards a black car, then turns around to face me. Dropping a light kiss to my nose, he opens the passenger door.

"You hold all the cards tonight, Kara. You have the power here. Please don't forget that."

Chapter 7

I CLIMB INTO the flashy, black sports car that is parked next to my old-as-the-hills Fiesta. I stare at the interior in awe and smooth my hands over the leather seat, slowly dragging my fingertips across the supple surface. My bum slides a little, due to the lack of friction between the gorgeous dress and the sumptuous leather. I pull on my seat belt and let out a long, deep, controlled breath. The boot slams shut, and I jolt. Sloan slips off his jacket and passes it to me, as he folds himself into the driver's seat. Gripping the jacket in my hands, I can smell him all over it. The pheromones he gives off are addictive. The uncontrollable urge to bring it to my face and sniff it until I'm appeased is far too great. Honestly, I'm not sure how I manage to hold myself back.

I observe him unobtrusively from the corner of my eye. His concentration is fixed on the road ahead, except I don't fail to notice the way he sucks his bottom lip between his teeth and drifts off in deep thought. I hold onto my seat belt tightly, not sure if being with him, when he is only half here, as such, is a good idea. I tilt my head towards the window and watch the night pass by, all the while studying Sloan's reflection in the glass, who alternates between chewing his lips to pursing them together.

Thirty minutes later, after he has defied every compulsory speed limit in the land, we are driving through the countryside. The silence is uncomfortable and heavy, and I decide to lift the mood slightly. "So, are we going to the hotel?" I enquire optimistically, since it was there that we had first met.

"No," he says unquestionably. It's now my turn to purse my lips hard. I can already feel myself becoming snappy again. Is it too much to ask for a straightforward answer?

God, I'm so frustrated.

At least I think that's what I am. Nevertheless, whatever it is, he is the cause of that, too.

Veering off the country lane, we eventually stop at a massive set of black, domineering, wrought iron gates. They lead to what looks like the entrance to an exceptionally grand property. I narrow my eyes and suddenly feel sick. *Is this his house?* He presses something on the dash, the whirring sound of electricity echoes and the gates open in front of us, welcoming us over the threshold. He eases the car forward, and I gaze out of the window at the surrounding beauty, until I see a house situated half a mile or so in front of us. Eventually, he slows to a stop at the end of the drive, which turns into a circle in front of the house. Well, actually, it's a mansion, a huge one, and I'd be lying if I said I wasn't equally enthralled and terrified by it. It is a large, weathered-looking sandstone building. The exterior is old, but loved, and very well presented. It is double fronted and symmetrical in every way, with a large wooden door taking pride of place between two stone columns and beautifully manicured, round, topiary trees.

He parks in between a Mercedes and a Range Rover. There are numerous other luxury cars parked, as well as a few bikes. He quickly comes around to my side to help me out. He might have been a bit of an arse tonight, but unlike his sister, he still has manners, which makes him even more attractive. But I have to stop thinking like this! *He* is for one night only.

A large, warm hand settles on the small of my back, guiding me towards the front door. My mouth drops open, and I swallow as much air as I'm able, as electricity causes every hair follicle and nerve ending to stand to attention. I'm so confused by his ability to make me feel different; I don't think I'll ever be able to think straight when he's near me. As the door gets closer, the realisation of what I finally plan to do tonight hits me like a ten-ton lorry. My eyes expand in fear, and I halt, unable to move any further.

He stares at me, his face full of worry. "What's wrong?"

"Nothing," I breathe out. I run my hand over my neck, tugging at the invisible noose around it. I'm unable to draw in enough air, and my throat constricts rapidly, to the point of causing actual pain. I look deep into his eyes, silently pleading with him.

Can I really do this? Can I really indulge in casual sex for the first time and not expect anything after?

"You have nothing to worry about with me, Kara, I will always respect your wishes. I wasn't lying when I said you hold all the cards tonight." He removes a key from his pocket and inserts it into the door. My breathing is still erratic and worsens even more so when the door creaks and opens.

Just breathe. I can do this, I think to myself, running my sweaty palms over the back of the dress.

Sloan guides me inside and closes the door behind us. He drops my bag to the floor and enfolds me in his arms. I grasp him, tugging him as close as physically possible. His hand rides up my back until his fingers draw tiny circles in between my shoulder blades. Any other time this might have induced me to scream bloody murder, but all I can focus on is the sound of my breathing under his maddening, provoking caress.

In and out. In and out. Deep and even.

No amount of therapy has ever come close to eradicating my fear of tight spaces or being touched, but inexplicably, he has already succeeded in obliterating one of my two aversions. It probably didn't help my plight that I never fully disclosed the true reasons why I feared either so much. I close my eyes, letting the memory fade away, and lose myself in the sensation of his strong muscles bunching together underneath his shirt.

God, he still smells good, too.

It feels like an eternity passes by until he releases me again. I tear myself from him as fast as I can, trying not to make a show of myself. *Too late.* His eyes narrow knowingly. He sees me - the real me - and I don't like. Not one bit.

He continues to study me closely, so much so, it's making me uncomfortable to even breathe in front of him. I turn and walk through the large open space until my jaw virtually hits the floor. There is an imposing central staircase in the middle, and I'm ashamed to say, the hallway and its adjacent corridor, are larger than the entire floor space of my flat combined. I tilt my head over my shoulder to see Sloan locking the front door behind us. Floor to ceiling pillars frame it, and it looks spectacular and breath-taking. I smile shyly and look back to the large, square hallway again. Beautiful, long, dark wood tables grace the walls on either side, and large vases hold an array of perfectly arranged flowers on the centres. Upon closer inspection, I realise they are exactly the same flowers that currently hold pride of place on my coffee table. I turn, and he grins at me

"I like these ones the best," I say, studying the blooms. I carefully touch the pink sloping heads which are not in my arrangement at home. I have no clue what they are.

"They're called Fritillaria Meleagris, or Snake Heads. See how they're shaped?"

"Snake Heads…very romantic," I deadpan, and he laughs.

"Very."

Electricity soars through me unexpectedly, and I let out a breath as he brushes past, ensuring he touches me. He holds out his hand, and I sigh overwhelmed. Sliding my hand into his, his fingers curl and squeeze reassuringly. I consciously control my breathing, still trying to figure out why I'm not experiencing the usual cold sweat running the length of my spine each time he touches me. I've been trying to figure it out for the last week, but to no avail.

I allow him to guide me down the long hallway into the living room. Again, my eyes enlarge in astonishment at the beauty of it and its contents. The room is neutral beiges, and is furnished with three dark brown leather sofas, dark tables, and a large open fireplace. I stand in the centre and rotate a full three hundred and sixty. Taking in everything all over again, seeing things I missed the first time around when my eyes barely skimmed the area.

"No TV?" I ask a little shocked, but I guess someone like him probably doesn't have time to sit around and waste the days away.

"Not in here, but I do have one in the living room next door. If you tell me you want to watch the soaps tonight, we're in trouble!" he taunts playfully, arching a dark brow.

I scoff, then laugh. The soaps have got nothing on my life. Not by a long shot!

Coming back to my starting position, Sloan is slowly walking towards me, and he holds out his arms. Moving into them, he wraps them tight around me and kisses the top of my head. He pushes back and gives me a smile that makes my heart flutter. I close my eyes, savouring his warmth which is fading rapidly. I'm sure I am swaying on the spot from the tiny intoxication of him. I shake my head; I have officially lost my mind. I've just willingly offered myself to him, maybe not in *that* way, but I willingly walked into his arms…and I liked it, more than liked, actually.

I wanted it.

I want him…

Holy shit, did I just admit that to myself?

Deep in my pensive state, I'm half aware he is leading me out of the living room and down the hallway. My eyes flick from one door to the next, wondering what lies behind them. The paintings on the walls are beautiful; old and new, classical and temporary, and I think that I might have seen have a few of them on The Antiques Roadshow not so long back. I halt to observe them properly, not that

I'm an art connoisseur and would know what I was inspecting them for. Sloan saunters towards me with his hands in his pockets. He stands behind me and then wraps his arms around my middle again. Instinctively, I lean back onto his shoulder, and it feels like the most natural thing in the world.

"Do you like it?" I nod, and murmur *yes* to him. "I'm not particularly keen, but maybe I'll give it another chance since you appreciate it. Come on," he says, holding me to his side and guiding us the last few feet of the hallway.

He stops us in front of a door, unlocks it and guides us inside. There is glimmer across the floor, and I squint trying to make out what it is. The light comes on, and a beautiful indoor pool illuminates in the vast space. The reflection of the water ripples off the surface and onto the pale grey tiled walls.

"Feel free to use this anytime you like, just let me know you're in here, for your own safety, of course," he grins at me, and I return it.

"Thank you, but I didn't pack a swimsuit. It's probably safe to say I actually don't even own one."

"Well, we will have to rectify that, won't we? Preferably sooner rather than later." He turns the lights off, and I take one last longing look at the dark pool before leaving.

One of the last doors leads into a large modern kitchen. Lights sparkle and reflect hypnotically in the distance through the large, imposing patio doors that run the length of the wall. I rotate just in time to see him jog up some stairs that are located just opposite the kitchen door, and he disappears.

I sigh, this is so much more than I thought it would be. I didn't expect when we walked out of my front door this evening, I would see *this*. I'm having a hard time comprehending what he is hoping to achieve by bringing me here. I watch the doorway until I grow tired, then mosey deeper into the kitchen while I wait for him. White, high gloss units and cupboards line it, accentuated by the black, marble worktops that sparkle under the cupboard lights. It's sparse, with nothing on display, not even a kettle. It reminds me of a show home. Lifeless and hollow. I run my finger along the worktops; they are cold under touch. I appreciate the irony, for the majority of my life, I too, have been cold, lifeless, and hollow.

Minutes later, I hear a light tapping, and Sloan comes jogging back down the stairs. His shadow from the upstairs light casts downwards as he moves. Entering the kitchen again, he stops in front of me, takes my clutch bag and places it on one of the bar stools. He lifts me up and sets me down on the worktop, and I flinch as the marble chills my backside to the bone. Even through the thick, gorgeous fabric of the dress, it's still unforgivingly cold. He gives me an all-knowing smile as he rounds the centre island to the fridge. He moves with such agility; I can't help but imagine how it would feel for him to move against me. My cheeks flush, and my palms start to sweat. I let out a little gasp as my centre fills with moisture. He turns and grins at me, smirking with full understanding. He then roots around in the fridge, removes various plastic tubs and puts them in the microwave. I arch my brow when he turns back to me.

"I ordered some food when you were packing. Security brought it in."

Is there nothing that escapes him?

I also have to question how I neglected to see security when we approached the vast gates outside. I think I need to start paying better attention to my surroundings from now on.

I hop down from the worktop, and I slide off my shoes. I tiptoe to the patio doors and place my palms flat on the glass, lost in the lights flickering through the darkness and the tree line outside. The world looks serene, almost beautiful.

Shame that in the harsh light of day it is anything but.

I am about to walk away when his presence surrounds me, and his stunning image reflects on the glass in front of me. I lift my hand to the pane and outline his form with my finger. Without shame, his breathing speeds up behind me as I trace him. A hand slowly wraps around my neck and jaw, and he gently coerces me to look at him. I turn around the same moment he holds a glass of wine out to me. Eager to cool down, I take a long sip. The liquid feels fantastic against my parched throat. He watches me assiduously as I lift the glass to my mouth again. Cradling it against my bottom lip, I slowly tip it up and swallow.

I observe him unapologetically, his eyes close, and he exhales; slow and meticulous. I revel in the fact he undoubtedly feels something more than I assumed he did. He is just as affected by me, as I am by him. I can't suppress the smile that tugs on my lips when I notice his fists bunch up. He wants to touch me, and if he does, I know I will never want him to stop. I still have no concept of when I stopped wanting never to be touched, as opposed to wanting him to touch me all the time.

His resolve wanes, and he finally gives in to the urge. His fingers stroke my skin and his free hand works its way down my neck to my arm. His beautiful features constrict marginally as he skims past the area that Danny had mauled over an hour ago, and a fantastic shudder runs through my body. Taking an audible, deep breath, he finally returns to my shoulder and traces my collarbone with feather-light strokes. I stare into his eyes; they are black, darkened with desire. There is no doubt in my mind that tonight is going to play out exactly as I anticipated. He leans towards me, and I willingly angle my head to expose more of my neck. He gently sucks the base, and his breath sears my skin. My entire body flushes, and I feel wet and needy in all the right places.

I close my eyes and lose myself in the moment, while an all-consuming heat starts to claw its way throughout my body. The sound of a glass being put down somewhere echoes around me, then mine is removed from my hand. Two large, warm, hands work from my shoulders to my neck. Strong fingers securely hold me at the nape, as dexterous thumbs draw small circles between my jaw and ear. Warm air blows gently against my right cheek, and snaps me back to reality, as my eyes fly wide open. Sloan is breathing hard against me, his expression is full of passion and hunger, and right now, all I want him to do is act upon it. I want him to push me up against the glass and devour me.

To hell with selling the dress, he can rip it off me if he so wishes!

I want him.

I want him all of him.

Then the microwave pings.

Damn it!

We sit in uncomfortable silence as we eat, neither of us daring to utter a single word. The air around us is thick, crackling with tension. It has been deepening since he pulled me away from the window, unable to contain his evident arousal. Now, he's taken to watching me a little too diligently, making me very mindful of his all-seeing, assessing eyes.

Feeling slightly self-conscious, I drop my fork to the plate, and he glances over my barely touched food. I'm more than a little hungry, but the desire sweeping over my extremely inexperienced body is doing funny things to my stomach. It's giving me an appetite for something I don't want to put a name to, but know exactly what it is. And it's something I never thought I would.

"Something wrong with dinner?"

"No, it's great. I'm...full." I lie blatantly. I could've told him the truth, but that would open up a can of worms I'm not willing to share until I absolutely have to. I'm not about to tell him that I'm inexperienced. Well, I will eventually, but not tonight, not unless...

He murmurs something randomly and gently sets his own fork down. "Hmm." He leans over with the bottle of wine to refill my glass.

"So, I want to talk about what happened earlier tonight, and who he is," he says nonchalantly, but the tightness around his eyes gives him away. I take stock of my thoughts and almost laugh out loud. He isn't inviting me to talk, he's inadvertently telling me I have to.

Just like he doesn't like being told no, he also doesn't like the truth being consciously omitted from him. Unfortunately, he doesn't have that advantage, yet. He might have my respect, but he doesn't have my trust. It's not something I throw around easily; it's something you have to earn from me.

"He's nobody; he doesn't matter." I divert my eyes away and look behind him. I stare at the high gloss cupboards over his head, pretending the light reflecting off them isn't actually blinding me in this white and clinical, cold looking space.

"Well, I say he does matter. He assaulted you in your own home, and that shit doesn't fly with me, baby."

I open my mouth to speak and subsequently shut it firmly. Then again, I am not exactly one for keeping my mouth shut. "Well, thank you for your perfect timing, but it wasn't necessary. I would have gotten rid of him, *eventually,*" I mutter, taking a sip of wine, knowing my table lamp would never be intimidating enough to get rid of him. Nevertheless, I've learnt not to depend on anyone to keep me safe. Even if I have to use inanimate objects to assist in my bidding.

He crosses his arms over his chest, the muscles of his shoulders and biceps stretch the fabric of his shirt mouth-wateringly. The veins in his neck strain under his poorly concealed anger. I gaze at him, mesmerised, and if I wasn't so annoyed, I might have taken this as an opportunity to start whatever was really going on here.

His lips form a tight line when he realises I'm not going to impart any truths. "You know, I can't help you if you don't tell me, Kara." His face softens as the last letter of my name rolls off his tongue.

I stare at him; his eyes wide, his expression hopeful. My heart rate climbs, realising this is probably the look he gives every poor woman who is unable to fend for herself. My personal self-defence has always been attitude. It is, and always has been, a fundamental layer of the wall that surrounds me. I use my acumen; I'm not a fighter. Truthfully, I've been defenceless my whole life. And I finally conceded it this evening, when Danny attempted to rape me. Tears threaten as the harsh truth hits me like a bucket of cold water.

I will always be a victim.

I quickly bring my hand to my mouth and, finally, let it in that I *am* going to tell him. It's a realisation that both shocks and comforts me in equal measure.

"He's my landlord," I confess in defeat, knowing I already lost the fight no sooner had he asked the question. "Sam was supposed to give him the rent money last week and didn't." I look down at my plate, not wanting to see his face when he figures out I'm not good enough for him. I don't want his pity, just the same way I don't want him to think I'm only after his money.

"When last week, and how many weeks?" he asks before he picks up his fork and continues eating.

"Monday, and three," I whisper timidly. His hand tenses around his cutlery, and I catch his fleeting look of frustration as his jaw twitches furiously. There is no doubt in my mind he has just done a quick monetary calculation of how much we owe.

"Right."

He doesn't even look at me, as he abruptly jumps up from his stool and waltzes out of the room. I hear heavy footsteps pound up the stairs. My hand clutches my belly, and I think I'm going to be sick. *Violently.* He has just seen me for what I really am - well and truly out of his league.

Long minutes pass before he returns. He slaps a cheque book on the island and flips it open. "How much?" he asks nonchalantly, as though he makes it a daily good deed to give money to women verging on the edge of homelessness and destitution.

I have never once depended on anyone to give me money, not as an adult, and I won't be starting now. I'm not blind; I can see what's around me, the way he lives, the clothes he wears, and the car he drives. I know he's disgustingly rich, but it's not his money that I want, and it never will be.

"No, no, no! I don't want that! That's not why I am here!" I shout.

He ignores me and starts to write out the cheque, leaving the obvious parts blank. He hands it to me with an unreadable expression.

"No! You're insulting and humiliating me!" Tears glaze my eyes, and I quickly clamber down from the stool. I slide my feet back into the heels, grab my clutch, and scuttle down the long corridor to the front door.

Bending down to retrieve my overnight bag from the foot of the staircase, a strong, firm arm encircles my waist and lifts me up and back. His free arm travels behind my knees, and suddenly, I'm airborne. Carrying me into the living room, my heart feels like it's going to explode. He lowers himself onto one of the sofas with me in his lap. I try to wiggle out, but he grips me tighter, and slowly moves his head from side to side. I ignore him, still trying in vain to prise myself away.

"Please take me home," my voice quivers.

"No," he replies firmly

I struggle in his hold, my bum rubbing against his growing hardness. Looking into his face, he doesn't appear impressed with my escape attempt, so I shift some more, trying to extricate myself from the confines of his powerful arms that I have no leverage or strength against.

"Please, stop!" he commands. I quit wiggling instantly. His voice ripples through me; heightening emotions and feelings that have no right to be aware or heightened right now.

"Baby, I didn't mean to cause you any offence with the cheque. I want to help, that's all. Please don't leave."

I turn to answer him, but before I know it, his mouth is on mine. His kiss isn't gentle. It's hard and unforgiving, devouring me with equal amounts of passion and pain. It's also the perfect catalyst for the heat slowly burning me from the inside out to stoke higher. One hand snakes its way up my side and the other massages my inner thigh. I moan into his mouth, and he uses this as an opportunity to take advantage, while his tongue dances intimately with mine. The rhythm is intense and all-consuming. He lifts my body up, hitching my dress further up my legs as he goes. I swing my thigh over and position it on the side of his. I really don't have a clue of what I'm doing; instinct alone is guiding me into the unknown. My soft, aching breasts are crushed against his hard chest as I straddle him. His hands at the back of my thighs tease and trace their way up to my arse, while he licks, nips, and sucks on my bottom lip. I inch back a little to watch his eyes; they are growing darker and hazy again with each second that ticks by.

My hands delve straight into his hair, and I tug the strands between my fingers, loving how soft it is, wondering how it would feel brushing across my stomach and other unmentionable areas. Pulling him closer, needing to feel more, he deepens the kiss; harder, firmer, stronger. I pull my hair from the band securing it and let it cascade around my shoulders, and instantly, his hands are wrapped in it.

Falling headfirst into the abyss I can't seem to turn my back on, I relax against him. He is both soft and hard, and by God, I want to stay like this with him forever. My eyes shoot open with that piece of truth.

Forever.

There is a faint possibility that one day I might have one.

With his hand cupping my neck, his mouth lingers at the base of my throat, touching and tasting, learning the contours of my skin. He leans me back a little, and his teeth softly nip a track across my jaw, as his tongue soothes my skin from the tiny incisions. His chest rises and falls rhythmically, powerfully, with each touch until he settles and gently withdraws from me. A broad smile stretches across his face, and it's enough to make me believe he wants more than I had initially compromised with him.

"I've wanted to do that since the first time I saw you." One hand is still on my back, and the other strokes the hair away from my face. "When you walked through my hotel door…I had no idea. I had no idea it would be like this; that *you* would be like this. So perfect." Something shifts in his midnight pools, and I can't quite put my finger on the true extent of what he's trying to say - albeit inadvertently. "I expected another drugged-up girl coming for her, but you...you surprised me." I stare into his eyes, and they radiate his honesty, except they're still holding something back. Whereas I, on the other hand, have lost all ability to reply.

"And then at the function. My sister wasn't too impressed…" He smirks.

I press my hands to his chest, attempting to garner some distance between us, but he only allows me a few inches. I have no desire to hear about his ungrateful, bitchy sibling, and my anger is gradually rising from deep within. I'm not a complete moron, I know I'm not in their league, but I have feelings too, goddamn him!

He smiles knowingly and shakes his head. "No, please don't misunderstand. She had a date lined up for the evening, but he was required elsewhere. I knew my sister really wanted to go, so I decided to attend at the last minute."

His hands knead my behind before one creeps up to the middle of my back. He lifts us both off the sofa, heads out of the living room and up the stairs. I smile half-hearted, too far gone to break down what he is saying. What I am fully aware of though, is the fact that I should be running from the madness he has unleashed in me, not allowing him to take me upstairs willingly.

"Actually, I was only going to annoy her, but then I saw the one thing I have wanted for so lo..." He pauses halfway up with a slightly worried expression. The unfinished statement is unmistakable, but I cannot pick it apart and analyse it right now. "I saw you; I wanted you. It's one of the best decisions I've ever made."

This man wanted me? *No, I don't think so.* Wanted to screw me more like!

His face crumples a little. "No, I want you in a way you will never fully understand. If I get to have you underneath me, screaming my name as I fuck you into next year, that's just a bonus." My eyes widen, and my mouth drops open. I'm truly at a loss for words by the bluntness of his. I wonder if now is the right time to tell him I'm a borderline virgin…

He finally drops me on my feet when we reach the landing. I quickly look around at the numerous dark wood doors. "Bedrooms," he says, quickly pointing at each one in turn. "Bathroom, dressing room, games room, gym, and-" He halts and eyes me, a sly smile tugging at his mouth. "The master bedroom," he says confidently, clutching my hand and leading me inside.

He switches on the lights, and I'm pleased with the sight before me. Very much like the man himself, the room is magnificent. The bed is massive and imposing, taking centre stage in the middle of the vast space. The dark linen of the duvet and curtains match the colour of the wall behind it, contrasting the light cream of the surrounding walls, and the thick, plush rug. Sloan's hand curls hard around mine, moving me towards the faux French doors. Just like the kitchen, they are also made up of large, imposing glass panes.

Again, I gaze out, taking in the beautiful, darkened countryside, peppered with lights from adjacent properties.

I barely have time to think, when he hoists me up and walks me into the centre of the room. He lowers me onto the bed and looms over me, a perceptive smile stretching lazily across his face. Bathed in the light being emitted from the bedside lamp, he really is the most beautiful man I have ever seen. Putting his weight on one hand, his fingertips tease the side of my face, making my skin tingle and shiver. He watches me with a gaze so intense, I have no time to react, or even register the death of the tender moment when it becomes lost in the pull of passion. He instantly snaps out of it, and starts to take what he wants from me.

He slams his mouth over mine with such ferocity, I feel it right down to my toes. I bring my legs up and hook them over his denim-covered hips. One hand grabs my leg, and he positions it higher, lowering his groin to mine. Meeting his fluid movements, I'm breathless at the invasion of him. I know I've lost my mind the moment I bind my arms around him and guide him down to me, relishing the way I'm caged under his delicious heaviness. I tilt my hips up to gain a more comfortable position, and his erection grows against my apex. It's a sensation that is setting off fireworks inside me. I moan into his open, inquisitive mouth, and his lips move more frantically, more urgent. I claw at the shirt on his back. I want it gone. I want to experience bare skin against mine, consensually, for the very first time. I want this with him, and him alone. I tug his shirt from his jeans and start to unbutton it. He lifts us simultaneously, his forearm under my arse so that I am sitting up, and he is kneeling before me. He assists in helping to remove his clothing, before pushing me back down with a satisfied smile.

Nervously, I glide my hands over the smooth skin of his back, memorising the defined curves of his taut muscles. I stroke him higher until I reach his nape, and twist the strands of hair between my fingers, over and over. His groans of approval empower me, and my lips move from his mouth to his jaw. I slowly venture down his neck, savouring each lick, never wanting this to end.

His arm slides under my back, and he rolls us over until I'm on top, straddling his hips. His palms run up the fronts of my thighs, hooking the hem of my dress. Suddenly, he pulls it over my head, leaving me in next to nothing, except the black sexy heels he so desperately wants to hear me scream in. He draws in a sharp breath, when he sees I am already braless due to the fitting of the dress and wearing the black thong he insisted I bring earlier. His hooded lids ensnare me, and it feels good to know I'm desired. Every body part quivers feverishly as he leans in, kisses me fiercely, and then pulls back, leaving me wanting more. He does this repeatedly, tempting and then taking away, until I am on the verge of begging.

And beg I will, whether he likes it or not. He will be the only one who will ever get the privilege of hearing me do something that is so disgusting to me. With him, I'm not begging to end the pain of hurting. With him, I am begging to end the pain of wanting; of needing something so unbridled and basic.

"I want more." I'm just able to articulate.

"I know, and I'm going to be the only one who will ever give it to you. Make no mistake of that," he grins, knowing exactly what effect this is having on me. This is madness I can't translate.

His lips drag against my collarbone, slowly tasting each little patch of skin he can find. I moan out continuously, unable to slap a lid on the arousal licking every cell under my skin. His hands ride up my sides until he touches my heavy and tender breasts. I jerk under him as his thumbs slowly circle my nipples, which are already hard and inviting. God, I never imagined it would be this good.

"Wrap your legs around me again, Kara. Feel what I do to you," he whispers against the swell of my breast. The sound reverberates against my aching flesh. I do as he asks, and his mouth encloses a nipple. I let out a gasp at how amazing it feels. My legs tighten as he lavishes my hardened nub with his tongue, sucking and nipping, over and over. He rolls my tender point between his teeth, pulling it into his lips and letting go with a pop. I'm too lost in sensation as he moves to the other side, administering the same treatment until I feel senseless and out of control. Instinctively raising my hips, trying to find release from the desire that is riddling my body, I can feel the hardness of his erection against my groin. I know all it would take is the removal of a few pieces of unwanted clothing, and how I do want to rip those jeans off and see him for the very first time.

He lifts up on his knees, bringing me with him, and my legs cinch harder around his hips. I hear the low growl in the back of his throat the moment he lowers us back down together. I cry into his mouth, while his fingers slide leisurely up my chest and then track back down my forearms, causing the small hairs on them to stand upright. In the heat of desire, I feel my hands being raised above my head. The metal of the headboard slides against the front of my wrists, and I flinch at its icy coldness. Sloan coils his fingers in mine and wraps them around the metal.

"Hold on, baby," he says softly, gauging my comfort level. My arms are heavy, dropping just above my head. My fingers twist and turn on the cold, hard iron, while the cool, crisp fabric of the pillowcase tickles the fine hair of my forearms as they rest comfortably in place.

The mattress shifts under us, and he works his mouth down my body again. Over my lips, neck, and down to the hollow between my breasts, which I have just found out are incredibly sensitive. His mouth is methodical and skilled, gliding down my stomach. He slides his hands from around my waist and positions them on the small of my back, raising my lower half from the mattress. His tongue stills, before it circles around the inside of my hollow belly button, before moving further. He lets out a deep, bass growl, and pauses at the elastic of my thong. I can already feel how wet he's made me. I always thought when the time came, I wouldn't care, but now I feel incredibly self-conscious. God, I'm actually embarrassed. I wiggle, uncomfortable, and my eyes find his. He lowers me back down and places a hand on my abdomen. Gently, he starts to massage away the worry and fear, stopping any further anxiety. He peers at me through his long, dark lashes, and his eyes smoulder. The heat is blissfully evident, and I silently beg him to act upon it.

And thankfully, he does.

The lace is pulled down my thighs in seconds. Sloan growls again, as he scans me up and down, and catches sight of my bare flesh. I feel exposed, and bizarrely, I love every second of it. And it's all because of him. Most of the sexual encounters of my adult life have been attempted one-night stands. But in my heart, I knew I'd never be able to follow it through. But this? This is something I would never have imagined.

My conscious comes up for air once again, telling me to be cautious. While I fully comprehend I might be ruined after this, I cannot think about that now, not with him. Not when this single moment - one I have waited my whole adult life for - is finally within reach.

I close my eyes, enjoying his fingers running from my lower stomach, deep down to the place I want to feel them the most. They delicately explore me, causing my hips to jerk on first contact, as he dips into my delicate folds, stroking and learning, almost pained and uncertain. His tender, reserved touch, in such an intimate moment, feels like he's waiting for something. His breath fans against me, and I know his mouth isn't too far behind.

"Open your eyes, baby. I want to see you." I flick my heavy lids back. His beautiful features appear to have shifted to almost feral. Combined with his dark, exotic eyes, ruffled hair, and flushed cheeks, he's the embodiment of perfection. He stops, mildly hesitant for some reason. Eventually, after a long pause of vacillation, he grins and shamelessly starts to play with me again. His fingers search me, all the while he watches intensely, gauging my reaction to each touch. My breathing is laboured, and I know it won't take long.

"Fuck," he says, a finger teasing my opening. He strokes up and down, spreading my arousal over me. I drop my hands from the headboard and twist them in the pillowcase, streamlining my focus, as my impending orgasm begins to build.

"Sloan, *please*," I whimper at the sensation rocking my entire being. His eyes flash in bewilderment, his fingers halt instantly, and he looks taken aback.

"I told you, you will never have to do that with me," he breathes out firmly.

His head drops back down and blows a long line of air against my sex. A delicious shudder tears through me. My body feels amazing, re-born, as he drags his talented fingers over my clitoris. My breathing is hard and erratic, and I feel myself becoming more pliable with each flick and touch.

"Jesus, you're so wet, baby," he murmurs, shocked and equally satisfied against my clit.

I relax further until he suddenly takes one long lick, stopping at my opening and dipping inside. My body arches off the bed, but his hand comes back down to steady me. I'm more than ready to cry out, and I do, until I am subdued by his mouth sucking at my folds and two fingers sliding deep inside.

"Oh, my God!" I cry out. It's exquisite and satisfying, and I moan with complete abandon as his fingers thrust in and out in a controlled, rhythmic pace. His actions are so gentle, it's almost painful. My body bows of its own accord, feeling him work wonders with that skilled mouth he possesses.

Just as my body prepares itself to explode, strong arms circle my knees, and he places my legs over his shoulders, running his hands from the black heels to the juncture between my thighs. His fingers stroke me repeatedly, and the small movements prove to be my undoing. The fire licks higher and higher, as he slowly slides three fingers inside me, stretching me internally, using a scissor motion to familiarise me with the foreign sensation. I keen unashamed, while his teeth softly nibble my clit. The feeling is deep and my body trembles and throbs, as my first ever, real orgasm starts to consume me whole.

"God, you're so tight," he hisses into my seeping flesh. "And finally, all mine."

Shocked, I tilt my head down, and I'm lost for words when my eyes make contact with his. The look on his face is ravenous, and I'm fully aware of exactly how he's feeling.

His words are temporarily forgotten as I cry out softly, splintering into a million pieces around his gifted fingers and tongue. My hands leave the coolness of the sheets and firmly cradle his head, bringing him closer to me, wanting to feel more of him all over me, and more importantly, inside me.

"Oh, God! Please, don't stop…don't stop!"

Methodically, his hands and mouth move in trained unison, and I continue to ride the waves of pleasure he has incited from within. It's a pleasure that is threatening to break me beautifully. He moans hoarsely, the sound vibrates from his lips to my over-stimulated skin. My body convulses and carries me to the end, wringing out the desire.

Eventually, my climax steadily subsides, and he continues his ministrations gently, easing me back down from my high. With a grin, he lightly grazes my swollen folds and drops one last kiss to my heat. He gently lowers my legs down, one at a time, swiping his tongue once again, before he shifts away. The emptiness is extraordinary, and immediately apparent.

He crawls up the bed, only stopping when we are face to face. I shuffle closer to his side, and his free hand covers mine, guiding it down my body. I hesitate, but I know I can't fight it. He has given me a little taste of intimacy, and I appreciate now I can never go back to the way I was. I know this amazing man will always leave me wanting more. He stares at my face a little confused. I bite my lip, knowing what his intention is. I know exactly what he is wondering – *how many in my past* - and I'm not ready to go there. *Not now.* In a motion to distract, I bring one hand around his head, pulling him in for a quick kiss, before lowering my hand until it's joined with his, our fingers massage, and dip in and out of my heat simultaneously.

"Good girl," he approves. He watches wide-eyed at our hands joined together intimately. "You are so fucking amazing." His eyelids droop, and then his fingers pump inside me again, leaving me to stimulate myself. My breathing peaks, and I know I'm ready to come again. Sloan lowers his head to mine and kisses me, hard and passionately. His clever tongue invades in my mouth, and I can taste myself on him. I moan against him, content, trapped in his clutches. He separates himself from me, our lips are barely fractions apart, and his eyes are wild and alive.

"Come," he commands with a laboured breath. I scream out for the second time, or maybe it's the third – I've lost count - as my body falls apart spectacularly. His fingers continue to pump furiously while I spiral out of control. Shutting my eyes, I throw my head back and allow myself to let go.

"Eyes open, baby," I hear him whisper against my face. My eyes flutter open instantly, to find him watching me with complete fascination and awe. "I want to watch you when you come. I want to look into your eyes. *Every. Single. Time.*"

Oh, god!

I keep my eyes open, as the last of my orgasm rips through my core and splinters at the very heart of me. His declaration of truth is not what I expected him to say, but now that it's out there, what would I do with it?

When the delicious shudders finally die away, I press myself tight against him, and then it hits me. I look deep into his eyes. "You didn't..." I can't even say the words. He chuckles lightly, pressing a single kiss to my cheek.

"Just watching you is enough, my love."

Even though I have no idea what to do, I move my hand over his length - which is still rock hard - but he stops me short. "No. Not tonight. Tonight was only ever going to be for you." He eases out of his jeans and his erection tents menacingly in his boxers. I gaze at it rapt and unsure. He reaches down my legs and removes my heels. Holding them up, he gives me a confident smile at his achievement.

Well, he did make me scream in only them. Smugly, he tosses them to the floor, pulls the sheet over us, and tucks me close against him.

"Sleep, my love."

My love?

He has now said it twice in a matter of minutes. My mind is already overwhelmed with how he plays my body to perfection, considering I've had no consensual sexual contact before, and now this. I inhale deeply, hoping to clear my head. Eventually, he switches off the light, and I fall asleep to the sound of his content breathing.

Chapter 8

I WAKE UP entangled in the thick, luxurious cotton sheets. I rub my eyes, and slowly glance around the bedside table for a clock. I sigh - there isn't one. I open my eyes wider and smile. Last night was amazing - amazing for me at least. I've never woken up in someone else's bed before. Most of the time I couldn't even get there in the first place. Stretching a little, my body is fully sated and happy, albeit a little tender in my intimate places. Last night was my first proper sexual experience. And while I didn't want to relive what had occurred in my past, I know if Sloan decides he wants to see me again, I will have to tell him. Or, at least lie convincingly.

I release a frustrated breath. *Why is my life so hard?*

I stare up at the ceiling and think back.

Over the years I have spent a lot of time living inside my own head – isolation was the only safe haven I knew. Except it's not a good place to seek solace when you are as damaged as they come. I don't usually allow my mind to regress. I've never really had a reason to until recently. This man has brought about a change in me, and I'm not entirely sure how I've allowed it to happen. I gave him consent to touch me, to penetrate me, to use his body to give pleasure to mine. Even more unexplainable, I want him to do it again. I rub my legs together, remembering what it felt like to have his mouth on the parts of me that had been tainted and traumatised, and seemingly, left for dead.

The sheets twist against my body, and I gasp; this is his bed.

Oh, shit!

Carefully sweeping my hand over the other side, it's empty and cold. He must have woken up a while ago. Gathering the sheet against my chest, I lift up carefully. I trail my eyes over the floor, looking for my discarded dress and knickers. I frown; they are gone. The floor is clear - not even his clothes remain. I pull the sheet around myself and drag my happily used body into the en-suite. It's beautiful. Marble from floor to ceiling, with a large walk-in glass shower cubicle and a separate whirlpool bath.

Standing at the double sink vanity, I study my reflection while washing my hands. I look different. It's not something that is manifesting inside my head. I really do look different; content and settled. Satisfied.

I smile and reach for a toothbrush. My heart stops. *What the hell?!* I look from left to right over the vanity and notice my moisturiser and deodorant sitting next to his, in between the two sinks. My eyes narrow looking at the toothbrush in my hand. It is mine. Not a new one, but actually *mine*. The one I had packed last night. The one that's in my bag...

Red flags start to fly. The acid in my stomach churns, and the resulting bile cuts a path up to my throat. Looking at my personal things sat innocently next to his, causes fear to run through me that I haven't experienced in a long time.

Possession.

Throwing the toothbrush into the sink, I quickly dry my hands, and pad back into the bedroom. I breathe out in relief as I catch sight of my overnight bag. I pick it up, put it on the bed and open it. *It's empty*. "What the fuck?" I swear to myself, as I open and close it again, needing to make sure I haven't imagined it. *I haven't.*

Yanking open the top drawer of the dresser; I pull out one of his t-shirts and slip it over my head. If my toiletries are now residing in his bathroom, then where the hell are my clothes? Panic comes over me in waves, and I quickly run out onto the landing, towards the room he indicated was a dressing room last night. Pushing the double doors open with force, I flick the light switch, and the room illuminates.

My stomach flips and recoils.

Oh, holy fucking hell!

It's not a dressing room at all. It's the size of a small clothing store, and it looks like one, too. Oak fixtures grace the space, presenting every item beautifully. Row upon row of suits, all materials, and all colours, line the rails like a boutique. One side appears to be formal and business wear, the other side casual. I walk deeper into the room, which is bigger than my bedroom, and skim my fingers over the garments. I slowly edge back in awe, until my body is stopped by the island in the middle. I look down over my shoulder and notice the multiple boxes of cufflinks, watches, and other accessories. Rolex is a name I'm aware of, but would never know what one looked like up close. *Until now.*

I slide down the unit and sit on the floor, my arms around my knees. I stretch the t-shirt over them, trying to absorb it all. This guy is rich. I mean he is stinking, filthy rich, whereas I'm just a poor girl who can't scrape enough money together to pay her rent. Actually, that isn't entirely true – I can afford the rent, if only Sam would stop secretly snorting it up her bloody nose.

Rocking on my knees, I'm a little girl lost in the middle of a rich man's land. A sob rises up from my throat, and shame overcomes me. I've never been one for material things, they've never interested me at all. But being here, in this multi-million-pound mansion, complete with luxurious furnishings and housing what could easily be some of the most expensive accessories known to man, I feel it more than ever. I've never asked for money, and I've never wanted it, but at the same time, I don't want someone feeling sorry for what little I do have. It also explains the reason why he looked so disgusted when he saw where I lived last night.

The large doors squeak from the other side of the room, and I tilt my head to find Sloan standing there. He is dressed in a white t-shirt, and blue, faded, ripped jeans. His hair is dishevelled and sexy as hell. God, if I didn't feel so pathetic and distraught at present, I would've hauled myself right into his arms and asked him to devour me senseless amid the lush surroundings. The smile on his face is cut short when he looks into my eyes. His features tighten, and he slowly approaches. His advance is far from predatory, it screams sympathy. And I hate it.

"Morning," he greets softly, getting down to my level and sitting next to me. His hand tugs on the t-shirt gently, and he smiles. "You look good in this. I'll have to remember to buy more just for you." I scoff. He need not bother, there's a distinct possibility I won't be here again after today.

"Sorry," I whisper. "I couldn't find my things. You've moved them." My tone might be slightly accusatory, but who on earth touches someone else's effects, let alone literally moves them into their house after only one night?!

He sighs. "I just thought you would feel more at home, rather than this being just a one-night stand."

"But this *is* a one-night stand, Sloan." I divert my eyes, so he doesn't see that secretly, I do want more than one night with him. The thought forms a lump in my throat. "Look, I just want my things so I can get dressed and go home." I look over his shoulder at nothing of significance. Anything is better than to see the look on his face, especially if the hardness building in his body is any indication.

Tilting my chin up, he shakes his head. "Let's have breakfast, and we can talk about *this*," he says, moving his hand between us. My lips press together tightly, defiantly. I want to argue and fight back, and say there is no *this*, but I know I will lose. Instead, I remain taciturn and nod.

Leaving the room in silent defeat, Sloan follows closely behind me. His warm breath tickles the back of my neck, as we venture through the landing and then downstairs into the kitchen. My nose registers food long before my eyes do. The whole floor smells of a full English. I pull a stool out, but he grasps my hand and leads me into another room which adjoins the kitchen. I had somehow missed this room last night, but breakfast is laid out beautifully on the large dining table. He pulls out a seat and takes the one next to it. He leaves, and then comes back with two plates, both piled high with the same amount.

"Leave whatever you can't eat. I'm not used to this. I've never really cooked for anybody before."

I gape at him. "What? Really?"

He gives me a small smile and shakes his head. "No, I don't have relationships, not like this, anyway. Commitment isn't really my thing, but...never mind." He doesn't look away, but he also doesn't elaborate further. His eyes can't hide the sadness that is forming in them. Deciding it's better not to push the subject, I raise the fork to my mouth.

"So, how long have you lived with Miss Jones?" My brow furrows at the mention of her name.

"A few years, but we've been friends since we were little. Why? And how do you know her last name? She wasn't in a fit condition to offer it when she was unconscious at the hotel, and I certainly haven't mentioned it."

"I make it my business to know. Like I do everything else," he answers quickly and ever so coolly. "I also know that her life is not in a good place at the moment. She had more than alcohol running through her veins on Monday night." He looks at me questioningly.

I bite my lip. No point in pretending it wasn't happening anymore. "I know," I reply quietly, looking down at my plate. I have only had a couple of mouthfuls, but I push it away feeling sick.

"She's the real reason that bastard attacked you last night. She needs help before she brings you down with her. I did a few checks on her. Are you aware she owes money all over to some rather unsavoury types? Coke isn't the only bad thing she's doing."

My mouth drops open in shock, and right now, I fucking hate him. "Is that even legal? Are you allowed to run checks on random people?" I begin to get up, but he slaps his hand over mine.

"I am when sluts are fucking Johns and pimps in *my* hotel." His hand hardens, and I give up the fight. I lower back into my seat and glare at him.

"You don't know that for certain!" I pray to God that he isn't right, but something tells me he wouldn't lie to me, not about this.

Would he?

"I do. Trust me, she looked a hell of a lot worse when I first saw her that night." He rubs his hand over mine and squeezes. "Look, I know you're upset, but this affects you. I'm just glad that she was in my hotel and not somewhere else. Not everyone is decent enough not to take advantage of a woman in that state."

I want to cry; I want to hate him. I want to hold him and thank him. He's making me feel too much.

And, of course, he's right. Someone else would have taken advantage of her. As naive as he seems to think I am, it may come as a surprise to him, but I am well aware of what she was doing for money in *his* hotel, and what could have happened to her elsewhere.

And then the words dawn on me.

I quickly rotate my head around the room. "*My hotel*? As in, *you* own the hotel?" I ask, shocked. Well, that would explain the million pound plus mansion I'm currently dining in. It also explains what Sam was going on about when she asked me if I thought the hotel's owner was okay. She knew.

"Yes." A fraction of a smile creeps onto his face, but then it evaporates just as fast. "Didn't you know that already?" he insinuates in a way that makes me extremely uncomfortable. His tone is now cold; snide and accusatory.

I shake my head, trying to wrap my thoughts around the sudden change in his temperament. "No, I didn't."

He leans back in his chair and tents his hands together at his lips, thinking. "You really don't know anything about the hotel or me?"

"No, seriously. Should I?" I stare blankly at the fine china in front of me, peering intermittently through my lashes. My appetite diminished around about the same time he started his line of questioning. He doesn't respond, but I identify his sigh of relief, even with my head down. It makes me wonder what he doesn't want me to find out.

When he remains quiet, I take it upon myself to break the silence. "Well, I guess that explains all of this." I motion my hand to the heavens. "And the car. I mean, I imagined you must be successful, but I didn't think the hotel was yours. I thought you were a guest." I watch as he stands and offers his hand to me. I take it without hesitation, and tiptoe behind him into the living room.

We sit next to each other on the sofa, and the anxiety radiates off of him, while my thoughts drown in his revelations. I start to fidget, but he quickly lifts me onto him and restrains me effortlessly. "I'm going take a huge chance here. I've been honest and told you that I don't do relationships, but I would like to try - with you. No woman has ever been in this house, only you. I've never had two toothbrushes in my bathroom, or shared my drawers with lace knickers. If I want a woman in my bed, I take her to a room at the hotel, but never my private suite. You are also the only woman who has been there, too, with the exception of Miss Jones, of course."

"Sloan, I appreciate your honesty, I really do. And I mean no offence, but you seem to have moved me in upstairs. This is too soon, far too soon. I mean, be reasonable, we've only just met, and we don't know the first thing about each other. This is crazy! I don't even know how old you are! *Oh, my god*, how old are you?"

"I'm twenty-seven, Kara. Too old for you?"

"No, I've just turned twenty-three. A four-year difference isn't bad."

"Baby, when you walked into my hotel suite last week, I expected… Well, you know what I expected, but there you were. You were so wary of me and guarded. You see, I've never had to deal with that before. I also know that you don't expect anything from me, and that is a rarity these days," he pauses, considering his words before he speaks again. "I want to see you again. I want more than just one night with you. A lot more, if you want the complete truth."

"I-I really don't think that's a good idea, not for me anyway," I reply softly, my heart racing as I lie about wanting this. His brow quirks, requesting me to clarify. "You're you, and I'm… Well, I'm nobody." His eyes narrow as I mumble quietly, and I know he's annoyed. The silence is killing me, but the ring of his mobile breaks the discomfort. He gently lifts me off his lap and walks out into the hallway. He lurks barely outside the door with his back to me as he answers it.

"I don't care. You tell him if that shit happens again, there will be consequences. I'm tired of cleaning up the bastard's crap. I won't tolerate it anymore!" he shouts, then pauses, listening to whoever is on the other end. "Again, I do not care! How many times do I have to say it? Tell him he can take her somewhere else, do not bother the doc. I told you; I am through with it." Again, he stops. "Fine, do what you must, but tell him I want to speak to him." Then he hangs up. I notice his fingers grip the phone like he wants to break it in half.

The vision of him, angry and unguarded, transports me back to a place that exists only in my nightmares. A place where a hand grips my wrist and another pummels my face. A place where binds cut into me until I bleed and feel numb. Until I pass out under the pain of a single prick…

I'm lost in my reoccurring, personal nightmare, when he returns and approaches with purpose. "Your things are in the bottom dresser drawer in the bedroom. I'm going to take a shower," he says tersely. He walks towards the door and halts, his large frame hovers in the opening. "Want to wash my back?" His eyebrows raise with meaning.

I flush my head of my cruel past, and my cheeks blush so hard, it prompts the heat to seep down my neck. It's then I remember I need to get out of here. I glance away slightly and tell him no. His face twists in annoyance, but he walks back towards me and kisses me hard.

"I won't be long. Make yourself at home." He jogs out of the room, and I listen as he runs heavily up the stairs. I wait until I hear the bedroom door open and close, then follow him up.

In the bedroom, the water resounds as I quickly rummage through the bottom drawer and pull out my things. Tugging on my clean underwear, followed by the jeans and shirt I had packed last night, I'm glad I brought my tatty old tennis shoes – there's no way I'm making a great escape in those killer heels. I huff out a frustrated breath; some of my stuff is still in the bathroom. The bathroom *he* is currently in. Screw it, a toothbrush and deodorant are cheap enough to replace. I dart out of the bedroom, down the stairs and into the hallway.

Picking up my jacket and keys, I locate my clutch and pull out my phone. Last night comes back to haunt me, when I see the blank cheque he had written for me safely deposited inside my bag. I run my hand over my forehead and remove the offending paper.

What part of no didn't he understand last night? What part of my mortification did he neglect to notice?

Back in the kitchen, I search through a few drawers until I find what I'm looking for. Quickly writing him a note, I leave the cheque beside it on the worktop.

Loitering silently in the hallway, I turn slowly, memorising everything, knowing I shall never see any of this again. I look up to the ceiling, seeing through it like it's made of glass, and I can see him clearly. It's not only the house I won't be seeing again. My stomach churns at the painful admission.

In the space of just over one week and one incredibly amazing night, he has gotten under my skin in a way I fear I won't ever be able to eradicate. I never dreamed it could be possible for me to feel such things as he did to me last night. Or maybe it's because I've never allowed myself to entertain the notion I could have a future with someone. The water shuts off, and I hear quiet movements. Picking up my bag, I quickly race to the door and close it quietly behind me.

The jog up the driveway takes an eternity, but I don't dare turn around. I wait for the sound of his voice or his footsteps on the loose gravel behind me, but they never come. Minutes later, I reach the security cabin just before the imposing gates. The guard manning the booth eyes me with unashamed interest. I cross over to him and ask him for the address. His eyes narrow, and flicker between me and the house. I'm intentionally giving him my best pleading look, hoping he will crack and defy his boss. There is not a shred of doubt in my mind that Sloan has schooled him to ensure no one gets in without authority, and in turn, that may also mean that no one gets out. The guard sighs before offering to call a taxi for me. He shakes his head discreetly and picks up the phone.

I sit and wait for the taxi to arrive. Although I know I shouldn't, since I actually can't afford it. Somehow, I have to find the rent money today, and I very much doubt cutting open the base of the sofa for loose change is going to cover it. My foot taps nervously against the pavement. All I want is to get home and forget all about ever meeting this incredible man, who seems to have my stomach in knots.

Finally, the taxi arrives, and I climb in and give my address. Taking a final look at the mansion, my eyes skim over the structure and the surrounding lawns and gardens. My lungs let out a deep breath when I see Sloan running up the driveway with a crazed look on his face. Shame ripples through me, and I turn away. Risking a glance back, I watch a very angry looking Sloan speak with the guard, who is waving his arms in my retreating direction. I slump into the seat and realise I'm running again. But this time, I'm leaving behind a man who has given me a taste of something I thought I would never have.

He has given me hope.

Walking through the residents' car park, I scan the vehicles to see if Danny's car is present. I don't see it, but it doesn't mean he's not here. I quicken my pace to the entrance and jog up the stairs two at a time. The burn in my thighs is a shock; I never normally feel anything. But truthfully, I'm well aware my aberrant activities of last night are the real reason behind my sudden discomfort.

I reach my door and drop my bag down as I enter. Locking and bolting the door behind me, I test the handle, determined not to have a repeat performance of last night. The flat is filled with the scent of cigarettes and stale alcohol and is suspiciously quiet, until I hear Sam's giggling flow down the hallway. I pinch my nose in both nausea and infuriation, knowing the unavoidable will undoubtedly materialise as soon as she steps out of her room.

Unzipping my bag, I remove the clothes I'd packed haphazardly and shove them into the washing machine. I groan when I realise I've left the dress and shoes behind. It's probably a good job, really - they are safer with their rightful owner. Although it means I won't be selling them to keep a roof over my head, after all.

Except, that's not why I'm so pissed off right now.

Pouring a mug of tea, I slouch against the worktop and mentally berate myself for being such a stupid, insecure idiot. The sounds emanating through the flat make me wish I'd never ran away from Sloan so fast this morning. I pick up my clutch, dig out my purse and other essentials, and transfer them back into my usual bag. I palm my phone, and my eyes cross when I notice it isn't switched on. That's odd; I never turn it off. I sip my tea slowly and wait for it to power up.

My eyes drift from the phone to the direction of Sam's room, at the same moment, a male voice moans loudly. I shudder and squeeze my eyes shut, fighting back the tears. It's all too much. I leave the steaming mug on the table, gather my things together and walk out.

I trudge down the stairs, my concentration is split between the phone screen and the next step. Finally, it's on, and my mouth falls open - five missed calls and six messages. I scan through the messages; one from Sam to say she has *company*, and four from Sloan. Staring at his unread messages, I still need to find out how he'd obtained my number in the first place. Unsurprisingly, all the missed calls are from him, too.

I scan through each text. They all pretty much read the same: *why did you leave; where are you; please call back; we need to talk.*

Stopping on the stairs, I inhale deeply, and it isn't pacifying in the slightest. My old therapist had taken me through these breathing exercises many times. Every attempt to calm myself was futile back then, and it hasn't gotten any better with time. Her preferred breathing techniques never worked for me, they only made me feel worse. She was confident that all I needed was time.

Eight years and counting.

I scroll through my phone list until I find her name. Seconds away from doing the unthinkable, and calling her office to book an appointment - without being put under outside duress to do so - Sloan's name suddenly appears on the screen. I pout at the handset. This is the reason why it's switched off; he has put his freaking number in. He probably did some snooping while he was at it, too. I contemplate ignoring him, but deep inside, I know he won't give up, he's already told me so.

It also doesn't help that my heart is hammering away so hard inside my chest, I fear I'm either going to stumble down the stairs, or have a heart attack.

Admitting defeat, I answer softly. "Hi."

Embarrassment pulses through me. Even though I want to tell him I'm sorry for running out, I'm also a little pissed he feels the need to call and text me incessantly. I knew what I was getting into when I agreed to see him last night. He'd had his fun, *or maybe not*, but I'd definitely had mine.

"I'm outside your building waiting for you. I just knocked on your door, and a naked man answered!" Oh fuck, he sounds livid. I scrunch my nose up, imagining what must have greeted him only moments ago. I'm so happy that I'm already on my way out, and didn't have to witness that little showdown. "I'm not leaving until we talk." Then he hangs up.

Shifting from foot to foot, I dally on the staircase and debate my options. There are only two ways out of the building; the front door, where Sloan is waiting, most likely with all the calmness of a raging bull, or through the back, where Danny's office is. I puff out, exasperated and out of options, but know I am better off taking my chances with Mr Unpredictable.

Stepping out of the main door, the sun finally begins to burst through the dark clouds. Across the car park, a black limo sits waiting. The door opens, and Sloan climbs out. He doesn't move, just stands and watches, until he eventually crooks his finger and motions me towards him. Considering what he has just discovered in my flat, I don't dare keep him waiting. Striding across the tarmac, I stop a few feet in front of him, out of arms reach. He has got me feeling so much, I need distance. He closes the limo door, and it drives away.

He's devoid of any facial expression, and now I'm just plain confused. I expected him to be shouting at me, because that was usually the case whenever I did something men didn't like, namely my father. It is also the unspoken truth as to why I never got involved, or even really made much of an attempt to. I can't be hurt if my heart belongs to only me.

I drink in every curve, flaw, and line. Committing him to memory, just in case this definitely is the last time I will lay my eyes on him. His hair is still a little damp and messy. A black blazer encases his shoulders, his white shirt stretches over his hard chest, and the faded, grey jeans define every inch of his thighs. His look is completed perfectly with worn, black, partly laced biker boots. I swallow hard, and my body flushes unforgivingly in his presence.

Stepping a little closer to him, I still don't understand why he is here. This wasn't supposed to happen; he's not meant to be chasing after me. But he is. And, although it might be premature to wish, I'm hoping he hasn't changed his mind, and he still wants something more than I was comfortable with an hour ago. Coming closer, his hand runs through his hair, and he grips my shoulders. It's not painful, but it's strong enough to tell me that he isn't going anywhere. It tells me he came back here for me.

A powerful, unknown emotion bubbles in the recess of my stomach. It is the first time I have felt this strange, yet welcoming sensation. It's peculiar and addictive, and I can't rationalise it. His hands trail innocuously down my arms and then curl around my fingers. He drops one of my hands and positions himself at my side. He keeps my other palm firmly in his, and his touch relaxes me for the second time in as many hours.

"Let's walk."

Chapter 9

SILENCE CONSUMES US as we stroll side by side. My thoughts are plagued by the events of the last week since he made his meteor sized impact on my life. My world used to be regimented; structured and controlled. A week ago, I was just another nameless face in a sea of people. No one saw me, no one even looked. Now I'm being actively pursued by a man who has no qualms about pushing his way in unapologetically.

Eventually, the rundown buildings of the area I live in blend into the landscape behind us, and the lush green lawn of a small, equally rundown park, comes into view. Sloan guides us over to an empty bench, sits down and pats the space beside him. Never letting go of his hand, I sigh and settle next to him.

He is deep in thought as we sit. He doesn't look at me, just gazes at the people passing by; couples, dog walkers, families. His silence is suffocating, and I'm undecided if I should break the ice first or wait until he is ready to open his mouth. I shift on the wooden bench as the sound of his voice breaks the quiet.

"My mother used to take me to Hyde Park when I was young. It was my favourite place in the whole world. Well, that and the Natural History Museum." A small laugh leaves his lips. I bite back the urge to smile, imagining a little boy with unruly dark hair desperate to see dinosaurs and all the other extinct stuffed animals. I turn to him, curious as to why he's sharing this, but he still doesn't look at me. I need to break the thick tension hanging between us. I need to ask questions that will give me plausible answers. I need to do something because he's too quiet, and he has been since we left the flat.

"What do you want from me, Sloan?" I ask, letting out a deep breath.

He cocks his head, and the sun highlights his features beautifully. I swallow down the saliva pooling at the back of my mouth from the way his body basks in the glow of the morning rays. No matter how much I try to deny it, I want him, more than anything else I've ever wanted before.

"I want you to trust me, Kara." He strokes his finger over my cheek. "Why did you run this morning?" he queries gently. His soft caress lulls me into what might possibly be a false sense of security.

"Scared, I guess." I look away from him because I cannot let him see the shame in my eyes. I'm not scared of him; I'm scared of the hidden truths he will uncover, facts I buried long ago.

"Why? Because of the things I said?" I nod, and he palms my shoulder and pulls me closer to him. "Look at me. You made a valid point this morning; you don't know me. When I first saw you, I recognised the loneliness I saw inside you, because I feel it, too. I know there's something in your past that terrifies you, but please give us a chance. Give *me* a chance." He looks at me in earnest. In the short space of time I have known him, he has never worn this look of vulnerability before. I'm not even sure if he's aware he is doing it.

But what I find even more frightening, is that a part of me wants to trust him, to give him a chance, albeit a little too willingly. He's taking a big risk with me, one that will have severe repercussions if the darker aspects of my life have any involvement.

I hesitate with my response. Gazing into his eyes, they reflect a million unspoken promises. Slowly nodding my head, I'm already well aware that if I didn't want him, I wouldn't be here at all. In my heart, I know I finally deserve to have a chance at living and dreaming.

"Yes," I confirm quietly. "But there are things I need you to understand first." He presses me to him, kissing my forehead. He withdraws, and his expression beseeches me to continue. The hope in his eyes is overwhelming, and for a split second, I fail to remember what it is I want to say.

"I'm not like you. Rich, I mean. I have nothing to give, but I will not ask for anything in return, either. You take a chance on me as I am, or not at all. I mean it. I won't have anyone thinking I'm only chasing after your money. I won't. I might be worthless, but I have my p-"

"Pride. I know a lot about that. Kara, I will never humiliate you in any way. But at the same time, if I want to buy you something, I want you to accept it graciously. I appreciate how difficult that will be for you, but please, humour me." He gives me a smile that almost stops my heart.

"Okay," I whisper, giving him comfort, failing to disclose that whenever the time does come, I fully intend to fight him tooth and nail.

"So, now I'd like to talk about Samantha." I roll my eyes, knowing exactly where he is going with this. Suddenly, the tense atmosphere that had just dissipated rears its ugly head again. His long sigh is indicative he's well aware there is no conversation to be had here. Still, we both know he's going to chip away at it slowly until I break from the pressure and spill my guts.

"Well, I don't. I'm tired of talking about her, even to her. She doesn't listen. My aunt thinks I should move in with her for a while, and a friend has also offered me a place to stay, if I need it."

"Well, that's a little reassuring, but I'm still concerned."

I don't reply. Instead, I focus on a couple of kids kicking a football back and forth with their father. I shut my eyes tight, and my well-constructed shield is penetrated by the harsh memories of my life with both Sam and my own father. I breathe deeply, fighting to keep my mind composed and balanced.

"Just give me an honest answer - is it normal for a naked man to be answering your door?"

I shrug my shoulders as if I don't know. He raises his dark brows at me, daring me to lie, but I can't lie to him because I would just be shooting myself in the foot. He's already admitted to running illegal checks on Sam, it wouldn't surprise me if he'd done the same to me, too. After all, he did seem to know things about me that were impossible. He pouts as I quickly engineer a credible response that will mollify him. Everything I'm coming up with is ludicrous. Realising I'll have to be honest; my only line of defence is that I can't control Sam's actions. She's a grown woman, and even if it does irritate the shit out of me the way she swans through life without a care in the world, she's free. I can't control the scoff that pre-empts my throat as I finally turn to face him. I'm annoyed, and the folding of his arms confirms he is, too.

"No, she isn't supposed to bring anyone back. She seems to be forgetting that a lot lately. Although I didn't see the guy this morning, I heard him loud and clear, but nothing could be worse than the wannabe Kray Brothers a week or so ago." I sound flippant like it's a regular, daily occurrence in my pitiful existence, to have a long stream of random men in our home. Truthfully, I'm scared to death. Not for her, for me.

"*The Kray Brothers*?" He sounds amused. I'm not.

"Yeah, two guys, both dark-haired and large, really large. One was called…" I pinch my nose, furiously racking my brain for his name. "Dean? David? No, Deacon! That's it, Deacon. I can't remember the other one." I risk another quick peek at him, and his entire body stiffens instantly.

"*Deacon*? Deacon was in your flat?" He grabs my arms, and his fingers cut through my jacket into my skin. His eyes are wide, and his nostrils flare out disproportionately. "Are you sure? You're absolutely sure he was called Deacon?" he asks urgently, shaking my shoulders a little. I stare, stunned by the unexpected change in his demeanour. He lets go of me and drags his hand through his hair, until it comes to rest on his open mouth and chin, covering them, like he's hiding a secret.

"Hmm, do you know him?" I ask curiously. One hand is still pressing tight and unforgivingly into my shoulder, and I can already feel the numbness start to take effect.

He dips his chin down, and his voice is low, defeated, even. "Yeah. Yeah, I know him."

I let out a surprised gasp from his revelation. He tugs me into his lap, roughly turning my face towards his in his cupped hands. He looks around the public park with suspicion and uncertainty, before tilting his head close to mine.

"If he comes back to your flat, you leave. Okay?"

"Why? Who is he?" I scrunch my face up in confusion and disgust. I only agreed to *try* something with him less than half an hour ago, now he's giving me orders!

"Look, just trust me. If he shows up, you call me, and I'll come and get you."

"Look, I don't th-"

"Damn it, Kara! Just trust me!"

"Why? I don't understand!" I cry.

"I don't want him anywhere near you. Ever!"

He lifts us up from the bench, steadies me on my feet. His face hardens, and tension rolls off him in waves. Agitated, he swipes his hand over the back of his neck, gripping his nape momentarily. Placing his hands on his hips, his jacket stretches while he waits impatiently for the answer he wants to hear.

My anger is steadily rising, and his own patience finally wears thin as he brings his mobile to his ear. I don't hear him at all, the rush of blood in my ears is too strong to concentrate on anything else. As always, my life isn't mine again. Another man is about to take control of it.

Sloan slips the phone back into his jacket pocket and strengthens his hold on me. His arm is strong around my waist as he marches us across the park at double speed towards the stationary limo. His driver opens the door. "Miss Petersen, Mr Foster," he greets, tipping his head. Thanking him, I curl into the back of the car while Sloan speaks with him. Minutes pass by before he slides in beside me and shuts the door with a dull thud.

The exterior of the hotel eventually comes into view a short while later. I look over at the restaurant placard outside, remembering the time I had stood right in front of that menu board. My heart rate slows, thinking back to those lost, lonely days, prior to Marie finding me at the kitchen door - a homeless, frightened, starving child.

Sloan jumps out of the car, not bothering to wait for his door to be opened. He holds his hand out to me, giving me a small smile when I grasp it without arguing. Mindlessly, I enter the hotel beside him. He is now deep in thought, and it doesn't take a genius to know he isn't happy. His stunning face displays a hardness that tells me something has just turned the axis of his world. Instinctively, I know our last conversation is most likely the cause of that shift.

My breathing turns into laboured, short breaths, the moment I register he is walking me towards the bank of lifts. I tug at his hand, and he stops instantly. His jaw grinds upon seeing my fear. My eyes haze over at the chime of its arrival and the doors open. I tilt my head softly, my expression exposing my absolute repugnance of the damn things. We stare at each other as the doors close again, leaving us standing in the lobby.

"Why don't you like lifts?" he asks quietly, as another set of doors open, allowing a waiting couple entry. The man motions for us to enter, but Sloan waves him off, allowing the doors to close firmly again. He lets go of my hand and brings his arms around my body, shifting us away from prying eyes and ears. He sulks a little waiting for me to share the first of my many demons.

"Not lifts, as such, just small confined spaces. Cupboards, cubbyholes, lifts…tight spaces in general," I reply. My body deflates a little under the exposure of my honest answer. My response is barely audible, but I know he heard every word clearly, as though I had screamed them in his face. I drop my head down and start to chew on my nails. It's a dirty habit, but I'm too ashamed to lift my eyes to meet his.

He breathes out sharply and brings his large hands under my arms, forcing me to at him. "Why don't you like confined spaces?" His eyes narrow to slits, but the flash of secrecy and awareness inside them doesn't escape me. I stare at him. The way he slants his head sympathetically causes panic to claw at my insides, and I jerk away furiously. If I couldn't share this shit with my old shrink, I couldn't possibly do the same with him, not this early in whatever *this* is. He snorts out exasperated, but doesn't let me go. The ringing sound of doom chimes out in the small area once more, and he holds me firmly, pretty much forcing me to board it.

Just breathe. In and out. In and out.

I count to myself as the box begins to ascend under us. The sensation is like having an itch you can't scratch. I close my eyes and sink back against the lift wall. I know Sloan is watching me. I don't need to see him to know he is scrutinising my actions. This is the first time an outsider has seen one of the many weaknesses I conceal. I let out a sigh of relief when the lift finally comes to a stop, and the doors slowly open.

I feel anxious as I stand outside the penthouse. My skin is more than a little moist, and my clothes are sticking in various places. It may have only been minutes, but it could have been lifetimes for me. Sloan holds the door open, and I shuffle through. His breath blows a line through my hair, and if I turn, I know there will only be inches between us. He's close, too close. Stepping away from him, I turn and watch him discard his jacket, phone, and wallet on the table.

My head is all over the place, and I can't seem to get my thoughts in a collective row. Leaving him to engage the security system, I head straight into the kitchen and grab a bottle of water from the fridge. The contents are almost drained, when strong arms encircle me, and I gasp at the unexpected intrusion. Turning inside them, I come face to face with his dark, desire laden eyes. Out of nowhere, I stretch up on my toes and place a bold kiss on the base of his neck, where a few buttons of his shirt are open, and he grunts deeply.

With a smile, he lifts me into his arms, carries me up the stairs and into the bedroom. Placing me on the bed with more care than necessary, I stay as I am, merely watching him, watching me. His hands firmly grasp his hips, and his head drops to one side. He is studying me for all intent and purposes, and for the first time in my life, I'm completely aware that I'm desired and wanted.

And I'm very, very nervous.

I crawl towards him on my hands and knees, appearing outwardly brave. I reach his belt first and bite my lip as I unbuckle it, and leave it hanging open. I run my hands up his chest, bringing them to rest on his shoulders. Stretching up on my knees, my fingers fidget with his shirt buttons, until, that too, hangs open, exposing his perfectly ripped chest.

My tongue darts across my lips taking in the sight of him. God, how I want him. His shirt and belt are unfastened, and his stomach and chest muscles contract with each heavy intake of breath. He slowly puts one knee on the bed, and his hands move over me. He begins at my jaw, moving both palms with synchronised precision; across my shoulders, over my breasts, down my waist, and finally, resting on my hips.

The bed dips further when he places more of his weight on it. With one arm locked around my back, and the other just under my backside, I feel secure. But in a flash, I'm falling backwards, safe in his arms. I blink up at his face - the one that has been the subject of my nightly fantasies for the last week - as he steadies his hands on either side of my head, effectively caging me under him. There is nowhere I can go, and no other place I'd rather be. I want everything he is willing to give me. I want everything that he is going to make me feel. I've been inwardly dead for so long, I'm fearful this enlightenment will ultimately become the true death of me. He will give me the world - I can only pray he doesn't take it away when he decides he's had enough.

My teeth tug on my lip; timid and apprehensive. The angel and devil on my shoulders debate whether this will lead to heaven or hell. I batten down my fears, and am placated when his lips lower towards mine. He pauses just inches above me and smiles.

"Ready to finish what we started last night?"

I squeeze my shaky thighs together, feeling wet and desirous in the place I need him the most. No man has ever invoked such a reaction from me before. Then again, no man has ever consensually touched me to gain a reaction. My heart stops, and I know I have to tell him before we progress any further.

"Sloan?" My palm caresses his cheek. He arches his brows in silent response, but doesn't say a word. "I haven't...haven't done this...in a long time. Only once, very long ago…" I confess quietly, relieved not to be carrying the burden any longer. It might not have been the whole truth, but it was a fraction of it.

His fingers twirl around a lock of my hair, while his lips graze the inside of my forearm. My skin flushes and tingles from his touch alone. He lets go of the strands, and the heel of his hand rests lightly on my breastbone.

"How long?" His brows arch again, as he delicately palms my chest, waiting patiently.

I chew on my lip further and contemplate lying. But considering he can tell when I'm lying, I decide it'll be easier in the long run to be honest. I hope to God he won't be disgusted, if - *when* - he finds out the whole soul-destroying truth.

"Eight years."

His look of surprise and satisfaction allows hope to spring up and flourish in my chest. I'm equally hopeful when I see a smile starting at the corner of his mouth.

"Eight years, huh?"

I might be imagining it, but, bizarrely, he's not even shocked. His blasé, nonchalant attitude to my darkest confession makes me nervous for entirely different reasons.

"Bad experience?" Now there's something about his tone that makes me worry my lip.

"Something like that. It was…different. I just want you to know, in case I seem inexperienced." I drop my eyes from him, not wanting to see his dissatisfaction. I'm not stupid; I know he's experienced. He's probably been with plenty of women, but I don't want him to compare me to anyone else. I have a more than a legitimate reason as to why I have no idea about sex or relationships. Sadly, I just can't impart that truth without having to explain the facts. The ones that blend so well into fiction, I can't pick them apart anymore or compartmentalise them further.

Tilting my chin up, he grins. "We can wait, there's no rush whatsoever."

Staring into his eyes, I'm more than ready to speak the words that terrify me. "I want this," I verbalise my true thoughts. "I want you,"

Passion and desire spread over his beautiful features, and I finally let out the breath lodged deep in my throat. I grasp his face in my hands, kissing him with abandon, thankful he hasn't asked me to leave. I loosen my grip and smile, enthralled. An entirely new feeling rises up in my chest, one that I dare not allow to develop any further than it already has in the last twenty-four hours.

"I will always respect you. We'll go slowly, okay?" He kisses me again. "So, are you ready to finish what we started last night?" I nod enthusiastically, knowing that although I'm technically not a virgin, emotionally and mentally, I still am.

"Remember, you will never have to beg me for anything." His face is firm and determined. "I want you to tell me what you want. If I do something you don't like, we'll try something new. I don't want you to be afraid of me." He strokes down my middle, from neck to navel, then back up again, and the feeling is maddening.

"Tell me, Kara. Tell me what you want," his says in a whisper. It is breathy and hoarse, and the sexiest thing I have ever heard.

My mouth parts slightly and my tongue slides over my top lip in anticipation. My breath is stolen from me when his determined lips possess mine. I move against him as he sucks and nibbles to the point of losing my mind. He licks the seam of my mouth, and I open for him willingly. My tongue thrusts its way in and out rhythmically with his. The sensations he is bringing out of me can only be described as wanton, and I throw my arms around him, guiding him. I need more of him. Inside, I'm screaming for him.

My body begins to move against his, and my hips lift up in search of him. The denim covering our bodies adds to the friction, while every pelvic roll matches what his tongue is doing inside my mouth. I close my eyes and revel in the raptures that are bubbling, waiting to explode into a million pieces, until I cry out intensely. Sloan lifts up from me, and my eyes open instantly to see what's wrong.

He kneels back on his knees, removes his shirt and throws it behind him. He really is the embodiment of beautiful, and I raise myself up so I can watch the show, but instead, he gets off the bed and goes into the en-suite. Returning, he tosses a few condom packets on the bed.

"Tell me what you want, Kara." He unfastens his jeans and lets them drop to the floor. My mouth and lips dry out, yet I'm salivating undeniably for this insanely sexy man in front of me. "Say the words, baby. Tell me what you need."

He closes the distance between us and lifts my shirt up. I raise my arms dutifully, and he divests me of it. He cranes his head back in admiration, then slides his hands down my body to my jeans. Deft fingers have them undone and around my ankles in seconds. I wiggle out of them, and he kicks them aside.

Time vanishes as we stare hungrily at each other; appreciating, wanting. Casting my gaze over his broad, densely defined shoulders, down to his chiselled abs, my eyes water when I catch the bulge in his boxers, which are now tented from his arousal. Biting the inside of my cheek, I force my eyes down to his strong muscular thighs.

Dread starts to chomp away at me, and I fear I might not be able to do this after all. I stare at his feet for a long time, not wanting him to witness the uncertainty that is overwhelming me. Staring at him, there's something about this gorgeous, barefoot man I just can't seem to fathom, or turn away from.

"I don't know what I like," I mumble, thoroughly embarrassed.

"Okay, baby, I know this isn't technically your first time, but as far as I am concerned, it is, so we'll treat it as such. Tell me, Kara." My heart starts to beat so hard I fear it might break free of my body. Strong fingers stroke from my collarbone, up and up, until they tip my chin. I lift my head ensuring we are face to face, and the dark desire of Sloan's eyes render me immobile.

"I told you, I don't know! I've never-"

"Do you want me?" he asks firmly, and I nod, timidly. "Do you want me to touch you?" I nod again, this time a little more eager. "Then tell me, Kara. Tell me how to touch you, baby." He pulls me to him, and his hard length presses deep into my stomach. I visibly swallow at the size of it.

I take his hand and bring it to my chest. "I want you inside me," I breathe out. "I want to feel you inside me, and all over me." I stare at him a little more confidently. "I've wanted you since the first moment I saw you, right here, in this hotel suite."

One side of his mouth curls and he growls out satisfied. "I will give you what you want, and more - on one condition."

My eyebrows rise in contemplation of what rule he's about to enforce. If there is one thing in my life I know well, it's rules.

I wait.

"You don't run later."

I smile; he doesn't need to know I have no intention of running. In fact, I knew the moment he turned up outside my door this morning I would never want to leave him. The unspoken truth is that he is it for me. He's the only one. After less than a week of knowing him, I know it unequivocally. It also justifies my theory further that he has already ruined me after only one moment of intimacy. I allowed him to do those things to me last night, and I'm not ashamed to admit I enjoyed them.

I enjoyed him.

His lips are mere fractions from mine as he speaks softly against my mouth. "Remember, you want it, you ask for it. But you will never beg me."

And then his lips claim mine.

Chapter 10

STRONG HANDS TENDERLY stroke down my back to my arse, learning my undiscovered, erogenous zones, beneath the sheer fabric of my lace knickers. I glide my arms over his shoulders, and my legs automatically cinch his waist. Frantically, my mouth moves with his as his erection throbs at my core, pressing deliciously against my wet heat.

His lips warm mine with fervour, and my mouth parts to give him full, unrestricted access. Accepting my invitation, the muscle of his tongue swipes fluidly against mine. The noises escaping from his throat encourage me, and I match him audibly with every stroke.

My mind is disseminated with abandon, my body fulfilling many unbridled fantasies I'd had about this moment for so long, but never dared to believe one day it would materialise. I moan into his mouth, preoccupied with all the things I want to do to him - and what I want him to do to me.

The air around us shifts, and he directs us back to the bed. From the corner of my eye, I can see the twinkling lights of London outside, but I'm too far gone in my heightened sexual state to tell him to draw the curtains. I'm definitely no exhibitionist, but suddenly, I feel more exposed than ever. Sensing my fears, his lips move to my ear, licking the delicate skin beneath it. My body heat goes up a notch, when a stream of warm breath touches my neck.

"Nobody can see us up here, baby."

His tongue outlines the cartilage of my ear, before nipping my lobe. I moan in desperation, while one hand travels from my behind to my mid-back. His nimble fingers skim across my stomach, and I stifle a giggle as he fumbles and curses, trying to locate my bra fastener. I recognise his frustration and decide to end his misery.

"It's at the front," I tell him breathlessly. His eyes glint wickedly before they grow darker.

With one last kiss to my lips, he works his own over my chin, sucking at the curve underneath as he moves towards my neck. I tip my head back slightly, giving him more room for manoeuvre. It isn't a selfless act; this alone has the power to make me unravel spectacularly.

He resumes his journey south, making the most of every inch of bare skin along the way. His lips leave my body until they no longer touch me, and it's just his tongue, taking long licks from my neck to my collarbone. My legs spasm impossibly harder with the pleasure of each small conquest. He growls out several times, and my limbs grip and release him continually. I'm desperately trying to achieve something more and hold on to rational thought simultaneously.

He finally reaches the valley between my breasts, and places a simple kiss just above my central bra fastener. His midnight blues reflect in mine, piquing my attention, anticipating his next move. He grins, taking the plastic clasp between his teeth. Mesmerised by the sight of him, he snaps it, and my breasts bounce free from their confines. I watch as the fabric falls and languishes at the sides of my rib cage. He leans forward, forcing me to lean back, as he openly peruses me, before peeling the obliterated bra down my arms. I observe his actions, helplessly enraptured, until he throws it to the floor like a used tissue.

In the midst of desire intoxicating me, infusing my mind and holding me prisoner, it takes long minutes to register his knee is now nestled between my legs, close to my sex. I brace one leg to steady myself, keeping the other curled around his calf. His thigh shifts, causing mine to spread wider. Completely exposed to his lustful gaze, a flood of heady sensation develops between my spread limbs. I accept his solicitation, rocking my hips up, rubbing myself on his thigh.

"All in good time, baby." He repositions me as per his choosing. Assessing me, admiring me. Inside, all I want to do is cover myself, but I resist the urge because he makes me feel something I can't openly admit to. *Yet.*

"Sloan..."

I stretch my hand up to him, and his body looms over mine. The hardness of him makes me react further, and I feel my knickers becoming undeniably wet. Talented hands tease up and down my centre, from sternum to groin, over and over. His eyes are filled with unspoken questions; questions of what he will do to me, or questions of whether I will let him. I gauge his expression with an open mind. I allowed him to take control last night. I allowed him to take me to a place I didn't think I would ever be able to feel comfortable in. But I'm glad I did. It was amazing, and I definitely want more of whatever he is willing to give me.

The sound of fabric stretching catches my attention. Looking down at my hips, the flimsy material that was once my knickers are being torn clean from my body. He holds up the shredded remains of the lace, and his eyes convey mischief, whilst a boyish smile creeps lazily over his lips. I can't help but reciprocate the look when he tosses my shredded underwear aside.

"We won't be needing those again tonight," he states proudly.

I continue to watch, holding myself up on my elbows, while he nudges my thighs again. He closes his eyes and breathes in, sighing out content through his nose. A shudder ripples through me as his lids open; his pupils are dilated and irrefutably heavy.

I let out a shocked yelp when he pulls me down the bed by the backs of my knees and adjusts his position in anticipation. A flush of heat surges through me, and I stare up at the ceiling, my mind speculating wildly at what is finally going to be a reality. I can feel his breath on me, and I know he won't make me wait. *Hopefully.*

I cry out the instant his teeth drag across the overly sensitive skin of my inner thigh. He soothes the area with warm, wet kisses, and my body clenches anxiously, silently demanding more. I raise my hips up, showing him what I want. Instead of reciprocating, he chuckles softly, gliding his body up mine, until we are eye to eye again.

"Greedy girl. All good things come to those who wait," he admonishes playfully, wrapping my hair around his fist.

"I'm through waiting, ple-" His finger over my mouth scuppers my impending begging. He rolls his eyes, and I brazenly roll my hips up to him.

His mouth smashes against mine, and I grip his shoulders, my fingers digging into his flesh for leverage. He kisses me so hard, I fear my lips may bruise from the invasion. His hands support my head firmly in place, just the way he likes, as he continues to plunder and ravish my mouth. One hand tightens in my hair again, holding my head from behind, whilst he brings himself over my breast. His talented fingers roll my nipple until it forms a hard tip. Circling it leisurely, his mouth swallows my moans. My body temperature begins to rise, and he slowly trails his other hand over me, seeking out my neglected nipple. Again, he rolls, pinches, and nips, until, it too, peaks to the point of pleasurable pain. He ventures lower, leaving my mouth both breathless and empty. His tongue draws wet circles repeatedly as the heat builds rapidly. His lips graze around my areola, sucking with such rigour, my hand pressures the back of his head. I don't want him to move, it's too incredible for words. Knowing I'm enjoying this, he gives me a little smirk and grunt, then switches sides again. Fingering my sucked nipple, the moisture from his mouth encourages the tangible pulse originating from deep within. I arch into him, as he sucks and nips relentlessly.

With his free hand, a fingertip runs the length of my middle, stopping and circling my belly button, before dropping further down. Cupping my sex, my body bows harder, and my hips roll in desperation against his hand.

"Ah, God!" I scream out.

My eyes flutter open and shut, feeling his fingers memorising my shape. His hand leaves me temporarily, until I feel a finger circle and linger at my opening. I rock my hips up again, thus assisting in its insertion. I moan with approval, and slowly, he starts to fill me, his finger working in my wet heat with determination.

Due to my earlier confession, I expected him to treat me like glass, but he doesn't. He isn't rough in the slightest, just extremely sure of what he can do, and I'm grateful for it.

I tug on the pillows behind me, levitating my back higher. I want to watch him. I want to see everything he does to me. His black, ravenous eyes meet mine from between my thighs. They smoulder undeniably, drenching me more than I ever dreamed possible. His mouth lowers, and I recognise his smirk before his tongue flicks over and over. I cry out, enjoying the way he sucks my nub with determination.

Unlike last night, everything about his conduct today is determined. He is making a statement. He is claiming me.

He extracts his finger, and I stare, automatically licking my lips as he pops it into his mouth. His cheeks flush, and his sparkling eyes glaze over and hood heavily. And it is the most erotic thing I've witnessed. With that vision deeply embedded, I wonder what it would be like to reciprocate. The thought sticks in my mind and refuses to budge, and I fear I may come just by thinking about it.

I watch intently, with bated breath, as he rubs down the back of my knees and bends them up slightly. He lets out a pained groan, then lowers his head back to my centre again. My hips elevate in a jerking motion, the instant his tongue slides across my opening again.

"So wet and delicious...and finally all mine."

The warmth against my folds is taking me over the edge faster than I want it to. His tongue pushes in and out incessantly, until my body allows the release I'm concentrating on and craving for. I cry out loud, coming with more force and intensity than I have ever done manually. Instead of stopping, he continues, until I feel the need to push him away to regain some composure, but at the same time, I don't want to stop this hedonistic sensation welcoming me into its world again.

Crying out, his tongue eases down and slowly withdraws from me. I throw my arm over my face, attempting to control my breathing. No use, I'm already gone; lost in this crazy passion he is unleashing from the pit of my soul. My heart knows I will never be able to fight him or his intense desire, not even if I wanted to. The result is truly dangerous and truly breath-taking.

The sound of the packet ripping causes my eyes to open wide, and I throw my arm down and stare at him.

"Sloan, I don't think I can." I know I definitely can't withstand another one of those orgasms.

"Baby, you can and you will," he says huskily, before reaching up to kiss me. "I'll stop if you ask me to. Promise me, you will tell me." I nod my head, but it's not enough for him. "I want to hear you say it."

"I promise I will, but I know you won't hurt me, even if this will be the death of me," I say flatly, and he chuckles beautifully.

I run my hands up his chest and hold his cheeks in either palm. With his crown ready and waiting at my entrance, he massages my backside. Staring intensely into the eyes penetrating my soul, he eases himself inside, pulling me towards him gently.

We stare at each other as he slides deeper into my depths. The instant reaction is amazing. He feels perfect filling me, even the slight burn is gratifying. I drop my thighs over his arse, letting them linger rather than wrapping them. He reaches forward, effectively climbing up my body. The movement causes him to throb hard inside me, and I quiver against his chest. The back of his hand strokes my cheek and tears of hope build behind my eyes. My heart almost breaks when I see the conflict raging inside his.

"Kara, I..."

Seeing his uncertainty, and fearful he may end this before it begins, I find my voice again. "Take me, Sloan," I whisper, but he remains still inside my aching core. Unsure what to do, I rub the inside of my thigh against his leg, urging him to move.

"I thought you would never ask," he sighs out. "But if I hurt you in any way-" I don't allow him to finish, and quickly press my lips to his to placate him, waiting for him to make me his. I don't have to wait long until he eventually starts to rotate his hips in a circular motion. I place one hand on his chest and press the other to the headboard, realising I will need the extra support before this journey is through.

His body is rigid; tight against mine, and smooth chest muscles rub my nipples deliciously. One of his hand's presses over mine on the leather headboard and the other disappears between us, searching. He plays with me flagrantly, thrusting out to the edge, then sliding back in again. Each time he touches somewhere deeper inside me that intensifies my impending climax.

Enjoying the deep-seated vibrations rocking me internally, I learn that when I raise my hips up, they strengthen. I smile to myself with that newly formed piece of education and start to meet him thrust for thrust. He shudders inside me numerous times, but never climaxes. I coil my legs around him, encouraging him closer, feeling him elongate deep within. I squeeze as tight as possible, but still can't seem to get enough.

He pulls up until he is almost kneeling. He grasps me firmly as he positions me and holds me close to him. My chest is hard against his; his heart beating wildly. I'm sat on his thighs, and he's buried to the hilt. He lifts me up and down on his hard, throbbing shaft effortlessly, hitting me deep inside, massaging places I never knew existed. My body stretches the moment he finally groans out and gives in to his release. He comes with a growl, and I feel him jerk inside me. I smile as my own body builds up for the inevitable.

"Come," he commands me, and I obey with pleasure.

I fall back, curling my fingers into the sheets until they are numb. I'm a little too loud, and I really don't care. I moan over and over, as the elusive tidal waves of ecstasy carry me away with them. My eyes never deviate from his while he roars out the last of his release. I rejoice he is smiling as we ease down from the most amazing natural high.

My body is tucked against his, and I stare up at the ceiling, trying to catch my breath. I can't help but laugh at the amazing transformation I've undergone in the last seven days. My one and only past experience didn't give me much hope for a future, or even the ability to perform even the most innocent of sexual acts, but I love this feeling and the hum rolling through me. I love it even more with a man who enjoys giving it to me. Or maybe it's just the man himself that makes me feel this way?

"Did I hurt you?" His fingertip grazes the skin between my breasts. His look of contentment makes me happy.

"No, you feel amazing. *You* made *me* feel amazing."

"Good, because I'm not done with you yet, not even close. Trust me?" He grins like a naughty schoolboy, and I smile and lift my brows in over-exaggeration. I have no time to catch my breath, as he leans over and rolls us until I am on top.

Looking at the ruffled bedsheets to see where I can find leverage, I baulk. "Sloan, I don't know what I'm doing," I mutter, a little embarrassed and a lot worried. I know my inexperience will be hideously apparent this way. He grips my waist and guides me onto him. He lifts me up and down, studying me with such veneration, I feel my heart pound frantically. He holds my body gently, his large hands guiding me, until I find my own unique rhythm. Circling my pelvis on his centre, his breath lapses momentarily.

"That's it, baby," he groans out, relaxing his hands on my hips. "Ride me."

Lying on top of Sloan, I watch, satisfied, at the rise and fall of his chest with each intake of breath. I trace every hard line from his waist up, committing to memory every ridge and flaw. Damn, he is beautiful. Even I'm not oblivious to the realisation that I am in imminent danger of falling too fast, too soon. I've never believed you can fall in love at first sight, and I don't know if I am, but the things I'm feeling for this incredible man have started to make me question my own better judgement.

"Penny for your thoughts, my love?" he murmurs quietly in my ear, kissing my neck.

"Just thinking."

"About?"

"You. Me. This. *Us*. Plenty going on up here." I point to my head, and he chuckles against my throat.

His fingers start to draw long fluid lines up and down my spine. The gentleness of his touch induces a shiver to build and run under my skin in time with his caress. His hand drifts lower and kneads my behind softly. I gaze at his dark head of hair and sigh in relief. Closing my eyes, I never want to let this feeling go.

For the first time in my adult life, I am just happy to feel something with another human being. I've never managed to get close to someone before. My fear of being hurt has never allowed me to. So to be here, bare in his arms, is a breakthrough. It might not have been the way most first times - or second times, in my case - happen, but to me it was perfect, and I wouldn't change it even if I could.

I gently nuzzle against him, and he lifts his head, holding my gaze with his. I still, and apprehension grips me when his finger dips down between my cheeks and strokes around my backside. My eyes widen in astonishment, but I don't say a word.

His finger continues to move around the area, and I shut off completely. I honestly don't know if I am able to let him do that to me, not this soon anyway. My reaction causes his jaw to tighten, and the veins in his neck start to bulge out. I place my finger over his mouth the same time his lips begin to part. I refuse to break eye contact with him, until my mobile rings from somewhere on the floor, puncturing our beautiful post-coital silence.

Pulling myself from his body, I wince discreetly at the loss of his heat. Hunting down my jeans, I fish out my still ringing phone and sit on the edge of the bed.

My father.

Wonderful.

I let it go to voicemail and throw it on the duvet. I drop my head in my hands, contemplating, watching Sloan from the corner of my eye. He picks up the phone, and his mouth contorts when he looks at the screen. I sigh out, knowing he is going to ask who *Ian* is, yet it never comes.

"What to talk about it?" His finger trails up my shoulder, but whereas I should be feeling goosebumps and lust-filled shivers, I feel nothing.

The moment is dead and gone.

"No."

I leave him naked in bed and pad into the bathroom, closing the door firmly behind me.

I'm soaking in the bath when the door opens, and Sloan stands before me in all his male, naked glory. I look away from him, not because I want to, but because I don't want him to see the pain the call has induced in me.

For years I've been hurting, and my father is always the reason behind it. I'm tired of picking up the pieces of his life whenever he screws up. It's a regular occurrence and shouldn't come as a surprise to me. Some may think I'm being selfish, but the truth is, he's made me this way. The things he did; things he permitted to be done. I blink back a tear at the thought of a father who never loved me enough to protect my innocence from evil.

The water level rises as Sloan's climbs in. He rubs my shoulder, and I slide forward, giving him enough room to nestle his beautiful hard body behind mine. He glides his hands over my arms, and I fall back against him and let go.

"Talk to me, Kara." There's no tone in his voice, and I wonder what has brought this on. Surely it wasn't just by looking at my missed call?

He pulls me back to him and lays his forearms over my stomach. His hand reaches up and massages my belly with determination, but I know what he's trying to do. He's trying to coerce me into a moment of weakness. He's trying to get me to react. To make me feel so secure that I will lose my rationality and spill the demons of my past.

"Tell me about your childhood," he probes again, no doubt realising that if he starts off with a simple subject, the rest might flow smoothly. Little does he know he couldn't have picked something worse to discuss.

I think back to the good times of my childhood, not that there were many of those, but I have to impart something. I'm sure as hell not going to confess the uglier aspects of my life.

"Well, we didn't have a lot of money, but my mum did the best she could." That should appease him.

"Hmm hmm, go on," he murmurs. Water flows down my back, and he delicately rubs a flannel over my skin.

"She would take me to the park to feed the ducks. Apparently, I drove her crazy about it." I did; I loved the ducks. I even loved when the gaggle of vicious geese would chase after me. I was carefree and innocent back then. It wasn't until later in my life I found out the truth about why she always took me there. It was a means to escape the violence and drugs, not that I remembered. Once it used to be my happy place, now I'm unable to think of it without bile scorching my throat.

He stops and turns me around with ease. Water spills over the sides and sloshes down on the marble floor. He searches my face carefully, and I have to close my eyes. He can't see me like this; broken, tearful and still able to love my parents, who have taught me first-hand that love hurts.

"Open your eyes, baby." I do as he asks, but try to avoid looking at him. "One day you will tell me. Not today, but I want you to trust me enough to be honest. I know something has happened in your past that closes you off, I don't know what," he says calmly. "Although I can imagine, and trust me, I'm not in a good place when I do. Please just allow me to look after you, let me take care of you, that's all I ask."

I press my lips together and nod. I lack conviction, even in my own mind. No one has ever really looked after me before. No one except for Marie, of course. And I'm not entirely sure I can relinquish my complete trust and happiness to this rich playboy, regardless of how much he believes in this.

Sliding around, I lean back against his chest. One day I will tell him, and maybe then I might stop hurting. Although the second the truth left my lips, I would still be in a world of devastation, because he will be gone.

Nobody wants damaged goods.

And I'm that and more.

Chapter 11

"SO, WHAT DO you like?" Sloan tilts his head from around the fridge door. I lift up to see him and shrug my shoulders.

"Anything. I'm not fussy, as long as it's not wet or smoked fish. You know, fishy fish."

"Fishy fish?" He's dying to laugh at me. If his face wasn't giving him away, the tone of his voice is. "Well, how about chicken? Stir-fry maybe?"

I smile and nod. Picking myself up off the floor, I slowly move into the kitchen. I stop instantly when I see an array of different pots and pans covering every available inch of the worktop.

"Are you expecting a battalion for dinner tonight?" I ask, on the verge of bursting into a fit of laughter.

He turns and gives me a pouty look. "There's no need for sarcasm. I told you, I don't cook, but I'm also enough of a gentleman not to expect my lady to eat takeaway every night, so here you have it," he says with his hands on his hips, looking at everything closely. "You know, I can run a company successfully, but not a kitchen." He grabs the wok and pours a large slug of oil into it.

I shake my head at the chaos surrounding him, roll up my sleeves, and walk towards the fridge. I pull out the chicken and vegetables, and gather them in my arms. Turning back to the worktop, my eyes move from one unnecessary object to another. I sigh and slide the pans out of the way. I drop the food down and pass the chicken, onions, and peppers, to Sloan. Doing a quick mental inventory, I loudly collect up all the equipment he doesn't need and pile them up on the island worktop. He turns and smiles, before he makes quick work of putting them back in their rightful homes.

"Why is it a grown man of twenty-seven has never cooked before? I find it very hard to believe." He looks a little lost, but doesn't answer. "What about your sister and your parents? Have you never made them dinner before?" The knife stops chopping. The only sound in the kitchen - between my hesitant breaths and his quick intake of air - is the oil sizzling away in the pan.

He lowers the heat on the hob and turns to me. "No, my parents are dead, and Charlie won't touch anything I make for her." The sadness in his eyes stabs at my chest. I've said the wrong thing, and my heart feels weighted down instantly.

"I'm so sorry, Sloan. I had no idea." I apologise, rubbing my hands together nervously. He approaches me with caution and kisses my forehead.

"Please don't be sorry, you didn't know. I've never really shared anything about my life with anyone. I learned many years ago not to let anyone in, or maybe I stopped letting people in. Take your pick, same difference." He gives me a knowing look. It's fleeting, but it was definitely there. His eyes turn serious as they rake over my entire body, and I shiver. "I did once. I let someone in, and then they were gone. The effects have been long-lasting. Until now." I bite my lip at his statement. I know all about long-lasting effects and living life alone for fear of being the victim again. He watches me as I commit his words to memory. Turning slowly, he flicks the heat back on, and the oil starts to bubble again as he throws the chicken into the wok.

"So, if you've never cooked for anyone before, who made breakfast for me this morning?" I query, perching myself on one of the stools at the island, needing to lift the palpable and awkward atmosphere circulating between us.

He gives me a sheepish look. "I had it delivered in."

"Oh."

"Yeah, oh. You'd be amazed at what you can get for the right price. Sorry, I just wanted to impress you. I guess I've failed."

"No, I'm impressed all right. I've never had that kind of takeaway for breakfast." Unable to contain myself, I laugh. The whole scenario is just too comical not to.

"You can stop laughing now," he says thoroughly embarrassed.

"Okay, so your sister won't eat anything you make?" He grins and quirks his brows up. "Well, what makes you think I will? I've got to admit you're not exactly selling it to me here." He lobs the onions and peppers into the pan, gives it a quick stir and walks towards me. He spins me around and braces his hands on the marble behind me.

"Really?" He smirks, and I can feel my legs weakening. "I guarantee I can convince you. What are you willing to bet?" I suck in my lips. I'm not a betting person, but I'm willing to bet my future happiness that he can convince me.

And convince me he does.

His lips linger briefly over mine, before they track a slow path down my chin to my throat. He bends in front of me, and I moan out, letting my head fall back. He slides his hand inside my top, and his fingers brush over my nipple continuously as he fondles my already aching breasts, until he pulls the material aside and takes it into his mouth. I'm panting out, experiencing a sudden light-headedness. My hand moves up to his hair, tugging forcefully to hold him in place, while my other slaps hard on the cold surface. I close my eyes, as one of his hands runs up my leg and slides underneath the shorts I nabbed from his dresser. His fingertips find my entrance, and I mellow, as my burgeoning climax starts to breathe life into me. I'm just about ready to come when he stops.

Oh, my God, he just fucking stopped!

My eyes widen in disbelief, and my mouth falls open. He laughs, sucks his fingers, and turns to the sink to wash his hands. I glare at him; a quivering, unsatisfied wreck. He throws the tea towel at me, and I scowl. I'm thoroughly turned on, unfulfilled, and absolutely pissed off.

"I'm willing to bet an evening of mindless, senseless, body shattering orgasms that you eat my dinner. So much so, the little appetiser you just had? Well, you won't get the rest until after." He grins and brings his hand to my face. I want to hit him so much. I also want to press his hand against the part of me desperate for release.

"Satisfied?"

"Not in the slightest!" I spit out fiercely. He cups my face and kisses me, before returning to the hob. Then he starts to hum to himself. He knows I'm pissed off, and I do nothing to hide it. I stomp out of the kitchen and into the living room. He's watching me from behind the island, and I do my utmost to make sure he knows I'm definitely not satisfied.

Not knowing what to do with myself, I flick through the television channels for a good fifteen minutes or so. Over one hundred channels and there's nothing on. Switching it off, I put the remote down on the table and plod back across to the kitchen.

Sloan is just serving the stir-fry and rice. He carries them over to the dining table and pulls a chair out for me. Sliding into it, I give him an unsatisfied, sweet smile as he pushes me back in. Holding my plate up, I sniff it a little. It smells okay, it doesn't look bad, and

I'm so hungry right now, I'd eat anything that was put in front of me.

Sloan returns with a bottle of champagne and a couple of flutes. He pops the cork on the bottle, and I wait to see how much damage it will cause. Like a true professional, it doesn't even bounce over the table. I guess he has plenty of experience with that, too. He pours me a glass, and I raise it to his.

"What are we celebrating?" I ask, dying to have a sip of whatever this is. I've had champagne before at events, although it wouldn't surprise me if it was cheap, since it never tasted that good.

"To firsts," he says. "May we have more than we've already experienced together." I cross my eyes at him. I think it's lovely he's saying it, but I don't understand why.

"Well, since you're now wondering - our first meeting, our first dinner, our first real relationship... Our first time together. To firsts, and if you're *still* wondering, I have plenty of other firsts we can experience, too." I grin at him; his insinuation isn't lost in the ether. I know exactly what other *firsts* he is referring to.

"To first relationships," I say, clinking my glass against his.

Sloan puts his down and looks between our plates. I prod my fork into the chicken and stab it up with some red pepper. It actually tastes really good. I'm impressed. I glance at Sloan to give him my seal of approval, and he grins again.

"Tonight might be the first trip to the hospital for us, too," he mutters.

Amused, I shake my head at his ability to ease the sexually charged tension which has been rife between us, since he brought me so close to the edge, and then pulled me back again.

"Tell me more about you. I'm intrigued."

I'm lounging in front of the fire on a thick, sumptuous, faux fur rug, with my third glass of champagne in hand. I'm not really a big drinker, heaven knows an alcoholic father will do that to you, but it has glided down my neck far too easily tonight. Sloan hasn't commented on it, so I'm not sure if he wants me drunk so I'll confess my sins, or if he just wants me partially intoxicated, so I don't remember to ask him to confess his.

His hand snakes up and down my back. "What do you want to know?" If he's worried, he doesn't sound it. Not even close.

"Everything. Starting with the reason why you have that gorgeous mansion, surrounded by beautiful views of the countryside, and yet you seem to prefer to live in this equally gorgeous hotel suite, surrounded by the hustle and bustle of the city," I say into my glass. "I know which one I'd prefer to live in." I hiccup as the bubbles tickle my throat. He laughs and kisses my shoulder blade, before letting out a loud sigh.

"It's not that I don't want to live there, it just holds too many memories. Besides, it's far too big for one person." I turn to him, and he gives me a small smile and an equally small, uncommitted lift of his shoulders. Sitting upright, I cross my legs and put my glass between them. He observes my action suspiciously.

"Well, why did you take me there if it makes you so uncomfortable?" I hiccup again.

Reaching for me, he kisses the back of my hand reverently. "Because I wanted to see how you would fit. The way you would react to it, and hopefully… Well, I guess I wanted your approval." My moderately champagne fogged brain sobers instantly.

"Excuse me?"

"You heard me. Playing dumb doesn't suit you, Kara. You're a smart, strong woman. It's what attracted me in the first place, so please don't act like you're not. Anyway, like I said, you heard me. Loud and clear."

"I apologise, I did, and it was you talking out of your mind. You don't know anything about me." I pick up my glass and drain the remaining liquid, as my eyes search around for the rest of the bottle.

"Oh, but I do know you." He tips the rest of his drink back, then reaches behind him, exposing the object of my hunting.

"Why, because you look into my eyes and see sorrow and pain in them? That isn't knowing someone. It's called empathy. It's what makes us human. Well, some of us at least," I mutter under my breath, remembering the one who had no empathy at all when I screamed for him to stop at the top of my lungs.

I pour myself another glass, and he gives me a critical, disapproving look. He takes the glass from me and virtually drains it on my behalf. I don't protest; it's probably for the best, considering I have hiccups and my head is feeling a little effervescent and disorderly.

"No, it's not that." He refills my glass halfway and hands it back to me.

"Look, I don't play games, especially not this kind. I appreciate I'm not one of your rich socialite girlfriends, but if all I am to you is a cheap, quick shag, then there's no point in pretending otherwise. I told you-"

"Don't do that!" he says severely, and throws his hands up in frustration.

"Do, what?" I counter sternly back.

"*That.* Putting yourself down, making yourself seem less worthy of something than some cheap, gold-digging whore! To me you're worth a million of those women," he says. Absolute sincerity fixes in his eyes, and I feel embarrassed that I have just compared myself to something he very clearly despises.

"Sloan, be reasonable! You hardly know-" His lips slam against mine, and he claims my mouth without giving me the chance to finish. He pouts, and I push him back; I was enjoying our *getting to know you* chat. My fingers are pressed against his chest, and I dig them in a little harder, inducing his huff to be replaced by a groan.

"Kiss me."

I shake my head in astonishment. He sulks, and I admit defeat, giving him a light peck on the lips. He tries to deepen it, but again, I push him away.

"Touch me."

I give him a broad smile. "I'm already touching you." I admit; I like this new game he wants to play. Or maybe it's the new, sensual side of myself, the one that didn't exist until recently, that is making me participate. I fumble with his buttons, and he holds his arms out, willing me to undress him.

His head tilts down, and he murmurs, "Kiss me again, Kara." My steadfastness in this game is slipping. He might have told me I held all the cards, but this is his game now, and he is definitely dealing the deck.

Grabbing the back of his neck, I pull him towards me quickly, devouring his mouth with my own. His lips part, allowing me to lead, and I swipe my tongue against his. The heat growing between us is threatening to turn my logic and reasoning to ash. With one last lash of my tongue, I lean back; flushed, turned on, and still very unsatisfied.

Sloan sits on his haunches in front of me. The warm flames of the fire behind me cast shadows over his face. He is both light and dark. His eyes look smoky in the dull glow of the room. "Fuck me, baby."

"Sloan, I-" I don't finish, because he obviously doesn't listen, and I start to stand. I'm feeling the urge to run since he has just upped the stakes. Honestly, I wouldn't know how to fuck a man if someone showed me. My one and only true experience is with him - and it was this afternoon. I haven't somehow miraculously managed to obtain a multitude of experience in the last six hours. "I don't know how. I already told you I-I-"

"No room for indecision here, my love, so you better get used to it," he says, dragging me back down to his knees. He presses me against his hard torso, using his hand on the small of my back to steer me where he wants me. "You're going to fuck me, and I'm going to enjoy it." He's right, there is no indecision. *For him.*

"I beg your pardon?" I ask in shock. Shocked, that he seems to have developed a form of acute amnesia, in the same space of time he seems to think I have developed into a wanton sex goddess. The one thing it has done is make me more vocal.

He grunts and rocks me over his hardness. He runs his hand over my hair and breathes out. "Well, the way I see it, the only man who is ever going to be under, over, on, or inside you, is me. There are times when I will want to make love to you, and there are times I will want to fuck you into next year, and vice versa. So, the sooner you learn how to take me the way *you* want to, the easier this will be. Like I said - no indecision."

"You're fucking delusional!" I reply, feeling the alcohol ripple through me, laced with potent levels of desire. His idea of mental empathy might be half-arsed, but his idea of physical empathy definitely isn't. But I'm not divulging that titbit of *need to know* information to him.

"No, I'm merely fucking honest. I'm also very, very confident that no one else has ever made you react this way; never turned you on this way. No one, but me, has ever seen the way your skin perspires and flushes a stunning shade of deep pink when you're aroused. The way your eyes haze over and turn from the beautiful green I love so much, to a dull grey, induced by pure desire. The way your lips part in anticipation, just dying to be touched and tasted. And most definitely, not the way your body coils and tightens when you're ready for release. And no one, but me, ever will." I blush, feeling my body starting to change in exactly the way he has just described.

He smirks with awareness. "Now, what do you think about our second time in front of this fire, with a little champagne?"

Oh…!

My body heats, and it's not the flames behind me that are causing my blood to boil rapidly. His hand wraps around the back of my neck, and he hastily pulls me into him. He steals my breath away as he kisses me, and I moan into it. My hands come around his back, scratching against the muscles flexing underneath my fingertips.

"Arms up," he says into my mouth. My arms shoot up immediately, and he pulls the t-shirt over my head. He leans me back and sucks my areola into his mouth. I instantly turn boneless at the contact, as he lavishes me with his undivided attention. The sound of something lightly thudding against the floor behind me compels me to turn, but Sloan grunts out, and I abandon my inquisition.

He leans forward, and my legs wrap around his hips. My back slowly touches the silky, softness of the rug, and my head is met with a soft cushion. I adjust myself to get comfortable, as strong hands run up my thighs, and I bend my knee, letting it fall to the side. The look of complete appreciation and longing makes me wet and ready. Sloan's hands stop at the top of my legs, and he moves them around to the insides. Gripping my inner thighs securely, he swipes his thumbs over my increasingly swollen folds, allowing one to drag deep into me. He brings the offending thumb up to his mouth and licks the moisture from it. Midnight blues eyes turn molten and smoulder undeniably, as he closes his lids. I stare, spellbound and compelled.

He lets out a loud, ear-piercing growl and grabs the elastic band of my shorts. He wrenches them down my legs and goes in for the kill. He spreads out my thighs wide, bending down and running his nose over my sensitised area. He grunts repeatedly, but doesn't do anything other than examine me with very uncomfortable precision. I relax back in my fizzy wine stupor, enjoying his fingers separating me until his tongue unexpectedly presses inside, and I cry out at the sensation of him taking me like this again. He moves in and out, over and over, pushing me towards the edge of sanity. Unable to control myself, I scream out gutturally, and my body explodes underneath him. We both already knew it wouldn't take much; I've been on the verge of coming since he turned up the heat in the kitchen.

"No other man will ever see this, but me," he states firmly from between my thighs.

I throw out my arm, and it hits the almost empty bottle. I glance down, and Sloan's head pops up. His passion-laden face curves into a mischievous grin. He quickly pushes off his jeans and digs into the pocket for a condom. I shake my head at his knack of being prepared. Except, it wasn't being prepared at all, and we both know it. He rolls the latex over his rock-hard length and pulls me to him. Crooking his finger at me to lift up, I do. He pulls me back onto his knees, and puts my hand over his hot shaft as he grabs the bottle.

"Put me inside you, baby," he requests hoarsely.

I run my hand up and down his length, my aching core is silently crying out for him. I lift up and guide him into my opening. I start to push down on him, and he takes a long swallow from the bottle and puts it down. Positioning his hands under my arse when I'm fully seated, he lifts me up and brings me back down hard. My lips part and a moan of desirous discomfort leaves my throat. He closes his mouth over mine, and he transfers the liquid between us. He continues to move my body up and down on him, almost painfully, as the fizz flows down my throat.

My head is thrown back each time he slams me back onto him. The discomfort is mild and subsiding, but I will definitely feel the lingering effects in the morning. Teeth graze against my collarbone, and he starts to nip at the swell of my breasts.

"Harder, baby," he pleads. Between his hands and my hips, I give him what he wants. He wanted me to fuck him; he's getting his wish. I lift up and down, hard and fast. He gives out an ear-splitting roar and fills me completely. Dropping my head to his sweat covered chest, I kiss the base of his neck. I'm panting like crazy. It's going to take a long time for me to control my breathing after this.

His hands cradle my face. "No other man will ever make you come like this." I close my eyes in veneration.

"Never. There will be no other man but you, Sloan. Never," I say, not recognising the sound of my own voice, or the girl that I have turned into. This isn't me; this isn't who I am. It frightens the shit out of me that I have gone from no sex to an abundance of it in no time at all. Except, inside maybe this *is* who I'm meant to be. He kisses me hard and my eyes open, like I'm seeing him for the first time. He's beautiful, perfect, and dare I say, mine?

He takes another swig from the bottle and pulls the back of my head to feed me again. The alcohol runs freely down my throat. Sloan's eyes are open, and he kisses me, never breaking contact. He kisses a wet trail down my neck, and I feel the urgent need to cool off. I pick up the bottle and take a mouthful. The sucking on my chest stops, and I lower my head to look at him. My lips are still around the glass neck, and his eyes are huge. This was another first he was talking about. I put the bottle back down and nervously suck on my bottom lip. Face to face with me, he rubs his thumb over my lips. I kiss the pad, and he exhales.

"Ever?" he asks.

I shake my head no.

"Good." He smiles gloriously. It obviously pleases him to know there is at least still one thing pure and innocent about me that will only ever be his.

His hand snakes down to my behind, and his fingers gently play between my cheeks. "Here?" he murmurs.

"No," I whisper. He strikes quick and drags me close, kissing me with such turbulence and fire, I can feel it right down to my toes.

When he finally raises his eyes back to me, they are dark again. "You're mine, Kara. I'm your first everything, and I will be your last. One experience eight years ago doesn't count, because he will never see you the way I do. Say it, baby."

Staring deeply into his irises, I know mine will reflect my sadness. One experience eight years ago might not count to him, but it was a debauched act that I will live with forever. Regardless of how much I think I've blocked it out, it lies just below the surface. *Waiting.* Aside from that, he's right; I am his, because he's the only one who has ever been able to touch me. Because I have waited my whole life to find that one person who fits me perfectly. I just never envisaged it would be someone like him.

Sloan tilts my chin up, waiting for me to say it.

"I'm yours."

"Good girl."

His hands drift down my waist to hold me, as he slides out and pushes back in. Nudging his head into the curve of my neck, he starts to suck as I massage my fingers through his hair and look towards the fire. Overcome with enlightenment, I'm content yet conflicted by the unspoken truth of my suppressed feelings.

Eventually, my back arches, and I moan as Sloan works me into a frenzy. The heat in my body deepens, and I cry out again when he roars and fills me.

The heat of the flames stoke higher and higher, and I'm not far behind them.

"Hello?" Marie answers on the first ring.

I'm sitting balled up on the bathroom floor, cocooned in a plush, fluffy robe that is saturated in Sloan's unique, unmistakable scent. "Hi, it's me," I reply sheepishly. I need to talk to her. I need to tell her what I experienced today.

"Hi, honey, are you okay?" The concern in her voice is amplified over the receiver, and a sigh of agitation drifts across the line.

"I'm fine, really, I am. I just need to talk to you about something."

"Okay, what is it, honey? Oh, God, is it Sam again?"

"No, no, no," I mumble, wondering how I'm going to get the words out. I bite the inside of my cheek; at twenty-three I should be able to tell her that I've finally had sex for the first time. But shit, they just won't come out.

She waits.

I still don't know how to say it.

"Kara? Kara, what's going on? Where are you?" she asks full of worry.

"I'm with Sloan Foster." I don't think it requires any further explanation - not if her sharp hiss of breath is anything to go by.

"Oh, baby, did he hurt you?" she queries gently, breaking the long, deathly silence. She knows what I'm trying to say without even asking.

"No, no, he was – *is* – amazing," I whisper. "Marie, he can touch me. I let him touch me, and I liked it." The sound of her content sigh that I have finally found someone, echoes in my ear.

"Honey, that's great, really it is. Just promise me it was safe…and consensual." The last words bleed into my heart painfully.

"It was safe, and consensual, and perfect, and I want him, Marie. I want him so bad, even I don't understand why. He makes me feel so much; emotionally, mentally, and yes, sexually. From the first moment he touched me, when I came here to collect Sam, I've wanted him. Does it make me a slut because I've only known him for seven days?" I hold my breath, terrified she will think poorly of me. I feel ashamed, and I know I shouldn't.

"Kara, no, of course not! Before today, you've only ever had one sexual experience, albeit not something that I would personally class it as. Kara, one real sexual partner in your short life, does not make you a slut. You're twenty-three. There are women in the world your age who have probably been with hundreds of different men! You're definitely not ones of those girls! You just needed to find the right man for you. Honey, I always told you that one day he would enter your life, and here he is! It's what you've always wanted. I know you'll never admit it, but I see you. The one thing you want most in the world is unconditional love, and not the type I give you, but the type that comes from someone who doesn't look at you as damaged. And you're not, Kara, I hope you finally see that now. You're strong and beautiful, and I'm proud to call you mine." Tears collect at the back of my eyes.

The door swings open, and Sloan stands there, smiling, until he sees I'm on the phone. He puts his hand up apologetically and slips back out.

"Marie, I need to go. I just wanted to talk to someone, and I don't think Sam would be interested."

"No, I agree. Not that I mind, I'd rather know than not know, but why didn't you call Soph?" My head leans back against the tiled wall.

"Because she wouldn't understand. Nobody understands."

"Oh, honey, I love you so much. We risked a lot to get here, but you were worth that risk and more. Now, I'm not the only one who realises how much you're worth."

"I love you," I whisper pathetically. It was something we said to each other very little, if at all. We didn't need words to confirm it.

"And I, you. Take care and call me."

"I will," I say, after hanging up.

The door swings open again, and Sloan invades the room for a second time. "Sorry, I didn't mean to walk in."

I shake my head. "No, it's okay, I was just calling my aunt." He takes my hand and leads me out of the main bathroom and down the stairs. He constantly turns and looks at me, as he guides me into the kitchen. He picks me up and drops me onto one of the stools, then turns and starts to rummage through the fridge. He pulls out the large half-eaten cheesecake I had spotted in there earlier.

"Dessert?" he queries, handing me a spoon. I smile as I cut into the biscuit and cream cheese. My eyes close involuntarily, savouring the first bite. I let out a little moan of pleasure at the combined tastes and textures exploding in my mouth. The sound of metal clattering pinches my eyes back open, and I see Sloan hastily retrieving his spoon from the dessert plate. I arch a brow, as he gives me a sexy grin and clears his throat.

"How about our third time with a little cheesecake?"

I smile, shake my head and take another slow, laborious bite, ensuring I moan again when the spoonful of heaven enters my mouth.

"I bet I can convince you!" His eyes sparkle beautifully with his statement.

There's no doubt in my mind he can.

Chapter 12

I'M CURLED UP on the sofa, reading a magazine, when a sharp knock resounds on the suite door. Sloan pads leisurely through the living room to answer it, like he hasn't got a care in the world. I watch in awe at this amazing man moving with such grace and agility. For someone who has so much, I still find it surprising that I haven't seen someone waiting on him hand and foot these last few days.

Reappearing minutes later, he's followed by a tall, incredibly muscular, dark-haired guy, who looks, quite simply, plain scary. His features are strong and masculine. Like Sloan, he's stunning, but not in the traditional sense. There is a raw ruggedness to his features, yet he oozes confidence. Standing next to Sloan, there is an air of seniority in his stance and composure. There is also something about him that I can't quite put my finger on. It's the same weird calmness I experienced the first night I met Sloan.

"Walker, this is Kara Petersen," Sloan introduces us. Quickly moving back to my side, he places a protective arm around my shoulder. I tug on my robe, feeling slightly awkward in my relatively undressed state. Even though I am fully covered, I feel extremely exposed in this stranger's presence.

"Hello, Ms Petersen," Walker greets, outwardly appraising me from head to toe. His look isn't one of sexual interest, more of surprise and curiosity.

A look of unspoken truth passes between them, and I watch them both diligently from beneath my lashes, as a silent conversation is carried out with looks alone. I narrow my eyes, wondering what I'm not permitted to hear.

"I'm guessing this isn't a social call," Sloan finally says to Walker, while pouring a glass of brandy and then taking a sip.

Walker looks down at me, and back to Sloan before he answers. "No. I didn't want to disturb you, but there's been an *incident*," he replies, crossing his arms over his huge chest. "There's another one."

Inspecting Walker closely, I realise he is the same man Sloan's sister was dancing with at the function. It all makes sense now as to why he would let her dance with someone else, especially considering she was a little tipsy at the time.

Not listening to what they are saying, I notice he really is a lot bigger than Sloan. His dark hair is cropped close, and there are a few speckles of gold highlighting it. Old scars and stress lines mar his handsome face. I can tell he's older than Sloan's twenty-seven years, and I peg him at early to mid-thirties, maybe.

Sloan sighs out in irritation. His arm then grips my shoulder tighter, and his muscles flex and tense. "The same room? Is she..." He turns to me with concern, gauging my response to what is being openly discussed.

"Yeah, and she's conscious, thankfully. We just can't get to her to see if she's okay. Every time one of the boys goes in, she starts screaming hysterically. I'm out of choices, and don't know what to do with her." Walker says, worried. "I can get one of the female staff to come up. Your call, of course, except it will cause questions to arise, but it might be the only option we have."

Sloan drops his arm from my shoulder and picks up my hand. I easily identify the look of significance that passes between them again, and I close my eyes, praying they won't ask me to do what I think they're going to.

"Baby, there's a girl downstairs, and she's not good. Remember how Sam was?" he whispers to me, kissing my knuckles.

I chortle. *How could I forget?*

My gaze drifts over to the sofa, replaying the memory of Sam lying there banged up and broken, knowing now it was Sloan and Walker who had bandaged her up. Her body is still bruised from whatever had happened to her. Fortunately, she spared me the details of the event itself, either because she didn't want to talk about it, or she just doesn't remember. I don't know which.

"I won't be gone long. Just call security if you need anything, and I'll be straight back up." His hands roam over my face. Although it's affectionate, I sense he is thinking about what he has to go and deal with, knowing only a week ago my best friend was in more or less the same condition.

Considering briefly what I'm about to offer, I brace myself for the inquisition. I always knew the day would come when I had to fight my own demons. I just never thought I would be confronting them in front of a man, whom I was starting to trust more than I should be comfortable with, after only seven days.

"Has nobody gone in to see how she is?" I look towards Walker, and he shakes his head.

"No. Like I said, we've tried, but she screams and won't co-operate."

The silence is palpable, until I speak again. "Okay, I'll do it. Give me a few minutes, I just need to…"

I slide out from under Sloan's arm, but he holds onto my hand. I look into his eyes, knowing he will see the conflict in mine.

"Please, don't ask me," I whisper out, and he lets me go.

My head is swimming as I head towards the stairs. Heaving myself up them, I walk with a heavy heart and the weight of the world on my shoulders into the bedroom. Grabbing my clothes, I dress quickly, straighten up and inhale deeply. Catching my reflection in the mirror, suddenly I'm fifteen all over again. A shudder flows through me, escorting me back to the night of my fifteenth birthday. That night was the worst of my life. It altered me forever. It was the night my existence became null and void. It was also the night the foundations of my invisible wall were constructed. At the time, I didn't actually remember all of the assault, only fragments here and there, and what the doctors had confirmed while I was hospitalised in the weeks that proceeded it. Eventually, the majority did come flooding back, and I forced myself to become immune and block it all out entirely. Up until recently, I'd done a damn fine job in forgetting.

Taking one last long look at myself, I have to wonder how the most perfect day of my life has managed to morph into what I know will develop into another less than perfect night.

I consciously eavesdrop at the top of the staircase, listening to Walker talk to Sloan. "CCTV captured them going in, but he left a few hours before she was found, kid. We haven't been able to locate him. I guess I hoped she would be in the same condition as the other one. I mean, at least we would be able to get her some medical attention if she was out of it." Walker pauses. "I might be stating the fucking obvious here, but is it really wise for her to go in there?"

"I don't know, but refusing her now will just open up a can of worms. Is Stuart here yet?"

I strain my head further, desperate to know what they're insinuating. I know the longer I stay here, the more at risk I am of hearing something I really don't want to. Inside, instinct tells me I'm more involved here than I'm aware of.

"Yeah, he's just arrived, and he's not happy. He had to get his bitch of a colleague to take over his surgery. He said he'll add it to the rest of the shit you still owe him for." Sloan lets out an unamused chuckle. "Kid, I know this isn't something to dredge up now, but do you think she'll-"

"I don't know." He cuts him off. "I guess we'll find out soon, won't we?"

Sloan's silhouette paces up and down in the living room repeatedly. He's nervous - that much is obvious. I watch undetected from my vantage point on the stairs, silently rebuking myself for what I've just volunteered for. My foot presses against the top step, and it creaks under me. Sloan halts mid-step when he sees me skulking in the shadows. Giving me a tight, strained smile, he holds out his hand. I descend and move towards him until I am close enough for him to tug me into his arms. His face is filled with apprehension, and he frowns a little as his lips gently graze my forehead. Drawing away from me, I can see and feel the stiffness in his posture. Aware we have an audience, I glance back at Walker, but he isn't actually looking at me, he's staring at Sloan conscientiously, pinning him with a troubled expression.

After taking the stairs down from the penthouse suite, we stop outside one of the rooms on the fourth floor. Walker knocks firmly, and the door opens. A tall man, with a shock of dark red hair, appears on the other side. He instantly motions Sloan towards a corner, and they start to speak in hushed tones. Sloan turns to me, even though the man is still talking to him, and he flicks his finger up, stopping his companion mid-sentence.

"Baby, I'll be just a minute," he says, and signals for me to wait with Walker. The emptiness is discernible the second his hand leaves mine. I glance around the room, noting the other men talking in subdued whispers. Walker is stood next to a man carrying a medical case, who I presume is the doctor. There are also three other men waiting.

Walker gestures me towards him. "Kara, this is Stuart Andrews. He's the doc, and also a very good friend of Sloan's." I divert my attention to the tall, blond man who is well over six foot. His arms look broad, gripping his medical supplies. His eyes narrow on me, and I shuffle restlessly. Again, his look is more of curiosity and recognition, rather than surprise. Studying me hard, he now looks as though he's seen a ghost, and is dying to ask me a thousand questions to which he already knows the answers.

"Hi," I greet him quietly. Stuart smiles, but doesn't reply. Instead, he gives a wide-eyed look to Walker, who subsequently ignores him and introduces me to the rest of them.

"Kara, this is Simon Parker, Jake Evans and Devlin Walker." He points out the triumvirate of tall, built men. "And when they've finished talking, you'll meet Thomas Fox over there," he says, jerking his head at Sloan and the redheaded man, who are now deep in conversation. I look back at the three in front of me, and they each carry the same expression Stuart had. I shuffle and turn away, my nerves getting the better of me under their scrutiny. I might be wrong, but lodged deep, somewhere in the back of my troubled mind, I feel something faint, something that had diminished a long time ago.

There is something about these men I can't quite put my finger on...

Even though they all appear friendly enough, I wonder what Sloan does to warrant such a small army of rather large, partially intimidating, and seemingly dedicated friends. I straighten up, hoping to appear more assertive than I actually feel in such a testosterone-filled space.

I'm about to speak, when feminine sobs ring out like alarm bells from further inside the suite. I turn to where the noise originated from, then pin my eyes back on Sloan, narrowing them in question. He rubs the side of his face and walks towards me.

"Come with me." He gently takes my hand, and we slowly walk down the small corridor in the suite. "You don't have to go in there if you don't want to. I really don't want you seeing this, but we need Doc to take a look at her." His tone is near enough begging me. I give him a quick nod, and he kisses my crown. "Thank you," he says, as we stop outside what I guess is the bedroom door. I take a breath when he turns the handle and opens it slowly.

Words fail me.

She has either put up a really good fight, or suffered really badly.

I'm in momentary shock at the sight of the room. I don't need to see the condition of the girl because the scene speaks volumes. The bedsheets and duvet are strewn all over; torn and splattered with blood. A table has been upended and lays on its side. Edging in further, there is crunching under my feet. Looking down, I can just make out the remnants of a glass lamp that is shattered all over the floor. I touch my forehead, now wishing I'd asked questions back upstairs.

What the hell does he allow to happen in this fucking hotel?

The sobs ring out again, and I throw my head back and pierce him with a glare. I'm confident I can't do this. My palms begin to sweat profusely, and I rub them over my thighs. A hundred different emotions bubble up inside, but the only one I can pick out is anger. My hands curl into fists, I want to hit something, *anything*. Anything to take away her pain. And mine.

The soft cries of distress claim back my control, and I walk through the door, slamming it shut behind me. The room is dark, and it takes a minute for my eyes to adjust to the blackness. The soft light of the moon bleeds through a crack in the curtains. As I pull them back, a soft shuffle of fabric resounds to my right. Looking over, I see her properly for the first time. Flicking on the remaining intact lamp, my heart breaks for the young woman cowering in the tiny space between the bed and the table. Her face is extremely pretty, even more so, if it wasn't so badly swollen and covered with dried blood. I crouch down and sit in front of her. She rocks on her knees, and my heart not only breaks, it obliterates.

My mind leaves my body, mentally turning back time to the moment I was the one cowering in the cubbyhole. I hear the voices, I see the shaded faces, but I don't see me, not the real me. Just the girl I was so long ago - broken, bloodied, abused…

Raped.

The woman's soft cries resonate loudly in my ears, and I focus my attention back on her. Reaching out hesitantly, I wait to see if she reciprocates. She studies me cautiously. Finally assured I mean her no harm; she stretches her arm out. Defying the prickle I know I'll endure for the first time in days, I touch my fingers to hers, while tears stream down my face. She gently eases herself out of the space and wraps her arms around me. Usually, I don't tolerate hugging in any form, especially from someone I've never met before, but this feels different. Probably because I can relate. She gazes at me through dead eyes, seeming to sense I understand her pain.

I sit with her, letting her cry into my neck with abandon. I hold and comfort her the best I can, all the while ignoring the dull sting coursing wildly through my body. But my best, evidently, will never be good enough.

My only saving grace is that I had found a way to shut most of my own pain out, and mentally survive for the best part of the last decade. I have lived through hell and come out the other side - albeit not completely unscathed and whole. I know exactly what she is going through, having been here before. Many times before, in various different guises. Whether it be the rape that transformed me, or the beatings at the hands of those I couldn't see. Of course, it no longer matters, because they all now live under a cloud of ambiguity, which is slowly filtering through my self-imposed mental fortress.

Eventually, her tears subside, and I peer down at her. Her voice cracks when she speaks. "I want to go to sleep." I nod and help her up onto the bed. Pulling the partially red saturated covers back, she climbs under them, and I tuck them down the side and turn away. My stomach somersaults, absorbing the vision of her wrapped in the sheets, covered in what I assume is her blood, and most likely her assailant's semen.

"Please, don't leave me," she begs. I give her a pathetic and weak smile, unsure if I'm able to pull off the role of protector, when I've experienced being the victim far too often. Carefully, I lie on top of the duvet, mindful of what I'm actually lying in.

"Emily," she says. Her voice is low and quiet, but gruff with tears. "My name is Emily."

"Hi, Emily. I'm Kara."

Her lips curve marginally, but her eyes are closing fast, and shortly afterwards, she falls asleep. I wait for her breathing to even out and then, as stealthily as I can, I climb off the bed and leave the room. My hand seizes the handle, and I look back at her. She is completely out of it. And completely destroyed.

I linger in the doorway of the living room. Sloan is talking with Walker and Thomas, and the other four men are all still present. I clear my throat, and seven pairs of eyes all turn towards me.

"You son of a bitch! You could have fucking warned me how bad she might be! Instead, you let me come down here and see that!" I motion my hand towards the bedroom door. I stomp towards him, breathing fire. "She's in there broken and beaten! It doesn't matter what she may or may not have done, nobody deserves *that!*"

Sloan is on me in seconds. His hands hold my wrists firmly. "Sit, we need to talk." His eyes never leave mine, and his face is full of guilt and regret. I look between the six other guys and narrow my eyes in suspicion.

"No!" I hiss at him. "*You* need to talk! Who the hell is she?"

"She was a guest last night," he replies, still not meeting my glare. He's lying to me. I can spot it a mile off. I should know, having perfected the art many years ago.

"A guest or a prostitute?" Something is definitely going on here, I sensed as much when he spoke of Sam's situation earlier. I wait for his response, but as expected, he doesn't answer me.

"Okay. Who the hell did that to her?" I study each of the men, they all carry innocent but disturbed expressions. "Who?" I shout again, until I remember poor Emily sleeping less than thirty feet away. My fist clenches and my nails dig into my palm, indenting the flesh into tiny crescent moons. Closing the door, I pad further into the living room and rotate on my heels until I'm facing them all.

"Baby, listen to me. She wouldn't let anyone in the room. She started screaming when any of my guys went in. What was I supposed to do? I'm sorry to bring you here, but something tells me this doesn't shock you." Concern etches across his face as he stands with hands on his hips. My anger boils, because I know this man has the ability to see through me in a way no one else ever has. He can see right down to the depths of my soul.

"You made the choice to come down here, remember?" he whispers. I glare at him, too lost in my own decade-old memories.

"You could have told me upstairs," I mumble quietly to myself. "And I never had a choice."

His arms unexpectedly come around me, and my eyes flash from him to the others in the room. He tugs my chin between his finger and thumb. "What do you mean, '*you never had a choice*'?" I shake out of his grip and turn away defiantly. "Kara?"

"No," I reply with insolence, raising my eyes to his. My lips form a tight line, and I realise all eyes are now on me. Some are wide, whereas others are sympathetic. Sloan's jaw twitches uncontrollably, and he gives me a once over. He's not a stupid man, I know he will eventually figure it out.

We face-off in uneasy silence until the dark-skinned, very stunning man named Parker approaches, running his hand over his closely shorn hair.

"Boss, what do you want us to do with her? She doesn't want the police. The only one she has even let in there without screaming to high heaven is your girl."

His girl? I'm not quite sure I can be called that just yet, even if I do feel it to be extremely accurate after our very erotic interludes today. I'm also not sure I actually want to be the bearer of that name, considering this is the second time I've seen a defenceless woman beaten black and blue in his hotel.

Then enlightenment impinges.

"Is it the same person who hurt Sam?" I ask, looking between the men expectantly. They all glance down. Sloan starts to open his mouth, but I raise my hand.

"Don't, I already have my answer."

The silence beckons all over again, until movement sounds from outside the room. The door opens, and the slip of a girl stands there. Her puffy face is deathly pale, counting the seven, larger than life, men.

"Hi, Emily," I say lightly, hoping she won't regress. Her arms circle around her body, secure and tight. The tears form in my eyes but refuse to come out. No, I *must* remain strong for a girl I'll probably never see again after tonight.

"Can you help me?" She motions for me to approach. Her face still bores the same terrified look, before she quickly disappears again. I take a deep breath and start to follow her. Looking back at Sloan, I'm in disbelief when he mouths *thank you* to me, and I see the stunned reactions of his friends.

Without a word, I leave the room, and find Emily in the bathroom. She looks weakly at me, and I turn on the taps to run the bath for her. Turning around, allowing her to keep whatever little dignity she still has left intact, she undresses and climbs in. Her whimpers of soreness, induced by the hot water enveloping her battered skin, is like a bullet to my chest.

When she starts to bath herself, her diminutive whines of pain are excruciating. My emotions are a little too raw, and amplified further, by aiding Emily to wash the blood from her hair and body. It's too reminiscent of times gone by, and I'm anxious to get the hell out of here, but at the same time, I also feel obliged to stay. Finally, unable to withstand it any longer, I excuse myself and head back into the living room.

As I enter, I see her clothes on the nearby table. The labels are all high-end designer, and no doubt, very expensive. It's a poor and nasty thought, but prostitution really does seem to pay. She is apparently better off than I am, or at least she was, prior to stepping into this hotel suite.

"Are these hers?"

"No, they're yours," Sloan says reticently. He folds his arms over his broad chest, ready for the impending argument I don't allow to materialise. Thomas and Parker, who are both flanking either side of him, watch with zeal, awaiting my retort. Casting my gaze over the other men, they too, all appear to be waiting for something to blow up between us. Between Sloan's steadfast look and my quickly developing infuriation, it's a possibility.

"Sloan, in case you forgot our conversation from earlier today, trust me, these are definitely not mine!" I almost laugh out loud, shocking even myself that I am still relatively calm and collected.

He pushes out his chest in arrogance. "Yes, they are. They're from your side of the walk-in."

My side of the walk-in? My flat is too small for a broom cupboard, never mind a bloody walk-in wardrobe! I make a mental note to ask him where on earth this invisible designer wardrobe of mine actually is! Pausing, my mind rewinds back to this morning and the designer dressing room at his house. I mentally scream, knowing that eventually, I will have to take another look in there, if I get a second chance. I also need to grow a harder backbone, and then have a serious chat with him about resisting the urge to spend his money on me. If we ever get back upstairs, that is.

My lips start to part, ready to protest, but I shut it down just as quickly. My mouth is parched from watching his stance. His entire posture radiates confidence. Confidence that is getting harder and harder to resist. I clear my head at the way my thoughts are deviating, and hurry back to Emily.

She is compliant as I help her get dressed. She sits in silence, contemplating, before she finally speaks. "He hurt me," she whispers. I lean forward, resting my elbows on my knees. "He hurt me really bad."

The tears start to fall down her cheeks and my heart tenses against my rib cage. I really don't want to hear what she's obviously desperate to confide. I consider myself fortunate that Sam kindly spared me the details, but having survived the same agony, I harden myself to listen and subsequently deal with it.

"Do you want to talk about it?" I silently pray she doesn't. She twists her hands together, then folds them on her lap. "Emily? Did he…r-rape you?"

She chews her lip and her chin trembles. She offers a quick nod, and I edge closer to her, as she stands and brings her arms around me.

"Was there more than one?" I can barely control my own tears as she resumes crying again. My hand runs to the back of her head, and I stroke it over and over, trying to reassure her.

"Just one, but there was another man with him, and he just left me with him. Please don't leave me with *them*," her voice shatters. My own mind delves back, deeper into the dark side that is too black and murky to even recall accurately.

"Emily, the men outside are here to help you. One of them owns this hotel, and another is a doctor. Would you mind if he examines you? I'll be just outside the room, I promise." The silence is palpable, until she finally consents.

I tap on the living room door and wave Stuart over. He approaches me and puts his hand on my shoulder. I flinch instantly, his touch is familiar, but I know that is impossible. Realising his action, he quickly removes it and apologises.

"She was raped. There were two, but the other one apparently just left her with whoever did it. How can someone do that?" I ask, knowing how easy it was for my own parents to turn the other way, rather than fight to preserve my innocence.

"Jesus Christ! The poor girl." Stuart looks up at the ceiling, but I can still see his eyes water. He quickly turns back to Walker; whose expression is murderous. "I know this is hard for you, but will you come in with me?" He waits for my answer. Shit. I know I can't refuse him, not when he's looking at me so expectantly.

Walking side by side with Stuart back into the bedroom, Emily is curled in a ball on the bed, her knees up to her chest.

Stuart sets down his medical case and closes the door behind us.

I stand motionless in front of the window that dominates the penthouse living room, with my palms flat against the glass. I stare past the lights in the distance, wondering if there is another broken woman, or man, suffering the same misfortune as Emily right now. Possibly at the hands of the same heartless bastard?

Sloan is in his office with the guys from earlier and the police. Two officers had arrived an hour ago, assisted by a couple of community support officers, ready to take statements from Emily. As they already anticipated, she refused to talk. She admitted she feared retribution from her attacker. She knew who had done it, but was too terrified to make a formal statement. My mind floods back to her. I wanted to know if she was okay - no - I *needed* to know. I didn't want her to be left alone, dealing with it in silence, the same way I had once been.

The room eventually fills with bodies again, and Sloan shows the police out of his office. They look around suspiciously before the taller one's gaze lingers on me for the longest minute of my life. Dressed in reasonably decent looking suits, these are not your average police who would normally attend a rape scene. Walker shakes the hand of the taller one with warm familiarity, while Sloan speaks to the shorter of the two. Sensing I'm watching him, he leaves the conversation mid-sentence, walks over, and wraps me in his arms.

"Thank you for what you did this evening. I know how hard it must have been for you." He kisses the top of my head, and I recoil at his words. Words which are almost identical to what Stuart had said to me earlier.

I rotate gradually to see Thomas showing the officers out of the suite. Parker and Devlin are sat on one sofa, with Walker and Jake opposite. Stuart looks dejected, standing with his back to the kitchen. Sloan then turns to face them all head-on.

"I want you to find him. Now! I don't care what you do, or how you do it. You find that son of a bitch!" The anger in his voice leaves no room for fuck-ups. "I also want one of you with Charlie at all times. She doesn't go out alone; I don't give a shit how much she complains." Groans rise up from the room.

Who the hell is Charlie?

Catching my confused expression, he clarifies with a grin. "My sister, Charlotte."

No explanation needed there then.

There is also no doubt in my mind, that she *will* most likely fight against this enforced custody he's bestowing upon her without her prior knowledge.

"When these guys decide who has the good fortune of watching her," his gaze fixes on Jake briefly, then back to me, "you will get to meet her properly." His hand caresses my jaw tenderly, and I ease my body against him, as someone clears their throat.

Embarrassed by the audience, I eye the other guys, and their looks of intrigue are firmly back in place again. I admit, I too, am equally fascinated just observing *them*. I'm dying to know what I'm missing between all the expressive glances and looks of interest.

I turn back to Sloan. "I've already met her, remember?" Not an event I will forget in a hurry, nor do I want to re-enact it in the foreseeable future, either. I've never met such a spoilt, pain in the arse, in my entire life.

Sloan chuckles softly. "Yeah, she's a law unto herself. But I promise you, she will be nothing like she was at the function. Her bark really is worse than her bite. Trust me."

Trust.

That was such a big word between us right now, and not one I could personally put a lot of faith in.

The stress of the night lingers thickly, until Walker finally excuses them all, and we are left alone.

Under the running stream of hot water, I take a long glance down the length of my body. I have scrubbed at my skin irrepressibly, and now I'm red raw. The glass door slides open, and Sloan enters. His face is hard when he sees the state of my poor flesh. Although he doesn't say anything, I know he's displeased. But rather than reprimanding me, he just holds me close.

"One day, will you tell me?" I don't reply; I just let him comfort me until my skin prunes.

He tends to me attentively, before finally wrapping a towel around his waist. He carries me into the bedroom and sits me on the bed. Lying on his side, he draws me down to him; his front to my back. The tears silently stream from my eyes as I lie still against him. His fingers stroke continually over my hip, but his ability to soothe me is lost tonight.

I'm ashamed to say it, but I want to run from him. It's the only thing I know how to do efficiently.

"Please, don't," he whispers, knowing precisely what I'm thinking.

I press back into him, then slide my hand over his, bringing it across my stomach. "Just hold me."

"Always," he says, his velvet voice drifting further away. "I've got you. I've got you."

My eyes are heavy, and the darkness claims me not long after.

Chapter 13

"PLEASE, DON'T. NO, I don't want to! Please, please I'll be good, I promise. I don't want to. I don't want to!"

"Kara!"

A voice tugs at my subconscious, but the darkness has me bound and terrified. "Kara, wake up!" Again, it calls to me. Familiar, so familiar…

"It hurts. God, it hurts!"

"Baby, WAKE UP!"

My eyes shoot open to find Sloan hovering over me, shaking me.

Inexplicably subjected to some of the darker aspects of what I shoved aside forever, my body goes into survival mode, and I literally fly off the bed. I slip on my own feet and land hard on my behind. Sloan freezes in shock at my display of craziness, but his reaction is the least of my worries right now. I scramble backwards until my spine hits something solid, and I can go no further. I sit with my legs bent, my head resting on my knees. I'm panting like I've been denied the right to breathe. The t-shirt I can't even remember putting on, is damp with sweat and sticking to me. I pull at it, trying to feel the cool air on my skin.

"Baby, calm down! Talk to me, please," he implores, crouching down next to me, circling his hands over mine. He looks scared out of his mind. I rub the remnants of sleep from my eyes, and notice he is dressed for work.

"I can't!" My voice finds its purpose, even though my lungs feel like they failing and unable to draw in enough oxygen.

"Can't or won't?" His tone is soft and comforting, but I don't reply. He starts to speak again, but I don't hear a word of it. I wish I could tell him everything. Someday I would, but not today. I raise my head and look into his eyes. There is no emotion there whatsoever; his poker face is excellent, and I curse mine for not being better.

He breathes out with concern. "It's seven o'clock. I need to get to an early breakfast meeting. Are you going to work today?" His fingers drift to my jaw, massaging gently, trying to assist in reducing my stress levels.

"Yes," I sigh out. "But I don't have any clothes here. I need to go back home, if it's not too much trouble." I drag myself up, and he places his large hands on my shoulders, effectively stopping me. Giving me a chaste kiss, he grins. Rotating me around, he guides us to the walk-in wardrobe doors on the other side of the room and opens them.

Holy shit!

I tip-toe into the room - which is virtually a smaller scale, mirror image, of the one at his house - and lose all ability to formulate coherent thought and sentence. All of his clothes adorn the room perfectly, nothing seemingly out of place. His secondary display of fancy watches and cufflinks are clumped together at one side of the centre island. Upon closer inspection, his expensive things look to have been swiped aside haphazardly, and the other half of the island is bare - waiting to be filled no less. I stare in suspicion. He flashes me a smile I had last witnessed over champagne and cheesecake yesterday evening. It's the same one that can induce instant tingling from head to toe. I sigh, defeated. He gives me a pleased look and raises my hand to his mouth, kissing the back of it over and over.

Ignoring his attempt at dissuading my annoyance, I take a closer look at the clothes and notice that one side is female attire. I walk towards the rails and pull the hangers aside. Each garment carries an expensive price tag. Risking a look at a few of them, my limbs become a little unstable, and I'm ready to hit the floor. The few items I have looked at so far cost nearly a thousand pounds!

"Whose are these?" I squeak out.

Sloan confidently cocks his head to one side. "Yours."

"Mine? Huh! Well, at least now I know where my expensive, designer wardrobe is," I mutter rhetorically. Peeking at him, he actually looks contrite. *For once.*

I've never had anything bought for me, except for when I was younger and unable to provide for myself. I even refused Marie buying things for me after a couple of months in her care, and paid her for what I needed in manual labour. Now, I have nearly half a room filled with designer stuff that I neither asked for, nor wanted, from a man I'm basically just sharing my body with.

I squeeze my eyes shut, reverting back to my conversation with Marie. Yes, I'm sharing my body with him, but due to the reality and severity of my condition, I know he'll be the only one. He didn't need to make me say it last night, because physically, it's already a done deal.

Spying a stunning mac, I prise it from the rail. It's short and black, and I'm instantly in love with it. After giving it a thorough examination, I gently slide it back onto the rail and run my hand over the adjoining garments. I pace to the back of the generously sized room, my line of sight swayed by the shoe racks, which house shoes and boots in every heel height and colour imaginable.

He moves behind me and wraps his arms around my waist, securely linking his fingers together over my belly button. His chin rests on my shoulder, and his lips tickle my jaw. "Try them on. Anything you don't want, we can send back."

"Sloan, I'll still be trying all this stuff on when I'm fifty!" I pick up the Jimmy Choo peep-toe heels I had left behind. They are sat on their lonesome on a shelf above the rest. "When did you do all this?" I step back, trying to gather my wits.

"The other day. My sister likes to shop," he replies with amusement.

I gasp out a laugh. "Your sister went shopping for me?! Did she have an aneurysm and forget how despicably she treated me a few days ago? I appreciate I was just the lowly waitress, but still."

He hoists me up and drops me onto the empty side of the island. Impulsively, I tuck my legs around his waist. "She's coming by later. She can be a little overprotective at first, but trust me, you'll like her."

And there's that word again.

Trust.

Never have five letters held so much weight.

"Look, you get ready for work, and I'll get George to take you." I open my mouth to fight, but he places his finger on it. "No arguments. Gracious, remember?" He walks out of the room, but stops. "The only time I will ever tell you no, is when I think you're unreasonable, or unknowingly compromising or jeopardising yourself. Understand? I'll see you tonight." He doesn't look at me as he says it, and equally, he doesn't wait for my response, before he is out of sight.

Wrapped in a towel, I style my hair into a low ponytail and apply my makeup minimally. I'm not out to impress anyone, not even him.

My mind is still trying to decipher what on earth he actually sees in me, considering I'm forgettable in every sense of the word.

Back in my own personal boutique, I bite the inside of my cheek, not entirely sure what to wear. The choice is vast, and I'm truly lost and disorientated with it all. I wouldn't have any clue how to coordinate if my life depended on it.

Browsing through the garments, I finally decide on a charcoal coloured shift dress. It's fitted to perfection, and I turn in the mirror to judge myself. Wow, it really is amazing what something well fitted can do, I muse. Switching my attention to the shoes, I pick out a pair of navy, three-inch heels and slip my feet into them. To finish off the look, I choose a navy, short fitted jacket, and a belt of the same colour. I still in front of the mirror, not recognising the well-presented woman reflecting back at me.

The suite phone rings, and I answer it – it's the concierge advising my car is waiting downstairs. I brace myself for the lift, deciding I may need to make a long-overdue appointment with my old therapist to work through this fear, and hopefully, finally conquer it. I know it would please Sloan not to have to deal with my borderline neurosis each time I'm faced with one. Even though this was only meant to be one night, I know he wants it to last longer.

Truthfully, I do, too.

Counting from the moment I get on board to the moment I rush off, relief floods through me when the doors open in the lobby. I scurry across the gleaming tiles, my heels clicking on the marble. The security guard appraises me with a curt nod as I dash outside. I slide into the car and stare mindlessly out of the window, watching the busy streets of London flicker by, until it stops in front of my building. I thank Sloan's driver, and quickly march inside.

Flinging my bag under the desk, I frown when my eyes settle upon the piles of papers that are waiting innocuously for me. At least the distraction of work will stop me from thinking about the events of this morning, and even more frightening, those of last night. I can't figure out what I find more disturbing; the fact there are some serious safety issues at his hotel, or the fact his friends seem to see through me the same way he does. The only reassuring event that arose yesterday was his honesty, when he told me there would be no one but him, before claiming me on his living room floor – repeatedly.

Acknowledging that crucial little fact, which has crept back inside my head every so often throughout the morning, a part of me feels at peace with the decision I've settled on regarding him.

The sound of the electronic door release catches my attention. I have spent the morning shifting through overdue invoices, outstanding correspondence, and generally putting my files back in order. *Again.* I finally risk a glance at the clock, as the front door closes and locks itself; it's one thirty, and I haven't even had a cup of tea yet.

"Oh, my!" I raise my head to find Sophie approaching the side of my desk, looking me up and down with approval. "Do tell!"

"Who the hell let you in here?" I ask playfully.

"The sexy beast on the floor below. A little eyelash fluttering goes a long way!" she all but sings to me.

The sexy beast in question is a sole practitioner accountant. Marie uses him to balance the books and make Her Majesty's Inland Revenue happy. I, on the other hand, never usually see him, but Soph never fails to lock him down like a heat-seeking missile whenever she stops by impromptu.

"So, come on, what gives?"

I give her a perplexed look, wondering what she's leaning towards, then realise I'm not wearing my usual cheap crap attire. I shrug my shoulders, pretending I have no idea what she's talking about. She isn't convinced, and I wouldn't be either. She reads me perfectly and obviously decides not to go there.

"Hey," I begin, trying to appear normal, and unaffected by the latest turn of events in my usually uneventful life. But quite frankly, I can't deviate my thoughts beyond them at the moment. "Want to grab some lunch together?"

"Sorry, I can't. I have a meeting with the head of the department and the *arsehole* shortly. I just needed to get out of the office, so I used my lunch hour to come and see you. You know, clear my head before my three o'clock bollocking!" She turns to leave, but stops and looks back. "You look really good, Kara. It's nice to see you happy at last." She smiles broadly, and I reciprocate the gesture with a thank you as she leaves.

I pick up my bag and rummage around inside for my mobile. I haven't checked it since early last night, before all of Sloan's drama invaded my life like a wrecking ball. I unlock it, and there are a few messages from Sam telling me the usual - that she won't be home; a couple from Sloan, asking what time I want his driver to pick me up; and lastly, one from my father. I open it to see what he has to say for himself today.

It's a choice I promptly regret.

Call me, sweets. I need that goddamn fucking money! Call me, now!

I study the short message at length, re-reading it again and again. I guess a part of me hopes that the more I look at it, it might miraculously change. I'm on the verge of calling, in the hope my mum will answer – it's been a while since I have spoken to her - but contemplate if it's really a wise decision. I blow out a shaky breath and prepare to dial, when the screen flashes up with a private number.

"Hello?" I ask tentatively.

"Hi, is this Kara Petersen?" The voice is female and cheery. I'm half inclined to hang up, since I have more pressing matters at hand, quite literally. I'm in no mood to chat about upgrading my current phone contract, or investing in new double glazing, and I doubt very much they can put a conservatory on a fifth-floor flat.

"Yes, speaking," I respond firmly. I don't like surprises, and I definitely don't appreciate unknown or private numbers calling my very private, unknown, number.

"Oh, hi! Sorry, I shouldn't have just called you. I'm Charlie Emerson, Sloan's sister."

Ah ha, the bitch!

How the hell did she get my number?

I shake my head. I'm seriously going to kill him! Well, maybe not quite, he's too damn beautiful and sexy to cause bodily harm to, but he could have at least warned me. Given me some advance notice he had given it to her. She was meant to be coming to the hotel later today, not calling me for…*why is she calling me?*

"Erm, hi. Sorry, how did you get my number?" I try not to sound too discourteous and vexed, but she really is the last person I want to speak to.

"Walker gave it to me," she says, very matter of fact.

"Right..." I guess I'm not committing GBH, after all, tonight. But how did Walker get my number? I only met him last night…

I roll my eyes, feeling my control slipping. This shit is getting weirder and weirder by the minute. My life has done a full circle in the space of seven days. Sloan's giving out my number left and right, and I still need to find out how *he* had gotten hold of it in the first place.

"Sorry, I don't want to be rude," I'm such a liar, "but I am just going out for lunch. Can we talk another time, you know, maybe when you see Sloan later?" My brain starts to work overtime; I'll have to make up a really good excuse not to be there tonight.

"Actually, I wanted to talk to you." She's all niceness and light now. Not only rude, but apparently, she has insufferable memory loss, too. "I'm outside your building, come down now! I'm starving!" She giggles, then the line goes dead.

My God, is nothing sacred anymore? First, my number, and now she's outside the bloody office, commandeering my one and only lunch hour! I don't think she appreciates that not all of us have the luxury of being able to swan around all day and still have a healthy bank balance to show for it. Some of us only get that single hour in the middle of the day to savour, and she has just claimed mine!

I grab my things and run into the toilets. Sitting my bag on the sink, I do a quick check of my appearance. My face and hair are acceptable, *I think*. I can't guarantee they're up to Miss Emerson's standards, but unfortunately, they will have to do, and she will have to tolerate it. I quickly smooth my clothes, but this gives me little comfort. She can't possibly make any derogatory comment regarding them considering she had bought them.

Feeling both anxious and weary, I make my way down the stairs for my lunch date with doom. Opening the main door, I halt in my tracks at the sight before me. Gone is the made up to the nines, strawberry blonde; in her place, is a girl who looks remarkably young, wearing skinny jeans, ballet flats, and a longline top. Her jacket nests in the crook of her arm along with her bag. I sigh. Even I have to admit, she has good taste. It must be a genetic trait; I mentally acknowledge and grin to myself.

"Hi," I greet her as brightly as I can muster. She inspects me up and down, boldly appraising me, and then she drags me into a quick hug. I stiffen and force myself to relax. Physically, I have nothing to fear from this girl, but it seems invasion of privacy and personal space is hereditary, and unheard of to her, too.

She inches back a few feet, full-on admiring my appearance. I blush a little under the scrutiny of the passers-by who are gaping at us, and the spectacle she is causing.

"Oh, I knew you would look good in these! I'm so jealous! I looked absolutely ridiculous when I tried them on, but Sloan told me to buy the best and – wow - the woman really does make the clothes!" she gushes at me. My mouth drops open in shock that she has just publicly appraised me.

She folds her arm over mine and trots us towards a waiting car. The dull prickle spreads over my arm and down my spine. The only reassurance I have is that we will be in the car within minutes, and her skin will no longer be in contact with mine.

I shuffle in the seat, dreading what will undoubtedly be an excruciating lunch, with a woman who detested me on sight a little over a week ago. The driver of the car throws his head back, and Walker gives me a huge Cheshire cat grin, while Jake - who is sitting next to him – smiles, albeit a little more subdued.

"Hi, Kara. Sorry about this one," Jake says, jerking his thumb to Charlie. "She just wouldn't shut up until Walker gave her your number." He looks at me pitifully, and I roll my eyes; she probably didn't give them much of a choice.

"Oh, stop it! You'd think grown men have the inability to say no, wouldn't you? Anyone would think I put a gun to his head, for crying out loud!"

The car begins to move, and I settle in as Charlie demonstrates the ability to talk the hind legs off a horse.

"…I mean, it's bad enough that I have Jake following me around all day. I, at least need someone to share the pain with, right?" She stares pointedly at me, nodding her head frantically for my support. "But secretly, I like that he does," she whispers, leaning into me.

"Uh-huh," I agree, not knowing whether to laugh or cry, while praying to God to get me out of here.

The restaurant she has booked for lunch is, without a doubt, going to cost me a full days' pay. I try to fight her, but Charlie refuses, insisting her brother can afford it, and that he would have premature heart failure if we paid. She giggles, but I feel sick just thinking about it. She flashes the same smile that Sloan does, and I realise I will never be able to stand up to either of them - however long they may be present in my life.

I study the menu, and my eyes physically hurt when I see the starter prices alone – it's a good job Sloan's going to be paying after all. She insists I must order two starters and a main, since the plates are always tiny. After giving the waiter our preferred choices, I glance around the room, and note Jake and Walker are sat ordering lunch on the opposite side. Walker gives us a little wave, and I quickly continue my perusal of the other patrons. They are all dressed impeccably, and I can't help but compare what I'm wearing; I feel like I belong here, dressed like this.

"So, I want to say I'm sorry, you know, for how I spoke to you last week." Charlie's face turns serious, and I, in turn, become ridged. I hope Sloan hasn't forced her to apologise.

"Did he tell you to say sorry?" I utter, before I even realise what I've said. I reach for my glass; my throat is scratchy and dry, and feels like it's about to close up.

"No. Well, yeah, sorry. I guess I just thought you were only interested in his money. I was really annoyed when he sent me shopping for all that stuff last Wednesday…"

She titters on, but my eyes widen at her confession. I gulp down another mouthful of water. He sent her shopping before I'd even agreed to *try* with him? He's not in his right mind!

"I mean, I love to shop, who doesn't, but shopping for someone that might only be around for a week? *That*, I don't like."

"*A week*?" I pry, attempting to refocus myself.

"Yeah. He never sees anyone longer than a week. Well, what I actually mean is, he dates the same woman a few times, mostly within the same week, and then he moves on. He treats them well, but he doesn't keep them. Never has, well except… Anyway, with you, I can't figure him out."

Well, how on earth do you respond to that?!

I am saved the effort of fabricating my reply when our food arrives at the table. She's right; the portions are tiny. She gives me a knowing smile, and I laugh out loud. If I'm to be one hundred per cent honest, it feels great to be out with someone my own age who is carefree, and who doesn't know all about my calamitous life.

An hour later, we finish lunch and Charlie insists she has me driven back. I refuse the offer; my own two feet will get me there quicker than driving through lunchtime traffic. I thank her, and she makes me promise to call her and arrange to meet up again. I drop Marie a text, letting her know I'll be a little late back. She responds immediately, telling me not to rush.

I quickly walk back to the office and fish my security card from my bag, turning it inside my palm. The office building comes into view, and I stop abruptly in the middle of the street. I shrink back against the wall and walk slowly backwards. The larger of Sam's latest male friends is idling suspiciously at the entrance. I can't remember which one he is, but that fact is irrelevant. It's more than coincidence he's here. My heart starts to beat a little faster, and my feet instantly move. I duck into the alleyway that houses the bins before he notices me. I fumble for my phone and hit Sloan's number with ferocity. He picks up on the second ring.

"Hey, baby. Did you have a nice lunch with my sister?" Ah, shit, he sounds so happy. How do I tell him who's currently loitering with intent outside the building without causing him to panic?

"Actually, I did. You were right by the way; she is really nice."

"Good. I want you to like her. Walker has already given me grief about the extent she lowered herself to to obtain your number," he laughs.

Pot, kettle and bloody black! But it's unimportant right now.

"Look, I don't want you to be alarmed, but one of those men is at the front of my work building. You know, one of those guys that was in my flat with Sam?" His sharp intake of breath indicates that he does remember our conversation, and I thank my lucky stars he is diligent in that respect.

"Baby, where are you?" His tone is hard and cold, leaving no room for ambivalence.

"I'm in an alleyway at the side of the building. I don't think he saw me."

"Good. Stay where you are. I'll have someone come and get you."

"Sloan, seriously, I need to get back to work!"

"No, you need to stay where you are! Call your boss now, tell them you were followed, and you're going home." He's verging on shouting, and I can clearly picture him becoming frustrated on the other end due to my response.

"No! I will not lie to her!" I whisper-shout back at him, before crouching back down. I'm sabotaging myself the longer this call goes on, because I know my pitch will get higher and higher, until we are screaming at each other.

"Kara, it's not a lie! Now, please, amuse me!" I don't reply, and so he continues. "Okay, I wasn't going to tell you this, but Emily was discharged from the hospital last night. Two hours later, she was re-admitted with her wrists wide open. Fortunately, they managed to save her. I will not risk you! Not now, not ever! So, please, call your boss and wait for my guy to arrive. You do whatever it takes to stay safe."

I slouch back against the wall to support myself. "Oh, my God! That poor girl." My eyes water just thinking about her, and what relevance it has on my sad situation. My sobs shake my body and resound quietly, echoing in the deserted alleyway.

"Shush, it's okay, baby. Just hold tight, Walker's on his way for you. Please, just stay hidden and alert, if anything happens to you..."

"Okay," I say in defeat and hang up.

I quickly call Marie and tell her I have a problem with Sam to contend with. I hate lying to her when she has been so good to me. She tells me not to worry and to let her know what happens. I end the call and lean my head back on the wall. Curling myself up behind the bin, I wait for my rescuer to arrive, and silently pray I'm not found in the meantime.

Checking my watch for the hundredth time, a car screeches to a halt, and the driver's door is thrown wide open. I crane my head further around the industrial-sized bin concealing me, and my shoulders drop in relief, observing Walker take long, determined strides down the alley. I shuffle away slightly as he reaches for me. I don't want him to touch me, but he ignores the way I shrink back and wraps his arm around my shoulders. The usual awareness that accompanies contact is quickly pushed aside, as my eyes catch sight of the gun holstered under his jacket.

He ushers me into the car, and I glance at the building entrance, just in time for my eyes to lock with those of the unwanted visitor. The large man's brows arch, and he looks pissed. Walker slams the door behind me and jogs to the other side. He climbs in and engages the locks. He mutters something as the other guy starts moving towards us with purpose. Pressing on the clutch and accelerator, the car speeds out into traffic.

I ease back into the seat and close my eyes. I just want to disappear, and forget all the shit that makes up my miserable half-life.

Chapter 14

WALKER HOLDS THE door open for me to exit the car. My body is irrefutably heavy getting out. Entering the building, I have no idea where I'm going. My eyes scan over the internal structure with admiration; steel and glass, sleek and modern. It's a complete contrast to the hotel, but still screams wealth and power. Walker strides in front of me confidently. He doesn't bother to stop at the security desk, and something tells me no one would ever expect him to.

I follow him dutifully to the lifts, and like clockwork, trepidation comes back with a vengeance. He gives me a look of concern, followed swiftly by sympathy. I roll my eyes infuriated. It's abundantly clear that Sloan has imparted my fear of confined spaces, and his small smile verifies this as we enter. Counting in my head, the lift commences to take us up to the fiftieth floor. I keep my eyes shut, and my back pressed tight against the chrome rail the entire time. The second the doors open, I hotfoot it out of the box.

My anxiety of the lift is replaced by my anxiety of Sloan's work environment. The first thing I'm confronted with is beautiful oak furniture, and even more glass, this time, etched with *Emerson & Foster*. I spin around to look at Walker, who seems completely unfazed. But, then again, he wouldn't be, he works for Sloan. In what capacity, I'm still not too sure given he is carrying. I put it away, along with all the rest of the unanswered questions I still need to corner Sloan on at some point in the foreseeable future.

A well-dressed woman in her early fifties is sat at the reception desk. The brass name plaque, Gloria Truman, glints under the lights. She greets us warmly and tells us to go straight through. Walker winks and guides us towards some large, highly polished, double doors at the end of the small corridor.

One of the doors swings open, and Sloan appears. Striding with vigour, his expression is pained, but lifts a little when he sees I'm still in one piece. He ignores everyone else present, and his hands come up to my cheeks, cradling my head affectionately. He stares deep into my eyes, examining them for God knows what. He finally breaks the connection, and I turn away. I can see the inquisitive look on his receptionist's face, whereas Walker, on the other hand, doesn't seem to care either way.

"She was where you said she'd be," Walker tells him. "He saw her get in the car, though." He then walks away.

Sloan grips my hand and guides me into the room he had emerged from. He closes the door and locks it with an air of finality. I gawk in awe as soon as I enter. It's reminiscent of his penthouse suite. Full, glass walls, line one side of the office. His desk is centred in the middle, with thick files stacked on either side and covered in what appears to be unfinished work.

"What is it you actually do?" I mumble, scrunching my nose up slightly, absorbing the scene of organised chaos. "And what is your obsession with glass?"

His warm breath tickles the back of my neck. Large, warm hands snake up the sides of my waist possessively. "God, I was so worried about you. I cancelled all my meetings for the rest of the day. I couldn't concentrate until I knew you were safe..." His soft lips move down the column of my neck. "Away from *him*."

"You didn't have to do that," I tell him, falling deeper under his spell.

His arms curve their way around my stomach and hips. He hitches my dress up my thighs, and I arch my back to him. The size of his erection against my behind encourages my pelvis to rotate, pressing as far back as his hardness will allow. I need more of him. *All of him.* He growls low in this throat. The sound is guttural and filled with want, making me wet and compliant. He drops the material back down and lifts me with only his arm around my waist.

Manoeuvring us over to his desk, I place my hands down between the papers and documents strewn over the top. Cool air skims my skin, and my dress is hiked up over my hips, until I'm practically naked from the waist down. In one swift move, my knickers are pooled at my feet. I lean further forward, lifting my behind up invitingly, still unsure of what I'm actually doing. He exhales, satisfied with my position. The sound of metal and fabric being adjusted fills the room, and my legs part wider the instant his hand pats my thigh. Willingly, I oblige. I want this; I need this.

"How do you feel?"

"A little sore, but not as much as I thought."

My fingertips claw at the papers, and the sound of foil being torn open fills the air. His bulbous tip teases my opening. Positioning himself behind me, one hand is firmly holding my lower abdomen, the other braces my shoulder. Seconds later, he buries himself inside, sliding through my wetness effortlessly. The sensation is beyond words; the slow burn indescribable.

Gradually building up his speed, moving in and out of me with reverence, I press my hands onto the wood to support myself. With each thrust, the desk edge hits my pubic bone. It should be painful, but it isn't, because I'm unable to think of anything, except the man behind me, claiming me as his own, yet again. The fire inside me is soaring out of control, and my skin perspires with each pelvic roll. My breathing is erratic and all over the place. Deep down, I feel the start of the end devouring me. I push back against him, meeting him each time he plunges back inside. My head lulls forward, until it lands on the desk. Sloan starts to move faster, slamming into my body harder and deeper. I pant out, splaying my fingers wide on the desktop, my face millimetres from the wood. My body starts to shudder, and finally, I'm overcome with euphoria.

"Sloan, don't stop!"

He moans from behind and jerks inside me. I feel his length pulsate and engorge, ploughing into me a few more times before he stills and groans out his release. He stays sheathed inside my soft walls as our combined breathing slows down. I barely register his fingers searching for my clit until he begins to rub circles leisurely over my hardened nub. I toss my head back with abandon, not knowing how I'm going to control myself if I climax again. His weight bears down on my back, and his fingers speed up. The tell-tale signs of my body beginning to prepare itself for pleasure again tingle inside my core. I raise my head and moan out his name, rejoicing in the sensation ripping through me. It creeps deep into every crevice and cell of my being, leaving me boneless and breathless. He never shifts from me, remaining as hard as steel, while I let go.

I cross my arms over the desk and rest my head on them, coaxing myself back down to earth. I feel his emptiness as he starts to withdraw from me. I don't have the energy to pull my dress back down after that. Beyond ashamed, I remain in my current position - bent over his desk, with my bare behind exposed.

I draw back slightly when cold, wet fabric cleans me with gentle proficiency. I clench the instant it grazes across the scar on my inner thigh. He breathes in quickly, moving the flannel across the whitened wound again. Tilting my head, my eyes met his. They are now filled with anger. I close mine, not wanting to get into this with him. I turn, and he pulls my dress down, adjusting and smoothing the fabric against my thighs, making me look presentable again.

Looking down, he's still hard and covered. His trousers are open at the fly, and his shirt is all over. He picks up a handful of tissues from the box on his desk and wraps the used condom in them, and strides over to a small private bathroom. I listen in a foggy haze, as he discards the tissues, and the water starts to run and then shuts off.

Returning, he approaches me with a look of apprehension. I offer him a small smile, and he tucks me against him, carrying me the length of the room towards a leather sofa in the far corner. He sits down with me in his lap. I wiggle against him, placing my head on his shoulder. He jerks to life under the friction, but my eyes are already closing of their own accord.

"Kara?" His tone is calming; deep, rich, and hypnotic. My tired eyes flutter open to find his beautiful, masculine features primed with a seductive smile.

"Hmm?" I can't verbalise any further in my current post-orgasmic bliss. He cups my cheeks and kisses the tip of my nose.

"Are you on contraception?"

"Hmm, hmm."

"Good to know."

I rest against him, falling into a welcome sleep. His words ramble around my head until my brain re-engages, and I snap back to reality.

"Sloan, my aunt put me on it years ago. She didn't do it to give me free rein, it was a *just in case* precaution. I've never stopped taking it – *just in case.* I was also checked eight years ago, after… Well, I'm clean. I've had further checks since, and they all came back fine. I haven't had any sexual partners, except you, but if you want me to get tested again, I will." I stare at him, wondering what he's thinking. Although I have never actually had sex with anyone but him in the last eight years, he has to agree. Irrespective of the fact I have been tested many times over the years - twice a year, every year, to be precise - my past still dictates everything I do, and this situation is no exception in my eyes.

"Baby, I'm glad, but I don't need you to get checked again. I trust you. You will be happy to know that I'm also clean." His arms surround me. "I don't want anything between us ever again. I want to be able to feel you when I slide inside you. I want to feel your body contract around mine when you come." My skin flushes, and I melt further into him.

My body is sated, and my eyes flutter sleepily. The impending prospect of rest is too great to ignore, and the darkness beckons me to join it. I drift away, listening to his steady, strong heartbeat against my cheek, with a new realisation in my heart.

I wake up with my face pressed into the supple, soft leather. Looking around drowsily, I'm still in Sloan's office, still on the sofa, which is the last place I remember. Except, the office is now empty, and I'm very much alone. Stretching with gratification, I quickly glance around, until my eyes catch where my knickers lay ominously on a small filing cabinet. I scarper to them and promptly slip them back on.

Wondering what to do with myself, I move around his desk. Dragging my fingertip over the wood, I slide into his large leather chair and stretch my arms flat over the top. I lift my head towards the door as low voices speak outside. It then opens, and the man himself strides in, confident as ever. He pins me with an arrogant and cocky, self-assured grin.

God, would I ever tire of looking at him? Or wanting him, as a matter of fact?

"You look good at my desk, baby, but not as good as you do on it." One eyebrow lifts, and he grins boyishly at me.

My heart skips a beat at my beautiful Adonis. How on earth can this man want to be with broken, damaged, little old me? I clear my head quickly. I don't need my brain conjuring up a million and one different reasons to end this through foolishness or insecurity.

"Actually, I wasn't on it, I was over it," I clarify, rounding the desk and perching myself on the front.

"True, but that can be rectified," he declares, with a wicked spark in his eyes, prising my legs as far apart as my dress will allow.

"Hmm," I murmur seductively. I fear I won't be leaving his office anytime soon if he gets his way. "How long was I asleep for?" I query, deliberately changing the subject. We need something more than sex to define this relationship, or otherwise, it will be a hopeless cause.

"A few hours. Don't worry, Gloria was under strict instruction not to let anyone in here, except me. You were perfectly safe." His arms creep me around me. "Hungry?"

Feeling ready to keel over, I reply in the affirmative. I haven't eaten since lunch, and that couldn't exactly be called a meal, regardless of the fact that I had two starters *and* a main.

"Come on, I'm leaving early. Let's grab something to eat, go home, and then make love until the early hours. Sound good?" I pause with his hand on my back. My skin flash boils under his statement. I would love to feel him against me, and inside me, for hours. I would also like to sleep in my own bed tonight. But ultimately, I'd like to know why I can't stop wanting him so badly, that my body physically aches for him and makes me agree to anything he suggests.

"Sloan, don't you think this is moving a little too fast? I mean, technically, we've only been seeing each other for a few days. I haven't slept in my own bed for three nights now."

"No, I think this speed is perfectly acceptable, Kara."

He directs me towards the lifts, and Gloria looks on, bestowing a genuine smile at me. A young woman is standing next to her now, and she is glowering at me in disgust. Sloan bids them goodnight, and the woman's scowl has now morphed into a hundred-watt smile - just for him. I roll my eyes at her blatant display of immaturity and turn away.

I shift my weight between my feet anxiously in the centre of the lift. The doors close, and Sloan pulls me the few feet to him, devouring my mouth as we descend. Our limbs tangle together; our lips fuse as one. I'm too lost in him to think about my usual fears. His passion transfers to me and courses through my veins powerfully. I lean deeper into him and allow him to take what he wants because I know I'll forever be putty in his hands. Minutes later, the doors open, and he escorts me out, still patting down my clothes to ensure I look presentable to the masses.

"At least now I know how to get you to relax in lifts." He raises his brows suggestively and smiles.

Outside, the car is waiting, and we climb in, resuming what we halted only minutes earlier.

Chapter 15

WE PULL UP outside a small, upmarket bistro. It appears relatively secluded and private. Sloan gently takes my hand in his, as I peruse the menu affixed to the pillar at the front of the establishment. He opens the door, and my senses are immediately assaulted by the smell of fresh herbs, cheese, and pasta.

Heavenly.

"Sloan! What the hell? Where have you been?" A guy dressed in black and white chef's overalls bounds towards us. He tackles Sloan and captures him in a man hug. I smile at the closeness of their greeting. There's no doubt they know each other very well.

"I'm good, really good. I would've come by sooner, but you know the business doesn't run itself." Sloan sits and introduces me. "Kara, this is Ethan. He used to be my head chef at the hotel, before deciding I wasn't good enough to work for any more!"

"Yeah, whatever, Foster!" Ethan laughs out.

"Hi, it's a pleasure to meet you." I hold out my hand, bracing myself for the burn.

Ethan smiles, but there is confusion in his eyes. Taking my hand, he kisses my knuckles. "No, the pleasure's all mine." Ethan's eyes square back on Sloan, looking at him inquisitively. Sloan grins and passes me a menu.

"So, what's good here?" I ask, scanning the mains.

"Everything!" Ethan exclaims, arms wide and exaggerated. I giggle softly at his enthusiasm.

Sloan orders *the usual*, and I opt for the cannelloni. Ethan returns a few minutes later with a bottle of wine and a young waiter to serve us. He watches us curiously for a long moment, then retreats back into his kitchen.

I'm dying to ask what's so strange, but I'm too frightened to, until I remember Charlie's ramblings earlier today. *A week. Sloan never sees anyone longer than a week.*

I admire him discreetly, sipping his wine. His eyes sweep over the dessert menu, and then back to me with a scandalous grin. Detecting he is being watched, he quickly replaces it with a vacant expression.

"Dessert?" I query.

"Already had it." He grins lazily at me. I nod, feeling the blush cover my face and spread down my neck.

"Is it true you don't see anyone for longer than a week?" I ask, flustered, a little too blunt, and very untactfully.

I'd like to say I'm just curious, but I know the real cause behind my questioning. Secretly, I'm concerned that it could mean my time is up in a few days. This is ridiculous. A few days ago, *he* was just going to be a one-night stand, now *I* am worried that I may not have him for longer than a week.

"Ah, my beloved sister has never been able to keep her mouth shut."

"Sorry, it's not my place to ask. Please forget about it."

Resigned, I divert my eyes to the handful of diners quietly conversing with each other. I risk a little look back at him, his jaw is tense, and the vein in his neck is taut and protruding. He finally opens his mouth to speak, but the young waiter returns with a plate of bread rolls. Not wanting to dissect Charlie's revelation with him any further, I hastily snatch a roll and pull it apart. It's melt in the mouth good. If these are anything to go by, I expect the food will be fantastic.

Two hours later, a couple of bottles of wine and some inane small talk - where we both avoided questions that revolved around our pasts, and he is very good at changing the subject whenever the conversation flowed to his exes - we are outside, waiting for the car to arrive. Ethan waits with us, conversing quietly with Sloan.

"You'll have to come by more often, and ensure you bring the lovely Kara with you." I feel my face flush deep red when Ethan kisses the back of my hand again. Sloan's features tighten slightly, and I pull back quickly, trying not to appear too rude. Sloan shakes his friend's hand and grunts his goodbye, as the car stops in front of us. Silence envelops the small space as we travel back to the hotel.

"Sloan, I need to go home tonight," I tell him, watching the lights of the city pass by.

"Why? You have everything you need at the hotel and my house."

"Just…because!" Because I haven't been home for days, because my clothes are there, because it is my home. *Because I'm not good enough for you.* My true sentiments race through my brain with the many reasons I could convey, but I know none of them will ever be good enough for him to change his mind.

"It's not safe there, Kara." His fingers dig into my hand that he is gripping to the point of cutting off my circulation. I turn to him, the muscles in his neck contract wildly, his jaw is stiff, and I fear if he clenches it any longer, it might shatter into pieces.

"It's my home! We've only known each other a week, and you're already acting as though you own me," I spit out, and snatch back my hand. Folding my arms over my stomach angrily, I turn to the window and blow out a silent breath.

I hate this.

I hate that men thought they could control everything - including me.

I had lived this way once, and I'll be damned if I allow it to happen again. Unlike before, how I lived now was of my choosing. I made my decisions, and if they were wrong, it was on my head, and I would live with the consequences.

"Fine!" he hisses out. He presses a button and the privacy glass slides down. "George, we need to take Ms Petersen home, if you don't mind."

So, when he's pissed off or not getting his own way, I'm *Ms Petersen.*

"Yes, sir," George replies instantly, and the glass slides back up.

"*Ms Petersen?*" I emphasise, fixing my eyes on his with an unwavering determination that has nothing to do with being confident. His face is blank, and he just shrugs his shoulders.

Fine, he can have it his way!

Right now, he is officially my one-night stand. *Don't call me, I'll call you.* Two can play this fucking game! Time and time again, I'd already proven to myself I didn't need anyone to hold me up in life, and I wasn't about to start bucking that trend.

The car draws to a stop outside my building, and relief floods through me. The atmosphere has been suffocating and intense since I announced I wanted to go home. Sloan has neither spoken, nor acknowledged my presence at all. Whilst the separation feels painful in a way that constricts sharply in my chest, I'm unsure whether it is my heart breaking, or the anger that is quickly gathering prominence.

Still, I will not allow myself to get caught up in his silly games. He has subtly shown his true colours a few times, and I'm not, under any circumstances whatsoever, going to become this man's plaything. I will not be bossed around, told what to do, or talked to like I'm a child. I should have known the moment he showed an interest in me that was otherworldly in my eyes. I should have known when he ordered me to lie to Marie. And I definitely should have known the instant he showered me with expensive things that cost more than I earned in months. I was too blinded by it all - by him.

I should have known better.

Sadly, I have failed myself in that regard.

Although I promised I wouldn't run, does he really expect me to stick around and follow his every command? I know next to nothing about him, and he isn't exactly forthcoming with information. Even at dinner, he avoided the questions of his occupation and fidelity like the plague.

I open the door before George is even out of his seat. I try to avoid looking back as I slam it shut, and do what may possibly be classed as the walk of shame, albeit three days late, into the communal entrance. I pause at the main door, opening it wide enough to ensure I will have to turn around to close it. Why I'm doing this to myself, I have no idea. I'm only going to hurt myself in the long run. Sloan's window is still raised, and I can't see him due to the dark tinting.

I hold my head high in defiance. Pretending I was fine has become second nature in my life. I learnt how to hide the truth and become invisible incredibly well. I had learnt it the first time when I was barely just a teenager. When you grow up in a house with a man like my father, you had to. It was the only means of escape. Not physically, just mentally and emotionally.

I kick off my shoes and scale the stairs quickly. I count the flights on my way up, each one taking me towards the safety of home. I let out the breath lodged in my throat and turn my key in the door. Inside, I lock all the bolts that have magically appeared over the last few days since I've not been here. Three guesses who has commissioned those in my absence.

Without turning the lights on, I tiptoe to the window. I roll my eyes, realising I'm in stealth mode for no apparent reason. Looking down to the street, the limo is still parked in the same spot it had been a few minutes ago. Standing in the silence and darkness, I stare idly at the car. Why hasn't he already left? What is he expecting from me? That I will run back out there and wrap myself around him? No, I need space from him. I need to regroup and move on.

Alone.

Sighing in defeat, I admit I shall fail this task. Even my thoughts lack faith and conviction.

I raise my finger to my lip and trace it, reminiscing at his touch. The way his lips caress mine and his unique taste. My hand drifts down my neck, remembering the way he claimed me in his bed and on his living room floor. I squeeze my eyes shut, trying to push out the unbridled, but definitely not unwanted visions. Tonight, I know sleep will elude me. No matter what I do from now on, he'll always be with me. He has invaded my head both consciously and subconsciously. He has taken over completely, leaving me afraid for my own mentality.

Glancing at the clock on the coffee table, he has been sat there for over thirty minutes now. I'm about to turn, when I notice the taillights illuminate, and finally drives away. I wait and watch as the car becomes nothing but red spots in the distance.

Climbing into bed, the flat is abnormally quiet. After three days of sleeping alongside Sloan, I appreciate it will be hard to readjust to sleeping alone again. As much as I want to live my life the way I please, a part of me – a really big part of me - wants him to be consistent within it.

Proving I really am in big trouble when it comes to Sloan Foster.

"Shush! You might wake her!" Sam's drunken voice is loud in the silence of the flat, waking me with a jolt.

"I thought you said she hasn't been here for days?"

"She hasn't, but you never know. Come on, hurry up already!"

The sound of a zip accompanies the voices, quickly followed by the sound of furniture scraping.

"Oh, yeah, I'm gonna fuck the shit out of you until you can't walk!" The unidentified male shouts out.

The sound of Sam's giggling, and heavy footsteps passing outside my bedroom, are too much. I turn the clock around – it's three thirty in the morning. I get up, creep to my door and wedge the chair from my dresser against it.

Sam's door slams hard, and minutes later, her squeals and moans resound so loudly, I fear the neighbours might even wake up. I flop back down and yank the pillow over my head, pummelling my fist against the mattress in frustration.

In the two years we have lived together, we respected each other not to bring any man back home to spend the night. Now, it seems that rule is genuinely null and void. I stare aimlessly and wide-eyed at the ceiling, as they go at it for hours and hours.

A lone tear flees me when I drift back to my bedroom in Manchester. The late-night parties, the couples in the adjacent rooms, and the bleary-eyed school mornings that raised alarm bells with my teachers. Sam was on a dangerous path. She was becoming what we both swore we never would - she was becoming our parents.

The sharp, shrill, electronic beep of the alarm rings out constantly. I slam my arm over the wretched device to turn it off. The last time I looked, it had been nearly five o'clock. Somewhere between then and now, I have miraculously managed to sleep for a few hours. I rise wearily, experiencing more fatigue now than I had last night. The flat is deathly quiet, and I pray she has sent her loud, loquacious, playmate home already.

I quickly shower and dress. Tying my damp hair into a ponytail, I don't bother applying any makeup. It would take a lot more than concealer to purge myself of these dark circles this morning.

Ready to leave, I assess myself in the mirror; the skirt and blouse I am wearing are in great need of throwing out, and my shoes need re-heeling. I stare lovingly at the clothes I wore last night. I make a mental note to have them dry cleaned when I got paid at the end of the month. It would be expensive, but they're worth it. I pick them up and fold them with care, storing them in the bottom of my wardrobe. They are my reminder of Sloan. It's dangerous to torture myself in such a way, but I have to keep something tangible to touch; to remember he wasn't just a dream I had fabricated in the obscure recesses of my damaged and disorderly mind.

Chapter 16

WELL, I'VE ACTUALLY done it.

I've survived almost a full morning without any drama or controversy.

I arrived at work early this morning, my guilty speech ready and waiting to be aired. I stopped by Marie's office first thing to beg, grovel, and apologise profusely about yesterday. I omitted the absolute truth of nearly being accosted by Sam's latest squeeze, and instead, laid all the blame at her door. Whilst I wasn't exactly lying - it is Sam's fault he's hanging around - it still made me feel shitty. Marie did the usual, telling me that sooner or later I would need to have a serious heart to heart with her. I didn't counter, we both knew that wasn't going to happen. Historically, Sam would always let her problems fester until they came to a head, and then we had no choice but to deal with them. A leopard doesn't change its spots.

I sit staring out of the window, absorbed in the personal hell I'm currently being dragged into. I've kept my head down all morning and accomplished more than I've achieved in days. Admittedly, this is also linked to the fact I need to force my brain around something other than last night. Not to mention a man who has some insane notion of compassion within relationships.

Marie had left earlier for a meeting with a potential client, and that meant I was now alone, with nothing except an empty desk, an uninspiring silence, and my own head for company.

Stretching my legs out, I slip off my heels and pace the room. Ever since Sloan left last night, he's all I have thought about. Needless to say, he hasn't called me, and I haven't made a move to call him. As much as I desperately want to, I'm not that kind of girl. Or at least I wasn't, until he coaxed her out of my self-inflicted darkness and into his light.

I won't pretend; I'm hurting from this isolation.

I know he's pissed, but he's asking for commitment I'm not sure I can give him. Apart from my father, I've never lived with a man before. Even growing up under Marie's roof, she never once brought a man home, as a matter of fact, I can't ever recall her going out on a date. Some might say it doesn't matter, but it's a huge leap of faith for me.

Holding my mug to my chest, I slowly walk up and down, concentrating on the invisible line marked out in front of my toes. Sloan wants a part of me I don't know if I can freely give. Actually, no, I know I can give it, I'm positive I can. I might have been forsaken back then, but I came out of the other side with a firm belief that true, unconditional love, still existed, and that one day, I would be worthy of being in receipt of it.

Slouching back in my chair, I grab my mobile and scroll through the phone book. My thumb hovers over his name, and my breathing quickens. What would I say to him? Would he want to hear from me? Would he expect me to apologise for last night? I chuck it back down, thoroughly fucking depressed.

Resting on my elbows, I slide my thumb over my philtrum, over and over. At the back of my open eyes, I can see him leaning over me, the flames of the fire highlighting his skin, colouring him with the warm, comforting shades of autumn.

Something has started to descend over me lately. It bleeds right into my soul while running through my veins in a gallop. I absolutely loathe being touched. I despise it with a passion of a million fiery suns, but with Sloan, I'm never quite satisfied – I can never seem to get enough of him. I've never tolerated physical contact, even the tiniest flick of a finger screws with my head, but inexplicably, he entices a side of my personality I wasn't aware belonged to me. Deep inside, I feel I've been waiting for him my whole life. I've never been wanton, sexual, needy, and I sure as hell haven't sat waiting around for my phone to ring. I've been considered asexual my entire adult life. Although it has never been clinically confirmed, it was personal. It meant I didn't have to justify my actions. If my life hadn't been turned on its head a week ago, I would've been fairly happy to live out my days with a dull ache in my heart, knowing I deserved more than what I'd been given. Ignorance would've been bliss, having never experienced anything different. Except, I can't hide anymore, because I've been seen and claimed by a man, who will take what he desires regardless of the consequences.

Considering my own consequences, I stare back at my phone and place my finger over his name. My eyes are heavy, and I do the unthinkable; I tap the screen. The phone starts ringing, and I can taste the acid bubbling up my throat. Terrified of being rejected, I quickly disconnect the call and put the phone back down on the desk. Seconds later, it vibrates across the small empty space. I leave it to ring and vibrate continuously, until it has worked its way from one side of my desk to the other, in no time whatsoever.

The office landline starts to sound, and I hesitate to answer it. It can't possibly be him; I didn't give him the number. It's laughable, I never gave him my mobile number, either, but he still managed to give it out to all and sundry for me.

"Good morning, Dawson's Catering," I answer, in the cheeriest phone voice I possess. There is a long pause, and it doesn't fill me with hope as to who might be on the other end.

"Kara?" Sophie's voice filters through my ear, and I let out a huge sigh.

"Soph, why are you calling me on the landline?"

"I'm ditching for the rest of the day. I've had enough of being fucking shouted at. He thinks I'm puking my guts up for England. My throat hurts from the retching noises I've had to make. Meet me at The Swan in ten." She hangs up, and I stare at the handset in astonishment. Sophie never plays hooky. It must be something serious to make her fake it.

I slide into my coat and slip my heels back on. Reaching up to lock the window, I notice there is a black Range Rover parked next to my car, and an identical one in grey on the other side. I curse up a storm, realising my reverse out might be a little tight and precarious. It's not that I'm a bad driver, it's the fact that my little piece of rust always gets boxed in by the big boys.

I turn my phone in my hand as I walk towards my car. The big black monster is sat idling with the engine running, whilst the dark grey one appears to be empty. I squeeze in between the vehicles to gain access to my door. I can't hold in the laugh that escapes me when I notice that the bonnets of the Range Rovers are the same height as my roof. Feeling bold, I turn towards the large black one. The windows are the darkest tint I have ever seen on a car, and I'm pretty sure they're not legal. As I raise my eyes to the passenger window and stand for a few minutes, someone guns the engine from inside. I yelp in shock - there's no need for bloody rudeness. Climbing into my car, my blood is pumping through my veins furiously. I back out slowly, making sure I don't scratch either vehicle. I manage not to incite any chaos, and drive towards my local, hoping there is a space left that I can squeeze into.

I push open the door of the pub and look around for Sophie. She's not here yet. Remembering I still owe her lunch, I approach the bar and wait to be served. I pull out my phone to call her, only to find that Sloan has tried calling me a further four times. I gasp sceptically, and place my phone on the sticky, ale covered bar.

"Afternoon, love. What can I get you?"

Locking eyes with the barman, and he smiles, waiting for me to give him my request. A gust of wind rolls in from the front door that has just welcomed another patron, and my phone starts to vibrate. I can't concentrate on my phone doing a jig in front of me, the cold chill wrapping around my legs, and the sound of the door hinges groaning back into place. I look up at the man again, but I don't see his eyes. Instead, I see bottles of champagne lining a shelf behind him. My body simultaneously heats and sags.

I grasp my phone. *Should I call him?*

"Miss?"

I smile apologetically at the barman. "Sorry, two waters, please."

"Oh, hell no! I want the biggest glass of the highest percentage red wine that you can legally sell me! Better still, just give me the whole damn bottle! There is not enough vino in this world today. And you, Little Miss Water, can have a spritzer!" Sophie throws her arms around me, and my body turns to stone underneath her. If she notices my terse posture, she hides it well.

"Soph, I'm driving," I say, rolling my eyes.

She huffs out with over-exaggeration. "Fine, give her a non-alcoholic wine on the rocks!" I pull away from her, and she picks up her large red wine, followed by the bottle, and stomps over to a vacant table.

"That's £18.45, love." I hand twenty quid over to him.

A man stands at the side of me and his arm brushes against mine. My breathing quickens, and eases down slowly. I'm too scared to turn. I know it isn't Sloan, because his touch is pacifying and calm, but bizarrely, this innocuous brush isn't a million miles off, either.

The bartender passes me back my change, and a pound coin rolls over the counter to the man next to me. His quick fingers stop it, and he picks it up as I turn to him. The familiar blond man grins at me, and I smile and bring my hand to my face.

"Hello, Stuart," I greet him.

He tilts his head to one side. "Hello, *Ms Petersen*," he replies. I bristle slightly, he's just used exactly the same tone Sloan had last night. Stuart holds the solitary pound in front of me, I take it and slip it back into my purse. "So, dare I ask what is so bad that you are drinking at lunch?"

"Oh, I'm not. I'm driving, so I'm going to be the sober shoulder to cry on. It's my friend who's going to drown her sorrows in a bottle of red," I say, motioning my head to where Sophie is nursing what looks like her second glass in the space of five minutes. Her head suddenly pops up, and she grins and starts to stare longingly at Stuart. He smiles at her, and she gives him a flirty wave back, before giving me a look to get over to her.

"I better go and watch her. It's nice to see you again, Stuart."

"And you. Don't be a stranger, Kara." I watch him walk away to the other side of the pub, towards a table that is completely obscured by the lunchtime regulars hogging the bar, and every inch of available floor space.

"Who the hell is that?" Sophie virtually hollers on my approach.

I slide into a seat and grab my glass. "Stuart Andrews."

"Huh, and how do you know him? Oh, my God, is he the clothes man?"

I gasp and giggle at her assumption. "No, he's one of the clothes man's best friends. Oh, and he's also a doctor," I say, taking a sip while I study her reaction. She starts to chew on her lip. I can see the wheels turning inside her head already.

"A doctor, huh? Is he single?"

"Sophie! You faked a sickie today, verbally hauled me out of the office - of which I haven't even told Marie I'm not there - and now you're trying to get it on with someone I've met once! Come on, what's going on?" Sophie quickly downs the remaining contents of her glass and pours another one. I roll my eyes, knowing that I'm going to have to take her home, which is on the other side of the city from me.

"Same old, same old. I don't know, I just got fed up with being shouted at, so I thought, fuck it! And let's face it, I never, *ever*, call in sick, so they owe me one." I let out a single snort, although to be fair she does have a point. I'm lucky I work for someone who is amazing and as good as family. I know the ins and outs of the company Soph works for. Turning a blind eye is the order of every day there.

"I know it isn't practical, but maybe it's time to start looking for something else. Let's face it, your niche might be legal, but your skills are transferable," I say, doing the unthinkable and placing my hand over hers. I can forego the slight burn in the face of upset. She stares down at her hand with a look that speaks volumes. She's aware I don't tolerate touching.

"I know. I actually already started to look, and I've signed up with a couple of agencies. Hopefully, something will come out of it." She slouches back and stares sadly into her glass. I watch her for the longest time until her eyes move rapidly behind me. I grin a little watching her. I know she's checking out Stuart, and I don't blame her. It wasn't every day a handsome doctor crossed her path.

"Okay, so when did this place suddenly allow the entire books of GQ entrance?" I cross my eyes at her and tilt my head back.

Oh shit! My eyes widen, and I pick up my glass. I down it in one, wishing I had taken her advice and asked for something stronger.

"Kara, do you know them too?!" she asks from only a couple of feet away, but my mind is so hazy by the man filling my vision, she sounds distant.

I turn, and my fantasy is answered. Sloan is staring right at me with a pint in his hand, his eyes fixed firmly on me. I shift as his dark gaze holds me hostage. He gives me a little grin, and I instantly turn around with a huff.

"Is *he* the clothes man?" Sophie asks, her eyes are large and inquisitive. I drop my gaze to the table. "Oh, holy fuck, he is! Right, that's it! I want to know everything, and I mean *everything!* Come on, girly, spit it now!"

I groan.

"Kara!"

"Okay, okay! So, Sam got herself into trouble a few weeks back, and she ended up being banged up in his hotel suite." Sophie gives me a sceptical flick of her eyebrows. "No, not banged up like that! Let's just say, her lifestyle rumours - they're all true. Anyway, he took care of her, and then we left. That's it." I give her a nervous look, and she shakes her head.

"You're lying! Come on, I want details, now! I know you've had sex in the last week, you look different," she says with a wink. My mouth falls open, and she leans forward and tilts my chin up. "Oh, come on Kara, you think I don't know? For as long as we've known each other, you have never so much as looked at a man, and the way you're grinning right now, and you don't even know it, tells me everything."

"I'm not grinning!" She rolls her eyes and digs into her bag. Holding a little mirror up to my face, she's right - I am grinning. I'm hurt, I'm pissed off, and still grinning. I'm losing my mind slowly over him.

"Kara, I've known about your *condition* for years. I'm not blind, but I'm ecstatic that you have finally met someone. Go over there and talk to him!"

"Why? So you can flirt with the doc?"

"Of course! Come on!" She starts to stand.

"No, I can't. We had an argument last night, or rather a disagreement. Oh, I don't know. I have no experience with this."

"All the more reason to get your arse over there. Make up sex can be so good! Up, now!"

"What? No!" She veers around the table and waits, tapping her foot. Picking up the half-finished bottle and glass, she gives me a pointed look and nods in their direction. My stomach curdles, but I acquiesce, and she slowly walks me towards them.

"Hi."

I turn to see Stuart greeting Sophie. She gives him her best smile, and I can feel my face harden as I look over everyone at the table. Almost everyone I met the other night is present. I can't remember all their names, but I don't care. Sloan stands and holds his seat out for me.

"No, thank you," I respond curtly with a shake of my head. I can't forget last night as quickly as he can, and the way his hands tighten on the back of the chair, tells me he doesn't like my response, either. I look around the table again. Six pairs of male eyes do little to hide their intrigue. I have just committed a cardinal sin.

I have told him no.

"Kara, we need to talk," Sloan says, sliding my arm to him, and I snatch it back.

"No, we don't! And it's *Ms Petersen* to you, remember?" Collective breaths whistle around the table at my insolence, yet I still don't give a rat's arse.

"Come on, Soph, let's go!" I glare at her. She gives me a look that could kill me instantly. I know this is the first time in ages she has actually met someone decent, but I need to get out of here.

I need to run.

"Kara, just hear him out. For once, don't be so stubborn!" I want to slap her stupid right now.

Sloan chuckles, and I give him my best fucked off look. "You know, I really like your friend; she talks sense. I'm Sloan Foster, by the way," he says to Sophie, who smiles idiotically.

"Sophie Morgan, best friend, and speaker of sense! Nice to meet you!" I watch Sloan smile broadly, while all I want to do is pick up the wine bottle and club him with it. And her.

"Come on," he says, reclaiming my arm and hauling me away. The sound of laughing at the table is ringing in my ears.

Sloan marches us outside and around the back of the building. The beep of a car lock resounds, and he pushes me inside the back of a grey Range Rover. I roll my eyes thinking of the two that virtually blocked me in earlier. I slide over the seat, and Sloan folds himself in next to me. I grasp the handle on the other side, but the child locks kick in the moment I try to push it open. I cry out in frustration.

"How fucking dare you?! How dare you think that you can treat me like shit! You don't call, you don't text, you don't do anything, other than fuck me like a prostitute and make me feel like I've made the biggest, most foolish mistake of my whole fucking life!"

Sloan shakes his head furiously. He grabs hold of me, but I retaliate and thrash against him, throwing my arms out wildly. "Kara, stop it! STOP IT!" he roars out. His voice echoes around the cabin of the car, and I shrink back into the corner, insofar as it will allow.

"Oh, shit, baby, I'm sorry." He reaches for my shaking body. "I didn't mean to shout, but you were out of control just now." He finally manages to get leverage on me and pulls me over to him. He sits me on his lap and starts to stroke the side of my face and hair. "Kara, I was pissed off last night. I can't begin to explain to you, but I just can't bear to be away from you. I want you with me all the time."

I stare down at my legs and tug my skirt lower. His hand comes over mine and assists. "You didn't call," I whisper. "You just let me go. You didn't even try to stop me. Why didn't you stop me?"

He lets out a sigh. "Because you were frightened. If the roles were reversed, I would've been, too. I promise you, I sat in that car watching your flat, and all I wanted to do was break down your door and take you away from there. But I couldn't because I knew you needed time to think about what I'd said. I'm not lying baby; you'll never know what you mean to me. I really don't seem to be able to control myself anymore," he says, tilting my face to his.

"I don't think I can have this sort of relationship with you. I can't be left wondering when you're going to call, or when I might see you again, if I do or say something you don't like. It's damaging, and it's hurting me. I can't; I'm sorry. Please-"

His lips brush against mine, and I press my hands against his chest to stop him. He grips my wrists and moves my arms to my sides. His mouth becomes hot and powerful, lapping at me fervently. Time stops, and the windows begin to condense. I tug at his jacket, needing to feel him against me, but also needing to push him away. His hand runs down my chest and inside my top. His fingers grip the lace of my bra, then he stops abruptly. My mouth halts against his, and I open my eyes, petrified of what I might see.

"Kara, I told you I would always respect you. Taking you in the back of my car isn't respecting you. I can't do it. You deserve better than this." He starts to straighten up my bra and then my blouse. My body is hot and bothered, and I can't control the disgruntled sigh that exits my throat.

But he is correct about one thing; I do deserve better. I deserve better than what he is giving me right now.

I step out of the car, and he quickly follows. He holds my hand tight, and I try to shoo it away to no avail. Walking back towards the pub, he stops us before we enter and gives me a quick look up and down, checking again to make sure I'm not exposed. "Give me five minutes, then we can go home and talk properly about this. I'm tired of your constant need to push me away."

"Sloan, I can't-" I breathe out. His eyes close, as though he's in pain. His lips begin to part, but I don't allow him a second. "No, I can't do this anymore. These last couple of weeks have taken their toll on me, physically, mentally and emotionally. It's damaging me. *You* are damaging me. You don't mean to do it, but you are!" I admit, verging on tears, as I take the first step to remove him from my life permanently.

I drink him in for the last time; his smile, his touch, everything about him that fits me so well and so right, but I know that I will constantly be hanging on for him if I stay. The only way I know how to protect myself properly is to run. He glares at me and drops my hand.

I walk back inside, and the first thing I see is Sophie giggling away with Stuart and the rest of the guys. They all turn as soon as they see us approach.

"Ah, they've made up!" Sophie spits out playfully. I scowl at her. I don't react well to being the centre of attention, and that is exactly what she has just made me. I shouldn't have expected anything less - she's garrulous when inebriated.

"Sophie!" I shout at her, but she waves me off, before turning her attention back to Stuart.

A phone starts to ring, and Sloan pulls his out of his pocket. His grim, vexed face turns pale looking at the screen. He looks at Walker, then to me. "Sorry, but I've really got to take this. It's important. Go home, I'll call you when you've calmed down," he says harshly, walking out of the door with Walker hot on his heels.

"Don't bother," I whisper to his retreating back.

I say goodbye to Soph, who seems more than happy to be left with a table full of big, strong, handsome men, and quickly leave. With one foot out of the door, the grey Range Rover speeds out of the pub car park.

I stare blindly into space, and wonder what on earth could possibly have been so important that he didn't want me to know about.

Not that it really matters anymore.

I pull my phone from my pocket and start to type.

Chapter 17

PUSHING THE TROLLEY in front of me, I throw random shit in. I have enough chocolate and wine in there to keep me sick and paralytic for weeks. I don't want it, but I need it.

I need it, because I have just let the best thing in my world go with my full consent. I gave him no other explanation than the one I forced myself to admit to at the pub. It was hard to tell him he was damaging me, but it's the truth. And in the long run, he would obliterate me just as easily if I allowed him to. So instead, I let him go, with five simple words that couldn't be misconstrued.

Please don't contact me again

Tossing my stuff onto the conveyor belt, I shift on my heels and wait impatiently for the cashier to work faster. The intermittent beep of the scanner irritates me, but draws me into an internal quiet. All I have done since Sloan had a change of heart, and a personality transplant this afternoon, is break down what exactly happened.

My head is so full of unanswered questions and realisations.

I realise after only a few short weeks, I will never fully know him. Admittedly, I never expected him to tell me anything personal this soon, but it saddens me that I'd given him such a sacred part of myself, and at the first sign of strife, I don't hear a word from him, and then has the audacity to act like nothing really happened. I laugh mindlessly to myself. If this is what relationships do to you, I'm better off single. Nobody is worth this much heartache.

The woman scanning my food looks at me like I have two heads. I mumble to myself, convinced I'm stronger than before, yet my heart is full of sorrow. Feeling very self-conscious, I quickly pack my groceries, pay the lady, then leave.

After finally finding a space in the residents' car park, I remove the plastic bags from the boot. I've never quite mastered how to put the key in the lock, turn it, and balance bulging carrier bags simultaneously. Groaning loud in frustration, I accept defeat. Putting the bags on the ground, I slip the key into the lock.

I rotate on my heels when I see a flash reflect on the windowpane. A large black Range Rover is parked on the street opposite. I squint, wondering if it is the same one outside the office earlier. Its windows are too heavily tinted, so I have no clue who is driving. A shudder runs through me thinking back to my almost run-in with Sam's guy yesterday. Panic grips me, and I quickly pick up my bags and bolt inside. I lock the door behind me, although this will be of no use, since the majority of the residents failed to do so. I watch from behind the relative safety of the door, praying the 4x4 will drive off.

"Ah, if it isn't my favourite tenant!"

I turn sharply, drop the bags, and send food spilling across the floor. My breathing almost stops when I come face to face with Danny. I remain silent as we face each other for the first time in days. Neither of us attempts to move.

"Let me get those for you." Danny breaks the uncomfortable silence, and starts picking up my escaped groceries. Bagging the last stray orange, he holds both bags in his hands.

Every muscle clenches tight. Nobody is going to magically appear and protect me now. Eyeing him suspiciously, I stand as far away from him as I can, hoping he will just drop them and leave. I don't need his help, and I didn't ask for it, and after his indiscretion of trying to rape me in my own home, I'm more than dubious as to why he is being nice to me now.

Upon closer inspection, his face is still slightly red and swollen around his nose and cheeks, evidence of where Sloan had punched him. Under different circumstances, I might have felt sorry for him, but considering our volatile history - which managed to escalate to a terrifying level only days ago - all I feel is revulsion.

He looks sheepish, and takes the first step of many towards my flat. "Kara, I'm sorry about what happened the other night. I'd had a bit to drink, and I didn't have my head-on. I'm sorry."

Didn't have his head on, my arse!

I nod indifferently. There was nothing he could ever say, or do, that will erase what he did - what he tried to do. Truthfully, I was actually beginning to consider cutting my losses. His actions were just the icing on the cake. Well, him, Sam, and now Sloan.

Outside my door, he faces me. I don't move when he jerks his head in silent request that I open it. I turn the key with caution; it has never sounded so loud before. I cross the threshold into the small dim hallway, positioning the key in my hand, the sharp end pointing out between my fingers. *Just in case.* I expect Danny to follow me inside freely. Instead, he does what I don't expect – he waits outside. He smiles, sort of, and passes me the bags, one after the other. He then looks to leave, but stops and rotates back to me.

"Thanks for the rent, Kara. I admit I didn't expect that much. Sam turning more tricks than usual lately?" There's no amusement in his voice, and his face is serious. I narrow my eyes, absorbing his words. I'm dying to get rid of him, but his comment scratches the proverbial hitch.

"What do you mean, *turning tricks*, and when did the rent get paid? I certainly haven't paid it. I was actually going to bring it down tomorrow."

"The rent was paid in full, for six months, two days ago. I never expected that."

The tension headache that is building behind my eyes starts progressing towards my forehead. *Six months, in full*? I knew that Sam didn't have that kind of money, and there was no one else who would be so generous when it came to either of us. That only leaves one person I know who has no money issues whatsoever.

Sloan.

I mentally scream at myself. I might have tried to push him away, but he's still invading. Even if I never see him again, I would live here every day, knowing he had done this for us. For me, specifically.

"Okay," I say, letting out a deep breath, trying to control my raging emotions. "Return the money. I'll pay you tomorrow for what we owe you already, and next months' in full." Although I can't actually afford it, it was out there now. The less contact I have with Sloan, the stronger my sanity will be. Not to mention my heart, which is beginning to feel less and less alive by the minute.

"I can't return an electronic payment, Kara. Look at it this way, someone has done you a favour." My face screws up, livid at the thought of being indebted to him once again. "If I were you, I would take your seven weeks' worth of rent and get your girl off the streets. You tell her I don't take too kindly to visitors at all hours."

I glare at him. While the man is a disgusting, obnoxious, would-be rapist in my eyes, I needed to know the truth. The request must have been evident, when he sighs, looks around the hall, and leans in. "After what happened the other night, of which I am really sorry about, I noticed you haven't been back for a while-"

"Three days," I interrupt.

"Well, there has been more than three days' worth of men coming and going from here, if you understand what I'm saying? I can't have that here; it's bad, other tenants have complained. If she doesn't stop, I'm going to have to evict her..." He stares down, refusing to meet my gaze. He's saying would have to evict us both, since we jointly signed the tenancy agreement. I don't know whether I should laugh or cry.

"Thanks," I say dryly.

He doesn't wait for anything else and strolls back down the corridor to the lift. I slam the door behind me, deposit the bags on the kitchen floor, and dart towards Sam's door.

Three hours later, I stand in the middle of her room after rummaging through all of her personal belongings. I feel ghastly for doing this, but the time for turning a blind eye has been and gone. There is nothing to incriminate her or to imply she is prostituting herself. No hidden amounts of cash, no numbers, nothing. I sit on her bed with my head in my hands.

And for the first time in forever, I allow myself to crack.

I roll over in bed, hearing the front door slam sharply. I scramble up and hobble half-awake into the living room. Sam is sitting there with another man I've never seen before.

"Hi! I haven't seen you in so long, I thought you'd left!" she says sarcastically. For all her dramatics, she fails. *Miserably.*

I stand there, unmoving, studying her. She isn't the girl I grew up with. She's a complete stranger to me now. Gone is the girl who would coax me to sleep when life at home became unbearable. The one who knew my deepest, darkest fears and nightmares. In her place, is a woman who looks at least ten years older than she actually is, slowly becoming devoid of all emotion towards anyone but herself. Her skin is turning sallow, and her eyes are glassed over, undoubtedly from some intoxicating concoction. Everything that was being spelt out to me from Sophie, Marie, and even Danny, it's all true.

My feet find life and carry me into the kitchen. I rifle through the cupboards, looking for the bagels I'd absentmindedly thrown into one of them, hours after Danny dropped them at the door. Sam clears her throat, and grudgingly, I turn to her.

"So, Mr Millionaire found someone new and hung you out to dry, huh?" She's being a complete bitch, and I don't understand why.

"Actually, no, he didn't, not that you really care. What the hell is going on with you, Sam? I'm hearing all this stuff lately." She shrugs her shoulders, and I'm in disbelief at the nerve of her nonchalance. "What about him? Who's he?" Again, she just shrugs. I snort; I'm fed up with this game. "Okay. How about this? Are you fucking men for money in our home?" I scream at her.

She scoffs and jabs her finger at me. "*Me?* How dare you! So what if I am! I don't have a gazillionaire at my beck and call! You have no right to ask me that. The only difference between us, is that I earn mine honestly. You? You're no fucking better than me. You think because he takes you out to dinner in a designer dress, and fucks you afterwards in that fancy hotel of his, that you're not a slut? Trust me, Kara, you are!"

I slam my fist on the worktop. My decision has just been finalised.

I storm back into my room, and text Marie to ask if I can stay for a few days. Her reply in the affirmative is returned almost instantly. I quickly dress in whatever I can throw on my back fast enough, and stuff a few necessities into a bag. I lock my bedroom door behind me and heft the bag back into the living room. Sam is preoccupied, rubbing herself in the lap of the man she has brought home with her. Her eyes drift over me briefly, then she refocuses her attention back to her companion and licks his face with determination.

"The rent is paid for the next six months. I'll be back to get the rest of my stuff soon."

Sam completely ignores me, never removing her eyes from her guest. I haul my bag down the stairs, halting outside of Danny's office door. When he sees me through the glass, his face loses its colour.

"Danny, can you arrange to take me off the tenancy agreement? I'm gone."

He sighs and nods. I guess he already knew it would eventually come to this. "Yeah, I can arrange for it to happen. Do you want the rent money for the next six months?" I shake my head. I don't want anything. Not anymore.

"Kara, once I've got the contract sorted, I'll let you know. Give us a call if you need a hand moving anything." I nod and walk out.

I flatten my hands on the side of my car and breathe deeply. My gaze is captured by the same black car parked opposite the building, and my eyes narrow into slits. I'm tense as I get into my car and drive away, never losing sight of the 4x4. Obsessively, I flick my eyes between the road ahead and the ominous vehicle behind me. It keeps a steady pace a few cars back, and an anxious, unnerving feeling, erupts deep in my chest.

I keep a close, paranoid check on my rearview as I drive towards my teenage home. I pull up at a set of traffic lights and my phone beeps. Ensuring they are still on red, I flick the screen, and a text from Sloan appears.

Don't be ridiculous, Kara. I'm coming over now

I chuck the phone onto the back seat and laugh. He's right; I am ridiculous. I'm damn right idiotic and masochistic to permit myself to go through this torture with him again and again. And what for? A chance to experience love and pain?

I've already had enough pain to last me a lifetime.

And love? Well, love is the most painful bastard of them all.

It's raw, it's brutal, and it shows you it can swallow you whole and then spit you back out. I've been through this with my parents, and look where that got me. I can't go through it again, not with him. I don't want to end up hating him the way I do my father.

I pull up in the driveway and remove the key from the ignition. Flicking my eyes up, the Range Rover slows to a crawl and passes by in the rearview. Expecting it to stop, instead, it speeds up and disappears down the street. I drop my head against the steering wheel heavily. This was a mistake. Whoever was in the car had followed me here intentionally.

And I've brought them right to Marie's front door.

Fuck!

Chapter 18

MARIE FROWNS, AND stares down at the small wad of tenners as she hugs her mug between her hands. Her petite, fair features twist in disgust, looking between me and my money.

"I can't take that, honey. Please don't insult me by giving it to me. This will always be your home, you don't need to pay me board. I don't need it, put it away. Better still, go buy yourself something nice; you've earned it."

My eyes drop down to the money for a second and then back to her. She leans her head to one side, in a way that says this conversation is well and truly over. I stuff the cash back into my purse and drop it on the table.

I've been living with Marie for two weeks now. I've heard nothing from Sam, and even less from Sloan, except for one text I received when I walked through Marie's door:

WHERE THE FUCK ARE YOU?!

Other than that, he has respected my wishes ever since.

He hasn't contacted me.

Every now and again, I find myself daydreaming, looking at my phone, willing it to ring and for him to be the one calling. It has never materialised.

Whereas my beloved father, on the other hand, can always be relied upon to cause me pain from afar. I'm now receiving calls and texts on a daily basis. Each one the same as the last. Each one always about owing money, telling me to pay up in one, and then to run and hide in the next. And just like each message that preceded it, I delete the majority of them the minute they arrive.

Needless to say, Ian isn't the only thing providing me with unwanted strife. The black 4x4 that had followed me here two weeks ago, now seems to be tailing me at every opportunity; to work, to the supermarket, to the cash machine. It's always there, just a few cars behind mine. I haven't mentioned any of this to Marie, knowing she will mutate into overprotective mother mode and demand I go straight to the police.

Ejecting the bagel from the toaster, I smother it in lashings of chilli cream cheese. I devour it quickly and wish Marie goodbye. She reminds me that we have a function tonight, and I shout back that

I'll be there, still rubbing the sleep from my eyes, as I close the door behind me.

Over the last two weeks, I have also been picking up Sam's shifts, since she so conveniently hasn't shown up for work. So, not only am I full time in the office during the day, but I'm also waitressing part-time at night, too. To say I'm mentally and physically exhausted, is the understatement of the century. The lethargy that is currently taking up permanent residence in every muscle and cell, plus the dark bags under my eyes, are all a visual testament to this.

I stroll into the office and look around my now bare desk for the final time. Picking up the last two boxes, I climb the stairs up to the new office. Unbeknownst to me, Marie had been negotiating a new lease on a larger floor in the building for the last month. Since the event at the Emerson a couple of months back, there has been a huge demand for her services lately. *No surprises as to who has been recommending her to all and sundry.* So, now we needed more floor space, and possibly another member of office staff.

My phone buzzes a little after one thirty, and I'm surprised by how immersed I've been in working on the new floor plans. I reach for my phone and scan the screen. My heart all but stops, as Sloan's name appears in bright lights.

I've spent plenty of time letting his pearls of wisdom float around my head, unyielding and free, and out of everything he has ever said to me, one thing stands out clearly: *firsts*. I have conquered a few of these since he told me I was ridiculous. Finally, at the grand old age of twenty-three, I know what it's like to be used, dumped, and left heartbroken. These are three firsts I never imagined would bring me more pain than I already knew existed.

Unsure what to do, I stare at it numbly while it continues to vibrate in my open palm.

This is the moment I've been waiting for, for two long weeks. I have spent the last fourteen days hiding the pain he has unknowingly induced by not contacting me. For all my tough girl talk and bravado, the truth is, I want him. I miss him. I'd admitted it to myself the second night I spent without him when I woke up unable to breathe. It has become a nightly interference ever since.

Unable to form words that would make sense, I let the call go to voicemail. I figure if he is just making a routine *how are you* call, at least I will be able to listen to his velvet voice repeatedly, until I'm so depressed, I have no choice but to delete it.

Needing to clear my head, I make a quick call to Marie to say that I'm heading out for lunch. Then I call Sophie to see if she wants to meet. She tells me she can't since her desk is so full of crap, she can't see the wood for the trees.

Standing in the café, trying to come to a final decision on what to order, someone taps me on the shoulder. I jump, twist my head around sharply, and lock eyes with Walker.

"Hi," I say, turning back to the counter for my order to be taken.

Pulling out one of my many tenners, I slip the money over to the cashier. She quickly calculates my change and stretches across the glass serve over to pass it back to me. I rotate around to Walker, who is still a hairsbreadth away from me, and start to cut a small path through the lunchtime hoard that is blocking my escape. And touching me. I glance back to see if he notices my discomfort, but he gives nothing away. He appears large beyond belief in the vicinity of such a small place. I try to multi-task, by juggling my salad, shuffling through the abundance of bodies, and still keeping my eyes on the door. I jerk when his hand slips around my elbow, and he escorts me safely out of the shop. I'm more than curious as to why he is here. Do I dare ask him? I deliberate as I slip my change into my purse.

"Kara, we need to talk. How much time do you have?" His tone is speculative, and I judge the best course of action going forward.

"I have some time." He is inches from me. So close, in fact, the air shifts with each step he takes behind me. I stop, and finally make proper eye contact with him. He nods his head towards a black Range Rover, and I follow obediently.

"Take a seat," he tells me, holding open the passenger door. Moments later, he slips into the driver's side, draping his arm casually over the steering wheel. I try to ignore him and gaze impassively through the windscreen.

"So, how have you been?" he asks jovially, a hint of a smile curls his lips.

I lift my shoulders with insubordination, trying to come across unaffected, but inside I'm breaking. I toy with the idea of asking about Sloan, since he had called me not less than thirty minutes ago, but shove that notion back into its box when Walker's expression darkens significantly.

"He misses you; you know?" *No, actually, I don't know.*

I laugh out bitterly. "Never would have guessed. That's why I haven't heard from him in weeks." I skim over my clear salad box, needing a place to divert my eyes. I don't want him to see me saddened just by the mere mention of him.

"Kara, you told him to leave you alone, remember? Look, I'm not here to argue trivialities with you. He misses you; he does. The reason why he hasn't been in touch is that he's been in New York for the last few weeks on business."

"Well, maybe they don't have good reception there. Maybe that's why he used me, and I haven't heard from him since." I lay my full hate-filled glare on him. It's not Walker's fault, but I need to level my anger on someone, and unfortunately, he's here. His hand contracts on the steering wheel, clamping it with such force that his fingers whiten under the pressure.

"Goddamn it, Kara. Stop being so fucking stubborn, woman! You gave him an ultimatum, and he gave you the respect you rightly asked for and deserve. If you want an explanation, you need to ask him. I'm here as a friend, not just for him, but for you, too. He really misses you. He's had me staking out your flat like a criminal for the last two weeks just to make sure you're safe. He really doesn't like you being there, Kara." He lets out a deep rumbling breath, and his eyes come over serious. "I also know you haven't been at your place since he almost near broke the damn door down when you were being *ridiculous*. I haven't dared to tell him that you left, he's worried enough already. Hell, he sent me to your office today because you didn't answer his fucking call! Look, I know he can be all kinds of unreasonable and overbearing, but I've never seen it with anyone besides his family. He's a good guy, Kara. He cares more than you will ever understand."

I nod, but my head isn't in this conversation at all. I'm in a world of my own making, and suddenly, I've developed selective hearing, because all I can seem to focus on is the last sentence. The sound of horns blaring from drivers on the other side of the road disrupts my train of thought.

It also dawns on me that today is the first time in weeks I haven't seen the car that has been trailing me lately. Now, I understand why.

"Well, you really don't need to follow me around anymore. I'm fine, more than fine actually. So, if you please." I open the door and slide out, leaving him shocked and open-mouthed. As my feet touch the pavement, pounding comes around from the other side.

I raise my hand to my forehead, touching the spot where I can feel a headache starting to gather momentum. These last few weeks haven't been good to me. In between worrying about the next communication from my father, and being too frightened to turn on the six o'clock news in case Sam's body had been found in a shallow ditch, I'm now having to deal with Sloan ordering one of his guys to follow me at every turn.

"Kara, wait!" Walker shouts, jerking my hand firmly; so much so, I fear it may bruise from the pressure.

"No! He used me! Now, granted I may have gone into it with an open mind, but I allowed him to get under my skin. The first time I say no to him, he disappears off the face of the earth for two weeks! I can't live with that kind of uncertainty. God knows I have enough of my own shit to contend with, so I really don't need his adding to it!" I twist my wrist from his hold and shake some life back into it.

Walker watches me flicking my hand back and forth, his face is hard and repentant. "Kara, I'm so-"

"Don't say you're goddamn sorry! I've heard it my entire life, and I hate it! And another thing, stop following me. Everywhere I turn, you're there. The next time you decide to follow me to the supermarket, come inside and pay, then I might be fucking grateful!" I ignorantly turn my back on him, and head off towards the office.

I don't get very far when his hand slaps down on my shoulder. Again, I spin around, my body pulsating with anger at the invasion of my space. My mouth parts, ready to let whatever is inside my head come spewing out, without any regard as to who is nearby, or what I might say. I really don't give a shit anymore.

"Wait!" Walker's deep voice halts me. He stands, holding his palms up. "I haven't been following you. I've kept an eye on Sam and who she's been dealing with, and that's it. Your old landlord told me you were with your aunt, so I already knew you were safe. So, tell me, what the hell is going on because once Sloan hears this, he's gonna be fucking furious!"

I stare blankly into his eyes, trying to fathom in my own brain what the hell *is* going on. I think back to each time I have seen the 4x4. I glance across Walker's arm and study his car. Whilst it is a large Range Rover, unlike the one that had become my constant shadow, his is completely different. It's a different model entirely, and unlike the other one, the windows are a smoky grey, not black as night.

My breath lodges in my throat, and my hand starts to tremble. Walker's eyes fill with something that resembles anger. I sense his impending action before he commits it, and I begin to move away. Annoyed, he puts his arm around my shoulder and guides me back to the car. He eyes me suspiciously as my skin twitches under my clothes. Opening the door, he places me inside, pulls the seat belt over me, then strides back round to his side.

Relaxing my head against the leather rest, I watch, a prisoner trapped in my own head, as the world glides by the window at speed. My eyes itch, and my body feels heavy and tired, no doubt brought on by the shock of knowing Sloan does still care, in some shape or form, and having my worst fears confirmed that I'm definitely being stalked.

But by whom?

At some point during the ride, I doze off. Not surprising, considering I've been running on nothing more than adrenaline alone recently. A shudder runs through me, and I sense the abnormal pull of the lift bearing down on me.

The waters of my mouth run dry, and I squeeze Walker's shoulders tighter. I make a mental note to apologise to him for being so familiar, when I finally get my feet back on solid ground. I lick my dry, cracked lips, and twist my head to him.

Slowly opening my eyes, they dilate in shock when I see that it isn't Walker cradling me like a child, but Sloan. I scrunch my face up in anger, the tears I have barricaded in for the last few weeks finally threaten to destroy me. I shift in his arms, determined to be released. Staring into his eyes, just like mine, they are filled with sadness. But unlike his, mine are also silently pleading for him to put me down, but his hold doesn't waver. Instead, he grips me tighter than a snake subduing its prey before a kill.

I face him with a ferocious glare, one which leaves no room for vacillation. I want down, and I want it now. I am beyond pissed off; I am absolutely fucking furious. Sloan's face is still harder than granite; impenitent and unforgiving in the wake of my temporary detestation of him.

The doors ping open, and I thrash my limbs hard against his, but he still doesn't let go. He's holding me tight; guarding me, *controlling me.* He opens the suite door and carries me over the threshold like a groom does his bride. He kicks the door shut behind us harder than necessary. I let out a breath when he finally lowers me to my feet to engage the security system.

All my intentions of lashing out, of screaming at him, of running down the multitude of stairs to freedom, vanish. He taps in the last number and turns to me, glaring with an intensity I feel deep in every part of my soul. He slips out of his jacket and slackens his tie, as he strides into the living room. He pauses at the centre, his hands on his hips, his shoulders squared in the waistcoat he's wearing. Even under the expensive fabric of his trousers, I clearly see the way his thighs clench and hold him aloof.

Even after all these days of not seeing him, he still manages to provoke every torrent of emotion in my body, and I have to force myself not to run into his arms. I have to remember he made me promise not to run, yet he did just that.

Emotionally, he's hurt me more than anyone else ever has, maybe more than my own parents.

I close my eyes and purse my lips together impudently. My gaze leaves his, and I stare blindly through the domineering glass window. I don't see the sky, or the ominous, pluvial clouds rolling in, just his reflection. It's amazing what you can see when you don't really look for it. Right now, I know that if I do look at him - the real him, and the vulnerable side he doesn't show that often - it will break me. Actually, that's not true, because he's already broken me. He's broken my heart. But the ultimate betrayal he has unknowingly committed these last two weeks, is that he's broken my trust.

We stand silently for a long time. My eyes drift to the clock, and I stare at the second-hand ticking by slowly. Ironically, this is what my life has become since he forced his way in. Time ticking by until I saw him again. Time ticking by that I could never claw back. Time, whereby I was losing myself more and more under his spell.

Exhausted and hungry, I rotate in defeat. If he is just going to stand there like a statue that might shatter at any given moment, I'm done with it. Done with him involuntarily hurting me. Fed up, I shake my head and make my way towards the door. With my fingers gripping the handle, it's wishful thinking to believe I'm home free. As it turns in my hand, a big, rock-hard body slams into my back, and twists me around. I gasp at the pressure of the air leaving my lungs due to the unexpected impact.

Sloan picks me up and presses my back hard against the door. A strong arm cradles my waist, a knee nudges my thighs apart, and my body, traitorous as it is, obeys as my legs willingly wrap around him for support. His head drops within inches of mine, and his lips touch lightly over my collarbone.

I breathe him in; it's a smell that seeps through my nostrils at a demanding pace. My eyes are falling, laden with irrefutable passion. A passion he recognises instantly. His dark blues sparkle under the lights before turning hazy. His hand grips my chin, firm and commanding. His lips brush over my mouth, and honestly, all I want to do is open up and feel his tongue dance a slow, seductive tango with mine.

Instead, I stiffen.

I won't give him this. I can't give him this, because he will only build me up and then break me down all over again.

From the moment I first met him, he's slowly chipped away at my walls. He lodged himself in my life, ensuring I would need him. Obviously, he doesn't realise the effect on me, but when you're as broken as can be, and someone shows you something – *anything* - remotely resembling affection, you latch on quickly until they spit you back out.

Defiantly raising my head away, I lean back from his hard body, until my own risks becoming one with the door behind me. A low growl emanates from his throat, and he pinches either side of my jaw, twisting my head and neck, coercing me to look at him.

"Don't run from me, Kara." His fingers cut into my chin again, and his eyes darken by the second.

"I'm not running from you, Sloan. I can't run from something I've never had," I respond flatly. My chest is pumping rapidly with both anger and lust. The arm around my waist squeezes harder, and his fingers part and stretch across my lower back. He moves tentatively; stroking me, breaking me, making me fall - ensuring I will give in.

I close my eyes tight. *I can't fucking do this with him again!*

I've relied on my own self-preservation for so long, and he has the ability to annihilate it with just a simple look.

I begin to drop my legs from his around his hips, but instead of permitting me the freedom I desperately desire, he moves both hands to the backs of my knees and holds me hostage. I open my eyes, and watch the way his flood with both concern and want.

"Please, let me go," I beg, knowing it will disgust him. It's a piss poor effort to gain emancipation, and it's insulting to both of us, but I have no alternatives left to manipulate.

Something crosses in his eyes. He drops his hands from my body and brings them to rest on either side of my head. I slide myself down his hard frame, not missing the bulge at his groin when my stomach slides over it. He runs his hand through his already messed up hair. My stance against him falters, as defeat clouds his eyes. No matter how much I think I need to break free from whatever it is that inexplicably draws me to him, I cannot deny how he turns me on immensely.

I stoop under his arm and tiptoe into the centre of the living room. My eyes flit from the furniture, to the fabrics, to the accessories. I have to do something to take my mind off being in such close proximity to him. Kicking off my shoes, I curl my toes into the plush, cream rug, housed under the coffee table. Shrugging out of my jacket, I drape it over the arm of the sofa, before sitting down on the leather. The fabric connects with the back of my legs, making me stifle a moan from the way its coolness chills my overheated limbs.

The sofa dips next to me, and I tilt my head. Sloan reaches his hand out to me, but I just stare at it, as though touching it might be poisonous. Heaven knows the man is definitely hazardous to my health. His brooding features sadden when he realises I'm not accepting the gesture, and he drops his hand heavily. His body tenses and the muscles in his neck flex. I watch equally addicted and worn out, while he tries to regain his precious control.

I knew I was right when I asked him if he heard the word *no* a lot.

I incline back into the sofa, taking long controlled breaths, hoping he can't hear them. Suddenly my body is elevated, and I'm sitting across his lap. One hand coils around the back of my waist as the other secures around my front. His fingers outline my hipbone, before entwining together at my side, locking me in, and incarcerating me inside his arms.

He nuzzles his head into my neck, stroking his nose up and down my jaw. "I've missed you." His admission is so quiet, if I'd have been any further away, I probably wouldn't have heard it. My eyes slowly drift shut, and I take in a deep breath, replaying his words over, knowing I have to fight to keep my own precious control.

"Say something, Kara," he presses, in the same quiet, penetrating voice, that is now igniting the fire within I was certain had died out two weeks ago when he ran away from me.

I say the only thing that is in my head. The question that has cruelly played with me for too long. "Where have you been?"

He shifts me in his lap, re-arranging my legs, so I'm straddling his thighs. I adjust a fraction, and my core rubs against his growing hardness. Electricity runs through me at the simple, but most definitely erotic, of touches. I scoot back so I can see his face; I need answers. Answers I know he probably won't give me, but still, it's worth a shot.

"Business." One word, and no further elaboration.

And sadly, it's not enough to make it right.

I shake my head and pull away. Untangling my body from his, he lets his arms drop, and I get up. Reaching over to grab my jacket, I slip my heels back on.

Sloan slides to the edge of the sofa, his arm shoots out and wraps around my thigh. He reels me in slowly, and I approach him with restraint. I have no idea what the hell is going through that beautiful, unpredictable head of his. Varying degrees of emotions play across his features, but I don't dare try to fathom what he might be thinking or feeling. The prospect is far too daunting.

He stands and takes my jacket, before throwing it back down harshly. I want to protest at his action, but instead, I stay mute. He towers over me, and I swallow down the fact I'm losing my battle with self-endurance. I'm mesmerised, as he holds out my arm and his eyes work over every curve and imperfection I possess. With both hands on my neck, his fingers curve at my nape while firm thumbs draw lazy circles under my ears. He's massaging me into submission.

My eyes lock onto his, and seeing my reflection in his dark pools, subdues and calms me instantly. The sensations he is unknowingly assisting with are too much, and I close my eyes, as I fight against the raw and primal need for him. Opening them, for almost the last time, before impending fatigue drags me under, deep into the place I fear to dream in, a small smile plays on his lips. The feel of his body, hard and warm against mine, is exquisite. I try to stay alert, I really do, but I can't fight it anymore.

I want to sleep peacefully and never wake up. Not unless it's in the arms of a man I fear I may have fallen more than a little bit in love with.

Goddamn my foolish heart.

Chapter 19

SOMETHING SOFT CARESSES my back. The way it feels against my skin is divine, as I rotate and roll in the comfort of this amazing thing. The sensation is sublime, drifting up and down my spine softly, and electricity sparks to life every nerve ending and muscle inside me.

My eyes refuse to open, and I start to regress under his touch.

My mind pulls me back, and I recognise the room. Reaching out, I spread my hand over the duvet beneath me…

The acrid, stale smell, of cheap spirits and cigarettes fills the air to the point where I can't breathe. Bringing my hand to my throat, I press lightly and swallow, somehow hoping to appease the burn the stench is causing.

The sound of a door banging somewhere in the house raises my internal alarm bells. I know that sound all too well. I stumble off the bed, dragging a blanket with me. On my hands and knees, I crawl into the cubbyhole, wrap the soft material around me and lock myself in.

The sound of heavy footsteps snaps my half sleepy eyes back to the here and now. They enlarge, terrified with the creak that always accompanies the opening of my bedroom door. The handle hits the wall behind it, embedding into the plaster that has moulded itself into the shape of the metal over time.

The gruff sound of male voices resounds in my ears, all the while I cuddle into the blanket, and bring it over my head, hiding away in the dark. Protecting myself from things I shouldn't be ready to know yet.

The voices drift off and begin to fade. I reach down, feeling for my only true friend all these years, my ted. I may not be able to see him clearly, but I know one of his arms desperately needs mending. I begged mummy to sew it back on ages and ages ago, but she said I wasn't a good girl. She said only good girls have nice things. I snuggle deeper into the blanket, hugging ted to my heart and let my eyes close. I curl as far back into the cubbyhole as I can.

In a flash of light, I am suddenly hefted from my place of safety by my ponytail. I no longer cry out, because nobody comes to help me. The hand in my hair hurts so much, and the one around my wrist is painful, too. I don't look at my captor as I'm dragged into another room.

"Be a good girl now, Kara," my father's voice cajoles softly.

The blanket cocooning me is snatched away, and a hand reaches towards my throat.

My eyes dart open, and I bolt upright. My nails dig into my chest, as my mind makes me relive things I've vowed to keep hidden. Things that hurt me, and things that will eventually destroy me. Except, until recently, I've never remembered much about that fateful night. I had even subconsciously managed to forget all the shit that came before it. But this is all new to me. I have no idea if it's real, or if my mind is mutating to epic proportions, to the point where I make myself believe them to be real.

A finger trails up my spine, and I scramble off the bed, sweating and panting. Sloan jumps up immediately, and is now crouching at my feet. I drop my head to my bent legs, and rest my forehead on my knees.

This is the second time we have been in this position.

The sound of sobbing pierces the thick tension, and I listen carefully, only to recognise the sobs are my own. I raise my head slowly, not wanting this strong man to see the quivering wreck I disguise underneath my mouth and attitude.

Pain manifests in my chest, replaying over and over the scene that my subconscious decided to make me remember. It kills me that I can't factually say what had transpired all those years ago, and that is my biggest cause of concern. I have the scars and the hospital notes to validate the rape and beating, but it's times like these, I wish I could remember everything.

It's times like these, I wish I had never been so determined to make myself forget.

Warmth surrounds me, and a strong, bare chest presses at my back, as protective arms wrap around my abdomen. There is no playfulness in this hold. He is holding me for one reason and one reason alone; because I need it. And I want him to be the one here with me every time I do. I have no energy left in my body to fight, not when the darkness goes so deep I'm petrified I may lose myself within it.

Swallowing hard, opening myself up to those revelations, my body becomes pliable with each rocking motion he pacifies me with. The combined heat of his body and the strength of his arms coax me back into the same semi-darkness, and I allow him to escort me there.

The shrill sound of a phone ringing jolts me wide awake. I glance into deep blue eyes and the corners crinkle, yet his mouth still displays a tight line. He lifts us up from the floor and gently places me back on the bed. I pull the covers up to my neck and listen to his receding footsteps. I curl into a ball while he speaks to whoever dared to disturb the silence. Eventually, his voice drifts closer and closer. The smooth, deep tones of his words invade my ears, and I can't help but admire the strength he exudes in everything he does.

The door opens quietly, and he rests against the architrave; unmoving and watching intently. I twist my neck away from him and gaze out of the window. The dark clouds have given way to a calm, clear night closing in.

It's so ironic, I can't even laugh.

The mattress dips, and I drag my eyes over every perfect, masculine inch, as he eases himself against me. "Marie asked if you would give her a ring back." His fingers move up and down my jaw, stroking with veneration. His eyes are softer now, but he still gauges my expression closely with every tiny touch he bestows upon me. I nod, thoroughly consumed by the way his chest moves, the way the muted light defines his muscles, and the way I really want to lick from the fine line of hair on his stomach, to the corded muscles of his neck.

Then it hits me like a tonne of bricks.

Marie. Event. *Tonight.*

"Oh, bollocks!" I shout horrified, diffusing everything else clouding my judgement. I throw the covers off, but his large hand reaches over my breastbone and flattens me back down onto the bed.

"Don't worry, she said she has it covered."

I run my hands over my face, agitation has never been a good look on me. And considering it's now mixed with the aftermath of my darkest nightmares; I probably look like shit.

He pulls me into him, hooking my leg over his thigh. "Ready to talk yet?"

Am I ready to talk?

Maybe.

Am I ready to talk with him?

Hell, no!

He's the reason why all these memories are coming out to play. They only started to raise their ugly heads again after he bustled his way into my life a month ago.

I slowly move my head from side to side. His cheeks hollow, and the vein in his neck protrudes under his skin. I'm fully aware how frustrating this must be for him, but I can't talk about it, because the cold, harsh reality is, I'm not sure if what I remember is real, or whether my mind is playing cruel games. I've spent so long blocking all the fucked-up shit out, I can't actually decipher what is fact from fiction anymore.

His muscles tense against my skin, and the slight vibrations incite a reaction that scares the living daylights out of me. I raise my hand to his cheek, and brush his fine, five o'clock shadow. His skin is more tanned than what it was two weeks ago. His hair is a little longer, unrulier and ruffled, but it still makes him look sinfully sexy and delectable.

I touch my finger to his mouth, tracing over his upper lip and he kisses it tenderly. His eyes flick down to my wrist where my watch usually sits. At some point, he has removed it, and he's now staring like a madman at the scar that mars my skin. His head quickly drops to the other scar on my inner thigh. His thumb runs over the white mark, and his jaw clenches tighter and tighter, until I feel the need to mollify him of this hurt, and share with him what little I'm comfortable with.

"Do you know what it's like to feel pain, Sloan?" He nods once. "No, I mean true pain, *real pain*. Not the kind you get when someone slaps you, or breaks your heart, or tells you they don't care. I mean the kind that comes from others. The kind that is inflicted on you when you have no choice, and no hope in hell of defending yourself. The kind that others gain pleasure from." He stares at me; expressionless, motionless, cold. "Well, I do." I pull my wrist away from him and lay my hand over my stomach. "I know what it feels like to cower in the dark, and to hide in a cubbyhole. To fear sleep because you don't know what will happen. I know what true pain feels like."

His eyes narrow in anger, forming premature wrinkles at the corners. "Confined spaces," he mumbles, and I nod. He doesn't say anything further, and allows me to continue.

"To fear every moment. To be too scared to breathe in case someone hears you. *I know*," I whisper. I run my hand down his chest, and he shivers under my touch. I can't fathom if it's my actions, or my words, that have this effect on him.

I don't say anymore as I get up from the bed, pad into the bathroom and close the door behind me. I don't bother to lock it because I know the hurt man in the next room could take it down if he really wanted to. Sitting on the edge of the bath until it fills, I debate whether or not I've done the right thing in divulging that morsel of information.

Climbing in, the temperature of the water is scolding against my skin. I lean back and stare at the ceiling, my mind awash with sentiments that have been carefully controlled for the majority of my life. The light knock on the door escorts me back from my reverie. It creaks open, and Sloan stands in front of me, wearing only a pair of well-worn jogging pants that sit dangerously low on his narrow, defined hips. My eyes drift down to his abdomen, and I wait with bated breath, wondering if he will join me.

He doesn't.

Instead, he drags over a stool from the vanity, and starts to wash my hair. His touch is maddening, especially when I all I want at this moment in time, is for him to caress me and erase the aftershock of the past. The way his fingers work through the strands, massaging my scalp, do nothing to remove the anguish that makes my chest expand disproportionately. The feeling of dread and apprehension still squeezes furiously at my heart. The water runs down my back, and I shiver constantly. I look at him through damp lashes, not daring to face him full on. I know he would never hurt me, having witnessed first-hand the way he was with Emily, and previously with Sam.

Sloan Foster is truly a good man. So far, he's one of the best I have ever met. And he's one I know I don't deserve to call mine.

That is also one of the reasons why *I* never called him these last two weeks. He needs someone in his life that will make him happy; make him smile. That woman isn't me, and never would be. All I can bring to the table is pain and destruction. A tear rolls down my cheek as I mentally argue with myself. There's no use in lacing it with sugar and pretending I'm good enough for him; I never will be. And I'm only fooling myself if I believe otherwise.

The water drenching my hair and back stops. I drink him in, absorbing the way the overhead spotlights bathe him to the point where he looks almost ethereal. *My dark-haired angel.* I sigh at the visual of him, memorising every line and curve, as I glide my eyes down his front.

I motion towards the towel hanging from the rail, and he pulls it off and stretches it out for me. I rise slowly - any faster, and my legs will not support me. He wraps me up in the plush, soft cotton; it's divine and heavenly, brushing against my skin. He picks me up, and I rest my head on his shoulder as he carries me back into the bedroom. I find myself breathing in tune, learning his rhythm, because come morning, there is a distinct possibility he may disappear for weeks on end again.

Sloan leaves me on the bed, rubbing a towel over my hair, as he disappears into the walk-in wardrobe. He reappears minutes later, holding a long, dark blue gown. He places it over the chair, then ventures back in again. This time, he re-emerges holding a pair of shoes that match the dress perfectly. I watch in confusion as he repeats this process several times, each time returning with something new.

"Right, baby, I'm going to take a shower. *Please don't go anywhere*," he stresses. His hands cup my face, and his lips touch my forehead. "I won't be long." I watch in awe as he saunters back into the bathroom.

I pick up the dress delicately, and my eyes dilate at the beauty of the garment he has selected. I let the luxurious fabric ripple through my fingers, realising it's the same colour as his eyes. I inhale a few deep breaths to calm myself, then pick up the shoes. Holding one close to my chest, my tears begin to break again. I feel truly pathetic, and a long, outdrawn sigh escapes the confines of my throat.

Long, uncomfortable minutes pass, with only the sound of running water, until I hear voices, followed by feet pounding up the stairs.

The door flies open, and Charlie bounds into the room with a suit bag in her arms.

"Miss me?"

Mortified, I snatch up the other towel and hold it in front of myself. Two is definitely better than one right now. Seconds later, Jake enters. He, too, is holding a suit bag, while his other hand is laden with who knows what.

I'm just about to open my mouth and tell them to get the hell out, when Sloan exits the bathroom. My eyes roam over his practically naked, exquisite form, and the blood rushes to my face. His eyes dart between the three of us, and he quickly shuts down the distance and stands in front of me, shielding me from our unexpected guests.

"Goddamn you, Charlotte! I told you we would pick you up! Why do you never listen?"

What starts out quite harsh, disintegrates by the time the last word leaves his mouth. It's abundantly evident he adores his sister, and my heart melts further for this man who should be running in the opposite direction - well away from me.

"We?" I move out from behind him, and he slides his hands over my shoulders, pausing centimetres from me. My eyes flutter as he unknowingly intoxicates me. I wish Marie had told me that body wash and man was such a natural aphrodisiac. *That* was never mentioned when she tried to school me on the birds and the bees.

"Yes, *we*. *We* are attending an event tonight. *We* are going together." He puts his finger over my mouth, seeing my lips start to the part in protest. "Because, if you haven't already noticed, I'm making sure that *we* work. I've spent two, long, aching weeks without you, do you really think I'm going to miss out on anymore?" His eyes flash with all kinds of unspoken promises. There is heat in them that sears my own instantly.

"And just where are *we* going?" I ask, ignoring the last of his sentence. I pick up the dress and shoes without due care. Sloan doesn't answer me, he just shrugs coyly. He's a sly sod when he wants to be.

"No, no, no!" Charlie stomps towards me with purpose. She looks almost ready to rugby tackle me. "You need my help tonight. That's why we're here. I'm going to make you look fabulous!" Halting abruptly, she grabs the bag that Jake has brought in and then marches out, dragging it behind her.

"Please tell me you're not leaving me to get ready with her?" I ask horrified.

Sloan slaps his hand over his mouth, whereas Jake has no airs or graces, and laughs out loud. Very loud. He's roaring with such intensity, it causes Sloan's shoulders to move up and down. I shake my head slowly, snatch up the other towel and launch it at them. Sloan catches it effortlessly, wagging his finger at me in mock disgust. I give them my best glare. Unaffected, they both continue laughing, still amused with themselves.

Safety in numbers is in their favour right now.

"Bastards," I mutter, slamming the door behind me. Their raucous laughter accompanies me down the hallway, as I go in search of Miss Emerson.

Chapter 20

CHARLIE'S FACE IS as vacant, as her voice is silent.

I perform a mental victory dance at the beautiful stillness of the room at long last.

She's prodded and poked. She's lifted my hair up, down, to the side, to the back, and then repeated it all over again. *Numerous times*.

My patience was wearing thin as she debated what suited me best, and then finally got to work on my make-up. I breathed out a sigh of relief, until she approached me with a black eyeliner in her hand intended for my face.

I feared the moment I had to look at my reflection. It is something I do as little as possible. In my world, mirrors existed to ensure you could walk out of your door every morning. They were not something I could stand in front of and seek self-admiration from. Whenever I did, the reflection that greeted me was that of my fifteen-year-old self, not the woman I am today.

Charlie is still quiet as I cautiously step in front of the full-length mirror. I open my eyes, terrified I will look ridiculous, yet I stare in amazement at the woman reflecting back at me. And *she is*n't *me*.

My eyes are smoky perfection, the colour matching my dress and shoes perfectly. I flatten my hand over my hip, suppressing a nervous laugh. She was right - the clothes do make the woman. And this dress does really amazing things for my, normally, very plain figure.

I spin with pizazz to look at her, and she finally gives me an approving smile. "Well, I've got to hand it to him, he does have good taste. In clothes, as well as women. Well, only one woman." She winks.

I delicately touch my hair, which is styled into a side parting at the front, and a chic, low bun at the back. "What do you mean? Didn't you buy this with everything else?" I query, suddenly feeling a great urge to hug her for making me look better than I have ever managed to do.

"No, silly. I bought one very similar. *This*," her hand waves over the dress, "this is Sloan's choice. But I have no idea when he found the time to buy it. I mean, we've only just come back from New

York. It's absolutely stunning on you, though." She walks out, and I gawk at her retreating back.

So, these last two weeks had not been *business* after all. Although he has consciously lied to me, a huge weight lifts off my shoulders knowing Charlie had been with him and not some other woman.

I study every inch of my reflection, hoping Sloan will approve of my appearance. This isn't good for my state of mind. My resolve is quickly losing the battle, trying to determine what I think is the right decision for both of us.

When Charlie fails to return, I make my way downstairs. Each tap of my heels carries me closer and closer to the man I want to run from, but can't seem to let go of. I stop a couple of steps from the bottom, nervous and feeling very much out of my depth. Seconds later, he is in my sight. His eyes hood heavily, casually raking up and down my body, making me shiver with anticipation. I lick my lips, reciprocating his stare, and take note of his attire.

Why does he have to look so stunning?

He is dressed in a formal tux, including a real bow tie, which is currently laying undone around his neck. I'm at risk of swallowing my tongue when his palm darts out to me, and he smiles in awe. The adoration radiating from his eyes steals my breath away. He takes my hand in his, and guides me down the last few rungs. I follow closely behind him, feeling lightheaded from the way his fingers gently circle my palm continuously, and the pheromones he is emanating. He stops when Charlie and Jake both turn simultaneously in our direction.

Charlie is smiling broadly, and for the first time since the night I had to deal with her at the function, I realise that first impressions can sometimes be deceiving. I watch her eyes flick to her brother, and she perpetually holds his gaze. There is an unspoken conversation being carried out between the siblings, that neither Jake, nor I, are privy to.

I slide my hand from Sloan's and look around the room, trying to see where Charlie has put my clutch. My eyes locate it sitting innocently on the coffee table, next to something else that seriously demands my attention.

"Come here." Sloan starts to walk towards the table.

Nervous, I look at Charlie, who links her arm through Jake's, and turns to leave. Watching the two of them together, I wonder if there is more to their relationship than I originally thought. He stares at her with the same lust and intensity that Sloan bestows upon me.

"We'll be in the car," Jake says over his shoulder, giving me a sly wink. "By the way, you look stunning, Kara." Charlie beams up at him and then me, before gathering up some of her champagne coloured gown, and then they are gone.

The room is silent enough to hear a pin drop, as Sloan holds the mystery box in front of him. I mentally brace myself and edge closer. My eyes never leave his, and it's a miracle I'm not flat on my face, considering the monstrous high heels adorning my feet.

He reaches out, and affectionately strokes my ear, lingering on my lobe. "Hmm," he murmurs, smiling and shaking his head. "You look beautiful tonight, but these are too bare, my love." I'm holding on by a thread, all the while his fingers tickle the skin beneath my ear. He withdraws his hand and opens the box.

Oh. My. God!

My first reaction is to shut the lid firmly and lock them away. Breathless, and acutely aware of what this man's presence does to me, I begin to quiver, until his warm hand on the back of my neck massages away the tension forming there. He quietens and soothes me, as I silently run through the many reasons why I cannot wear what he is requesting me to. These are things I could never afford in a million years. It's more than apparent in this precise moment, that I don't belong in his world.

Sloan bends at the knees, dipping to stare intensely into my eyes. "You *do* belong here - with me. Please?"

My rib cage expands uncomfortably with each deep inhalation. I nod slowly, as he opens the box again and removes the first of the earrings. The diamonds glint and sparkle with each tiny movement, and I observe him attentively, concentrating on his task. He smiles each time his eyes catch mine. He tilts my head up gently, and looks from side to side, admiring the beauty of the stones.

His eyes lower again, and he gently removes the choker. It's almost too painful to feel him brush over my extremely sensitive skin and collarbone, as he takes full advantage of the situation. After positioning the multi-strand, diamond-encrusted piece, his concentration is unbreakable. He grins and strokes it reverently, and I catch myself falling deeper for him.

Finally, he extracts the matching bracelet. It dangles innocently and beautifully in his hand, while he holds my scarred wrist with his other. He secures it and holds out my arm. His thumb glides across the scar, and he carefully slides the bracelet over it.

He pulls me close to him, and yet again, my senses go into overload at his scent and strength. I lose some of my rationality, as his hands run over the satin of the dress, up to my bare shoulders. His lips press against mine, and his tongue plunges deep inside my mouth. My eyes begin to flutter in lust when his teeth tug at my bottom lip. He lets go, and I lick it involuntarily. He squeezes his eyes tight and groans.

No words are spoken as we exit the suite. I even manage to keep it together when faced with the prospect of the lift. He holds me close as we descend to the ground floor, diverting my awareness with an abundance of tender, chaste kisses.

Waiting in the lobby, Charlie and Jake are still hand in hand. They climb into one of the cars, and it sets off. Crossing over to George, he smiles warmly and tilts his head with approval. Safe inside the car, Sloan tugs me closer and strokes his hand over my arm. My skin tingles under the delicate touch of his fingers, and I smile shyly and turn to the window.

I might be fighting the internal battle in my head as to whether I should stay or go, but I can't deny the way my heart has finally come back to life after eight, long years.

The journey to the venue is short, and when we pull up outside, I'm shocked by what awaits us.

Lights flash constantly as we walk the red carpet into the hotel hosting the event. The calls and shouts from the waiting reporters and photographers are deafening.

I eye Sloan more than once, noticing each time I do, his face is growing tenser, and he actually looks ready to explode. I'm shouted at to pose and smile, but he holds me tight against him. I'm shaking a little from the intrusion of the whole circus. Cameras are being shoved in my face, and I'm forced to shift into his arm to avoid appearing in whatever trashy magazine they're reporting for.

Walking the gauntlet, I recognise a few faces that pass by us, and I do my best not to let my jaw hit the floor. The other less famous guests greet Sloan with familiarity and acknowledge my presence by his side. His face beams as he surveys my countenance. It is an odd feeling to be at such ease with myself, but I'm painfully aware he plays a big part in calming my inner storm.

Finally inside, Charlie motions to me. She makes our apologies to the men and hurries us towards the ladies' toilets. She looks into each cubicle, ensuring they're empty, before locking the entrance door.

"God! I hate this. Every bloody time! You'd think after all these years they would get tired of picturing us. We're nobodies! We just turn up because it's for charity, and Emerson and Foster make a substantial donation. It's not like our picture ends up in the trashy tabloids or anything. At best, we might get a tiny two by two in the back of a glossy that no one will ever look at!" She slicks her lips with gloss, smacks them together, and declares she is ready to go back out.

I hesitate at the door, subdued by the paparazzi, and the fact that my picture of holding Sloan in an intimate fashion might be viral in no time whatsoever. I feel physically sick. I'm overwhelmed by Charlie's statement, and terrified that my past will, no doubt, come back to haunt me if anyone decides to dig deeper and discovers my name.

She halts at the door; a sad expression replaces her happiness. "Whatever has happened in your life, Kara, don't let it win. Don't allow it to control your future. Never be too scared to live or dream because of it." A look passes over her glassy eyes. I can't put my finger on it, but something tells me that Charlie has also suffered somewhere in her own past. I clutch her hand, squeezing it for dear life, forgetting how much I despise it.

When we return, Sloan and Jake are talking quietly, and Walker is now with them. It's a miracle I recognise him in a suit. Just like Jake, he looks amazing in the perfectly fitted two-piece and bow tie. Charlie nudges me, and points over to a group of women, who are openly lusting after what could easily be the three most handsome men in the room. I grin and roll my eyes, listening to her mutter incoherently about cheap and cheerful.

Okay, so I admit it, I really do like her. *A lot.*

"Evening, Kara," Walker greets, and I smile shyly. Sloan moves to my side, placing a protective arm around me. Walker shakes his head in amusement. "Don't worry, kid, we all know she's yours," he drones out. "By the way, that *thing* you wanted doing - it's done." Sloan turns and glares at his friend.

"Kid?" I query. His eyes are still narrowed on Walker, but the man simply grins and walks away. Sloan shakes his head and laughs, then turns to me.

"He calls me it when he's pissed. Or happy, apparently. It's better than half-brit anyway."

My brow quirks. "Half-brit?"

"Yeah, Jake started calling me it in uni, because of my accent. It's blended in a lot over the years, but sometimes he and Devlin still call me it," he grins. I have no idea where his accent originates from, and I'm about to ask when he answers the unspoken question for me.

"My mum's a Londoner, and my dad was from Chicago."

I nod, dying to ask more, but leave it for now. There's plenty of time to discuss it later, so I slap the lid back on the imaginary box inside my head. He folds my arm into the crook of his, and rubs my wrist as we stroll through the crowd towards his sister.

Charlie looks radiant, standing proudly with Jake, her hand in his. The smile he gives her leaves no doubt in my mind as to what their relationship really is. A quick glance at Sloan and, he too, is now watching them closely. I curve my fingers around his hard bicep, and he grins at me.

"They've been together for a while. They first met when Jake and I were in uni. Charlie tried to hide it for years, but to no avail."

"Does it bother you?" I ask, continuing our synchronised stroll en-route to the main room.

"No, Jake's good for her. She drives him crazy, but he's always been there for her." Seeming to have relaxed somewhat, he continues. "And as much as it might have annoyed me back then, I would never deny her happiness." Looking ahead, I spy Charlie's silk-clad back disappear into the horde, with Jake following closely behind her.

Entering the room, I look over the tables; white silk covers them and the intricate centrepieces, made up of various varieties of lilies, are to die for. I've seen this type of function hundreds of times before, but now I'm no longer on the outside looking in. Sloan motions to a passing waiter and picks up two glasses from the tray. Handing one to me, he gives me the first genuine smile I have seen since we arrived.

"To our future, *Ms Petersen,*" he says, touching his glass to mine.

Lust darkens his eyes, and the heat of his stare penetrates deep inside me. I squirm a little, and my body begins to ache, the space between my thighs becoming excessively moist. He smirks at me, *knowingly*, understanding exactly how my body is reacting. Needing to cool off, I drain the glass dry. His eyebrow plucks up, and he inches closer.

"Don't drink too much. I want you lucid when I take you home tonight," he whispers seductively. My stomach is tied up in knots, anticipating what he has secretly planned for us later. He secures one hand on my hip and claims my lips. Heat rolls off him, and I cling to him for support.

I'm lost in the moment until the clearing of a throat pulls us apart.

A man in his late fifties is standing in front of us, with a very pissed off looking Walker. The muscles in Sloan's arm pull taut to the point of combustion, and I know I need to get away from whatever is brewing between them. I scan the room, hoping to see Charlie, but instead, I see someone else who makes me feel both happy, and very, very guilty.

Marie.

Running the show from the bar, assessing the attendees, she's giving out instructions to one of the waitresses. I tug discreetly on Sloan's sleeve. "I'm going to see Marie and grovel profusely!" I point to her, then gather up my long gown to avoid slipping. He doesn't say anything, just turns in the direction of my surrogate mother. His eyes scan the room quickly and cautiously, then he nods, kissing my forehead before I turn on my heels.

I catch Marie's attention while crossing the room. Her face is overflowing with happiness. I can't recall seeing her smile like this in the last seven years. I am nearly halfway there, when she jerks her head to the side. I turn in the direction she is indicating, seeing the hateful glares I'm receiving from a table full of women.

If scowls could kill, I think, trying hard not to look at them.

One of them stands, just as I am about to pass, effectively blocking me. She looks me up and down with undeniable disgust, like I'm nothing more than dirt on the sole of her shoe. I square my shoulders, pretending she doesn't affect me.

"So, you're her then! Well, I thought you would be better than this; prettier, less plain and forgettable, but you're nothing but an ugly fucking tart! You don't belong here, and you won't for much longer. Once he's had his fun and gets bored, he'll come back to the one woman that really matters!" The spiteful woman's eyes lock onto the diamonds adorning my body, and she gives me an evil smile. "Well, I guess you must be doing something right, after all!"

I look at the table of sneering women as salty tears prick my eyes. Enduring their pitiful stares, my heart sinks as I wonder how many of them he might have slept with. I have no room to judge, but the thought of him with any one of them, leaves a bitter taste in my mouth.

"*Kara?*" I shift to find Charlie behind me with Jake, both wearing expressions that would've turned the bitch to ashes if it was possible.

"Oh, get over it, Christy! He's not with you, and he never was. He told you this at the last function we attended, remember?" Charlie says with venom, edging closer to the woman. "Unlike you, she'll be in his life for more than a few hours at a time, because that's all you were to him - a toy; *a cheap, easy plaything!*" Her eyes are mere slits as she vents her anger for all to hear. "You were just a means to an end, you delusional, fucking slut!" This side of Charlie is more than a little scary, and it's a side of her even I'm backing away from.

Marie is now approaching the little showdown, looking angry. I scan my eyes across the room to find Sloan, also watching the debacle from afar with acute concern. He is completely ignoring the older gentleman, who seems to be oblivious he isn't paying him any attention. I send him a small smile to let him know that I'm okay, although I'm not. Far from it, actually. The tension in his face remains, but he acknowledges me with a little smile of his own.

With my guard down, a slim arm links through mine. I instinctively know who it is, but it doesn't ease the slight burn within. Marie guides us away from the table and stops at the bar, pulling out a couple of stools.

"I should be really angry with you, but it's impossible when you look this amazing and happy!" I sniff back my unshed tears. "Well, happy until that vapid bitch opened her mouth, I guess." She hands me a napkin, and I dab it over my eyes gently.

Walker appears at my side, and I still when his hand runs down my face in a fatherly fashion, catching the stray tears. It's painful to feel such affection, especially when my own father had never so much as noticed me growing up, unless it was for his own personal gain. He sure as hell never soothed the tears that he helped to create.

"Don't believe a single word she says, honey. She's infatuated with him, has been for years, and she'll stop at nothing to get him.

The man Sloan's speaking to is her father. His business isn't doing too well at the moment. It's on its knees, pretty much of the verge of going into administration. She needs to tread very carefully because the future of their company lies in Sloan's hands. He won't tolerate her talking to you like that, or anyone, for that matter," Walker explains, perching himself on a stool. He looks towards Sloan, and I follow. Judging by the look on his face, and that of his older companion, the conversation seems to have taken a serious turn.

"Please, don't tell him what she said," I plead. I may not like the bitch, but I'm not spiteful like her. I don't want to see anyone suffer due to a few hateful, jealous words.

He sighs and nods, before getting an eyeful of Marie Dawson.

"Oh, Marie, this is Walker. Walker, Marie," I introduce them, grateful for her presence.

"Marie, it's a pleasure to see you again, Angel." Walker turns his full attention to her, and she appears ready to commit murder. She gives him a shrewd look, then slowly moves her head from side to side. This only encourages him more, and he flashes his whites at her. She stands with her hands on her hips, one leg jutted out. Her whole stance is defensive, but I don't miss the glimmer of pride in her eyes as she catches him ogling her more than once. I put my hand over my mouth to conceal my laugh, and she glares at me.

"I wish I could say the same!" she replies, before turning around, flushed, and mumbles to the bartender for more champagne. She completely ignores him, but Walker seems unfazed. He winks, slaps her behind, and quickly becomes lost in the crowd.

"Marie?" I whisper, wanting to know what on earth just happened. She shakes her head, and hands me the glass.

"You know, I've met him a few times before you started seeing him. The first time was the night our paths first collided. It was only a brief meeting with the hotel manager, but Sloan was there, and he seemed really pissed off and angry at everything. To be honest, it didn't register with me who he was back then, he was really young, maybe eighteen or so. I honestly thought he was heartless - he certainly acted like a cold bastard," she says, looking over at him.

"The second time was for the Emerson event next month. He was openly horrendous! I wasn't happy to be catering for him at all. I was going to tell you what an arsehole he was, but you were having issues with Sam and Ian, and since that took precedence, I just let it go. Then the last meeting was when he replaced the original caterers at last month's event. He seemed to have mellowed a little, especially when I talked about you, but tonight he's completely different. I can't help but think you've played a part in that," she says, eyeing me lovingly. "He's quite popular. Famous even, in his circles, at least. I'm told the amount of money he donates to charity is extraordinary." Her admiration for his philanthropy is blatant.

I sip my champagne, unable to form any kind of response. I'd honestly forgotten she has met him before. She eyes me suspiciously, and I know she wants information about what's going on between us, but since it's all still very new to me, I'm not willing to share just yet.

"So, tell me how you know Walker?" I ask inquisitively.

She grins broadly. "Stop changing the subject. And no, I had nothing to do with it!"

"Nothing to do with what?" I challenge. *What is she hiding from me?*

She smiles innocently, before adding, "And no disrespect to you, you know I think you're stunning, always have, but what *are you* doing with him?"

Ah, nice subject change.

"I have absolutely no idea."

I'm far from offended by her statement, because, I too, am more than curious as to why he wants to be with me. I'm still waiting for something that will give me further significant insight.

"Well, I think you need to get back over to your man before she does." Pointing towards Sloan, I follow her finger to see Christy siding up to him, touching him. He looks furious and pushes her away. He says something to her that makes her look as though she has bit into a lemon. The small smile stealing across my lips fades quickly, and a new reaction shocks me to my core.

Jealously.

I want to rip the fake nails from her fingers and scream at her not to touch him! My hands clench together, trying to rid the vision of her openly pawing him. I shake my head, clearing my crazy, foreign thoughts. I have no right to be possessive over him; I'm not even sure what we are yet.

"He's not my man, Marie," I admit, dejectedly.

"No, honey, he is. The few times I've spoken to him, he's proven that he is. You just haven't accepted it yet."

"And when have you spoken to him?" She doesn't reply, just arches her eyebrows and taps her nose.

"Go, ask him to dance, and show every wealthy, unappreciative bitch in here that you have what they all want." I huff out a little too loudly at her absurd suggestion, but she just shoves me off the stool.

Walking towards him, every step booms in my ears. I fail to hear anything else, except the click of my heels and the blood rushing to my head. I drift through the crowd with my mind working overtime.

Why on earth is he with me?

Why did he bring me here tonight?

And just how successful is he?

I laugh to myself, remembering he never gave me a reply when I asked him what he actually did for a living. Instead, he diverted my attention with sex. I know he owns the hotel chain, but his office, *Emerson & Foster?* What does he do there? I make a mental note to quiz him about it later.

Not that it really matters to me, throughout my entire childhood I grew up poor. I don't care for his money, the dress on my back, or the diamonds he presented me with this evening. I don't need any of that stuff. The one thing I truly do need is unconditional love.

But will he still be able to give me that when the inevitable truth finally comes to light?

Only time will tell.

My eyes might be wide open, but I'm blind, until a pair of strong arms envelop and lift me. My toes trail on the surface of the marble floor, and I look up in delight as Sloan's blues pierce mine. Brushing my concerns aside, I grin at him as the big band starts to play Frank.

"Please, may I have this dance?" he whispers to me.

I decide it's time to play with him, and release some of the tension we have both been dealing with lately. Pursing my lips together, I make a face that says I'm thinking about it, and then nod with a smile.

"Thank goodness! I thought you were going to say the word I detest, and I'd have to dance with one of *them*!" He makes a horrified face towards the table Christy and her friends are sat at, and chuckles genuinely.

I smile and lean in closer. "I think we have gone over this before; you don't like the word *no*, and it's not a word you hear often. So, tell me, *Mr Foster*, what would you have done if I had said it?" He inhales harshly but doesn't respond.

I flatten myself against him, letting him know I never had any intention of turning him down. His partial erection strokes my stomach, and I quickly peek down between us. He softly brings my head back up to meet his seductive eyes. The look of adulation floors me, and I melt under his touch. He spins me effortlessly on the spot and leads us onto the dance floor.

Well, here goes nothing.

I'm not a natural dancer. There is not one iota of co-ordinated grace present in this body, so I'm putting my faith in him to make us look good - but I'm not about to tell him that.

"Just follow my lead, my gorgeous girl. I'll never let you fall." He supports my lower back, and I relax into him as a new song starts, and he takes control.

Four songs later, we're still on the dance floor. To my left, Jake and Charlie look like they have danced together a million times before. It warms my heart to see them like this. Watching them together, I'm painfully aware I wouldn't know how to make a relationship work. Not even if it was given to me with an instruction manual and an audio guide to boot.

A flurry of laughter drifts from my right, and I'm shocked to see that Walker is actually winning the battle with Marie. She leans into him, and he whispers something in her ear. Her face tints pink, and I look up to Sloan, who arches his brows and laughs out with surprise.

"Interesting," he says candidly. The look on his face speaks volumes; this is yet another piece of the complex web being weaved. There is definitely more going on here than he's letting on.

"What is?" I ask.

He twirls me around like a pro and then back to him. "Well, he's not normally like this. He prefers to stand on the sidelines and blend," he replies coyly.

"Sounds familiar." *Too familiar.* He stops my turn suddenly and moulds me to him. "I like to blend in, be unseen. It's easier to remain invisible," I confess sheepishly, trying to encourage him to move, so as not to draw any unnecessary attention to us.

"Why?" His hand on my back dips lower until it's riding the swell of my behind. "Why do you prefer to remain invisible?"

"Well, if they can't see you, they can't hurt you."

His face constricts, and a part of myself breaks at having to witness his pain. This is because of me, but I'm still strong enough, or secure enough, to let him in. I close my eyes, too scared to look anywhere else.

The song slows and finishes, and Sloan guides us towards an empty spot in the corner of the room.

"Let me in, Kara. Tell me what haunts you, baby." I want to. I really do, but I can't, not yet.

Not that it changes anything, because eventually, I'm going to lose him either way. I'm aware deep inside I'm just delaying the inevitable. One day, I'll be that broken girl again, picking up the pieces of my shattered soul. My heart is in turmoil, and I know I have to shut this down, sooner rather than later, if I am to protect myself. I snag a drink from a nearby waiter and down it in one. Sloan glares with a mixture of suspicion and concern. His eyes soften when he sees mine glass over.

"Please, talk to me," he begs.

"I thought you don't like begging."

"No, I don't like *you* begging. I make no apologies for wanting the best for you. I want to be the person who comforts you when you're sad, the one who picks you up when you fall. I want to be everything for you."

"No," I whisper. Feeling my conviction starting to diminish, I drag myself away from him. "You left me for two weeks after mauling me in the back of your car. You ran away from me, remember? You said you had business, but both Charlie and Walker confirmed you'd just come back from New York. I hate liars, Sloan! I hate them!" And I hate myself even more because that is exactly what I am doing; I'm withholding the truth. I'm omitting. I'm inadvertently lying.

He seizes my waist and attempts to close the gap. I quickly glance around to make sure nobody has witnessed my outburst, and thankfully, no one seems to care.

"I can't do this anymore! I've spent two weeks going out of my mind. Please understand that I can't become so dependent on you that I lose myself completely. I would like nothing more than to be with you, but I can't live with not knowing when you will drop me again. I'm pretty sure you can't give me what I want, and I'm positive I wouldn't even know how to make a relationship work. Please, just let me walk away with dignity and respect my wishes. You did it two weeks ago; you respected my request. Please, Sloan, let me have it again now."

And he does.

With an air of hostility and hurt, he lets go of my hand, and permits me to walk away from him.

I manage to make it outside fifteen minutes later, after being stopped by everyone asking if I'm okay. Naturally, my face betrays me and threatens to expose my pain. After convincing myself that I have lied effectively - and well - I find myself outside the hotel, wondering how I'm going to get home.

And more so, do I still have one?

A black limo pulls up in front of me while I contemplate. George steps out of the car and opens the door. "I'll take you home, Miss Petersen."

I want to object to his kind offer, but cannot afford to. I thank him and climb inside. He softly closes the door, and I rest my head against the window. I've fucked-up big time tonight, and quite possibly destroyed the best thing in my life.

Damn my wretched past, and the turmoil it still unearths inside me.

George starts the car and then speaks, "Where to, Sir?"

Sir?

I whip my head around, and Sloan leans forward from the shadows to speak with George. I whimper to myself at how ignorant and silly I've been. Of course, he wouldn't let me go home alone. Shame starts to grip me, and I feel sick and remorseful at the way I've behaved. There were no grounds to warrant it, other than my own insecurities. I'd just let whatever was in my head come out of my mouth without any consideration as to the consequences.

"The hotel, please." He stares at me questioningly, waiting for me to refuse. Instead, I shuffle up to him and snuggle into his side, seeking solace from his body heat. My head drops to his shoulder, and his arms fasten around me. He breathes in satisfied, and I've never felt so safe in my life.

"Please forgive me."

He kisses my forehead and tilts my chin up.

"I already have."

I kick off my shoes the instant George drops us outside the hotel. Sloan holds my heels and observes me with curious amusement, eying my bare feet, slapping on the impeccable, marble floors of his very expensive, plush hotel. He continues to study me meticulously on our approach to the lift. He doesn't make any attempt to touch me as we enter and the doors close, imprisoning us.

I grip the bar running around the box and count in my head, waiting for the tense feeling to come. Surprisingly, it doesn't. I admit, I still feel anxious, but I can't pinpoint exactly what has caused this transformation. Sloan eyes me speculatively, no doubt wondering the same. The doors ding open a short time later, and then we're standing outside the suite.

He whispers the code in my ear. "Remember it. You'll need it for future use." He kisses my knuckles as we go inside. My feet feel like lead weights, much like the rest of my body.

"Do you want to go to bed?"

Ah, of course he would ask that question! My brow lifts a little, and he shakes his head and smirks.

"To sleep! You have a one-track mind, my love." My mouth falls open, and he puts his finger under my chin to close it. "Come on, let's go to bed."

Hitching my gown up, he carries me upstairs while I cling tightly to the two glasses of water he insists on bringing up. He eases the tumblers from my hands and places them on the bedside table. Stopping to grab one of his t-shirts from the dresser, he moves us into the bathroom. Sitting me down on the vanity, he pulls something out of the drawers below.

I narrow my eyes at him. "Make-up remover? Are you cross-dressing at weekends, Mr Foster?"

He laughs out loud and seriously, it's good to see a more playful side of him. I've only witnessed it a few times previously with Walker and Jake, but it pleases me to know I can bring this hidden side out of him, too.

"Well, I figured since you would be spending more time here, I should make sure you have everything you need." I blow out my breath. He's presumptuous, I'll give him that. Understanding I'm a little vexed, he glances down at the drawer, and I follow suit.

My eyes scan over the toiletries, and I smile, feeling my annoyance dissipating swiftly. I'm touched that he has done this, until I see a familiar blue box, and my skin heats uncontrollably. *He has bought me goddamn tampons!* I raise my hands to my face, dying of embarrassment, but he taps them away.

"Baby, nothing to be ashamed about, it's natural. But no, I didn't go shopping for tampons." He grins and kisses my nose. "I sent Walker," he says coyly.

Flustered, I slap his arm playfully. He laughs and continues to concentrate on his task. I close my eyes, and allow him to finish divesting me of my artificial face. If only he could divest me of my mortification.

Ten, silent, minutes later, I'm finally on my own two feet, brushing my teeth, dressed in one of Sloan's oversized t-shirts. Still feeling a little awkward, I gaze up at him, and he stops mid-brush and strokes my cheek. It's such an innocent, yet intimate act - just watching him watching me. It pulls at my heartstrings in a way nothing else can. This is his normality, but I don't know if I dare to dream that it will eventually become mine, too.

I'm almost comfortable, when the other side of the bed dips and a strong, muscular arm draws me in. He rolls me over, so that I'm facing him, and positions my leg over his thigh, just like he has done on the previous night's we have spent together. My hand comes up to his bicep, and I ease my fingers over the strong muscle, admiring and loving how it feels under my caress.

My eyes are gritty and heavy, and I curl against him affectionately. For the first time in two weeks, I'm home. Thankful that tonight wasn't completely ruined by my stupidity, my body relaxes, and I begin to fall into the start of a much needed, deep and sated sleep.

His lips move against the top of my head, and the last thing I hear, before I give in, is a murmured revelation.

"I love you, *Ms Petersen.*"

Chapter 21

"FOLLOW MY VOICE, baby. Come to me. I won't let anyone hurt you ever again, my beautiful girl."

The words are soft in my ear, and I gently stir. I squint my eyes and smile, seeing his beautiful face suspended above me. For the first time in forever, I've slept soundly.

"Morning," I whisper. Sloan ducks down and tastes my lips. His kiss is soft and loving, and I crave the way his mouth teases and effortlessly coaxes mine into obedience.

He pulls back, grinning. "Good morning, my gorgeous girl."

Suddenly, I feel very shy with him. He's being careful with me, handling me with kid gloves, so I have to ask the question that's dancing in my mind. "Did I dream last night?"

"No, not at all." His voice says one thing, but his eyes tell me he's being duplicitous when they shift away from me.

Determined fingers skim over my neck and ride down the shirt covering my body. My flesh heats under the material, and I want nothing more than to strip us both of what little we have on. He seems to know what I'm thinking, because he lifts me up and diligently tugs the shirt over my head. He throws it behind him and gently lowers me back down.

He traces a finger down my stomach, and my breathing becomes shallow. Underneath his heavy lids, his eyes turn serious, when a look, one that promises more than I could ever dare to imagine, burns me with intensity.

"Last night, I had every intention of bringing you back here and making love to you until the sun came up."

"Sloan, you've made love to me a few times now, one night isn't going to make a difference."

He arches his brows. "No, baby. I've fucked you; I've never made love to you." His hand trails over my aching sex and into my sensitive folds. A finger slides inside, followed quickly by a second, and my core spasms with each penetration. Working myself against his hand, I groan the instant he leaves me empty and wanting. He brings his finger back up to his mouth and sucks it. I won't lie, it's a complete turn on to watch him taste me in such a way.

"Are we good, after last night?" His tone is serious, and I nod, needing to end this now, because after two weeks of yearning for him, I finally have him back, and I need him. I need to feel him inside me again.

"Make love to me, Sloan," I ask, trying not to sound like I'm begging. He will definitely not be impressed if he hears anything that remotely resembles it in such an intimate moment between us.

He stops immediately, deep in thought, before he says, "Promise me you won't walk out and not come back."

I hesitate. *How can he ask that much of me?*

"Promise me!" This time it's a command, one I know he won't let go until I give him the only answer that he deems acceptable.

I accede and whisper, "I promise."

No sooner have the words left my mouth, he's all over me. His hands roam my body thoroughly, memorising my shape all over again. His mouth is soft against mine, and I undulate into him, loving the way he fits me so perfectly; so right.

Somewhere in the suite, a phone starts to ring incessantly. Sloan groans out his aggravation at the shrill sound, but ignores it regardless. A drawer opens, and I meet his gaze, all the while he continues to claim my mouth. From the corner of my eye, I can see the condom packet in his hand. I pull away from him breathless. I know if I allow him to do this, to have me bare and unsheathed, I will truly belong to him. I will be his, and he will be mine.

"Sloan, I trust you. Call me foolish, but I trust you not to hurt me."

He searches my eyes, long and hard. "You are foolish," he says, and drops the packet to the floor, "because I would never hurt you." His hands cradle my face, and the kiss becomes firmer, deeper. He's showing me in actions what he cannot say in words. Words I'd heard last night - or at least what I think I may have heard last night… *I love you, Ms Petersen.*

With a renewed faith in the trust he so desperately wants from me, I close my eyes and worship the emotions rampaging through my heart. His mouth leaves mine, and slowly glides over my skin in a rhythmic motion. There isn't an inch of me he hasn't claimed with those gifted lips. I arch my back as they drag over my stomach, pausing to dip into my navel. My legs spread voluntarily, inviting him, willing him to go lower. Needing him to touch the very part of me that is screaming for him.

Crying out in pleasure, I can no longer resist the urge to watch him. He dips his mouth to my core, and covers my folds and clitoris completely. Everything south clenches to the point of shattering. He slides two fingers inside me, and like clockwork, my body throbs and primes itself for ecstasy the moment he curves them in my heat. My hands slide through his hair, and I tug at the strands, euphoria pulsating deep inside. I hold back as long as possible, until I can take any more. Shaking against him, my inner muscles cripple his fingers. He gives me a sexy grin as he extracts them and kneels between my legs. His tip teases at my opening. The sensation is intense when he starts to push himself in, a fraction at a time. He stretches me beautifully, and his expression alone is enough to make me come again. I purse my lips at the way he feels filling me; like pure silk and steel, both soft and hard.

He groans as I take him to the hilt. Pressing my head back onto the pillow, he starts to move inside me. He performs a flawless, circular motion with his hips, and I practically convulse off the bed. My body grinds against his fluidly, our pelvises meet and part sinuously. His mouth finds mine again, and his tongue emulates his penis, in a dance so intimate, it infuses every inch of me.

"*Kara…*" My name is a prayer from his lips, but he doesn't finish as fever overcomes him.

He tremors and elongates inside me. I stretch my arms around his back, bringing him closer. He pauses briefly, and I can feel his slick, hard shaft pulsating out of control. He raises one leg to his shoulder and holds it there, thrusting and penetrating to the point of madness. His breathing is fast and furious, and he roars out the release of his pent-up desire. Watching him let go is the breaking point that unravels me completely. Losing myself in the beautiful motion of his body making love to mine, I cry out against his neck. Reaching the pinnacle for a third time, my muscles milk him, hard and unforgiving, until neither of us can give any more.

Gradually, we float back down to reality together, and he slowly shifts, so that I'm on my side. His face is stunning; moist, flushed, and sated. His hands link behind my neck, and his sporadic breath blows over my face.

"Say the words, Kara," he commands. His darkened eyes level with mine, and I finally admit the terrifying truth to myself.

"I promise I won't leave." *Because I'm completely in love with you.*

Finally, I allow myself the luxury of letting another human being into my life.

Into my heart.

I only pray he doesn't rip it to shreds when he finally learns the horrifying truth.

With his hand firmly on my back, Sloan forces me into the shower. *Alone.* Literally pushing me into the bathroom, he honestly admits it's for his own benefit, rather than mine, saying he wouldn't be able to control himself. I openly giggle to myself, and lather up the shampoo in my hair. My fingers massage the strands, and sadly, I wish he was doing this for me. I linger under the hot stream for long, soothing minutes, before my hands begin to prune.

Wiping the condensation from the mirror, I reach down into *my drawer.* Kneeling on my shins, on the cold marble floor, I rummage through the contents to get a better idea of what's actually in there. I find all sorts of things I'd failed to notice last night, including more creams, lotions, and make-up, than I know what to do with.

Except, some of these items are not new…

Curiosity wins out, and I fish out the face powder. My own is worn down and desperately in need of replacing. But ever since Sam had become such a drain on my personal finances, shelter and nutrition prevailed over luxuries. Studying the compact closely, I screw my face up.

This powder is mine!

Seeing red, I continue to explore the deep recess of the drawer, my mounting fury expands to epic levels with each new find. I drop to my backside and kick out my legs.

He's moved me in for a second fucking time without my knowledge or consent!

I stomp back into the bedroom, ready to wring his neck. I grab my bag and dig into the inner pocket for my contraceptive pills. I come up empty, and I cry out in frustration. They were definitely in there yesterday! Throwing my bag down, I look around the room wide-eyed, searching for the all-important blister strip, wondering where he's put it. I rip open the drawer on the bedside table. Nothing. I repeat the action with each of the dresser drawers. Again, nothing. I turn in a small circle, and start to feel the panic seep up from deep inside - my pills are nowhere in sight. My eyes catch the light of the bathroom again, and I tilt my head in suspicion, hoping my fears are unfounded. I pray I don't find my pills in that drawer - or any drawer, as a matter of fact.

Poised in front of the vanity, the handle feels like fire in my hand. I debate whether or not I'm just being unduly irrational. Nevertheless, I'm pissed off he is playing a very dangerous game - one which could result in very serious, life-changing repercussions. I yank the drawer back open with more force than intended, but right now, I couldn't give a shit.

As suspected, inside the drawer is my half-used packet of pills. Relief courses through me, but it's tainted, because I'm angry – really fucking angry! The reason I always carry them with me is so that I'll never forget to take them. This behaviour is unacceptable.

Popping today's pill into my mouth, I put the blister strip back into the drawer and notice the new, unopened prescription boxes - the ones that should currently be residing in my underwear drawer at Marie's house. Confusion ripples through me in full force. I pull off the towel, wrap the bathrobe around me, and go in search of the man who knows no personal boundaries.

My senses are assailed by the aroma of a full English as soon as my foot leaves the bottom step. I swallow hard when he comes into view, moving around the kitchen with ease. He's barefoot, wearing only a pair of worn jeans that sit dangerously low on his slim, defined hips. His naked skin glows beautifully under the light, emphasising the toned and ripped muscles in his back and shoulders. His feet slap against the hard floor, while he moves from one worktop to the other. His arms and back bulge and flex when he reaches for the plates in a nearby top cabinet. I can't stop my wayward thoughts of wanting to run my mouth all over him – while my hands ache to wring his interfering neck.

He turns, and his lips curve at the corners into a smile that oozes pure sex and mischief. "Morning, again. And before you comment, I did actually cook this!" He motions for me to come hither, with that sinful, sexy grin and a crook of his finger. I don't. I'm beyond pissed with him, and I'm going to let him know just how much.

"Sloan, why are my contraceptive pills in your bathroom drawer?" I try to stay as calm as possible when he shrugs his shoulders in response.

Well, this is a first. I guess he doesn't like it when the shoe is on the other foot.

"Okay, how about this? What gives you the right to snoop through my things and put them in there? Or, better still - how the hell did you get hold of them in the first place?" I shout at him. My calm persona has flown with my reasoning. Whilst I care he appears so forlorn and guilty, he needs to understand boundaries since he has definitely overstepped mine. And the sooner he lets that information sink into his thick skull, the better.

His face flickers from hurt, to confusion, to justification. "I just felt that-"

"No, you need to respect that you can't control everything. All you've done is violate my space and lost a fraction of my trust. If you wanted me to put them in there, you should have asked me! I probably would have said yes! They live in my bag so I'll never forget to take them. I even have a daily reminder on my phone!" I slump onto one of the stools, giving him my fiercest glare.

Ignoring what I've said, he quickly steps around the island and pins my body to his. "You're very, very, sexy when you're angry." He roughly presses his lips to mine, and although my body is jumping up and down for joy, my head forbids me to participate. Realising I'm not giving in this time, he backs away marginally, but doesn't relax his hold.

"Stop it! I mean it! Consider the consequences of what you've done," I say firmly, slapping my hand on his chest as he leans closer once more.

"Maybe I'd like those consequences," he murmurs against me, his hand drifts to my stomach. I shake my head, the last thing either of us needs is an unplanned pregnancy. He kisses me again, and yet again, I pull back.

"No, we're not kissing and making up! We are going to talk about this rationally!" I push him back further, but my traitorous fingers caress his chest a little too intimately. He slams his hands on his hips, pushing out his bare, beautiful torso. I roll my eyes; he knows exactly what to do to make me submit, but not today.

Completely ignoring the word he hates, he grins. His eyes sparkle wickedly, before he says, "How about make up sex? We don't have to kiss!" My God, he's completely serious, and quite possibly delusional.

"No! No kissing and no make up sex, just talking! Starting with why you have my make-up, toiletries, and pills upstairs. Did you lift them from Marie's house?"

He starts to laugh.

"Oh, my God, you did!"

I lean against the worktop, thinking about how much time he would've had since yesterday afternoon and this morning. I'm so confused. There's no way he did it this morning, because he hasn't left the suite. And he couldn't have done it yesterday, because I was with him in the afternoon. There's no mistaking the fact he's ransacked my bag for my makeup and current packet of pills at some point, but my toiletries and prescription? They were all at home at Marie's...

And it all starts to make sense now.

It explains the way she was with Walker last night. She'd already met him after he was obviously ordered to fetch my stuff. She would've known he was coming to collect them. She also mentioned she'd spoken with Sloan a few times before...

Of course, she had nothing to do with it! She's such a liar - she was a first-hand participant!

I shake my head. "No, you didn't, but I'm going to kill her!"

Hearing him laugh wholeheartedly behind me, I run back upstairs, grab my phone from the dresser and run back down to the kitchen. I halt at the island, seeing Sloan's eyes droop heavily. His stare lodges at my middle, and his tongue darts across his lip. I look down to see that the robe has fallen away at the front, exposing me completely. I hastily re-wrap myself, much to his amusement, and he turns, humming in satisfaction.

"Sloan, shut up! I'm…really, really angry!" I say, climbing onto a stool, staring at his naked chest with longing. "And can you please put a goddamn shirt on your back?!"

"Not a chance, because I know you love what you see!" He laughs, and flexes his pectorals intentionally, both arousing and infuriating me.

"And get some lower bloody stools, too!" I cry out, chucking my mobile on the counter.

He places a full plate in front of me, and I gape at the amount of food. I arch my brows at him. It doesn't take a genius to calculate that I'm going to end up at least a stone or two heavier if I let him cook for me daily.

Kissing the top of my head, he grins beautifully. "Well, I figured that since you seem so determined to pick a fight today, you'll need your energy. And, considering I insist we have make up sex after said fight, I suggest you start eating, my love. And just to verify, you're going to need all the energy you can get."

Oh, he's so very matter of fact! He can be such a smug bastard when he wants to be! Then again, I recognised this trait the night he brazenly propositioned me at the function.

My mobile vibrates across the worktop, and Sloan picks it up. "Ian?"

"My lovely father," I say sarcastically. My annoyed arousal is now being pushed aside, and pure hatred is replacing it.

His face contorts, and he drops his fork. He reaches out and places his hand on my wrist, but I snatch it back. The last thing I want to do is discuss my lying, cheating, drunken father, who is up to his eyeballs in gambling debt, while my pathetic, spineless, no good mother, stands by and lets it all happen.

"Don't. He's not up for debate. *Ever*." He mutters a curse under his breath, removes his hand, and continues eating.

The phone rings constantly. His eyes flick from mine, to the phone, and back again, numerous times, until I can't stand the sound of it any longer. "What?" I scream into the handset.

Silence greets me on the other end.

"Kara? Honey?" My mother's fragile, timid voice breaks through, and I instantly fill with regret. I'm more than curious as to why she's calling, Dad spoke for her, always had. I know for a fact that hasn't changed in the years I've been gone.

"Sorry, Mum, I thought you were him," I apologise, absently moving the eggs around the plate with my fork. My vision is trained on Sloan, who seems wholly intrigued by my behaviour. He never takes his eyes off me, and I never look away.

"I'm sorry for calling, but your father...he's in trouble, Kara. There were men here last night." Her voice cracks and falters, then finally gives way to muffled tears. "They said they would come back and...and..."

"Mum, please don't cry!" I say, listening to her mumble on. This conversation existed under many different guises over the years, I'm not sure if I can still believe it any longer. I turn my head away to ask my next question. "How much does he owe this time?" I practically whisper.

"Five thousand," she replies shakily.

A shocked gasp leaves my mouth, and Sloan shifts uncomfortably in my peripheral vision. "I don't have that kind of money, Mum."

"I know. I just needed to... Oh, no, he's back! I have to go! I love you." Panic laces her thick northern accent. I want to scream in anger at what she has had to live through for years. I wish she would have just left with me eight years ago when I gave her a choice. It was the day I finally realised I was all alone in this life - not even the woman who gave birth to me cared enough to put me first.

"Mum? Mum!" I half-shout, but she's gone.

I stare at the phone, feeling guilty that I actually don't want to help her, because helping her means it benefits him. But am I really being unreasonable? Am I inadvertently punishing my mother for my father's idiocy? Yes, I am, but what else can I do? One doesn't exist without the other.

Sloan looks expectantly, waiting with patience, no doubt wanting me to share. I know I should just lie and leave it at that, but I also know he won't let sleeping dogs lie. I made him a promise not to leave again, and I don't doubt, in his mind, my promise also probably extends to revealing the true ugliness of a life that I have, so far, managed to avoid baring.

My fork drops on the plate; my appetite vanished the moment my dad's name appeared on my phone screen. We stare at each other with equal determination. He's waiting, whereas I'm trying my hardest to convince myself to be open with him. It's uncomfortable, but the call has left me with no other choice.

"My dad is an alcoholic, amongst other things. He uses and deals, and he's in trouble. My mum is..." The words lodge in my throat. God, why is it so hard to open up to him? Marie knows about this side of my life. She doesn't know all of it, but I was brave enough to tell her this. A cold sweat runs the length of me, from tip to toe, and I wonder what he will honestly think of me when I finish telling him. I inhale deeply and continue. "He owes money to a dealer, and it's more than I originally thought."

"How much?" he bites out.

"Five grand, apparently." I look down at my hands, twisting in my lap, as I whisper out the amount. It would be too painful to witness his look of disgust when he eventually realises that Christy was right about me.

All I am is an ugly, fucking tart. Plain and forgettable, with a questionable lineage.

"To whom?" his voice is calm. Too calm.

I raise my head up, surprised he is even considering discussing this. He deserves every ounce of my respect for not kicking me out already. I hesitate. How much information will he deem to be enough? And how much is classed as too much?

Taking a deep breath, I look straight into his eyes. "A man called Frankie Black. He's been in my dad's life for years. He's not...nice." A shiver tears through my body, remembering the first and last time I had seen him. He was darkness and evil personified in my mind, and nothing that anyone could ever say or do, would ever change my opinion regarding him. Sloan's eyes darken, a look of pure hate fills his beautiful face, and he frowns at me.

Oh shit, he thinks I want him to give me money.

I baulk and stand, knocking over the stool in my haste. I start to back away from the island one step at a time. "I'm sorry," I apologise in panic, still wringing my sweaty hands together. "I didn't tell you so that you would give me money." I take another step back, and he follows. "I told you because last night you made me promise not to leave. I respect you too much to hide this from you, especially since whenever he's in trouble, he ends up dragging me into it." My voice breaks under pressure. The tears slide down my cheeks until a few warm drops land on my forearm.

"Shush, don't cry, baby. It's okay." The heat of his body surrounds me, but fails to conciliate my distress. I try so hard to dam the tears, but nothing will stop them from tumbling down my face at an alarming rate.

"No, it's not okay! Every time I turn it around, he just drags me back down again. It's a vicious circle I'll never break free from. I'll never be free of him."

I bury my head against his chest. I'm ashamed of what my father has reduced me to over the years. He doesn't even need to talk to me to make me feel pain, just remembering has the same effect.

"I'll deal with it. Seriously, baby, don't cry for him. It kills me to see you cry. I'll make a few calls; plus, Walker knows people." He touches my face and tucks a stray strand behind my ear. "Are you going to work today?" I nod. "Okay, how about you go get dressed, and I'll drive you to the office. Sound good?" I back away slowly, but his expression is unreadable.

Should I be suspicious that when my world comes crashing down spectacularly, he acts like it is irrelevant? His reaction is almost like he expected it to happen at some point, and that he is, impossibly, already aware.

On my way up to the bedroom, I hear the low murmur of his deep, velvet tones. The mention of my father's name catches my attention, and I sit at the top of the stairs, blatantly eavesdropping. His voice sounds a little broken, and I instinctively put my hand on my heart where the pain is beginning to consume it.

The man who should have cared for me unconditionally, had caused me nothing but immense agony and torture, while the man downstairs was trying to make everything all right. Guilt weighs heavy for having such misgivings about his true intentions, and the pessimism that he would eventually hurt me.

"No, I want a full profile on him again! I want to know everything; where he works, drinks, eats. *Everything.*" He pauses. "I don't care. You do what you have to, John. He hurt Kara, remember?"

Full profile again?

He hurt me?

Remember what?

Confused and unable to listen to any more of his allusions, I walk mindlessly into the bedroom, kicking the door shut behind me.

My mobile vibrates, and Charlie's name fills the screen. "Hi," I answer, pulling out a black blouse and a pair of equally black trousers. My current mood is now black and gloomy, so this outfit is more than fitting.

"Have you seen it yet!?"

"Seen what?" My brow furrows.

She snorts. "The pictures. Online. You're viral!" Her voice drips with abundant excitement, but I can barely crack a smile.

"Oh, my God! Every blog site has pictures of you and my brother! They're all wondering who you are considering he never really dates, and anytime he does, he poses for few pictures, and that's it! There are like a hundred different photos of you two from last night!"

I scrunch my face up in exasperation. Do people not have lives of their own anymore that they have to intrude in mine?

I'm nothing.

I'm nobody.

"I haven't seen the pictures, Charlie, and I'm not sure if Sloan has, either."

Frustrated, and with my clothing choices in hand, I rotate to find Sloan loitering in the doorway. I mouth *Charlie* to him, and he rolls his eyes. He passes me his iPad, all the while she drones on about last night in my ear, but my attention is ingrained on the tablet.

Oh, shit!

"Sorry, Charlie, I've got to go! We'll talk later." I disconnect the call, and gape at the picture. A picture of us dancing, lost in each other's gaze. I stare in both shock and admiration. I can clearly understand why it is viral, now I'm seeing it with my own eyes. Sloan has me in a firm and tight embrace. It's so intimate, you can barely tell where our bodies start and end. His hand is on the small of my back, and the other is caressing my hair. He's looking at me lovingly, and I'm reciprocating his expression. The whole picture screams *mine*.

Then I read the unforgiving and slanderous text underneath it. The words insinuating I'm a gold digger who has done well and landed on her feet, jump right off the page. Tears prick my eyes as panic sets in. I rudely shove the tablet back at him, and he looks a bit put out.

I quickly dress and gather my things together. I fetch my pills from the bathroom, popping one in my mouth and putting the strip in my bag. He doesn't comment as he watches me, but I can see the pain stretching over his face.

"Kara, stop it!" I spin around on the spot to face him. "I've never once read anything that has been written about me, and trust me, there are some really shitty, fucked-up things you could easily dig up. I don't care what they've written about us, I just wanted to show you the picture. I wanted you to see what I see when I think about our relationship. *This*," he holds up the iPad, "this is what's real to me. This picture. *Us*."

I take another fleeting glance at the screen. "Last night, that redheaded bitch called me a tart, that I was plain and forgettable. She said you would get bored with me and leave. That you would go back to women like her, who have money and class." I shrug like it doesn't matter, but my heart is breaking, because deep down, I know she's right.

"She said what?" he shouts out furiously.

"No, it doesn't matter what she said. I'm not angry at you, or even her. I'm fucked off because everyone just automatically assumes that if you have nothing, then there must be an ulterior motive. I guess what I'm trying to say is that if anyone decides to dig deeper, and they find out about my parents…about my past, it will bring you shame and embarrassment. I don't want that for you."

"Kara, I hope you're not saying what I think you are."

"No, I made a promise, I'm not leaving. I'm just saying we need to be more careful. I don't want my life becoming a hindrance on yours." He nods, fully understanding my words, and I'm satisfied I have aired my fears out loud.

I pick up my bag, dig out my pills, and hold them up to him. "Please don't move them again without asking my permission. Otherwise, I'm getting a coil fitted!" I place them down on the bedside table.

"Thank you, my love." He smiles broadly as I walk back to him. Then he runs his finger down my cheek and tugs me into his body.

"Can you still take me to the office?"

"Of course. I'll take you anywhere in the world you want to go." He pulls out a t-shirt and drags it over his head, then leads us out of the suite.

"What do you think about seeing someone about your claustrophobia; this loathing you have of small spaces?" he suggests quietly, uncomfortably, while we wait for the lift to arrive.

I drop my head discreetly. It isn't claustrophobia or small spaces per se, it's the absolute loathing of things that happened after I was pulled out kicking and screaming; things I'd spent years in the aftermath forgetting.

I slowly raise my eyes to him. "Actually, I already have a therapist. Well, I did, not that she was much good. To be honest, sometimes it's just good to talk to someone who's not trying to analyse you." The doors open, and he gives me a sideways glance, then kisses my hand.

"You can always talk to me, you know."

"I-I know, but I'm just not ready. Sometimes I don't even know if what I remember is true. But I'll see someone if it makes you happy," I reply, staring at the inside of the doors, stroking his hand in mine, as we travel down to the car park. The doors open, and our footsteps echo in the deserted multi-storey.

"You're wrong by the way," he says firmly, striding across the tarmac to his Aston. He stops, pulls me tight into him, and caresses my cheek.

"About what?"

"Christy. She doesn't have class. She won't have fuck all by the time I'm finished with her, make no mistake of that." There is a menacing lilt in his tone, and I wince, thinking of what he will do, knowing he has dealings with the woman's father. I decide not to give it too much thought. Whilst I didn't want her to suffer financially, she talked to me like I was shit because I have what she wants, and that is unforgivable in my opinion.

Feeling a little better, I sway my hips intentionally, reaching the car first. The locks disengage, and I slide across the leather, wiggling unashamed. Sloan's features intensify, witnessing my action.

"Sure you don't want to try make up sex? There's no one down here," he suggests coyly, his voice husky and thick.

"Just the cameras," I mumble, rolling my eyes at his proposition, but I can't deny the flush of liquid heat in my tummy.

"Is that a no? Maybe tonight?" Astounded by his audacity, I slap away the hand creeping up my thigh.

"Eyes on the road, mister. There won't be make up anything if you kill us both."

"Don't worry, baby, you're safe with me. Besides, they might even have make up sex in heaven."

He drives out of the car park with ease and efficiency. I try my best not to look at him, so he won't see the smile I'm finding difficult to conceal.

I admit, I'm looking forward to make up sex tonight.

It's another first.

Relaxing back into the seat, an anxious, hollow sensation starts to strengthen in the pit of my stomach. I'm confident it isn't the intensity of being turned on, or the crazy butterflies of secretly being in love, because I have, at long last, experienced both individually.

This new feeling is different; it's a sense of foreboding, of something bad coming.

Instinctively, I know it won't be long, because nothing good ever lasts for me.

Chapter 22

I RAP MY nails on the desk, ignoring the negligible discomfort running up my wrists from my fingertips. Waiting impatiently for the computer to load, I meander through the rooms that now form part of the new office space.

My mind is so consumed with my current situation, and my new living arrangements, I don't hear the muffled click of Marie's heels against the floor. Nor do I notice her until she waves a hand in front of me, snapping me out of my fantasising about Sloan, and the foreign, distinguishable emotions I'm feeling for him.

"Earth to Kara!" she chides with a smile in place.

My eyes focus, and I start to stand. "Sorry..."

"Oh, no, you don't! He's that good, huh?" My cheeks blush when she wiggles her eyebrows and goes off to make some tea. "Sit, I'll bring it through."

Ten minutes later, I'm sat staring blankly at the pages the search engine has brought up. I'm entirely aware clicking through the articles I may be setting myself up for a fall. I browse the pictures of us together and smile a little, but my happiness is short-lived when I see the pictures of him with other women, including Christy. Overcoming my anger at seeing her face, I focus on the pictures of Sloan, and I'm truly mesmerised.

Row upon row are displayed, from newest to the oldest. He looks exactly the same as he does now, but he's ridged in each; cold and distant. Studying them, I finally understand what he was trying to prove this morning. The differences are discernible. On the older ones, he's completely passive; no smile or emotion. Whereas on ours, there is contentment in his face that touches his eyes. His smile, the one that can make me feel damp with desire, is fixed firmly in place on the majority of them. I lean back, finally coming to terms with what's right in front of me.

Marie places down the mug of tea, some thick looking files, and pulls up a chair to view the screen. "You know, I didn't want to say anything, but the night you covered for Sam, he asked me about you."

"When?" I ask, my attention still transfixed on his stunning face.

"Just after you went outside for a break, that's how he found you. He asked me where you'd gone. At first, I thought he was just looking for a bit of fun, but he was adamant that wasn't his intention at all. So, taking his word at face value, I told him where to find you." She sips her tea and clicks on the next picture, the one he had shown me this morning.

"What do you think, Marie? Do you think I am setting myself up for heartbreak?" I cradle the hot mug in my hands, the warmth heats me from the outside in.

"I don't know, honey, but when I spoke to him yesterday evening, and he said you were unwell, he sounded so worried and helpless. I honestly do think he cares a lot about you. I know it's hard for you with your past, especially with what happened, but I think it would be wrong to force him aside due to fear of the unknown." She clicks again, before arching her brows at me. "I'd even go so far as to say that man is actually in love with you. You, my angel, just need to decide what you're going to do about it." She steals a tiny glance, before looking back to the screen.

God, I love this woman so much. We rarely say the words to each other. Instead, it's a silent truth we both respected greatly.

"I don't even know that much about him. There's Charlie, his closest friend is Walker, and the rest of the guys, but other than that...I just don't know." I try to gauge her reaction. I don't want her to judge me for being with someone whom I've not engaged in any kind of serious conversation as to who he is, or where his money comes from.

"So, why don't you ask him, instead of sitting here fretting about it and scouring the internet for information?" she suggests logically.

"Marie, I asked him where he was for two weeks, all he said was *business*, but Charlie told me they had just come back from New York, and Walker had already confirmed the same." He's withholding something, but he's not stupid. Surely he has to know at some point I will find out the truth, especially considering my blossoming friendship with his sister.

Marie types Sloan's name into Wiki, and low and behold, a page dedicated to him appears on the screen. I scan the page looking for anything to shed some light, but nothing is out of place. Everything listed I have already seen on the gossip pages and blog sites. There is the standard information about the hotels, his work with the charity, and not much else. There are a few paragraphs written about his family; the death of his father when he was just a toddler, and lastly, his mother, who passed away around ten years ago - bizarrely only circa dates are listed.

I click on Charlie's link, and skim-read the information. It's an exact mirror image of her brother's, and frustratingly, it doesn't list anything out of the ordinary either. Even more frustrating, there's no information about who her father is at all, and I know it isn't Sloan's dad because the dates don't match up. Curiously, I scroll to the bottom of the screen, and note it was updated a few weeks ago.

As internet deficient as I am, I know Wiki is a public domain that anyone can update freely, whether the information is true or not. Anxiously, I wonder what information has been either added, amended, or deleted. I hit the back button to Sloan's page and scroll down again. Surprise, surprise, low and behold, his page had also been updated at the same time. I arch my brows towards Marie, whose lips turn down, and she shrugs.

"Come on, missy. No good will come out of looking at this." Marie switches the screen off, and hands me the thick file.

Blowing the hair out of my face, I step back and admire my accomplishments. The old filing cabinets, kindly left behind by the previous tenant, are now in an organised fashion and everything client-related is stored alphabetically, while everything financial, is in date order.

Marie had left me to solicit for new business after our chat this morning. As usual, I decided to stay and finish organising the last of the boxes which were still unopened from the move. Peeking at my watch, I expected her to be back by now. I glance at the door on my way into the kitchen, and a glimmer of gold, from the business plaque outside, catches my eye.

What had started as a little venture funded by her ex-husband, is now a successful events planning company. She hires temporarily when she needs to, or contracts with other companies she has formed relationships with over the years. The majority of the time, she actually runs it with her current team, which is made up of mostly part-timers, and me, of course. All in all, it works well.

The sound of the door closing, and voices speaking in hushed tones, piques my attention. I scrunch my face up and walk in the direction of the banter. Tilting my head around the architrave, I find Walker sprawled out on one of the leather sofas, in what will eventually become one of our two new meeting rooms. I bite back a smile when I notice Marie shift uncomfortably in her seat.

"Hello, Walker, what brings you here? Maybe plotting to steal a few more of my things from Marie's house, perhaps?" I ask, sarcastically. Marie's eyes narrow, and it takes all I have not to giggle. I didn't pull her up on it this morning because I knew she wouldn't have had any say in the matter. Walker probably barged his way in, taking what he wanted, just like Sloan does with me.

"No. I believe I got everything I was asked to yesterday, right after I left you with the kid. Actually, I came by to see if Marie wanted lunch." God, he's so confident, it should be a crime. Between him and Sloan, I fully appreciate no woman would ever stand a chance of refusing anything they may ask.

"Of course, she can!"

"No, no, I can't! I've only just come back in! I have to do the orders and call the caterers with the lists for this weekend."

"I've already done them," I reply with a satisfied smile. Satisfied, that the shoe is now on the other foot, and it's obviously not fitting very well.

Her eyes are slits and level at me grudgingly. If the entire scene wasn't so amusing, I might have cut her some slack, but after years of being alone, she needs to heed her own advice. God knows she has imparted enough of it on me as of late.

"Go! Now!" I gently push her in Walker's direction. He winks at me, and I nod, gratified with my achievement.

"Fine! Kara, remember to take your key and card if you go out. I don't know, maybe you could call Sloan!"

"Hell, no, woman! If she does that, he'll want lunch with us, and I see enough of his ugly face already!" Walker shouts back at me. He places his hand on the small of Marie's back and leads her out, while she stomps in front of him.

I've been sitting at my desk for the last half an hour, debating what I should do about the beautiful Mr Foster. The phone turning in my hand feels like hot coals.

Finally, I make the decision to call him and see if he wants lunch, but just as I'm about to dial, the screen flashes up *Sam*.

I curse at the empty room.

I haven't seen her in weeks, not since she called me a whore and I walked out. I also still haven't been back to the flat for my things, either.

"Hello, Sam," I answer, hesitant, and perplexed as to why she is finally contacting me.

"Hi, Kara, how are you?" I practically choke. She sounds as rough as shit, and she's asking how I am?!

"I'm fine, Sam, just fine. I'm sorry, but why are you calling me? You made it perfectly clear what you thought of me weeks ago." I rock back in my chair and swivel round to look out of the window.

"Kara, I'm in trouble. I need money."

I stand and raise the blind. "Sam, Sloan paid the rent in full for six months. So, tell me another one." I listen to her mumble through various reasons. She's lucky I didn't cut her off straight away.

My wayward gaze lands on a flashy, silver, BMW convertible, speeding down the street, showing off with its top down. It zooms into the office car park at a ridiculous speed, failing to observe the five miles per hour limit. My eyes turn frenzied when it doesn't look like it's going to slow down in time, and is on a collision course with my car. The driver slams on the brakes, sliding into the empty space next to my Fiesta. I press my face to the glass, astonished by the lunatic behind the wheel. I'm ready to scream out of the window at the arsehole, when Mr Foster climbs out of the small car with unmistakable confident. I let out a huff, shaking my head at his recklessness. I also can't help but lick my lips hungrily at the sight of him slackening his tie. He unbuttons his collar a few holes and straightens his waistcoat. My concentration is divided, observing the car's roof emerging from the back of the vehicle, and Sloan looking like a runway model, watching as it secures into place. Slipping off his glasses, he goes around to the passenger side and grabs his jacket, sliding into it effortlessly. The fabric stretches over his big arms and shoulders and, proud and unashamed, I watch, drinking him in, trying to quench my constant thirst for him.

"Kara, are you listening to me?" I blink as the shrill tone of Sam's voice pierces my ear canal. I know I have at least five minutes or so to get rid of her before he gets up here.

"Yeah, yeah, I am. Sam, I don't have any money." It's the truth; I'm just as poor as she is, and the little savings I had festered away over the years were not getting touched, unless it was life or death.

Or my mother.

Or worse – my father.

"Please, Kara, I'm begging you. Deacon said I need...he said that he would..." She starts to sob, and I pinch my nose. I'm finding it harder and harder to believe her lies, yet I can't shut her out. Unable to do anything other than stay on the line, I listen to a broken woman in distress for the second time in as many hours today.

Heavy steps enter the room, and I turn to see my beautiful man watching me. He stabs me with a look that can be interpreted a million different ways, but one that will always render me compliant to his will and stop my heart from functioning briefly.

He twirls a security card in his hand, sits in my seat, and pulls me into his lap. He nuzzles my neck, and his nose brushes a path up and down my sensitised skin. I tap his cheek to get his attention. He pins me with a far from innocent expression, and I shake my head at his inability to pretend he's unaware. Suddenly, he winks at me, then reaches under my shirt. I yelp out loud and slap his hand away, his eyes glaze over, and he construes this as a challenge to fondle me some more. His octopus hands are all over me. He lifts me easily and positions me to straddle his thighs. Holding me in linked hands at the curve of my backside, my front is pressed tight to his, revealing his current level of longing.

"Kara, are you still there? Is *he* with you?"

"No, he's not. Sam, I'm sorry, but I really can't help you."

Staring straight at Sloan, his eyes darken and turn cold. His playful demeanour vanishes, and his arms constrict around me. I place my palm flat on his chest, and plead with my eyes for him not to say or do anything. He takes the phone and puts it on speakerphone. I sigh at the intrusion, fearing what crap might leave Sam's mouth about my concealed past while he is listening.

"Kara, can't you ask Sloan? Say you need something, anything. I'm in fucking trouble!"

"No! You accused me of being like you. I will not do that. You know I don't care for money. Just sort your own shit out, because I was done with your antics two weeks ago!" Sloan is slowly nodding his head in approval, as he listens with determination.

"Fine! You know what, Kara? Don't come crying to me when he dumps you, because he will. I know all about him. He's dangerous. Deacon said..." The phone is dragged out of my hand and cut off by Sloan.

"Don't listen to her, baby. Not a single word she says."

"Sloan?" He squeezes his eyes together, letting out a breath before opening them. The anger that had been building is gone, and he's back to his usual self.

"Baby, I will tell you, I promise I will, but some of it isn't good, and some of it involves someone else. I have to make sure that person is fine with what you will hear. I promise you, but can we just leave it for now?"

I nod; at least it's something to look forward to.

Or, quite possibly, something I will regress from.

I wrap my arms around him and claim his lips, savouring the taste of him. He deepens the kiss, and I open my mouth, urging him to take advantage. His tongue runs the length of mine, then over my teeth. I'm breathless with anticipation, and I know if we carry on like this, we won't be able to stop. I pull away, panting softly. Curling my fingers in the back of his hair, I tilt his head to mine.

"What are you doing here? Don't you have work or meetings?" I ask. A change of conversation is definitely needed.

And possibly a cold shower, too.

"It's called lunch." He lifts me down and stands. Straightening up, he appears completely unaffected by our little rendezvous, although the partial bulge outlined on his trousers tells me otherwise.

I take in the sight of him; his perfectly fitted three-piece suit, his dark, dishevelled hair, and his lust filled eyes. There are plenty of other things I would like for lunch right now, but my stomach betrays me and growls. Sloan picks me up and wraps my legs around him. He stops, so I can pick up my handbag and lock the office door on the way out.

"I can walk, you know." A low, disgruntled sound leaves his throat, and I decide to let him have his fun. I love this side of him, especially now I'm seeing it more often.

We manage to manoeuvre from the building to the car park, with me coiled tightly around him. He finally places me on my feet as we get to his new car. My eyes take in its mechanical beauty, but it isn't very Sloan. It's far too small for his frame. Looking at it now, I'm surprised he actually managed to fit inside.

"Downgrading the Aston?" I muse flatly. He smirks and drops the key into my palm. He doesn't elaborate, just merely folds himself into the passenger seat and shuts the door. I stare at him, until he opens his door, followed by his mouth.

"You're driving, by the way." He tries to close the door again, but I grasp the top.

"Sloan, I can't drive your car. A, I'm not insured, and B, I might...I might crash the bloody thing!"

"Baby, just get in the car." He closes the door and watches me with amusement.

I linger alongside it for a good five minutes, mentally arguing with myself. Eventually, I stomp around to the driver's side and purposely throw my handbag at him, since there are no back seats. I slide inside and slam the door hard getting in. Staring him down, I wait for the admonishment to come - heaven knows I am vying for it with my current conduct and attitude.

"Quite finished?" He smiles.

"Piss off!"

"Well, this little temper tantrum is another first…for me, at least."

I scowl at him.

"Okay, key in the ignition, baby. Just take it slow, as much time as you need. Remember, there's more power here than you're used to." He settles into the seat, coolly slips on his aviators, and looks positively relaxed, albeit a bit cramped, whereas I'm a quivering wreck.

My knee shakes uncontrollably on the clutch as the car roars to life. Still in neutral, I position my seat, check my mirrors, and look around more times than I usually do. Finally satisfied, I ease up on the clutch, press down on the accelerator, and the car moves off slowly. I silently pray to Him above for quiet roads today.

Sloan doesn't say which direction to head in, so I just drive around, getting a feel for the car. It really is lovely to drive. Then again, anything is a step up from my rust bucket, with its questionable suspension and lack of everything, but this is truly gorgeous. I'm completely in love with it and dare I say, hoping he'll let me drive it again - provided I can handle the extra horsepower under the bonnet.

After spending an hour or so driving on dual carriageways, country lanes, and even undertaking a few junctions of the M25 - which is a truly terrifying experience in a shiny new car that isn't mine - Sloan eventually directs us towards a nearby dealership. I slowly reverse into an empty space outside the showroom, a smile of pride and satisfaction spreads over my cheeks.

"Do you like the car?"

I nod adamantly, but I'm not really paying attention. I'm too busy falling in love with the interior leather all over again.

What it must be like to be able to afford such stunning things.

My eyes cross when I see a man waiting just in front of the bonnet, wearing an identical smile to mine. Having already stepped out, Sloan is shaking his hand firmly. I follow, my legs resembling jelly, but in a good way. I look at the vehicle longingly, until I feel Sloan's presence in close proximity.

He moves behind me, wrapping his arms around my waist lovingly, securely linking his fingers together over my stomach. His chin rests on my shoulder, while his lips tickle my cheek.

"Are you sure you like it? Colour, specs, model?"

I nod enthusiastically again. I have no idea what they are, but who cares about all that crap really?

"Good, because it's yours, my gorgeous girl."

I whip around instantly. His smile is glorious, and my mouth forms a perfect O. The reality dawns on me that I have just unknowingly taken it for a test drive. I sigh, feeling my happiness diminish at the speed of light.

"Is it normal to test drive without someone from the showroom present?"

He shrugs noncommittally. "Maybe, maybe not, but they get a lot of business from us. And my credit's good." I snort. I never imagined that it wouldn't be.

I stare at the beautiful machine in front of me, but I can't give him the gracious acceptance I know he is expecting. I need him to know I didn't want this, that I don't want his money. I need him to understand how degrading this actually feels, that he has resorted to buying me a car, because mine isn't pretty enough, or new enough for him.

Automatically sensing my worry, he comforts me. "I know, baby. I'm just not overly comfortable with what you already have. I can't even begin to imagine you broken down in the middle of nowhere. Kara, I didn't do this for any other reason than your personal safety." I sigh and attempt to turn away, but he catches my face in his hands. "Look, every year your car fails its MOT, all you are doing is wasting good money on something bad, and eventually it will become unfixable. You promised me gracious, remember?"

"*Gracious* is giving me a bunch of flowers, or a box of chocolates, or even a new dress. It's not giving me a car that is worth more than what I will make in years!" I reply while he holds me firmly.

"Shush, baby, I know this is hurting your stubborn pride, but nothing you say will change the fact it's yours now. It's my gift to you. I've already told you; I make no apologies for wanting you to have the best of everything, and I have the resources to make it a reality." My fingers dig into his skin, as I grapple to feel more of him and still hold myself together.

"I should have known when I saw you pull up in it," I mumble into his chest. "I've seen your Mercedes, and you do love your precious Aston." I peer up at him, and he smiles, tipping my chin up.

"Oh, I don't know. This is little…" Kiss. "…and sexy…" Kiss. "…and very, very stunning." Kiss. He punctuates each word perfectly. "It's exquisite, beautiful, and comes in the most amazing package. Plus, it reminds me of you." His arms snake around me to the point of constriction, but it's a feeling I don't ever want to let go of. "And, I wouldn't mind taking it, or you, for a ride at all. In it, or on it, as a matter of fact." I slap him for the bluntness of his words.

He laughs carefree and kisses my forehead. "Let's have lunch. You can either argue with me later, or show me just how graciously happy you really are. I guess I don't need to remind you, but that makes two bouts of make up sex you now owe me!"

Chapter 23

SITTING IN THE restaurant at Sloan's hotel, I squirm uncomfortably in my seat, glancing around at the other patrons.

I watch with admiration and hunger, as the man I'm absolutely and unequivocally in love with, walks towards me, resembling a lion coming to claim his lioness. The way his body stretches under his clothing, and the way he confidently cuts a path through the other diners, has me salivating profusely. And I am not the only one affected. I cradle my wine glass and flick my eyes to the other women in the room. Regardless of age, they are also struck dumb, mesmerised by the visual of his inner strength and external beauty.

He sits as close as possible, and I sense his eyes rake over me. He starts to stroke my arm under the table, and I turn to him. My eyes feel irrefutably heavy, deepening with each tiny blink. I rub my legs together, feeling excessively wet and needy. I gulp back the wine and refill it moments later. I'm positive he can see the desire radiating from my eyes, and other concealed places.

"Good to know," he confirms, drawing his bottom lip in, while his thumb rubs over mine. I press my thighs together, and his eyes drop to the area while his lids hood heavily. They, like mine, are filled with awareness and longing.

"Sir, I'm sorry, but this table is reserved-"

"Afternoon, Arnold." Sloan holds his hand out to the impeccably dressed man. Arnold's face flushes with embarrassment, and he begins to apologise. "Please don't worry, Arnold. We didn't make any advance arrangements today, we apologise, but Laura said we can sit here. If it's a problem, we can move to another table instead."

"It's not a problem at all, Mr Foster," the older man replies, flustered.

"Arnold, this is Kara, my girlfriend. Kara, this is Arnold, he's the restaurant manager."

So, I'm officially his girlfriend now…

I offer my hand to Arnold, whose colour is now more pink than red, but he's still uncomfortable. "Very nice to meet you, Arnold." I greet him shyly, averting my head so he can't see my grimace upon contact.

"And you, Kara," he says. Kissing my hand in a very gentlemanlike manner, I stiffen as the burn travels up my arm. He then passes us a couple of leather-bound menus and makes a hasty retreat.

As we wait to order, Marie strides toward us with Walker following closely behind, his arm around her waist, whispering sweet nothings in her ear. Her smile is astounding, and I can honestly say I've never seen her this happy in the last seven and a half years. Sloan stands, kisses her cheek, and she sits opposite, with Walker on her left.

A waiter arrives, and we each order a main and a dessert. Noting that Marie and Walker also order lunch, I shake my head at my own shortcomings.

"You guys didn't go for lunch today, did you?"

"Uh-huh," Marie replies. "He just wanted us out of the way so he could give you the car, so we..." Her cheeks tint profusely. I hold my hand up for her to stop. There are certain things I really have no interest in hearing. Walker casually throws his arm around her, and chats in between mouthfuls of bread. The man doesn't seem to have a care in the world.

An hour passes by quickly, and I sip my wine slowly, already feeling the effects of afternoon drinking. The restaurant has thinned out somewhat, and we are the only diners left, apart from a couple at the far side of the room who appear to be in a heated conversation over a laptop.

Giggles rock out in the amiable silence, and I turn to see the attraction. Charlie hurries through the restaurant, her hands laden with bags. Sloan groans and scoots back in his seat. His hand touches mine, and electricity scorches every nerve ending starting in my palm. I turn away, knowing the colour dusting my cheeks is a few notches darker. I twine my fingers in his and rub gently with my thumb.

Charlie plops down in one of the empty seats, and we all focus our attention on her. She rolls her eyes, as she looks behind her at the empty doorway. Minutes later, Jake trudges through, frustrated and seemingly exhausted, carrying even more bags. He looks like a man who's spent many hours outside dressing rooms. I raise the napkin to my mouth and laugh into it. Walker shakes his head, and gets up to take a few bags from him.

"Thanks, pal." Jake drops into the last remaining seat and snatches the water carafe. He pours a tall glass and drains it dry. "You know, Sloan, it's a damn good job you're a millionaire, mate. This one could easily bankrupt you within a day! My feet are fucking killing me!"

"Excuse me, but these are not mine, *mate*! God, I wish they were!" Charlie pours herself a glass of wine and takes a long sip.

Marie turns to me with a questionable frown, then her eyes find Sloan. I, too, turn to him, and he is wearing a sheepish look. Rather than respond, he just takes a bite of his apple tart and averts his gaze. I purse my lips hard and stare at him.

"That's right, mister, you stay quiet! Kara, these are all yours by the way. *He* asked me to collect them. Although I must admit, Kelly and Victoria are very good at what they do."

"*Sloan*?"

"Hmm?"

"Who are Kelly and Victoria?" I ask. He gives me a quick flick of his brows and goes back to devouring his dessert. When it becomes apparent he's not going to answer, I look at Charlie. She rolls her eyes at her brother's display of feigning innocence.

"Kelly is the PS at Selfridges, and Victoria is the PS at Harvey Nicks."

"PS?" I query.

"Personal shopper. So, if anyone is bankrupting Sloan, it's going to be because of them, not me!" she says sarcastically. "More wine, Kara?" I nod furiously. She pours me a large glass, and I knock most of it back in one long swallow.

"Sloan?" He looks up with those wide, innocent, midnight blue eyes. "I have enough clothes to open my own shop - two, actually! Seriously, stop buying me stuff. *Please*." I'm under no illusion I have that begging look etched on my face, since I can definitely hear it in my tone. But at this moment, it's inconsequential.

"No," he states firmly. A collective groan resounds around the table, and Jake is rubbing his temple, while Walker crosses his arms over his chest.

"Kara, please don't go there, it won't work. Save yourself the time and effort. Just take what he gives. *Please*," Jake says, mimicking me.

I motion to the waiter for more wine. I hold my glass out with determination before the bottle is even in reach. I think this is my third glass, but I'm past counting because I need something to calm me down. Alcohol makes me brave, and that is also something else I need a lot of right now.

Eventually, the subject of money and clothes falls by the wayside, and the conversation works its way around the table, until Marie asks me if I like the car. I shift in my seat inconspicuously, sensing all eyes fix on me.

"I'm absolutely in love with the car, but I really don't need it." I observe Sloan, reiterating our conversation from a couple of hours ago. "My car runs just fine."

"Yeah, it does now. But let's face it, there are only so many times you can call it a bitch until she gives up the ghost!" Marie says, taking a sip of wine.

"True, but I'm quite sad to see her go to scrap, though. You know how hard I worked to pay for driving lessons and then the car," I say grudgingly, wondering if anyone at the table - apart from Marie and me - knows what it's like to really struggle financially and count every penny. Something tells me Sloan pays them very handsomely. But for what, I still don't know. I sigh, and Sloan's fingers curl around mine, pacifying me somewhat.

"Don't worry, Kara. We've already got a good home planned for her," Walker pipes up. "I've also got some money back at the office for you. It's not much, like five hundred quid, but I guess you already knew that anyway." I nod, knowing that was roughly what I would have expected, maybe a little less.

"Really? I can't believe someone actually bought it. I've got visions of some poor teenager breaking down in the dead of night somewhere."

"Hey, that car works fine! Park and I spent hours working on it. It's got new everything, a full service, I even MOT'ed it to make sure it was roadworthy. Trust me, there'll be no breaking down," Jake says loud and proud, while Charlie smiles at him adoringly.

"Well, I hate to break it to you, but it did refuse to start after I got it back from the hotel." I give Jake a small smile, and he huffs out, looking far from happy I have just burst his bubble.

I ease back into my seat and become a bystander in the conversation. I listen intently, but I'm quietly consumed. Today was just another normal day for me. Normal, until Sloan flew into the car park like a bat out of hell in shiny new wheels. *My* shiny new wheels. I breathe out a heavy, discreet lungful of air. My aim to fight him to the death on buying me expensive things has taken a back seat. No one, but Marie, seems to pick up on my current discomfort as she gives me a little grin. Everyone else is chatting animatedly among themselves, from the car to other inane small talk, and I catch certain words here and there.

Taking a small sip of wine, my attention is diverted from my inner ramblings when Sloan asks Walker how his, and Jake's new assignment is progressing. I unobtrusively glance up, to find Walker taking an unnoticeable peek towards Marie, and then he glares back at Sloan. Needless to say, the question remains unanswered. I wonder what the new definition of *assignment* actually is when it involves them…and why he seemingly doesn't want Marie knowing about it.

The alcohol flows through me, and I feel a little merry. It doesn't last long, and I instantly sober the moment Charlie ups the ante and announces she wants to go clubbing. Whilst Marie is courteous, although not happy, I feel anxious and just agree for the sake of it. It isn't something I've ever really indulged in, or been comfortable with, preferring to remain unseen…and untouched. It's not a situation I would ever put myself in willingly.

"No way!" Jake vetoes it straight away. Charlie pouts with huge doe eyes, but Jake isn't succumbing. "No. I'm not having some arsehole rubbing all over you! No. Never. Not happening!"

The other two men neither say nor do anything. Although I did notice how their postures harden at the announcement, and subsequently relaxed when Jake shut it down.

"Please, Jacob," she whines and presses her lips together. She knows how to get her own way; I'll give her that. I watch in amazement as she wears him down until he starts to work something over in his head.

"Okay, you can go clubbing-"

My stomach sinks at his words. For a minute there I thought I'd had a lucky escape.

"As long as we go with you!" His smile stretches endlessly, and Charlie's drops the moment she registers the compromise.

I catch Marie's eye, and she gives me a weak, unhappy shrug. Walker, on the other hand, is openly cursing.

"Char, you know I adore you, but I'm too freaking old for clubbing! Besides, Marie might not want to go." Marie's head flips towards him, and her eyes dart out as he lays the decision at her door. Charlie turns to Marie, who laughs with uncertainty, and then her eyes plead with mine. I train my gaze on the table, admiring the very insignificant, plain white tablecloth, until Sloan breaks the tension.

"Okay, we all go. Not my idea of fun, but I'm not about to let three beautiful women loose in a club." Charlie whoops with joy and Sloan turns back to me. "Sorry, babe, but she's hard to say no to," he whispers, and I nod. He'll never need to explain it to me.

Walker rises, saying he has to go. He holds out his hand to Marie, who takes it without qualm. "Oblivion? I'll call Rem to book us out the VIP." He nods at Sloan, then walks out hand in hand with Marie.

Oblivion is one of those exclusive clubs that has been open for a year or so. In good times gone by, Sam had tried numerous times to get me to go, but my disinterest and resilience triumphed.

Charlie shuffles round to my side of the table. "Oh, we are going to have so much fun! Just wait until you see the club! Sloan refurbished it, and it's absolutely amazing!"

"*What?* He owns that club?"

"Yeah, that, the hotels, shares in Walker Security, and some other stuff." She gazes at me in shock, finally understanding I really have no idea what her brother actually does. "Sorry, he didn't tell you, did he?" I shake my head.

"No, he didn't."

Sloan clears his throat, shooting an annoyed expression towards his sister and excuses us. He doesn't look at me as he grips my hand. I say my goodbyes to Jake and Charlie, who gladly hand over the mountains of bags. Sloan tugs me towards the lifts, and I pause, remembering the most significant purchase of the day.

"Sloan, we left the car parked outside the front door." And it isn't the first time I've done it, thinking back to our first meeting.

"Don't worry, it's been moved into one of our bays downstairs. It's perfectly safe. Come on."

Our bays? I shake my head, and let him take the heaviest bags from me. He guides me into the foyer, towards the dreaded lifts.

"Let's go and see how poor I am."

Chapter 24

PRISING MY BODY away from his, I scurry naked into the bathroom, desperate for a wee. I shut the door behind me and linger stock still in front of the mirror.

I look as thoroughly fucked as I feel.

My lips are tinted deep red and swollen, from him showing me how much he desired me. My skin is a delightful shade of pink, a result of the rush of blood, and the fire now smouldering inside. My body is boneless, weak from the multiple orgasms he challenged me with, as I modelled some of the beautiful items Charlie had picked up earlier today.

It was all going so well until his resolve cracked, and he confessed he couldn't take anymore. He dragged me to the bed wearing a barely-there silk bra, which didn't cover my breasts fully, and equally, did not offer any support whatsoever. The matching knickers were not up to much good, either.

Relieving myself quickly, I wash my hands and cover up with the robe hanging on the back of the door. Strolling back into the bedroom, Sloan is standing naked at the dresser with my mobile in his hand.

He is undeniably stunning in his full, naked glory. The evening April sun streams into the room, highlighting his lean, sexy, muscular frame. My eyes cast down his back, and I rejoice at the vision of his toned arse and thighs.

"What are you doing?" I ask cheerfully, strolling towards him. I bring my arms around him, linking my fingers at his stomach, leaning my head on the back of his shoulder.

"Reading." Blunt, one-word answers from him are never a good sign. That much I already knew.

I stretch up on my toes and peek over his shoulder, only to realise he's going through the text messages from my dad. All of them, including some particularly vile ones I had forgotten to delete - or rather didn't, so at least I had a reason to be consumed with revulsion for him.

"What the fuck? How dare you! You asked me to trust you, and yet you snoop through my messages?" I shout, stepping back.

"Kara, please don't get angry. I don't want you seeing him alone. If you need to, you call me. If I can't go with you, I'll get Walker, or Jake, or someone else if need be, but under no circumstances do you go alone. Same goes for Sam, if you have to see her, then someone goes with you. I've programmed in all the numbers you need. Walker and Jake's you already had. Dev, Tom, Parker, Rem, and the doc are now in there too, but Doc's the last resort. You work your way through them until someone answers. If no one answers, you call the police, understand?"

He really is an overbearing prick at times!

"Don't you think that's a little extreme? I know some of those messages are nasty, but he isn't going to do anything in broad daylight."

"I have my reasons, baby. Please, just say you will."

"Fine, I will!" I hiss out, pissed off, but decide submission is the best way to stop this conversation.

He rotates the phone in his hand, his expression thoughtful, deep and brooding. He swipes his finger over my cheek and withdraws quickly.

"What Sam said today," I say quietly, not wanting to change his mood. Of course, the playfulness has vanished, but his attitude is still friendly, regardless of my pissed off demeanour. "You promised me you would eventually be truthful. I'm not talking about hearing it now, but soon. Okay?"

"Okay." He places my phone back on the dresser and cups my face, studying me, judging me, maybe.

"So, do you really want to go clubbing with my sister?" A smile plays on his lips, and I shake my head.

"No. I really can't think of anything worse, but she's hard to say no to, right?" He laughs and kisses my swollen lips. "*Baby,*" I breathe the endearment into his mouth. It's a term he uses with me regularly, but it's the first time I've ever referred to him as it. Bizarrely, it feels natural, albeit a little strange, tumbling from my lips. The familiar tingle of pleasure courses through my body. He pulls back and leads me into the living room, sitting me on his lap after he gets himself comfortable. He stares at me for a long time, and his expression is one of conflict.

Then he does something I don't expect him to.

He starts to talk.

"Charlie is my half-sister, Kara. My mother remarried after my father died. The man she married was...*difficult*. A year later, Charlie arrived. She was so beautiful, like a little doll. My mother and I worshipped her. My stepdad, on the other hand, didn't give a shit about any of us, least of all his newborn daughter. After a while, he was out more and more, and rumours of his infidelity were rife. It became apparent the only reason he married my mother was for her money. Life wasn't easy. He already had children from his first marriage, and needless to say, none of us got on particularly well." He's calm as he confesses. His fingers delicately massage my hair and scalp. "My mother stayed unhappily married to him for years, until something happened that changed everything."

"Your mother died," I interrupt, remembering my own snooping. His fingers stop, and he turns my face to him, gliding his thumb over my cheek. His eyes are glassy and hollow. "Sorry, I looked you up on the internet after you showed me the picture of us at the ball," I admit thoroughly embarrassed, especially since I have just blown up at him for doing pretty much the same thing.

"My mother had cancer, but that wasn't why. Like I said, I need permission to tell you that part. Anyway, my mother eventually saw the light and divorced him. But it wasn't that easy, we still had to deal with the aftermath of it; his kids, his connections. He dragged us through the shit with him, until he realised no amount of shady solicitors or barristers were ever going to get him what he really wanted from the start - namely, my mother's money."

I curve my arm around him and press a kiss to his neck, while the suite's phone beeps incessantly. Neither of us moves to answer it.

"My mother fled back to the States after she was diagnosed. She filed for divorce and transferred all the companies to me. I was eighteen at the time, just starting uni. Aside from the hotels, which my mother's family - the Emerson's - built from scratch, we now co-own quite a lot of businesses, including John's - Walker Security - plus restaurants, bars, that kind of thing. Apart from the hotel, none of them bear the family name, and every side of the business is in my sole name. My mother didn't trust him. He'd have tried to take it all if Charlotte was on any of the legal documents."

Wow.

I press back, trying to make sense of everything. I didn't expect him to be so open today, just someday. I keep still and quiet, because he seems to be on a roll.

"Remember when you said that Sam had two men - the *Krays* - in your flat?" I nod. "Well, one of those men is Deacon. And the other man, Remy? His name is Jeremy James. He's a good friend of mine who tries to keep Deacon in line, although he doesn't realise it. Deacon runs prostitutes, baby. So, you see, when my guys found Sam that night, I saw red. I was incensed to the point where I wanted to kill him. Walker managed to get a few words out of your girl, and she mumbled she had called someone, so we waited while Doc patched her up. Eventually, you arrived. The way you looked at me like I was the reason she was in that condition, it killed me to think you'd hold me responsible for such despicable things." His fingers drift over my cheek, and I close my eyes, absorbing his touch.

"My mother once told me I'd meet someone who would steal my breath away one day. I knew exactly what she meant when I first saw you. I just can't explain why. I silently thanked God I managed to convince you to let George take you home, knowing you would have to come back for your car. I was undeniably pissed off when you sent the scrawny lad to collect it."

I duck my head and smile. "I was ashamed. What did you expect? I didn't want anything from you, apart from my car."

"I know that. I also managed to wrangle some information out of the guy, and found out you were single and where your office was. I even had Tommy on a bike tailing you for days – you never even noticed him. He said you were the most boring woman he had ever met." I drop my head again, crimson infusing my cheeks rapidly. "I was thrilled to hear you weren't like your friend."

"Hey!" I slap his chest lightly.

"Seriously, when I walked into that function room a week later, and I saw you, it was like all my Christmases and birthdays had come at once. Charlie was pissed off that I was ogling the waitress, and decided that she would show you we didn't tolerate gold-diggers."

"Oh, crap, no wonder why she hated me at first sight."

"No, hate is too strong a word. I guess if you think back to how she treats Christy, the things she said to her... Well, the truth is, Christy *is* a gold-digger. She wants a rich husband to keep her in the lap of luxury. It's also the reason why Charlie takes it upon herself every time she sees her to rub it in, albeit very cruelly. Like I said, she doesn't have class. My sister really does like you, you know. She was very impressed after you both had lunch. She called me and told me I had to keep you." He leans me back to look into my eyes. "It might not have escaped your attention, but she doesn't really have any friends. Although, I think she may have found two in you and Marie."

I smile, tears of happiness in my eyes. "I really like her, too. Maybe not at first, but I know now that she was trying to protect both of you. I admire that trait."

"Well, I guess the reason why I'm telling you all this, is that you need to be aware that if Deacon comes anywhere near you, you call me or one of the guys. If you can't do that, you run. I mean it. You run as fast as you fucking can."

"I promise, I will." I peek at him; his look is solemn as he tugs me closer to him. "What about this Jeremy guy? What if I see him?"

"Rem's a good guy. He won't always act it, but he is. But again, if you're out alone, and he's with Deacon, you don't act any differently towards him. You still call me."

"I will." I curl my legs and shift on his knees. His erection springs to life between us and I raise a questioning brow at him.

"I can't help it!" he says, flashing his whites at me.

"Try!" I laugh.

"Thank you for letting me buy you the car, by the way. I honestly thought you would fight me to the death. I'm still amazed you didn't."

"You didn't really give me a choice. Gracious, remember?" I toss his words back at him, but they are laced with sarcasm.

"Well, in the interest of being honest, I have to confess I bought it for you weeks ago." He drops his head down.

"When, weeks ago?" I narrow my eyes.

Sloan lifts his head and runs his finger down my nose. "When Jake and Parker spent nearly a full day repairing every fault that your car had. You shouldn't have even been driving it around full stop. Sorry, I know this is a lot to take in, but I bought it the day after George took you home. Please don't say a word, because I know you're dying to!"

I slouch back in both shock and admiration for the most perfect man I've ever met. "You were that confident I'd be back?"

"Positive. Not a doubt in my mind."

"You know, you could have just bought me another used car. I wouldn't have minded. It's just a piece of metal that gets me from A to B. I don't need anything fancy, especially not a convertible roadster that is currently parked downstairs in one of *our* bays."

"True, but what kind of man would I be if I let my woman drive around in something that could die at any moment?"

"Your woman? That sounds...official," I reply.

Today has been a whole lot of new for me. Another new first, too. It's the first time in my life I have ever been introduced as somebody's girlfriend. I have to admit, I like the sound of it. *A lot*.

"Hmm, you're mine Kara Petersen, and I'm never letting you go. Think of it as fate." He smiles gloriously, and I suddenly feel caught up in his words and the power behind them.

"Okay, since I am *officially* yours, how about you take me on an *official* date? We've never had a first date. I think we might have done this a little backwards."

"A date? What like dinner, the cinema, making love until the sun comes up? That kind of date?" His eyes glimmer seductively.

Oh, yeah, that sounds like a date to me.

"Yep, I mean, I understand if you can't, or you're too busy, but I'd like to. I can honestly say I've never been on a proper date in my entire life. I've had…disasters." I scrunch my nose up, as the medley of unfortunate memories come and go quickly.

"I find that very hard to believe, my love," he says, pulling me tighter.

I let out a laugh. "Seriously, it's true. I've never really allowed anyone close to me since..." Oh, shit! My mouth closes quickly as my brain re-engages. I've let whatever is in my head spew out from my lips in this perfect moment. I'm such an idiot. He can't know, not just yet. It will ruin everything.

Rather than stressing me to continue, he grips my hips and lifts us up from the sofa. He guides us into the kitchen, drops me on my feet, then digs around in the fridge.

"Well, since there isn't really anything in here that's edible, how about we have that first date right now?"

He braces his hands on the marble worktop and watches me. Shifting under his powerful gaze, his finger slowly indicates for me to approach. I saunter towards him slowly, a pronounced sway in my hips, and don't stop until his lips mould with mine.

Chapter 25

THE AIR CONDITIONING rumbles quietly around the room, while I absentmindedly input the figures for the last function. Cursing up a storm, I delete the last line and start to tap in the numbers yet again. I give up when I do them wrong for the fourth time. My focus is lacking lately, and it's all because of one man.

It has been a week since my first date with Sloan, and nine hours since the sixth. My body is in a constant state of arousal from his attentiveness, and my heart is well and truly in freefall.

I'm in love with him.

Pure and simple.

The cool chill induces me to shiver, as I stare at the same line over and over, unable to give it my complete, undivided attention. I drop my hands from the keyboard in irritation and push back in my seat. My eyes cast down to the car park through the open window, and I admire my little silver car longingly. The way it gleams in the sunlight screams *look at me*, much like the man who gifted it to me. I smile and unlock the top drawer of my desk, pulling out the notepad I keep hidden at the back.

Over the last week, I've been making notes, trying to remember the demons of my childhood and teenage years. Some of the events subconsciously unfold in ways I either can't remember accurately, or have blocked them out entirely to ensure I would never have to.

Opening the book where I last left off, I tap the pen on the next clean line. These notes are my life, there is nothing that has been left unwritten, and still, I keep adding to it. Each line I write, each memory I pull back to the surface, cleanses me. It releases another part of myself I have kept well hidden. I only hope that when the time comes, when I eventually hand this over to Sloan, he can forgive me for not confiding in him.

I'm lost in my words as my phone dances across the desk. Marie is late calling me; no doubt Walker is making her lose track of time again. Lately, I'm seeing less and less of her in the office. Walker is around more often than not, and they seem to have something serious going on. She's a hopeless liar, though. Every time I speak of him, she either brushes me off, or changes the subject. Still, I don't miss the blush that colours her cheeks adorably.

"Marie, where the hell have you been? Tell that man to let you up for air!" I admonish playfully.

I confess; I played a big part in making sure she spent time with him, even if she was hesitant. She's constantly pushing me towards Sloan, and even though she thinks he's amazing, I am still holding back. Just like her, I have to protect what little of my heart is still mine.

"Who the fuck is Marie, sweets?" My stomach reels and acid surges in my gut.

"Hi, what do you want?" For once, I'm relatively polite to him, not that he deserves pleasantries. Although, I concede it might be best to keep him on an even keel, otherwise my mum will suffer the brunt of his rage.

"Kara, sweets, we need to talk. I'm stood outside your flat, get your fucking arse over here, now!" His words drip with malice, and I frown in confusion.

"How did you know where I live?" I ask politely, keeping up the pretence.

"A little birdy told me, now stop fucking around and get over here!" The line goes dead.

I stuff the notepad and pen back into the drawer and lock it. I toy with the key, deliberating what to do. Looking pointedly at my mobile, I have the numbers of seven men who will be able to take my father down effortlessly. Except, I don't want Sloan, or any of them, to meet my father. *Ever*. Money would turn him into a disease that lingered. It would ensure he never went away.

I randomly bite my nails, fighting the internal battle with myself. I'm truly conflicted. I made a promise I would never see him alone, but I'm ashamed of who he is, so how can I call any of them? Bypassing the list, I pick up my phone, dial, and wait for it to be answered.

"Marie?"

"Oh, Kara! I got a bit side-tracked honey, but I won't be long!" she giggles, and Walker's voice seeps through the receiver.

Thought so.

"Look, don't come in, but I have to tell you something. Are you listening?"

"Sure, sure!" More giggling.

"Goddamn it, Marie! My father is at my old flat, and he wants to see me right now!" The line is deathly silent.

"Kara, don't even think about it! I'll be there in ten, so sit your arse back down and wait for me," Walker barks out, but my mind is already made up.

"Sorry, I can't. I have to go! I'm sorry." He bellows at me to fucking wait for him, but I hang up. I know he will inform Sloan, and they will both be pissed at me, but I have to do this.

Taking what I need, I lock up the office and run down the stairs. Disengaging the car locks, I slide in. Buckling up, I press the accelerator, then I'm gone. My phone is sat on the dashboard, sounding out continually. My heart heaves with both fear and pain – fear of what Ian might do, and pain that I'm breaking my promise to the man I love.

I mentally repeat over and over what I plan to say to Ian. Our spats over recent years were well practised. But not as well as the words I'd had in my head when I woke up in hospital eight years ago, a completely different person.

Pulling into the car park of my old flat, through the windscreen I see Danny standing defensively, shaking his head at my father. I inhale and get out of the car, clutching my phone tight in my hand. Strangely, the constant vibration soothes me, like knowing there is someone here with me.

Except, there is no one. I'm all alone.

The loose soil crunches under my feet, and my father's head spins in my direction. He watches me a little too closely. He looks over the car with interest and then at my attire. If only I'd known this morning he would be here, instead of being up north where he's meant to be, I would've worn my rattiest jeans and sweater. Since Marie and I had a meeting with a potential client - one which she didn't even show up for, I might add - here I am, in a designer dress and jacket that cost more than I'm comfortable with.

Leaving a good few feet between us, Danny gives me a look of sympathy as he stops trudging towards me. "He's been here for an hour, Kara. Him, and a big guy in that 4x4."

I acknowledge him and look at the car. My pulse hitches higher because I recognise that 4x4. It had vanished as soon as Sloan reappeared in my life. Although it's too heavily tinted to make out the shadow inside, instinctively, I know I'm in deep shit if whoever is in there decides to make an appearance.

"You look really good, sweets," my father praises, closing the gap. I lift my hand to stop him, and he halts. "What's wrong? No hug for daddy?" he adds sarcastically.

I don't expect him to understand my pain at being touched. He's spent the last eight years torturing me from afar. He has absolutely no idea of the long-lasting effects the final night under his roof has had on me. But I know it wasn't just that night, it was a culmination of everything. It was my entire childhood, the one I now had issues separating fantasy from reality.

"What are you doing here? I don't want you here," I say, squeezing the phone harder in my hand. "And who's that in the car with you?" I throw it out there, letting him know I'm aware he isn't here alone.

"He's insurance. Frankie wants his money, and his guy over there is here to make sure I pay up. If not, he's gonna take payment another way." I clearly remember from past experience the other ways in which payment would be taken - none of them were pleasant. "Come on, sweets, you're not exactly hurting for cash. I know you've got a rich guy waiting for you."

I turn to Danny, who shrugs. "Hey, don't give me that look! I didn't say anything to him."

A little birdy. Samantha.

"Look, I don't have any money, and I'll never ask Sloan for his, so you really are wasting your time coming here."

"Nah, I don't think so, sweets. You see, I know all about your guy, and I know he'll give you whatever you want. So ask him, because if you don't, it will only be you and your mother that suffer," Ian says, giving me a determined look, causing his face to crease further. Decades of abuse have aged him beyond his years, but today he looks older than ever.

I am about to answer when the sound of tyres and a car braking harshly forces me to turn. The car door is thrown wide open, and Walker climbs out. He strides over to us with more menace than I have witnessed from him in the past. I close my eyes, asphyxiated by guilt, and my hand comes up to my neck, needing some assistance to breathe. Walker assesses me, but his eyes darken significantly when he sees my dad. He stops by my side and takes my hand in his.

"Anything you have to say to her, you say it to me. And *you* should know I don't give a fuck!" Walker points at my father, whose posture drops by a few inches.

Ian stares at Walker, a spark of recognition flares in his eyes, and I wonder if they have met before. The 4x4 roars to life and my father begins to walk backwards towards it. "I'll be in touch, sweets," he says, never removing his eyes from Walker. The look of fear is evident.

"Don't fucking bother, bastard!" Walker shouts after him. Something in his stance makes me worry, as my father hops into the passenger seat and the car zooms off.

I let out the breath I'm holding and tilt on my heels. Biting the inside of my cheek, I raise my head to look at Walker. His nostrils flare in anger, and I start to open my mouth to apologise, but he cuts me off.

"Don't, Kara. Just don't." He looks at me in disgust and starts walking back to his car.

"I'm sorry I ruined your afternoon, but I had to... My mother..." I feel numb as his large frame stalks back towards me. His breath cuts a path through my hair, and I flinch.

"I don't think you realise what you've just done. You really don't have any idea who was in that car, do you? Remember the one that was following you?" I nod, remembering the fear it provoked in me every time I saw it. "Well, it was the same one! And trust me when I say you don't want to meet the fucking owner. You fucked-up, Kara! I'm afraid sorry just doesn't cut it this time, honey."

"Did you tell Sloan I was here?" Silence. "Did you?" I probe again when he remains tight-lipped.

"Of course, I didn't! He's my best friend, and you're his entire world." He looks hurt, and my chest constricts. I don't have the heart to walk away, especially when I have failed everyone so badly. Acid churns in my belly, and all I want to do is drop to my knees and cry.

"He's at the hotel, waiting for you to go home. I suggest you head straight back there." His eyes scan the area, apparently making sure my father and his accomplice are definitely gone.

The weight of the world rests on my shoulders as I watch Walker drive away. I walk mindlessly back to my car and slip inside. Locking the doors, I pause before tapping in Sloan's number.

"Baby..." he sighs out breathlessly on the other end.

"I miss you," I whisper. The long pause does not assist in easing my anguish.

"Come home to me, then." Tears choke my throat, and I realise this man might love me just as much as I do him, after all.

"Always." I disconnect before the first tear falls.

Sloan comes into view seconds after I enter the suite. His vest and jogging pants are soaked through with sweat. A pair of boxing gloves cover his hands, and he looks ready to go another ten rounds. I train my gaze to the floor. I'm so ashamed of what I've done; I can't even bring myself to look at him.

A large leather glove gently knocks under my chin, moving my face up to his. "I'm so pissed off right now, I can't think straight. The last time I felt this raw, I was almost too late." The calmness in his voice is terrifying, and I close my eyes because his words cut deep inside my heart.

He knows.

"Open your eyes, Kara."

I'm confused. How does he know I have done something I promised I wouldn't?

I slowly separate my lids, and he fills them completely. It's almost like I'm seeing him for the first time. His features are dark and feral. Untamed.

"Why did you disobey me?" My head sways to the side. Why did I? "I asked you to call one of us, but you didn't. You may think I'm being difficult, but I'm not. There's a reason why I made you promise, and you still broke it!"

I tread back from him; from his touch, from his stare. I can't let him know that Walker was there because he clearly hasn't told him yet.

"How did you know where I was?"

"Tracking devices on both your car and mobile." His voice is eerily calm, but his body is giving him away. I know he's fighting to keep control, and now he is starting to lose it.

I put my hands on my hips and narrow my eyes at him. His confession is such an invasion of my privacy. I am no longer ashamed of my own actions; I am more fucked off by his.

"What can I say? It's done, and I can't change it now. I'm sorry I didn't call you." My heart physically hurts beneath my rib cage, and I feel like I have been run over by a lorry. Nevertheless, I won't let him push me around when he shows no remorse in doing things that are borderline illegal.

"Sorry will not save you the next time he decides to fucking hurt you!" he bellows at me.

"What the hell are you talking about?" I start to whimper in fear. A glimmer of concern creeps into his eyes. He has said too much.

He stretches out to me, but I refuse. Finally tipping over the edge, he growls, rips the gloves from his hands, and launches them across the room. One rolls over the coffee table, taking a glass vase filled with flowers with it. It shatters into pieces on the floor.

I start to cry at his display of impending violence. Dodging his arm, I sprint up the stairs and lock myself in one of the spare rooms. Throwing myself onto the bed, his fists pound at the door repeatedly, demanding entrance.

I pull the duvet around me and lull myself to sleep. Cocooned inside it, I cry in fear, as all my senses are unforgivingly assaulted by my childhood demons.

The room is quiet as I lie on the bed. My body is exhausted and damaged beyond belief. The pain of the bruises is justification enough that I may not be able to walk properly tomorrow.

The sound of silence is a beautiful thing. I love the sound of nothing when it's there.

The banging has long since stopped, and I curl up with my book beside me. I had dropped it down when I ended up reading the same line more than once. I know I have to give in to sleep eventually, or I won't be able to stay awake in school tomorrow.

I hug the duvet closer and shut my eyes.

The nightmares are the same every night. Some mornings I would wake up with no memories of my dreams. Others, I'd shock myself awake with the fear that laced through my veins. Inevitably, I know I can't make it through to morning. Sometimes I wish I could. At least then I'd know the truth of what really happens to me when I am dreaming.

The pressure of fingers cutting into my stomach brings me back to reality. I instinctively drop my hand to them, attempting to push them away, but they stay firmly in place. I begin to shake my head, blinking and adjusting my eyes in the darkness. The man next to me is familiar, and I know I've been here previously.

But this time it's different.

The light penetrating the windows allows me to see his face. I have seen it before, but somewhere deep inside my head, I had chosen to forget. I guess if you can't remember, then it might not have really happened, only I know that isn't true.

His hand creeps up to my breasts, pausing momentarily in the middle. His breathing is hoarse and shallow, and I can feel how hard he is against my knee. I freeze when his hand rides up further, stopping at the base of my neck. His fingers twist until I feel the compression take effect on my throat. I can't breathe under the tension he is applying accurately to the centre, and dark spots start to colour my vision.

You can't survive without oxygen; I think to myself. And with that little piece of information, I don't fight. It might be the only way I'm ever going to be free.

His tongue licks up my cheek, and I swallow back the acid forming in the recess of my throat. It burns on the travel back down to my stomach; the taste is vile and sickening. Saliva envelops my mouth rapidly. It's my body's act of defence, and I swallow again when it pools copiously, and I'm unable to breathe.

Banging erupts at the door, and the man spins his head around, hollering at the impending invasion. "Stay the fuck out of here! I'm busy!" He turns to look at me, his hand exerting enough pressure on my chin that my jaw is becoming sore. "Isn't that right, sweets? That's what they call you, isn't it?" I don't answer him, and he doesn't push for my response any further.

Instead, his hand comes back down to my rib cage with more force than I'm able to stand. I cry out, and he laughs. It sounds perverted because it is. His other hand moves down to my lower abdomen, and his fingers are now inside my shorts. With one concise pull, he rips them clean from my body. The cheap material tearing is the only sound I hear over my cries; cries that I'm trying so hard to keep concealed. I whimper, unable to stay voiceless any longer.

I kick my legs out, but he is having none of it. He adjusts his body so that his knees are holding mine open. His hand fumbles with his trousers, and I close my eyes as the tears finally break through.

My breathing is erratic, and my body begins to shake from what I know is going to happen. It shouldn't be like this. Intuitively, I know it's not the first time, and it probably won't be the last. I know this, as my eyes open in horror, the instant he pushes inside me against my will. It burns, and I scream out in pain from the forced intrusion, as his hand comes over my mouth to silence me...

I jolt awake in the darkness. Haunted by my fears, my first reaction is to be in the light. I haphazardly feel for a lamp that I know isn't there.

Then the room is suddenly aglow.

I repeatedly squeeze my eyes open and shut, acclimatising to the brightness. Putting my hand on my face, I look around to see who's there, and Sloan is standing frozen, statue-like, in front of me. I can see from my current position that the wood around the door is fractured. *A lot like me,* I think mournfully. His right hand is fisted, and his knuckles are covered with blood. He looks crazy and out of control, and right now, I'm terrified of him.

This is the moment I know my life will change yet again. Except, this time, it won't be for the better. I fear any progress I've made in the last eight years, and more recently in the last few months, has just been cruelly snatched away, like it had never materialised in the first place.

"Get the fuck out now!" he screams at me.

My eyes widen in shock. "W-what?" I cry out, clutching at the covers in vain.

"I said, get. The fuck. Out! You fucking lied to me! All this time, I thought you were good, honest, but you're just like all the rest of them. How long did you think it could last? How long has he had you deceiving me?"

My head is shaking in misunderstanding and bewilderment. "I don't know who you're talking about!" I yell back, hot tears streaming down my cheeks.

"Deacon! You're one of his fucking sluts! I should have known, but your innocent act was just too fucking good! Now, get the fuck out, or I'll have you arrested. Move, now!" He stands aside and waits.

My tears burn my skin, as I scramble off the bed and drag myself out of the room. I can hear his steps behind me, but I don't look back. I can't. Gripping the rail tight, the void in my heart cracks further with every step I take. I can feel the heat of his anger radiating behind me. He's so close, I can smell his fury. I stop at the door and turn to him. His eyes are black and dead. Hesitantly, I reach out to him. I'm not stupid; I know this could go either way, but it might be the last chance I get to make this right.

"Don't you dare fucking touch me!" he growls back at me. His shoulders harden impossibly, and his muscles ripple with rage as he glowers at me.

"Whoever is feeding you these lies; I hope they're happy. It's obviously worked."

"More like you got fucking caught!" he spits back.

I'm so emotionally drained from my nightmare; I have no energy left to fight. His hatred for me is palpable and fills the room like nothing else ever has. It's so thick, I can almost taste it.

"I'm sorry, Sloan, for going to meet my dad and for whatever else I've supposedly done." Still, he says nothing. And since I have nothing left to lose, I go for broke.

"But mainly, I'm sorry because I fell in love with you. And that piece of my heart, the one thing I've kept protected for all these years, well, you have it, and now you've just destroyed it. You've destroyed me, and I'll never get that back. If you don't believe me, ask Marie. Aside from her, I've never loved anyone, maybe not even my own parents." I watch his eyes soften and glass over, my revelation puncturing deep inside him. In the same instant, he hardens again, and I know it's all over.

Not willing to let him bear witness to my breakdown, I stumble out of the suite. I stare at the lift button dumbly, but it will be too much to get in there right now, and so I race down the stairs. My fear of confined spaces was beginning to subside with each day I spent with him, whereas my nightmares were coming back with a vengeance, forcing me to relive them in droves.

I finally enter the foyer, one step in front of the other, trying to maintain the fraction of dignity I still have left intact. I reach the main door, and it opens for me. Walker and Marie both stand there laughing. They stop, and their smiles fade away instantly, recognising something isn't right.

Marie's hand steadies me. "Honey, what's wrong?"

I can't pretend any longer, and I collapse into her arms, crying hysterically, unable to breathe. Walker mumbles some expletive that even I'm not sure I would ever dare to repeat. Marie forces her key into my hand and tells me to go to her house. She pulls me close and guides me to George, who is waiting outside. His face crumples with concern, seeing my tear-stained cheeks and unmistakable red eyes.

I climb into the car and lie down across the seat, completely uncaring, and not taking one iota of safety into consideration. The leather is smooth and cooling under my body, as George drives me far away from the fallout.

Nothing has ever hurt this much. Not how many times I had been left to fend for myself, nor how many times I had been starved, hurt, abused, or raped in my own bed.

Nothing.

Love hurts.
Fact.
And my ravaged heart is living proof of that.

Chapter 26

THE SMALL, SQUARE room is sterile and clinical, with drab, off-white walls and standard, aged, discoloured blinds. The putrid smell of hospital disinfectant and death hangs thick in the air around me. The familiar woman sitting opposite is talking, but I don't hear a word she says, I only see her lips move.

There is a light tap on the door, and Marie steps inside the room. She pulls up a chair, sits next to me, and wraps a protective arm around my shoulders. I ease into her side and wish she had been there for me when I was growing up. If my own mother had been more like her, I wouldn't know things, or had seen things that my innocent eyes should've been shielded from. No, if Marie Dawson had been my mother, she would have clawed the eyes out of any bastard who dared to look at me the wrong way.

"Kara, are you listening to me?" the doctor's voice chips in with an aggravated tone.

I raise my head and lie. "Yes, I'm listening."

"Good. So, what did I say?" she asks, removing her wire-framed glasses and picking up her notebook.

I sigh and breathe out. "I'm sorry; I wasn't listening."

Marie's arm tightens around me, and I hear a soothing, shushing sound coming from her. Although it could be the sound of the last remaining pieces of my fractured heart still disintegrating into dust.

"That's quite alright, Kara. I know this is difficult. We will start again next week. Is Thursday at four o'clock good for you?" I nod and leave the room with Marie.

I sit in the passenger seat and watch the world go by. I have become good at reading people these last six weeks. It's amazing how much you can learn from just observing - and I've had plenty of time to just sit back and do just that. I shift and study Marie as she drives us home in silence.

Six weeks ago, she was blossoming. She was radiant and full of life, more so than she had ever been. No one had managed to break down the walls she had put up around herself after her ex-husband admitted to a string of affairs when they were married. Yet surprisingly, Walker succeeded with minimal effort. He brought her out into the open and showed her how good life could be. In the last six weeks, she has gone from seeing him, from what I can recall, most days, to maybe only twice a week, if that.

"So, are you going to start participating if you go back next week?"

"Hmm," I murmur my response, and she sighs. She knows me all too well.

She pulls up in the driveway and Walker is waiting, leaning against his Range Rover. She hesitates and looks at me. "Kara, if this is a problem for you, I can stop seeing him. You will always come first, you know that."

"No, don't do that," I whisper. "I like him, and he makes you happy. You deserve happiness, too." I kiss her cheek quickly and open the door.

"Sophie called for you earlier. Why don't you give her a ring? She's worried she hasn't heard from you lately." Marie hands me the wad of keys and gets out. She climbs into Walker's car, and he gives me a small, tight smile, before he gets in and drives away.

"Oh, my God, where have you been?" Sophie's voice is full of panic. It's uncharacteristic of me not to speak to her for weeks on end.

"Around," I say. I'm not up for telling her about my disastrous last six weeks.

After giving me an earful about laying low, she starts to rattle on about work and other commonplace crap. I smile and feign interest, glad that she can't see me.

"God, I've missed you," she coos.

Well, at least someone has.

I haven't heard anything at all from Sloan since the night he intentionally called me a whore, and brusquely threw me out onto the street. Even Walker avoids everything that is Sloan related whenever I see him, and Marie has also been unusually tight-lipped.

I have no idea what happened after she had put me in the car that day. All I know is that she and Walker had gone up to find out what had gone down. When she returned home a few hours later, she had a face like thunder, and was more than ready to kill someone. I was so lost and devastated, I didn't have the courage to ask, and Marie hasn't bothered to tell me.

So, in light of events of the last six weeks, I currently stand in the middle of nowhere. I'm just existing - barely.

"What do you think about getting together sometime this week? The girls are dying to see you. I'm not the only one who misses you, you know. Come on, a night out with us is exactly what you need," she coaxes gently, but I don't want to go out. Truthfully, I don't want to do anything, except stay at home and nurse my broken heart and mourn true love lost.

"What makes you think I need a night out," I pry. She knows I don't particularly like clubbing, which means she's heard something, and that snags my attention.

"Belated birthday drinks!"

"Soph, my birthday was months ago, besides we had drinks at the pub. Remember, when you were rubbing up against the doctor?"

"Ah, the doctor… Would you be angry if I went out with him?"

"No, why would I be?"

"He gave me his number and asked me to call him, so I just thought I'd ask you."

"Sophie, you don't need to ask for my permission, so please, just spit out whatever you know."

"Okay. So, I ran into Sam on Oxford Street yesterday, she was with some guy. She looks... Well she looks like shit if I'm honest. She also said you had split up with Sloan. She seemed quite pleased about it, actually. I'm sorry, Kara, but I thought you cut ties with her? And is it true?" She stops speaking, obviously waiting for my reply.

I pick my words carefully. Sam had something to do with what happened with Sloan, I'm sure of it, but I just don't know what. "I did… And it is."

She sighs loudly. "How about tomorrow, just a few drinks, nothing big, I promise. I'll come pick you up. Are you at Marie's?"

"Yep." I'm ready to hang up, until she speaks again.

"Kara, I'm sure whatever has happened, it will all work itself out. From what I saw, he adores you. I'll see you tomorrow."

I switch off the phone and hold it to my chest. I needed answers, and the only way I was going to get them was by talking to Sam. I dial the number for my old flat and, as expected, it goes straight to the answering machine. The message is the same one we had recorded together a couple of years ago. My eyes water a little when I think of all the good times we'd had.

But it all dies away when I repeat Sophie's words in my head.

She seemed quite pleased about it, actually.

Sam deliberately set me up. She embedded lies in Sloan's head and destroyed me in the process. I intentionally drop the phone to the floor and shift on the sofa, until I'm facing the back. Alone and tired, I bring my arms around myself, and stare numbly at the fabric in front of me.

Will I ever be free of pain and suffering?

"Kara? Are you there?"

The machine picks up the call, as I run from the bathroom, wrapped only in a towel, and reach for the handset.

"Hey, hi, I'm here," I answer.

"I'm going to stay with Walker tonight. Is that okay with you?" Marie asks hesitantly.

"Sure, why wouldn't it be?"

"I just wanted to make sure you were fine with it, that's all." I can hear the uncertain pitch in her voice.

I turn on the television and trawl through the channels. "It's fine. Just to let you know, I called Sophie, and I'm going out with her tomorrow. No point in wasting my heart away over someone who doesn't want me, is there?" I try to sound positive with my rhetorical question, but even I'm unconvinced. I hear her sigh gently, and then there is the long pause, which makes me even more uncomfortable.

"Well, that's great, honey. I'll see you in the morning."

"Okay, I'll-"

"Kara, if anyone shows up unexpectedly, you call me. I'm serious. Anyone." Her voice is firm, and I'm in two minds whether or not to query who she is talking about specifically. Since I am no longer in the inner circle, and privy to the workings of Sloan's complex mind these days, I don't know for definite if this is her laying down the law, or him.

"Yes, mother," I reply sarcastically.

"Good girl." Then she hangs up.

I busy myself by cleaning both the kitchen and living room. Having nothing better to occupy my time as of late, I tend to work my way through the house when dire boredom sets in. I'm just about to start on the bathroom when the doorbell rings like a warning bell, sounding around the house with a certain malevolence.

Lucky for me, the lights in the hallway are off, and that means I can at least see who is rudely disturbing my solitude, without them seeing me. Peering through the spy hole, Sam is outside. Normally, I wouldn't have been so worried - until Deacon's large frame steps out from the shadows behind her. I don't need to see him clearly to know it's him.

I lean back against the wall and the sound chimes through the house again. Leaving the bell to ring out continuously, I wrap my arms securely around myself and wait for them to leave. Eventually, she gets the message and trots back down the driveway, hopping into the waiting car, with him directly behind her.

I run around the house, checking all the locks on the doors and windows. Once I'm satisfied they're all closed and secure, I send Marie a quick message to let her know that we did indeed have unexpected visitors. I also ask if she knew they were going to be showing up here since she had inadvertently warned me.

An hour later, I still have no reply. I can't decide if it's because of Walker, or whether she knew this would happen tonight.

At least I can go to sleep with a clear conscience tonight, knowing I have done the right thing this time.

This time, I have kept my promise.

Chapter 27

THE SUN HAZES through the window, and I roll over in bed. My hand drifts to my mouth, and I think of all the times Sloan had kissed me awake in the morning. My mind does this a lot, it reminisces painfully. Anything that reminds me of him induces a heart-wrenching tug in my chest. It strains against my rib cage and causes my lungs to fail me momentarily.

This is a repercussion of being tragically in love with a man, who has not only broken your heart, but has shattered it into a million little pieces.

It's gone two in the afternoon when Marie finally resurfaces. I know I should have gone into the office this morning, but I honestly didn't have the courage to, especially considering Sam was at the door last night. It was suspicious, and somehow, she must have known I was flying solo and Marie wasn't home.

Marie drops her handbag on the sofa and comes over to me, wrapping her arms around me. I don't say anything as she holds me, although the distinctive chill makes its presence known.

"Thank you for calling me last night. I'm sorry I didn't get back to you." Her eyes shift from mine, and I know she's hiding something.

"Fine, but whatever it is you know, don't tell me. It makes me think of *him,* and I'm done with *him*. I can't exist knowing his every move, it hurts too much that we both breathe the same air. If you had heard the things he said to me, you would have ripped him a new one. Instead, you're in deep with him and Walker, and keeping things from me." She opens her mouth to defend herself, but I tear away from her and hold my hand up.

"No, I don't want to know. Whatever is going to happen, will. Between my father and Sam, I know it will. You can't protect me forever. I'm a big girl now, and I can handle this myself. I'm a survivor, remember? My past proves that I am."

She stands in shock as I turn to go grab my overnight bag. "Sophie has taken half a day's holiday, so I am going over to hers. Don't wait up, I'll see you tomorrow."

"Kara, please wait, we need to talk!" She sounds frantic and follows me to the door.

"No, we don't. I'm sorry, but I can't keep doing this! I'll never be able to move on until I stop thinking about him. He compared me to Sam for fuck sake! He called me a slut, then threw me out. Well, if that's what he thinks, then maybe that's what I'll be!" I want to scream out my frustration at her, but hold it back. This isn't her fault, but she isn't helping the situation by siding with him, either.

All I know is my heart aches for him, and knowing that she still sees him regularly, it's more than I'm able to cope with right now.

Standing in front of Sophie's full-length mirror, I groan. The dress I have on is akin to a belt. If I tug it up, it will expose my arse, and if I pull it down, it will flash my nipples.

"Don't you think this is a little too revealing, Soph?"

"No, I think you look sexy as hell! You need to start showing off that little figure of yours, instead of hiding it away." She gives me the same smile she did years ago when we went shopping with Marie for our end of year party dresses. I can still remember with vivid horror the red thing she threw at me, which I then discarded, and she subsequently ended up buying.

"No, I'm really not comfortable in this. It's definitely too revealing for me." Picking up my original choice, I commence peeling off the unbreathable second skin. I pull out my dressy black shorts, white flowing top and cream jacket. It's forecast to be reasonably warm tonight, and I want to feel cool, without drawing too much attention to myself.

In front of the mirror again, stare at the clothes I'm wearing. The clothes that *he* bought; the ones I'm now going to go out in. No matter how much I want to get past this, the truth is, I'll always live in some form of limbo regarding him. I can't move on, not until he is one hundred per cent honest about what happened that day, between my bolting up the stairs distraught, and however many hours later he broke down the bedroom door. We have unfinished business, and I'm fully aware I will never be able to move forward until he is completely truthful.

It also doesn't help that I'm so much in love with him, my heart carries a persistent, dull ache. Until I stop loving him, no one else stands a chance. And I know there will never be anyone else, because he is the only one who can illicit tranquillity within me. He's the only one who will ever be able to touch me, to kiss me, to love me.

I stare at myself and finally see the truth - I'm lost in my own life. The path I had mapped out so clearly and precisely has become tangled, and harder to navigate these last few months. Sloan had barged his way in with such ease and determination. He had grown to be such a big part of my world, then he removed himself from it just as quick. A few well thought out lies, and some ingenious planning on Sam's part had brought me - quite literally - to my knees.

Sophie throws her arm around me, staring at our reflections in the mirror. "Well, we look good!" I glance down at her. She is now wearing the dress I had discarded, just like so many years ago. Unlike me, she is out to get noticed tonight, whereas I just want one night where I can forget.

I just want to forget the only one I shall ever love.

Except, I know it will never happen.

Sophie leans over the bar and shouts our drinks order to the bartender. My eyes dart around the place, and I survey it with admiration. We are in the last place on earth where I want to be - Oblivion.

I had initially refused, but after Sophie's nonstop begging - which made me wonder whether or not she was privy that Sloan owned the place - I gave in. Now here, in a sea of people, I'm feeling both anxious and worried. What if Sloan is here tonight? What would I say to him if I do see him? And what would I do if he threw me out a second time?

Feeling the distress growing, I grab the drink Sophie hands me and down it in one. Her eyes widen, and she turns back around to get me another.

"Well, so much for not having a big night! We might be carrying you home if you go on like that!"

We move deeper into the crowd, and just as I had anticipated, the walls are matte black in the background of the strobe lightning that colours every person in its path. The other girls have already found a table, and we slide into the large leather seats.

There are three of them; Tina, Leanne, and Rebecca. They are girls Sophie and I went to college with. I've been out with them a few times over the years, and although they are some of the nicest girls I've met, I can't really relate to them.

"You guys look amazing!" Rebecca shouts, trying to be heard over the thumping beat of the speakers.

"Thanks," I say. "I love your dress, by the way." Rebecca is tiny, no more than five feet tall. She's half Japanese, and her skin tone is the most stunning I have ever seen. If I ever wanted to be someone else, she is that person. She grabs me by the hand and drags me onto the dance floor, ignoring my protests, which are drowned out by the loud music.

The beat pulsates through the club and through me. Time has all but stopped, and I don't know how long we've been here for. I have been on my feet for far too long, and they are cramping alarmingly at the height of the heels. I stumble, feeling a little light-headed, and march back over to the table, with a drunk Rebecca giggling under my arm.

Rocking on my feet, I pick up one of the glasses and drain it. I'm tired and becoming irritable. I'm also feeling the effects of the copious amounts of spirits and wine I have consumed. The only good thing about alcohol, not only does it make me brave, it dulls the distinct sensation of skin contact. Which is a positive tonight, since there is absolutely no avoiding it.

Shuffling on the spot, my eyes dart around the immediate space, and I spot two guys staring at our table. They lean into each, speaking while still looking at us. They're vaguely familiar, and I narrow my eyes, trying to work out where I have seen them before. The taller of the two winks at me, and I recognise him from the Emerson function all those months ago. I quickly turn my head, feeling nauseous.

"I'm off to the toilet, don't go anywhere!" I shout at the girls in my alcohol-infused stupor. I stumble again as I head towards the toilets.

The line for the ladies is ridiculous. I shift on my feet, desperate to relieve myself, when a familiar voice splinters my eardrums, sobering me immediately.

"...I can forgive him for his little indiscretion. Besides, he proved it last week by taking me to the E and F charity dinner. It was amazing, both during and after. The room was stunning, but the man was even better!"

"Are you not worried in case she shows up again? He's already dropped you once for her, she obviously means something to him that you don't."

"You bitch! Whose fucking side are you on? It doesn't matter now. I can honestly say I'm not worried, he said she was nobody! I told you, she was just a poor slut to fuck around with. She never belonged with him or in our world. At least he finally sees it now. He will always be mine, no poor, gold-digging, ugly little bitch like her is going to take him away from me!"

I duck down a little and turn back to see Christy chatting loudly, and animatedly, with another woman I recognise from the event Sloan had taken me to after he had vanished for weeks on end.

The line begins to move and is finally getting smaller. I'm truly thankful there are more than a couple of people separating us, so at least I won't run into her in the toilets.

"So, are you guys still going away?" Christy's friend asks her.

I bring my hand to my mouth in shock. Did I really mean so little that he could replace me so quickly? All I have done for the last six weeks is mourn the loss of him, and think of ways to keep my mind occupied so I didn't have to relive that awful day. Anything, so that I had something other than him to think about, and he was already seeing someone else? My heart constricts, and I inhale harshly.

Oh, my god, he must be sleeping with her, too!

I feel ashamed and pitiful that it took the one bitch I absolutely detest to throw it back in my face, to make me finally realise the reality at long last.

I *was* just a rich man's plaything - as I had initially suspected I would be when we first met.

Well, fuck him! The bastard doesn't deserve my love or my tears.

I finally gain entry to the ladies, quickly do what I have to, and then scarper back out. I look up to find my way through the throng of women still standing outside when my eyes inadvertently connect with hers. She looks at me like the cat who got all the cream. I maintain my posture and walk on by, but my arm is pulled back painfully. And by God, it burns like she has just set me on fire.

"Well, if it isn't the little fucking slut! How did you even get in here?" she goads, looking me up and down. "Make the most of it, because once he finds out you're here, he's going to go fucking apeshit! I would leave now if I were you."

I have to hand it to her, she's a first-class bitch who knows exactly where to strike.

"Oh, look! He even let you keep some of the clothes he so obviously bought because, let's face it, darling, you could never afford these!" she taunts with a grin, tugging at my sleeve.

We are now drawing an audience, and I just want to get as far away from here - *and her* - as I can. "Excuse me." I stare straight into her eyes. She throws her head to the side, whilst her friend giggles beside her. I raise my head and never bother looking back. Fighting against my newly acquired heartbreak, I push my way through the bodies back to where Sophie is sitting.

"Hey, we were wondering where you were! We have some new *friends*!" she coos emphatically. "Meet Carl and David." She beams at me.

I glance between the two guys who had been staring at us. Carl licks his lips like I'm something to eat.

"Hello again, Ka-ra," he says, clearly expressing the syllables again. He reaches out his hand and drags it over my arm. My skin crawls, and I ponder my next action for a moment, until he confidently puts his hand on my shoulder and squeezes. A cold sweat shoots through me, and I'm about to pull away, when I hear it.

"Kara?"

Staring beyond the irritating guy in front of me, Charlie is next to Jake, completely dumbstruck. Her voice sounds confused, but I don't understand why. Jake looks at me and then at Carl. He frowns, and quickly walks away. Compulsion forces me to follow the path he cuts through the horde of bodies into the VIP.

My mouth drops open when I see Christy draped all over Sloan, who appears to be listening enthusiastically to whatever she is saying. His arm is around her, and her mouth is at his ear. I see red when her lips tug on his lobe. The bastard isn't even pushing her away!

I'm such a fucking idiot!

Charlie begins to speak, but I don't hear a word of it. Either the music is too loud, or I'm so consumed with jealousy by the fact that he definitely has replaced me. *With her.*

My heart has now, well and truly, been fucking annihilated by him.

I glare, unmoving, as Jake pulls him away from the redheaded slut, and they both turn to me. Even from this distance, his face is full of pain. Abruptly, he starts to plough a resolute path through the people separating us. A small hand touches my arm, and I meet with Sophie's big, sympathetic eyes.

"Kara, I think it's time you talked to him."

I pull her away from prying ears and confess the truth. "He kicked me out, Sophie. He called me a slut, all because of lies that Sam told him. I'm not strong enough to talk to him. I love him, and he hates me."

"Oh, Kara." She holds me tight, and I let her.

"Walk away, Carl!" Sloan's voice booms over the crowd, coming closer.

"Oh, my God, I feel like I can't breathe! I have to get out of here!" I quickly move away from Sophie and make my way to the door.

"Kara, wait!" she calls after me.

I turn to her, but all I can see is him in my peripheral vision, watching me. Charlie is now in front of him, blocking his way, waving her hands at my retreating direction. She's furious from what I can tell. Sloan quickly strides from the table, and he's now barrelling towards me, virtually pushing people out of the way.

I quicken my pace, and pretty much run from the club. I have no phone on me since I never bothered to replace it when Sloan booted me out, and I don't remember seeing any phone boxes when we arrived.

Damn it!

I walk with intent, alone into the night. Relief washes over me when a taxi pulls up at the kerb.

"KARA!" Sloan hollers at me.

Checking the driver ID hanging from the rearview, I quickly get inside and lock the door. Sloan stands in front of the taxi, and slams his hands down on the bonnet. He pierces me with a crazed look, and the driver gives me one of sympathy. Seriously, he must have seen this type of scene hundreds of times before in his line of work, this is no different.

"Please, just drive," I plead. I can't mistake the pity in the driver's eyes staring back at mine in the mirror. He reverses the car a little, then inches forward. Sloan slams his hand on the bonnet again. The anger rolls over his face as the car starts to pull away. His palm slams against the window next to me, but I don't look at him. Instead, I stare straight ahead, as the car picks up speed and leaves him behind.

The streetlights flicker all around, and I relax back into the seat. The driver has been quiet the whole time, and I appreciate he hasn't attempted to make typical small talk.

The taxi speeds off as soon as I hand over the fare. Fidgeting with my bag, there is a Range Rover parked in the driveway. Great! Walker is here with Marie, and the lights are off. I imagine Sloan has already called him, and he'll be on his way over. It wouldn't shock me in the slightest.

I contemplate if Sophie would come away from the club if I called and asked her to. Then I remember I don't have a phone. Left with no other choice, I start to trudge up the path, and the car door opens. My stomach lurches when Sam slides out and blocks my way. Fear rolls through me, and my limbs feel weak. There is no way she is going to walk away for a second time. I cling to the key in my hand and debate whether I might be able to outrun her. I already know I can't since I'm slightly drunk.

"Hi, Kara," she greets coyly.

"Um, hi, Sam. What are you doing here?" My fists harden, and my body goes into fight or flight mode. I'm still weighing up my options when she starts to speak again.

"I want to see how you are. How is life after Mr Millionaire?" she sneers, and I know for certain she instigated the turmoil.

"Sam, I've had a long day, so, if you please-"

"Well, I wanted to talk yesterday, but you didn't answer the door last night." She grins knowingly, and waves a finger between me and the door, enjoying this game.

"I was asleep," I retort.

"No, no, no! You're lying!" she screams at me. "You were never really good at it, Kara. You haven't got any better with age, either." She shifts and the streetlamp illuminates her frame. Finally, I see her for what she really is. She's emaciated, having lost a significant amount of weight. Not the kind that I have lost in the whole *Sloan ripping my heart to shreds and stomping on it* debacle, but the kind that is induced through addiction. Her eyes are rimmed with dark circles, and her clothes look dirty and unkempt.

"Sam, I haven't got time for this. I'm tired, and Marie is waiting for me." I start to walk to the front door, but she stops me.

"You're lying again! Marie isn't here. *Fact*. She's out with that Neanderthal, Walker. So, tell me another one. Better still, tell him!"

Her eyes glisten with what I can only describe as glee, when I turn around to find Deacon behind me.

"No!" I cry out, as he tackles me and renders me immobile. Something lodges painfully in my back, and I start breathing hard. With one hand, he forcefully twists my head back to face him. He grunts and smiles demonically, and that's when I feel the all too familiar fist smack across my face. My body gives out from underneath me, and I slump to the ground, holding my cheek in agony, as hot blood trickles down my throat.

Deacon bends down in front of me, roughly grabs me under the arms and hauls me up. He runs his nose up my cheek and breathes in deep. I retch, but I'm unable to expel the vomit and bile in my oesophagus.

I start to kick out my arms and legs, drawing hidden strength from somewhere deep inside, but he subdues me by raising his fist again in warning, then slamming it against my cheek. I cry out as the impact creates a tidal wave of pain to careen through me. I grab my face, feeling the hot stream of blood flowing from my nose. One arm secures around my forearm, and he forces me into the car. Shoving me inside, the door slams shut, and the child locks kick in. I crawl back into the seat, and wrap my arms around myself as I sob.

"Shall I call him, or do you want me to go in person again?" Sam asks him, sliding into the front passenger seat.

"No, change of plan," Deacon responds with venom.

"What do you mean? What are you going to do with her?" Sam asks, a hint of panic is firm in her tone.

"Anything I fucking want!"

I close my eyes and sob harder, comprehending I will always be a victim.

"Deacon, no, you promised-"

"Shut the fuck up, you don't call the shots here!"

Sam cries out unexpectedly, and it's evident Deacon has just delivered a powerful blow somewhere on her body. Her whimpers of pain are loud and clear in my head, and if he can hurt her so easily, I know he will have no issues in showing me he's definitely calling the shots.

The interior lights switch off, and I'm back to where I have existed my entire life. Alone in the dark, cowering in fear, terrified of the unknown.

Once again, I have been left with a monster…

Author Note

Dying to find out what happens next? Download book two, Tormented, now!

Fractured is the first instalment in the series, and the story of Kara and Sloan develops and unravels throughout the first three books.

If you enjoyed this novel, please consider sparing a few moments to leave a review.

Follow Elle

If you wish to be notified of future releases, special offers, discounted books, ARC opportunities, and more, please click on the link below.

Subscribe to Elle's mailing list

Alternatively, you can connect with Elle on the following sites:

Website: www.ellecharles.com

Facebook: www.facebook.com/elle.charles

Twitter: www.twitter.com/@ellecharles

Bookbub: www.bookbub.com/authors/elle-charles

Instagram: www.instagram.com/elle.charlesauthor

Or by email:

elle.charlesauthor@gmail.com

elle@ellecharles.com

About the Author

Elle was born and raised in Yorkshire, England, where she still resides.

A self-confessed daydreamer, she loves to create strong, diverse characters, cocooned in opulent yet realistic settings that draw the reader in with every twist and turn, until the very last page.

A voracious reader for as long as she can remember, she is never without her beloved Kindle. When she is not absorbed in the newest release or a trusted classic, she can often be found huddled over her laptop, tapping away new ideas and plots for forthcoming works.

Works by Elle Charles

All titles are available to purchase exclusively through Amazon.

The Fractured Series:

Kara and Sloan

Fractured (Book 1)

Tormented (Book 2)

Aftermath (Book 2.5)

Liberated (Book 3)

Marie and John

Faithless (Book 4)

Made in the USA
Monee, IL
21 August 2021

76149497R00187